A VOTE FOR JESUS

A SATIRE ON CAMPAIGNING, CORRUPTION & POLITICAL CRUCIFIXION

JOHN BRIGGS

Uban Creek Books • Amsterdam, NY

Uban Creek Books, Amsterdam, NY

Printed by IngramSpark, La Vergne, Tennessee

Edited by New Author Editing, Amsterdam, NY

Cover Design by Pradeep Premalal, CoverCreators, Sri Lanka

Humor/Political Satire. A poor carpenter from Bethlehem, Pennsylvania encounters political corruption and powerful enemies when he takes on a veteran U.S. Senator.

ISBN: 978-1-7348101-0-3

Library of Congress Control Number: 2020905753

Inquiries: info@ubancreekbooks.com

*To my Left-Wing Laughs partner Mike Irwin
and the countless comedians
who, for years, have made fun of the way
campaigns are run*

CHAPTERS

AUTHOR'S NOTE

This book is meant to offend. Oh, not religious people or Christians or any of the usual suspects. No, it is meant to offend anyone who blindly calls this the greatest country on earth when our system defends the powerful, the rich, the corrupt, and then puts them in office. From the Electoral College to super PACs, gerrymandering to voter suppression, foreign interference to flat-out lies, our political campaigns find a way around the will of the people, which is why they desperately need to be attacked and altered. Oh, and satirized.

This book is also meant to offend those who believe Jesus is on their side. Have they read anything about him? Even a cursory understanding of his life shows that his beliefs ran the breadth of our political spectrum. And so, this story is not about the Jesus of a Second Coming or the son of God or any of that. No, this story takes place in a contemporary America in which Christianity does not exist. Jesus is just your average Joe thrown into our unruly system. You know, a poor carpenter with questionable parentage and a willingness to attack the powers that be. So, what did I come up with after applying my sharpened pen? Jesus wasn't conservative or liberal—he was anti-authority. And that's the one thing authority can never allow in power.

It's been said that a satirist should appear to have no stake in his story. Well, when it comes to religion, I don't. In fact, I find that religion interferes with my atheism. But then that's why I chose Jesus in the first place—I'm as guilty as they are in using his image to further my message. I believe that's another rule of satire: irony.

i

But our politicians so abuse Jesus it's as though Kierkegaard himself created a candidate. We've somehow developed a quintessentially American Jesus that politicians quote even when they don't believe a word he said. He's a means to their end, but if they truly believed in him, he'd be the end of their means.

So, there you have it. *A Vote for Jesus* is satire, pure and simple, which means it's probably the best way to understand our elections. All I can ask is that you enjoy the book and laugh at our system because heartfelt mockery remains one of our most powerful weapons in resisting it.

—Briggs

HE WHO IS FIRST...

Everything about Senator Herod Antipas, from his alabaster skin to his pointed head and rotunda-shaped midriff said he was a perfect fit for the halls of Congress. It was no surprise, then, when his standard-issue aide, barely able to grow facial hair, kept to the standard practice of bursting through the mahogany doors at the end of the senator's office as if the world were about to end.

"Someone new is entering the race!"

Herod scowled, wondering who dared to mount a challenge against him after thirty years in office. Likely someone better fit for a crown of thorns than his crown of gold. Still, he would watch the press conference. The sometimes-inquisitive press would seek comments to run in between rounds of canned commentary. Whether he used his time-tested and thoroughly clichéd response or something a decade fresher depended on what his opponent said.

Herod pushed himself up from his desk as his aide turned on the plasma-screen TV set deep in the cherry red cabinet along the wall. The senator lowered himself onto the pristine black couch, the treated hide groaning under his girth. His press secretary always referred to him as stout in the best possible sense of the word. She intended it to mean strong, but truth be told, he was stout in its most derogatory sense. At a hair over six-feet tall, he had a torso that resembled a square with the corners rounded off. He had once believed that a round or two of golf several times a week would take an inch off his waist, but he abandoned that when his staff, and then his physicians, started lying about his weight, which seemed far more agreeable than hitting the links. Now, undaunted by his appearance and unwilling to be svelte, Herod scooped a half-dozen chocolates from a bowl on the coffee table in front of him. The man on screen stood draped in a tailored dark blue suit and red tie over a light blue shirt. The whole ensemble resembled a majority of Herod's most conservative suits, which made him chuckle. He could already hear his response. *Why vote for a new man in an old suit? Vote experience. Vote Herod.*

Still, the man had a certain demographic appeal—early forties with a good tan, though the creases in his forehead spoke of someone who didn't achieve them in a tanning bed. They were produced by long hours outside. An avid outdoorsman? A man pushing the rough-and-ready angle? That could pull in a few right-leaning independents who loved L.L. Bean lumberjacks and ready-wear cowboys. Or was this man working a blue-collar angle? Some laborer who found the chutzpah to run. No, those people never had the money. Still, his age might capture some of the youth vote. Not that Herod worried about that. He hadn't kowtowed to the under-thirty crowd in thirty years and for good reason. Added to the certainties of death for everyone and taxes for the middle-class came the maxim that the young never showed up to vote.

The man's biggest detriment was his slightly receding hairline in front and curly hair on the sides. It probably looked natural in person but was terrible on TV. His team would dig up a frightening picture of him, maybe from a video capture, to use in their attack ads. Shouldn't take more than an hour.

Herod leaned forward and motioned for his aide to turn up the volume.

"Ladies and gentlemen of the press and the voters at home, I give you the man who will save our political system, the next senator from the great state of Pennsylvania, Jesus Christ!"

Herod nearly choked on his chocolate.

"That? That's my opponent? That...that hippie?!"

A rail-thin man in his early thirties with a scraggly beard and hair cascading around his shoulders, decked out in a casual corduroy jacket that would not be complete without the requisite patches on the elbows, strode to the podium and squinted through his right eye into the flashbulbs and camera lights shining in his face.

The aide laughed caustically. "Some people just don't know when they're beat."

"Shut up. Take notes."

The aide whipped out his phone to type in a shorthand Herod couldn't understand. As long as his aide translated it later, he didn't care. He was interested in something the young man couldn't translate: his opponent's body language.

Jesus grabbed each side of the podium like a preacher, a possessed man set to pound the pulpit. And like the preacher demanding the undivided attention of his parishioners, he did not speak until silence descended upon the pews. Until the clicking of the cameras abated and the reporters no longer rustled in their seats.

"Thank you, Peter, and members of the press. My name is Jesus Christ, and I am officially announcing my candidacy for the Senate of the United States." He paused as newspapermen scribbled away and bored on-air personalities waited for their turn to speak. "You might ask yourself why an unknown carpenter from Bethlehem seeks such an office. Because I know what it means to struggle. I know what it means to suffer. And most importantly, I know what it means to serve. I tell you, here and now, I come to serve and not be served. The man I seek to replace forgot that decades ago. It is time the people remind Herod Antipas of his place. That he is one of them and not above them."

Nothing new, thought the aide.

Nothing new, thought the newspapermen.

Nothing new, thought the pretty correspondents.

Nothing I can't handle, thought Herod, inherently recognizing a rookie mistake. This newcomer—this idiot, if he had to put a name to it—had invited a political animal to fight back. *He's playing dirty pool and I didn't even have to rack 'em up.*

Herod popped another chocolate into his mouth as Jesus continued. "We have a class in this country that believes it deserves power because it has privilege. They don't realize that power itself is a privilege. They think the working class should give them respect without them earning it. Well, I am here to tell you that I will earn their respect. I will help the poor and the sick, the meek and the merciful, for they deserve our compassion. But first, we must send a message to the Herods of this world: you may persecute the poor and the sick and the powerless, but they shall be rewarded. He who is first shall be last, and he who is last shall be first!"

Herod dug his fingers into the arm of his couch, his nails indenting the leather between the tarnished rivets. This was the fire and brimstone of a man possessed. A knight tilting at the dragons of old-guard politics. He did not plan to rail against Herod—he planned to embarrass him.

And that was another mistake.

Zealots arouse the passions of their supporters and enemies in equal measure, and Herod now bore the intensity of a lion in the Coliseum. Let his aide take notes. He would remember every word. A man like this Jesus could feed the media beast tomorrow and the next day and the next unless Herod's endless bag of baubles succeeded in distracting the magpie press chattering before this shiny new candidate.

Why do you think you can win?

"Americans love an underdog."

How can you beat Herod?

"Unexpected men are free to do unexpected things."

Have you done any polling?

"No, but there are those who expected my coming."

Do you have a constituency?

"Mankind."

A party?

"I am beholden to no one."

Do you have a team?

"I am sure a few will gather in my name."

Are you pro-life or pro-choice?

"Be fruitful and multiply."

Are you against the death penalty?

"Let he who is without sin cast the first stone."

What about gun ownership?

"Not all lawful things are good."

The military build-up?

"Better a patient person than a warrior."

What are you for?

"Justice."

Slick, thought the aide.

Slick, thought Peter.

Dangerous, thought Herod. *The man speaks his mind in sound bites. He has either been well-coached, or he's a natural. And God help me if he's a natural.*

The press had a different take. One or two slick answers did not make a candidate. They badgered the Senate hopeful for another forty-five minutes, expecting this political waif to melt under pressure. Yet, Jesus took it all in stride. He never bashed them without cause. Never called them liars for seeking the truth or attempting to better understand him and his still unformed policies.

Should the rich pay more taxes?

"A rich man will find it easier to pass through the eye of a needle than escape my tax plan."

What about immigrants?

"They are strangers, and we should take them in."

Tariffs on foreign goods?

"Don't wear foreign clothing, and one problem is solved."

His positions were scattered like lawn signs in a hurricane, but they had an unmistakable populism. Tax the rich, enrich the poor, stop the war, buy American. This man was as homegrown

Middle America as they came, but they expected nothing less from a carpenter raised on the Rust Belt's eastern edge.

That realization made Herod sweat. It wasn't his corpulence or the Corinthian leather that warmed him. It wasn't the balmy spring day or the suit that sat heavy on his shoulders. It was this man of the people. This would-be senator. This...

And then Jesus gave it to him. The Kumbaya moment. The let's-all-hold-hands-and-sing moment. He spoke of peace and harmony. Of laying down weapons and loving our enemies. He begged the armies of the world to beat their swords into plowshares and let the weak cry out, 'I am strong!' And when he'd gone too far for far too long, a solitary voice in the press corps yelled out, "And when is all this going to happen? The end of the world?"

The reporters laughed.

Herod laughed.

The aide laughed.

And Jesus laughed before giving them the smallest smile, one lost in the depths of his beard. "Let me tell you a story about ten virgins."

The reporters froze. There was no way he just said that, but in case he did, every TV camera in the room zoomed in for a close-up. For a story like this, you wanted a tight shot.

"A man was set to marry ten women. Five of the women were foolish, and five were wise."

Peter, off to the corner, slipped a hand up to his neck and flicked his fingers back and forth in what he believed to be a subtle gesture—a gesture that remained subtle only because anyone who should have noticed couldn't take his eyes off Jesus. The candidate caught it but chose to carry on. He was sure these reporters would appreciate his point if they could stop focusing on sound bites and snippets.

"On the day of the wedding, the bridegroom was delayed on business. The ten virgins were forced to wait."

Peter dropped his head into his hands. He knew a PR nightmare when he was having one.

"The five foolish women did not get extra oil for their lamps, while the five wise ones did. At midnight, the man arrived and said the wedding would happen without delay. The five wise virgins lit their lamps, but the five foolish ones could not. They went out to buy oil, but when they returned, they discovered they had missed the wedding and the bridegroom refused to marry them because they were foolish."

The press looked at each other with raised eyebrows and jaws askew, searching for meaning. They turned to Peter, but he looked at his shoes. If they could have peered through their camera lenses, they would have seen Herod methodically slipping a chocolate into his mouth as he enjoyed the fire and smoke that preceded a crash.

Peter stepped forward. "That's it, ladies and..."

Jesus cut him off. "What I mean is that this future will come someday. It may not come as soon as some would like, but it will come much sooner than we think if we all work together and don't act foolish."

Jesus at last nodded to Peter, the signal to end this memorable press conference.

Peter's voice faded as Jesus departed the press room. A young reporter near the door rose from his seat and touched Jesus on the sleeve. Innocent eyes peered out from wire-rimmed glasses wrapped at the ends by swoops of fine hair. His cherubic face proclaimed the sort of cub reporter built to cover fluffy features and local sports, not hard news, but Jesus looked beyond that because he recognized him. Knew him. Not by name or employer, but by personality.

Anyone sparkling with such naiveté could be trusted.

"Go ahead," said Jesus. "Ask your question."

The young man's eyes widened to span his face, his mouth struggling to get out his question. "Who...who are you?"

Jesus put a workman's hand on the boy's shoulder. The young man's pursuit of the truth kept his faith in the Fourth Estate alive, and so Jesus told him, and him alone, the truth.

"I am the way and the truth and the life."

The reporter stood there with his mouth agape. Had he heard that right? Did he just say he was "the life?"

"Uh…can I quote you?"

That was the best question yet. Of course he could quote him, if his editor would ever believe that a sane man said such a thing.

As it turned out, his editor would believe because contrary to what Jesus believed, he hadn't said it to the young man alone.

THE GOOD SHEPHERD

Herod leaned close to the TV. That was no small feat as he had to roll himself forward and off to the right at a forty-five-degree angle before tucking his legs to the base of the couch and pushing, but all that effort was worth it. He swore his opponent said, "I am the way and the truth and the life." What the hell did that mean? No matter how honest you were, saying you were the truth itself was a lie. No wonder this Jesus spoke like a madman—he was a madman. He had to be. Nobody but a madman would state his actual policy positions at his first press conference. Everyone knew that by taking a position you lost half the voters before you finished your sentence. If Jesus kept losing a half here and a half there, the only returns he'd see would be diminishing returns.

For Herod, however, that was the slow route. Catching him saying something asinine was the quickest way to dispose of an opponent.

Herod faced his aide. "Please tell me that was recorded."

"Of course, sir. Everything's recorded. Everything."

"Then play it back! Play it back!"

"Don't you want to see the rest of the press conference, sir? His campaign manager…"

"Screw the press conference! Play it back!"

"How far back?"

"To that reporter!"

The aide scrunched his tweezed eyebrows. At least two dozen reporters cajoled the candidate. Which one…which

9

one…it had to be the last one. The one that got his boss all excited. Had to be.

He hoped it had to be.

The aide rewound the DVR back ninety seconds, finishing a moment before Herod's press secretary stuck her head in the door. "Excuse me, sir—the press is clamoring for a statement. Do we have anything we want to say?"

"In a minute!" Herod barked. "In a minute!"

"Yes, sir." The press secretary closed the door with the softest possible click. After eighteen months on staff, she understood that silence was often the press secretary's greatest weapon. Some days, it was the quintessential definition of her job. Other days, it ranked just behind obfuscation.

"Found it, sir," said the aide.

"Well, turn up the volume! We barely heard it the first time."

The aide did as instructed before hitting play. And there it was, seemingly in slow motion.

Who are you?

I am the way and the truth and the life.

"He was on a hot mic, sir. A hot mic!"

The hot mic—the devil's plaything of politics. Even half-seasoned politicians knew that if a camera or mic or reporter was within a hundred feet of you, you played it cool and said exactly what you were supposed to. In fact, if anyone was near you—an aide, your wife, your mistress—you said exactly what you were supposed to. You couldn't trust those bastards either. You were always one disgruntled employee or divorce away from facing a scandal.

It was a lesson Herod learned the hard way: in public.

Twenty years ago he called a reporter "asshole" on a hot mic, broadcasting it to the audience in front of him and the audience at home. His team spun it the best they could, saying that such language—and such open contempt for the press—showed just how tough Herod was. That was the real him breaking through his crafted persona. It was a gamble his followers loved, covering his wager by sending the reporter thousands of emails and letters addressing him as "Dear Asshole." Herod gained the reprieve he needed, which allowed him to swear even more on the campaign trail and in the Senate chambers. His image transformed from daddy's boy to no-holds-barred brawler, and he never had to act tough to do it.

When you're a winner, the dice always come up sevens.

Herod's aide brought him back to the present. "What do we do with it, sir?"

"That's easy. We sit on it."

"Sit on it, sir? But that tape's gold."

"No, it's lead. It becomes gold when we catch him in a lie. That's when we show him saying he's the truth."

"Brilliant, sir."

Yeah, thought Herod. *Now all we have to do is catch him in a lie. But this is politics. That could happen before sundown.*

Herod scooped one last piece of chocolate from the crystal bowl. "Get our friend on the line. No one comes from nowhere. I want to know everything there is about that guy. In the meantime, I'm going to piss on my opponent's parade."

Peter Cephas stood opposite a dozen aggressive print reporters. The TV correspondents, who needed to get facetime before getting the facts, had already ducked outside to get on-air.

"I will be available to answer any of your questions, but please remember to pick up a copy of our itinerary on the way out. Tomorrow, Jesus will be at Hades Steel in Bethlehem…"

That's when the initial murmur turned into an onslaught.

Who are these virgins?

"It's just a parable, not an actual…"

Does Mr. Christ know these virgins?

"No, he doesn't know any virgins. I mean, maybe he does. I don't know. We never ask."

Why virgins/?

"The candidate misspoke. He meant…"

Are these virgins part of the campaign?

"They're not actually virgins. They're…"

Does Mr. Christ personally know they're not virgins?

"There are no virgins! It's a story. It's a para…"

Has Mr. Christ ensured they're not virgins?

"No, he…"

What does his wife think of this?

"Mr. Christ is not married."

Why ten bridesmaids? Does the candidate support polygamy?

"Of course not! He believes in the sanctity of marriage. His parents were married."

Does he respect women?

"Yes!"

Does he think virgins are foolish?

"No! Jesus loves virgins."

Does he support the Virginity Pledge?

"Now, that's a personal choice…"

Peter had enough of this insanity. The press tossed out questions just to make him look bad. And they were succeeding. Not only was he playing their game, he was playing on their field with their ball. The only good news was there were no TV cameras. They weren't necessary. Half the hands in the room held up cell phones taping every word. He'd be all over the Internet within the hour. Peter had his first viral hit and it made him sick.

The next few words exploded out of his mouth like a frat boy bringing up the evening's beer.

"It's a parable, people! Do you know what that is? There are no virgins, no bridesmaids, no groom. It's a parable!"

The press stared at him in strained silence until one of them asked the natural follow-up.

So…what does it mean?

Peter didn't know, but the last thing he could do as campaign manager was admit he didn't know what his candidate was talking about no matter how clueless he or the candidate appeared to be.

"Well, since you're not listening to me, I'll get the candidate himself out here to put this matter to rest."

Peter dashed offstage for the safety of the back room. The press shrugged. They knew he didn't know what it meant, but without him saying that, all they could write was, "It appeared Mr. Cephas was unsure what the parable meant," but they knew he didn't know. They weren't even sure the candidate knew, but they weren't leaving without finding out. Or without another messy quote. Whichever made better copy.

Peter found Jesus two feet inside the door to the back room enjoying orange juice in a paper cup. All the good cups in the office were placed in the press room for the reporters, leaving the staff—well, him, his brother Andrew, and Jesus—to use second-rate cups and plasticware. None of that surprised Peter. What shocked him was that Jesus was talking to a reporter. Alone. Without supervision. No candidate should ever be alone with a reporter. Always have witnesses!

But Peter didn't have time to explain why his candidate was making a press faux pas minutes after he himself made one. He had to put out this campfire in this room and the raging inferno down the hall. Fortunately, he knew how to put out two fires with one bucket. A bucket of ice-cold water called reality.

"You have to get out there. The press doesn't understand your parable. You have to explain it to them, or they'll get it wrong tomorrow."

"I don't see why. It's very straightforward. The five virgins who didn't get the oil…"

"Don't explain it to me, explain it to them! They're the ones who'll be telling the world about virgins tomorrow. Your whole message will be lost!"

Jesus couldn't imagine a fate worse than having his message lost, altered, or misunderstood. He placed his empty cup on the round Formica-topped table in the center of the room, patted

Peter on the shoulder, and said, "Let's go." He turned to the young reporter, "If you'll excuse me."

Peter and Jesus stepped out of the small room. To Peter's surprise, the young man didn't follow. *Must not be much of a reporter if he's going to miss this debacle.*

Jesus returned to the rostrum he left a few minutes ago, displaying the same confidence he had before. The room's instant silence brightened the glow in his eyes.

"I understand some of you don't fully understand my parable. That's my fault. I should have given you a better explanation. In the story, America represents the wedding, the voters are the bridesmaids, and the groom is the future. Some voters are wise and some are foolish. Those voters who know what we need to do to make this country a success will act to make that day happen. They will prepare. The foolish will not. They will fall for false promises and vainglorious boasts. And if the foolish win out, America, like the wedding, will be a disaster. It will come unexpectedly in the middle of the night, and half this country will grow scared, insecure, and angry. The American empire can succeed or succumb. It can be great, or it can collapse under the weight of its own malaise. The wise brides had their oil and were prepared. We must listen to the wisest among us."

The room stayed still for several uneasy seconds. Although the purpose of the parable had not been obvious, it was obvious that Jesus treated the reporters like intellectual equals. He gave them the chance to understand, and in explaining it with the utmost poise, had done so with the voters. He treated neither like his enemies. Or children.

Jesus gave them a faint smile to once again wrap up his portion of the press conference. "Thank you all for staying. I found this day invigorating, and I hope you found it enlightening. Good luck making your deadlines. I look forward to reading every story."

Jesus slipped from behind the podium and escorted Peter to the back room. They found the young reporter standing there, the door propped open against his chest, his face peering around the corner. The sparkle in his eyes indicated he caught every word after all.

"There is no darkness in yo—only light. I know what you mean when you say 'I am the way and the truth and the life.' You can actually do it. You can bring the haves and the have-nots together. You can ensure that those who sow and those who reap rejoice together!"

"You're quite the wordsmith," Jesus replied, ushering the young man into the room while giving him the most sincere smile. Someone finally understood him.

Peter closed the door behind them. He understood something, too. The power of those words that washed over you like an untamed flood could only come from one writer.

"You're John Patmos, right? *Bethlehem Star?*" The young man nodded. "I like your stuff. You give the news some insight. Some context. Hmmm..."

Jesus knew where Peter was going with his "Hmmm," but John was still in the dark.

"Jesus is right. You're good with words. How'd you like... how'd you like a job writing our speeches?"

Peter hesitated to ask because the campaign needed a friend in the media, even if it was the hometown paper. Still, he could use someone to keep Jesus on script without putting silly words in his mouth about virgins and bridegrooms and oil. It sounded more like an orgy than a wedding, and that was an image he didn't need after one day on the campaign trail. No, as much as Peter hated to admit it, the campaign needed John to write Jesus' story. This scribe could transform him from lowly carpenter to great communicator.

"So, what do you say?"

John looked down, pushing waves of hair behind his ears. A second later, he eyed the two men with the joy of a monk embracing nirvana. "I'll quit my job right now!"

Peter grabbed John's left arm before this grad student of a man could bolt past him.

"Wait! Give us a good story, then quit your job!"

Herod entered his press room greeting more than half the reporters by name. He shook hands as if this were a reunion of old friends. It wasn't, of course. They had it in for him—which only meant they were fair and not favorable—the exact opposite of what Herod wanted. Still, he treated them like family when it suited him, and right now, it suited him.

He stood in his usual spot, two steps to the right of center in the room. His staff assured him the lighting there was best, although they also told him he had no bad sides, right before telling the cameramen where to set up to make sure they didn't capture his bad side. Everything about the process was controlled, right down to the message. Herod had run it by his press secretary on the way out. She punched it up in places, giving him guaranteed keywords, until she was sure it didn't sound like he was insulting his opponent, even though that was all he planned on doing. He always said that backhanded compliments were still compliments if you didn't look into them. Passive-aggressive wasn't just the approach of overbearing mothers.

Herod faced the press corps, small as it was, for his rebuttal. The important thing was that they were the "A" team and not the second-stringers covering Jesus. Herod would get bigger headlines for sure. The small-market papers and various penny savers could pick up the leftovers the next day. Within twenty-four hours, he'd blanket the state.

"Thank you all for coming on such short notice. I know you all want to know what I think of my opponent. First, I welcome him into the race and look forward to a vigorous debate. A new candidate always strengthens our democracy."

Several reporters stifled yawns. Same spiel, different election. Little more than civil drivel. But with Herod, there was always a but. One shoe never dropped without the other already falling.

"But…"

There it was.

"But what of my opponent? Well…he's alright. But that's it. He's alright. Jesus is just alright." He smiled at the press, and then his press secretary. After all, she gave him the line, replacing his original headline, *Inexperienced Loser Enters Senate Race.* "I'm sure I'll like him. He seems like a very nice, though naïve, young man, and his plans for this great state are terrible. Dangerous even. We've heard them all a thousand times, and they've been rejected by the voters because they don't work."

With Herod's trenches established and set to repulse any attack, he brought out the offensive weapons: the sound bite, the political equivalent of the Gatling gun, rapid-fire quips destined to make copy on-air and in print, and most importantly, be believed by the gullible on social media.

"My opponent plans to raise taxes. My opponent wants to raise the deficit to pay for welfare. My opponent does not support our troops. I can't make it any clearer: he is not the right man for this job. I have been a senator long enough to get things done, and I will continue to work for the great people of this state. My opponent says he's a carpenter. Well, I'm sure he's a very good carpenter." Herod then smiled, hitting up the room for his big line. "I'd hire him to build my house, but I don't want him in the House—or the Senate." He paused, not to wait for the few chuckles he got, but so the TV crews would have the proper space to edit the film. "Thank you all for coming. There will be no questions at this time as I have a very important meeting to get to. But thank you again, and we'll talk plenty about the election in the coming months."

And Herod walked out of the room, ignoring the few questions thrown his way. The only thing he heard was his aide whisper, "I called our friend. You have a meeting in two hours. He says, 'Don't be late.'"

Herod placed his call exactly two hours later. He had his aide set three alarm clocks so he wouldn't miss it. And like clockwork, the CEO of Hades Steel answered the phone on the first ring in the husky tone that made him sound more like a phone sex operator than the leader of a Fortune 500 firm.

"What can I do for you, Senator?"

Herod always appreciated a man who respected his time but figured this was more because his friend had better things to do.

"I need to take advantage of your…"

"Connections?"

"Yes." Herod wasn't sure why he was sweating. He was a sitting senator and committee chair, yet he got the impression that this CEO could buy and sell him if he ever asked for too much. He was certain the tax cuts he helped procure for Hades Steel alone were more than enough to cover the cost, which didn't make it enough to cover his own backside.

"You've been very good to us over the years," said his friend, "and I reward loyalty. I won't even ask for anything in return, though I'm sure you'll discover certain legislation we'd like to see passed. Voting for it will earn you our gratitude."

"I'll look into it," said Herod, code for 'consider it done' and not the usual synonym for maybe. But that was the appropriate response to gratitude, which was code for 'campaign contribution.' Which was reasonable. Hades Steel and its subsidiaries stood to gain billions if that legislation passed. And what was the point of having a hundred billion dollars if you couldn't get a billion more?

"Good. Clear your mornings for our friends in the media. We'll also dig up every piece of information on this Mr. Christ, from his finances to his love life. You'll know everything you need to know. If he has a skeleton in his closet, we'll find it. If he doesn't, we'll skin him till he does."

"Thank you." Herod was sure skinning him was a metaphor for creating a skeleton, but with his friend, he was never sure. He only knew that those beads of sweat now trickled down his face and onto his collar.

"I am happy you don't want him removed from the race, Herod. That's very mature of you."

"He can run," said Herod, "I just want him beaten and bloodied in the process. After all, democracy must be preserved."

His friend chuckled. He liked sarcasm best when it was unexpected yet effective.

"I see he's going to be at your plant tomorrow. Perhaps…"

"Yes, and he will be allowed to speak to our workers as long as he stays outside the gates. We must give the appearance of being fair, Senator. After all, democracy must be preserved, and the best ones to preserve it are the ones who control it. I mean, who else has that kind of power?"

Herod nodded, which ordinarily would not work on the phone, but he knew his friend didn't expect an argument. Or care that he agreed.

"Your opponent is a man of the people," the CEO went on. "Be wary of him. I'll give you all the information you need to beat him, but the beating is up to you."

The line went dead without another word, leaving Herod to swim in the silence that followed. He missed the old days of the dial tone, the droning buzz telling you definitively the conversation had ended. For now, his only comfort was the bottle of wine he kept for emergencies, which could be anything from celebrating to commiserating. Tonight, he wasn't sure which to toast. He could celebrate his friend's monumental help or worry that, for the first time since his first campaign, he was in for a slog.

God, he needed a drink.

A drink, and a good woman.

That intern.

The one who danced at the office party. The one he couldn't take his eyes off of even after his wife stopped talking to him.

He tapped the intercom that went directly to her office.

"Would you come in here, Salome?"

He poured two glasses of wine instead of one. He'd made up his mind. It was a celebration.

GIVE & YOU SHALL RECEIVE

J esus and Peter stepped from the car, one clearly dressed for this event and the other underdressed but comfortable. The maroon awning stretched from the hotel to the sidewalk, offering shelter to dapper guests and sharp-suited valets in accessorized maroon vests, none of whom jumped up to park the car with the peeling brown paint that made it look as dull as a donkey. It was worth less than the tires on some of the luxury vehicles sitting in the main lot. Peter argued they should have arrived in a limousine or Bentley—something that said style and class. Something that said Jesus was a formidable candidate with powerful backing. He would have even taken a Mustang, a car that proclaimed power rather than this upgraded Pinto they parked by the curb. With any luck, it might be mistaken for trash and hauled away. Jesus, of course, would have none of it. It was his car and it had served him well for more than a decade. He was as loyal to it as it had been to him.

"It's my image," he said. "It makes me one of the people."

"Well, I hope those people show up when we need a push."

Jesus laughed and pointed out that they arrived at their destination without incident.

"Yeah," said Peter, "but also without being noticed." Which was not true. They had been noticed, but for all the wrong reasons. People pointed as they passed, and a tow truck followed them for several miles hoping to pick up business when they broke down. Peter was grateful they had not yet printed up bumper stickers to plaster all over the car like groupies on the road, though he realized those might hold the vehicle together, or at least cover up the rust spots.

Peter popped open the trunk and pulled out a camera bag before handing the keys to a valet who appeared to have drawn the short straw. As the young man ground the car into gear, Peter made a mental note to give him a big tip so that any stories or snide comments he told tomorrow of the shabby, would-be senator had a happy ending. A pound of generosity could always blunt an ounce of derision.

And that's what tonight was all about. Giving one thing to receive another.

Peter put a hand on his candidate's shoulder as they walked up the steps and through the brass-framed glass doors. "Remember, this is about money. They're here because they're curious. And because they hate Herod. Well, mostly because they hate Herod. That's the best way to gain support. It's also the best way to inspire them. Now, you can inspire them, but get the money. In fact, the more you inspire them, the more we get."

"I understand, but we don't need big money. If our supporters give us five or ten dollars, so be it. This will be a movement of the people."

Peter hung his head. This was going to be a tough sell, like Arctic ice vendor or liberal pundit on a conservative station.

"Look, a movement like that can win, but only if every single person in the movement gives. They won't. Ninety percent won't Take the big money when you can, or you'll be outspent like Herod's prince to your pauper."

"Have faith, Peter. People will rise up."

"I'm sure they will, but until they do, hit these people up for the big bucks. We'll call it start-up capital. They're only paying fifty dollars a plate, and that's still doubling our coffers. You get better known, we can make that five hundred a plate. Maybe five thousand. The catch is that you get better known through big money, and that money allows a hundred times more people to give you five- and ten-dollar donations. Got it?"

"Got it. Politics is a pyramid scheme."

Peter chuckled. He wouldn't have drawn it up that way, but it explained why powerbrokers threw money at politicians in order to make more money. "Yes, it is, but for a good cause. Follow the money is a good way to catch criminals. It's also a good way to get elected."

"So I can then become a criminal?"

Peter laughed the last few feet to the ballroom doors.

"That's good. Use that wit against Herod. Call him out."

The porter opened the glass-paneled doors draped in precision-cut, semi-sheer curtains. Twenty heads turned their way, each one above an elegant evening gown or black-tie tuxedo.

Yep, should have sprung for the monkey suit, thought Peter, who realized you don't connect with the poor at a rich man's event. Dress the part you're playing.

Jesus, on the other hand, entered with a broad smile and a wave to the room. Believing you're the way and the truth and the life bolsters your confidence. These donors might not have been his normal social circle, but if they helped him spread his message, he would forever call them friends.

A man in his mid-sixties wearing the best weave money could buy stood up to greet Jesus. He had a warm, firm handshake that showed how excited he was to have this candidate here. As he asked how Jesus wanted to be introduced, Peter stepped away to place the camera on a tripod in the back of the room. He thought he would have a minute or two to set everything up and get it rolling as these introductions usually ambled through a joke or two and excessive, even exuberant, praise for the guest of honor.

"Ladies and gentlemen," the man said, leaning into the microphone attached to the podium by a bendable stand, "our guest tonight needs no introduction because he's asked me not to give him one." This brought as many strange stares from the audience as nervous titters. "He says he will explain who he is. And so, without further ado, I give you the man of the hour and the next six years, Jesus Christ."

I have got to write him a better introduction, sighed Peter, racing to finish his one pre-show task. *Something with pizazz. Something that says he's a superstar and not the understudy to the county commissioner.*

Jesus reached the podium placed dead center on a parqueted dance floor as the speaker gave way, stepping to the side while leading the applause in a vain effort to bring the crowd to its feet. He failed, but it was not entirely his fault since it wasn't what any objective observer would call a crowd. A small gathering perhaps. A herd of well-heeled political paleophytes. But Jesus knew they could become believers because they showed up. They were the only ones who came here out of the hundreds of people invited, and so Jesus took the stage as if entering a stadium, shaking the man's hand and waving and pointing to individual supporters, connecting with every person in the room table by table. He thanked them without quieting them, knowing that twenty diehards could carry his spirit for days and his campaign for hours.

"Thank you so much for that generous welcome. I know you have come to hear me speak not because you are devoted followers but because you no longer believe in Herod or his cause." This was an understatement. These people would vote for nearly anyone else, and Jesus was anyone else. All they wanted to know was that he could stand up to Herod and make a fight of it. They could not abide seeing another idealist crushed under the weight of Herod's political machine. If this Jesus gave them hope, they would give him cash, the surest thing in America to prove commitment.

"I am tired of politicians being the lesser of two evils when the winner should be the greater of two goods. Every politician asks you to join his cause, but I will not, for I am here to join yours. I am here to be your voice in the wilderness when those in power will not listen. I ask not that you serve my cause, but that you let me serve yours. For I tell you now and forever that I come to serve and not be served."

Good, thought Peter. *Hammer that line home. We'll make that our campaign slogan.* He peered into the eyepiece of the video camera. *Damn, he lights up a room.* Almost literally, as this flea-market purchase bought with nearly the last of their campaign cash captured a glow around him.

"But enough about me. Tonight is about you because believe it or not, I know you. You are intolerant of cruelty and corruption and injustice, yet you see injustice every day. Herod turns his back on the poor. He does not see them fed or clothed or housed. You see the rich get tax cuts, and what do they get for this sacrifice?" Jesus paused as the audience gave him a chuckle, aligned with his subtle sarcasm. "Access to power. It is the way of our world. Give, and receive nothing. Receive, and receive more." Jesus shook his head. "But that is not what we want. Give and you shall receive. Take when you should give, and I promise you shall soon give twice as much as any other. Give when you should receive, and you shall receive twice as much!"

A man with an unruly gray beard and matching mop-top leaned over to Peter. "He's amazing. They love him."

Peter whispered back, "Wait until he gets going. They won't elect him—they'll anoint him."

"You know the people of whom I speak," Jesus said. "They rub elbows with the kings they make while scorning the poor on the streets. I know where you stand. You are not at a $2,000-a-plate dinner but here at a fifty-dollar-a-plate buffet. You are not here to cast aspersions, but to create anew! You are not here to impress, but to improve! You have come to give from the heart without taking for the stomach. You believe in the power of the people. And it is that faith that will carry us to victory. It is that faith that will move a mountain of red tape. Because I tell you the truth—if you have faith as small as a mustard seed, you can move a mountain. Say 'Move from here' and it will move! And Herod is that obstacle—the mountain before us!"

There was a small snicker as the paper-thin fasters of this audience recalled Herod's precipitous hips and bulging belly.

Jesus thought it best to move on without ad-libbing or dignifying his inadvertent joke, lest he make it funnier.

"We have people who spend every last dollar on lottery tickets. Tickets that represent the smallest possibility of hope because that hope is all they have left. And the nightly news pitches it right along, telling us the amounts like the carnival barkers they've become. Ten million, one hundred million, one billion! But I tell you this is no different than the man who hears of a treasure buried in a field and sells everything he owns to buy that land."

A murmur arose from the audience attempting to understand this comparison. Unlike his joke at Herod's expense, he would expand upon this. He had to if he wanted to avoid a repeat of the Ten Virgins Disaster.

"The man might never find that treasure because it is a rumor, or he does not know its location. He will die before he ever strikes it rich. We who have the means to help must help. A little from us is a lot to them."

The audience now murmured louder. Was Jesus calling for greater taxation? Charitable donations? Business investment? What exactly was his plan? Even the man next to Peter fell silent, wondering exactly how little he could give that would be a lot to someone else.

"Finally, let me say to you that whatever is true is pure, and we must reflect on those things. We must share what is noble. We must share what is best in this world. Whatever you see in me, put into practice. And our first step must be to remove Herod Antipas from office. He must learn what it means when I say he who is first shall be last, and he who is last shall be first! Rise up and be first! Thank you and goodnight!"

Jesus pounded the podium with his fist to accentuate his point. The audience gave him a hearty round of applause, beyond polite but short of enthusiastic. Two women, however, rose to their feet. One about his age, in a flowing blue gown and enchanting, if understated, diamond earrings and necklace—a woman of some wealth, but who retained her modesty by showing no need to flaunt it. The other was an elderly woman at the front table who struggled to stand but remained determined to do so. She needed to show those behind her that she believed in this message; that she would follow him no matter how slow her steps. She pushed up on her cane, her right hand planted on the back of her chair—until she stood there strengthened by her own accomplishment. The audience burst into greater applause, recognizing her devotion. The pain she endured on his behalf galvanized them to give more.

Jesus smiled at her. She had the inner strength he was looking for. This crowd would follow her lead. If she gave, so would they. Her strength made them stronger.

Peter, in the back of the room, pivoted the camera to catch this sudden standing ovation, zooming in like a TV crew to create the illusion of a much larger crowd, reshaping the room so that it appeared filled to the rafters.

This would look good online.

The man who introduced Jesus returned to say a few words, but Jesus was not ready to give up the spotlight. He stepped into the audience, personally thanking everyone for coming. Peter pulled out his cellphone and opened the camera, snapping candids of his candidate meeting the well-to-do. Well, the well-enough-to-do. They'd get a photographic keepsake of a handshake with the candidate in exchange for Jesus getting some cheap publicity. Cheap for the campaign, not so cheap for the donors.

By the time Peter reached Jesus, the guest of honor had been cornered by the evening's host. They shook hands as though the man would never let go.

"I'll tell you what, Mr. Christ, you get half as much done as you say you can, and you're worth every penny I'm giving you. I'm willing to go right up to the legal line for a campaign donation."

Chump change, thought Peter. *We need millions to win this election. Hell, we need millions to lose this election.*

"Thank you. Anything you can give. You're my kind of people."

Click.

Peter snapped a quick photo. He thought the man might let go if he had his memento, but he didn't take the hint. Peter raised an eyebrow while trying to hide the two fingers rubbing against his thumb, urging Jesus either to move on or ask for a greater sign of support. Jesus had to learn another rule of politics: Pumping the flesh meant pressing the wallet.

Jesus didn't take the hint either.

"Quite a spread you put out tonight."

"Oh, yes, the chicken was delicious, and the fish exquisite. Did you have some? I can get you a doggie bag…"

Oh, for the love of God, thought Peter. There was no greater sign of financial desperation than a candidate leaving a campaign event with a doggie bag. He might as well leave here with his worldly possessions wrapped in a handkerchief tied to a stick or publish a video of him eating shoe leather.

Peter stepped forward before the old man discussed place settings and how much the room cost to rent and what the weather would be on Wednesday. By the time he was done describing the beauty of the wall sconces and how he got the chef to work here because he was first cousin to his electrician's barber, the place would be empty. Jesus needed to make everyone in this room feel important if he wanted them to stay. He had to give of himself if he wanted them to give.

This led to another of Peter's Principles for Political Success: follow your campaign manager when he pulls you away no matter where he's going.

"Smile," Peter interjected, raising his camera to take one last picture. At least he'd make the man feel important without letting him get in a word. The man took the bait and posed for a cheesy photo that would never make the website. "Now, Mr. Christ really should meet a few other people."

"Of course, son," the man went on. "Don't let me keep you. I understand the candidate is busy…"

He was still saying goodbye when Jesus and Peter were five feet away. *What is it,* Peter wondered, *about people who have just enough money to think they're important but your time isn't?*

Peter ushered Jesus toward the exit before the evening's biggest catch escaped. Two more steps and the beguiling woman in the blue gown would have been out the door, forcing them to do this in the drafty hallway where no one—particularly the well-dressed—ever wanted to do business. Contributions were not meant to be observed by eavesdroppers and interlopers.

"Jesus Christ, may I introduce you to a very important person: Miss Mary Magdalene."

The woman offered a porcelain hand in the most professional way. Not the limp hand-over-wrist of an aristocrat, but the firm handshake of a tycoon. After a practiced three seconds, she let go of his hand and gave him a wry smile with a deep right dimple that matched her eyes: mischievous, but with a practiced quirk. He had no doubt she often used that to her advantage.

"It is a pleasure to meet you, Mr. Christ. That was the most impressive, if short, political speech I've ever seen. If you fire up the public this way, we'll be riding your coattails and not the other way around."

Click!

Peter flashed two more in rapid succession under the simple reasoning that you never let the photogenic get away. And Mary Magdalene was undeniably political clickbait.

"If there's any way I can support your campaign, please let me know." She paused as if waiting for instructions on which steps to take next. Toward him, or out the door.

"Whatever you can do to spread the word, Ms. Magdalene, will be greatly appreciated."

"Call me Mary."

Peter took another quick snapshot, if only to remind them he was here. Peter figured this political rule needed its own chapter: Make donors feel special but don't flirt with them. A candidate who gets caught voting for a lobbyist's pet cause after receiving millions makes page ten. Commit insider trading? Page five. Sleep with an intern/supporter/donor/campaign worker/lady you just met in a hotel ballroom, and you become a three-times-a-minute news crawl on the bottom of the screen with added thoughts by opinionated hosts and an extraneous review of the hotel which will mention the candidate had sex there.

"Miss Magdalene, we greatly appreciate your support, but even if you tell everyone you know, and they tell everyone they know, it will never reach all the people advertising can—and that doesn't come cheap."

"Mr. Cephas, isn't it? I will certainly give the campaign the maximum amount—allowed by law, of course."

This brought a smile to Peter's face. That was code for "there are plenty of other ways my money can help your campaign." If it weren't illegal, Peter would carry a list of PACs in his pocket.

"Thank you so much," said Jesus. "Just make sure not to give us a penny more."

"Yes," said Peter, who didn't want to broach the subject of too much money with a woman looking to give them too much money. And while he agreed that the billions pouring into PACs was pure lunacy, he was currently looking to run that particular asylum. But people didn't vote for campaign-finance reform. They voted on bread-and-butter issues. That is, bread and butter for themselves.

"Save your money for the poor," said Jesus. "Better charitable than political."

"My fortune," Magdalene added, "means I can do both."

This put an unmistakable twinkle in Jesus' eyes. "I love that you are on guard against greed."

Now it was Mary Magdalene's turn to smile, if by smile one added blushing cheeks and flitting eyelashes.

Yeah, they're flirting, thought Peter, *but it's harmless.* And he would think that for as long as the money came in.

"Alright, one more photo," announced Peter, knowing he'd get them in the best light when they were in the best mood. Jesus shook Mary's hand.

Click.

Mary put a hand on Jesus' shoulder.

Click.

Mary leaned in and put a cheek next to Jesus' bearded face.

Click.

Well, we can use two out of three. That third one will get too good a go-round in the rumor mill.

Delete.

Jesus finally stepped away, allowing Mary Magdalene, their newest—which was to say their only—major donor to depart for the evening but not before Peter slipped her his business card, complete with an address where she could send a check.

She placed it in her black beaded clutch and said her accountant would be in touch first thing in the morning.

Peter walked away smiling at just how easy that had been. The accountant! The man with the money. His favorite phrase next to slush fund.

Jesus returned to working the room. He took the hand of the elderly woman so determined to stand on her own. Peter readied his camera with one thought in mind: The senior demographic!

Click.

Jesus kissed her on the cheek, putting a big smile on her face.

Should have waited another second, thought Peter. *She's beaming now.*

Yes, Peter realized, kissing a senior citizen past the age of eighty was the political equivalent of kissing a baby, with one major upside: the elderly can vote. You had to wait for the baby by wading through three terms in the Senate—which Peter hoped Jesus would do.

"Thank you so much for coming," Jesus said, leading her toward the door.

"Young man, you take this twenty dollars and when my next check comes in, I'll see that it's twenty more."

"Thank you, ma'am, but please save it for yourself," he said, trying to roll the money back into her hands.

"I won't hear of it. You need it. If I could make it twenty thousand, I would. Anything to stop that wretched Herod.

The way he treats seniors. Privatizing Social Security. Medicare cuts. He ought to be ashamed of himself."

"With your help," Jesus said, "he will be. But I would be ashamed of myself if I took your money."

Peter jumped in, mastering a trick deep in the campaign manager's playbook: give the candidate a dirty look with one eye while charming supporters with the other. "Such a gracious lady. A woman giving when she should be receiving. You'll get back twice as much. Nay, ten times as much! Your faith in our Jesus will be rewarded. Greatly rewarded." Peter took her by the hand like the suave gentleman he could be and led her to the door while Jesus fought back a chuckle. Peter had used his own words against him in a brilliant display of spontaneous strategy.

Jesus tucked the bill in his jacket pocket.

But his campaign manager wasn't done yet. "Oh, it's raining, ma'am. Now, where's my umbrella?"

He hadn't brought an umbrella, but it was all part of the charm. Duplicitous yet effective charm. She appreciated the gesture and only half-expected the umbrella. It was precisely how politicians got away with broken campaign promises.

"Wait here, Mom," said a woman in her mid-forties coming up behind her. "I'll bring the car around."

Peter excused himself, saying she appeared to be in good hands. He headed back through the banquet door to pack up their equipment. The last thing he heard in the second before the door closed was, "Oh, don't bother, dear. I swear my arthritis is gone. I haven't felt this good in years."

WHAT SHE HAS DONE
WILL BE TOLD

P eter met Jesus in the hallway outside the banquet room, camera bag in hand. As they departed the hotel, a woman in a barely-there skirt and skimpier top gave them an inviting smile, or at least what she hoped passed for inviting. Jesus detected a mask of sorrow. Peter hardly detected her at all because they were too similar. Both were selling, not buying, tonight.

When the valet returned with their rumbling rust bucket, her smile diminished, but she fought bravely to keep it up. She shivered, stamping a foot to fight off the evening chill, a stilettoed version of chattering teeth. She glanced toward the hotel's grand entrance, desperate to get inside. The valets and managerial concierge knew this game. Get warm. Get fed. Get paid. Get laid. They would never let her inside unless accompanied by a paying guest willing to pay her way, too.

But in her eyes, Jesus saw the despondence of every last voter he hoped to reach. Her hunched shoulders and emaciated legs indicated a broken spirit, the only thing he could truly fix. The only way for the downtrodden to go was up.

"Peter, I'll meet you at Hades Steel tomorrow."

Peter, standing there with the driver's door open, shook his head. Oh, no, this was not happening. Peter had seen too many staffers make the mistake of ignoring a candidate's peccadilloes. They all seemed to have some perversion that needed covering up. He could put pressure on them to walk away—or better yet, run—but he was a campaign manager, not a personal manager. He could always say, "Well, at least the candidate wasn't cheating on his wife. It was an entirely consensual relationship that the candidate paid for."

And would pay for again and again.

Peter scooted around the back of the car, gripping the edges of Jesus' lapel. "Where do you think you're going? We have a big day ahead of us."

"She needs help, Peter."

"Then she can come to the office. Look, rule number one in politics: Never leave your candidate alone with a woman. Or a reporter. And definitely not a woman reporter."

"What if your candidate is a woman?" Jesus said, poking a hole in Peter's argument, but doing it with the greatest sincerity.

"Then vice versa, so vice doesn't happen. Or can't be claimed as happening."

"That's ridiculous. I can be trusted around a woman."

"Yeah, but maybe she can't be trusted around you. You're a good-looking guy, you know."

"Ha. I guess that means you won't need to change my image then." Jesus rubbed his chin through his beard. "Look, I appreciate your concern, but I'm sure I can resist her advances."

Peter knew Jesus was being glib, but that didn't stop him from pressing his argument. "I'd like to think you're strong, but you went into politics. Your back is naturally wea...uh... more flexible than others." Jesus stepped around Peter onto the sidewalk knowing he had to hurry before the woman, her patience grown thin by their bickering, left for the night. "You know, I bet she's not even a voter."

"Then we should get her registered."

"Hmph," said Peter, who had no better retort. "If the press gets a shot of you talking with her, you go to the top of the tabloids."

Jesus put a hand on Peter's shoulder. "If it worries you that much, park the car over there and keep an eye on us. I'm offering comfort, not cash."

"Fine," said Peter, heading toward the driver's seat. "But you should have been a social worker, not a politician."

"They're the same thing if you fulfill the social contract."

"Hmph," Peter said again as he climbed behind the wheel. He needed stronger arguments if he ever hoped to win a single disagreement with this candidate.

Peter pulled the car forward and executed a three-point turn as if to park before turning the wheel left and lighting up Jesus and the woman with the headlights. It wasn't subtle, but it was effective. They could not ignore his presence.

Jesus raised his right hand to block the light, but the woman squinted until giving up and shielding her eyes, too. Jesus placed his back to the headlights, cutting off the glare on the woman's face. Peter might want to see everything, but he never would until he gave away his suspicions. Until then, he'd cast his doubts like a heavy fishing net.

"Good evening," said Jesus, extending his hand.

"Hey," said the woman, unwilling to remove her hands from the warm spot under her armpits.

"My name's Jesus. What's yours?"

"Bethany."

"That's a beautiful name," Jesus said, though he sensed another mask. "So, what are you doing out here on a frigid night like this?"

"Trying to make some money."

Jesus shifted his eyes toward the hotel. "Seems to be the thing to do here."

He reached into his pocket and pulled out the twenty the old woman gave the campaign. She forced it into his hand to support a good cause, but this was a good cause, too.

"Here, take this."

The woman scoffed just above a whisper. "That won't get you anywhere."

"It isn't supposed to. It's to get you a bite to eat."

"I'm not a charity case. I'll work for it, but twenty bucks won't get you much."

Peter interrupted their conversation with a loud blast of his horn made all the louder as it echoed against the hotel in this half-empty parking lot.

"Unless your friend wants to join us. Maybe he's got some bread."

Every informality this woman used seem forced, unnatural. The street was not her native tongue.

"Bethany isn't your real name, is it?"

"Hey, nobody in this business uses their real name."

"I'm in a similar business, and I use my real name."

"Yeah? What business are you in?"

"Politics."

"Yeah, that business will screw you, too."

The woman laughed until the cold air seized her lungs. Her coughing turned to gasps and guttural choking noises. Jesus put his hand on her shoulder to steady her. "We should get you looked at by a doctor."

"No way I can afford that. That's another business that will screw you."

"I know. Free healthcare is my highest priority."

"Fat lot a good that does me now." The woman stared into his eyes. He meant well. It just meant nothing. "You know, my brother used to preach that, and it got him nowhere."

Jesus noticed that the woman's speech now reflected a refinement missing just moments ago.

"And who is your brother?"

The woman looked at the sidewalk, twisting the pointed tip of a once-fashionable shoe as if crushing a cigarette. She didn't want to answer because, although she had been willing to sleep with him, she never wanted to reveal anything about herself or her real life. But something about this man made her open up. Maybe because he fought for the same causes as her brother.

"Lazarus Larnaca."

Sympathy for this woman's plight tightened Jesus' cheeks. Peter honked again, but Jesus held up a finger, instructing him to hold on a minute longer.

35

"Your brother ran a terrific campaign against Herod. I supported many of his…"

"Yeah? Well, Herod destroyed him in that election. Killed his political career and eviscerated our family fortune. Now, my brother is too sick to work and I'm out here working the streets."

She fought back tears with fierce words, but her disgust was a plea. She was not beaten yet—not by Herod, not by the night, and not by the world. The despondent did not cry.

"You do know that I'm running against Herod?"

"Good for you. Now get out before you end up like my brother."

"I'm afraid I can't. While cruelty exists, I must carry on."

The woman pulled her top tighter as the wind picked up. She couldn't stay outside much longer. If there was no money here, she'd find someone else. Some sucker worried about her immediate future and not some better tomorrow. Maybe politics and prostitution were different after all. Politicians focused on the future at the expense of today. Prostitutes worried about today because there might not be a tomorrow.

"Is that twenty bucks to fight Herod?"

"Yes."

Bethany bit her lip. She wanted to snatch it. Tuck it away somewhere this Boy Scout would never grab it, but her ambitions gnawed at her. Damn it! She was no better than her brother. Politics is prostitution for greedy people, and she just couldn't do it. All that separated the world's oldest profession with its most ignoble was ethics. If she hadn't had them before, she had them now. "I…I need…"

"Here," Jesus said, wrapping her ice-stiff fingers around the bill.

"I told you—I don't take…"

"It's not charity. As of tomorrow, you work for my campaign. Consider this a small advance. We'll resurrect your family's fortunes yet."

The woman hung her head. Yep, another promise of a golden future, even if this politician was putting his money where his mouth was. But then selling insincerity was the mark of every successful candidate.

Sometimes the good ones rise above it.

Jesus walked toward the car, stopping to look at her before climbing in the passenger's seat. The headlights that framed her were dimmer than the halo that surrounded her.

She tucked the bill inside her blouse.

"My name's Mary."

Jesus smiled. "I've always liked that name. We'll see you tomorrow...Mary."

WORTHY OF HIS REWARD

Peter and Jesus, with Andrew at the wheel, sat in the backseat of Jesus' unmistakable clunker reviewing the morning papers. Peter grabbed more than a half-dozen copies from around the state while purchasing donuts by the full dozen this morning to give to the first shift at Hades Steel, a mere twenty minutes from the Bethlehem streets where Jesus entered the world.

"I'll give you the good news first. Patmos gave us a great write-up in *The Bethlehem Star*. 'Jesus Christ has come to transform us. He will lift our spirits and lead us from financial bondage. This reporter is convinced that Christ can destroy the plague we have set upon ourselves,' This is priceless. Golden. I'm sorry we offered him a job."

"That bad, huh?" said Jesus.

"Well, *The Philadelphia Inquisition* played it straight. *Political Unknown Declares Senate Candidacy.* Boring! Snoozefest if there ever was one. They go on to say you're inexperienced and seem confused at times. There's a little sidebar on the virgin thing, but nothing big."

"That's not bad," said Jesus, examining the rows of shuttered homes and bordered-up businesses that negated vague memories of the city's former prosperity.

"Yeah, but you're forgetting the first rule of journalism: If it bleeds, it leads, and that's exactly how the rest of the press is treating this—like it's got blood all over it. Look at the headlines: *Candidate's Weird Position on Virgins. Virginal Candidate Loves Virgins.* And *The Morning Star* went full tabloid: *Virgins Screw*

Candidate. Just fantastic. It hooks the reader with a sex scandal in which there's no sex and no promise of sex. I mean, that's the worst kind of sex scandal—one in which there's no actual sex. The only thing those virgins screwed is your chance of winning."

"It's not over yet, Peter. The people will come to understand what we stand for."

"You're right, it's not over. Not by a longshot. But we're in a deep hole. You're trending number one right now. It's twenty to seven and *The Morning Star* has more than two hundred comments on this story." Peter flipped open his phone to reveal the paper's homepage. "Make that two-twenty. No…two-thirty."

"Then everyone will know my name. I can take a joke as long as I get my message across."

Jesus' reassuring smile did little to reassure Peter. "You have to explain everything so that there is no misunderstanding. Treat everything like a vague parable without *CliffsNotes*. Just don't tell any actual vague parables."

"I'll do my best," replied Jesus, struggling not to tell Peter that he believed people understood the parables. Explanations only ruined their potency. They were like jokes—if you had to explain them, they weren't working.

"We're here," Andrew said over his shoulder. He parked the car along the curb closest to the razor-wire fences that gave the steel plant all the warmth of a gulag in winter.

"The way to beat this, Peter, is to meet the voters without fear. We can win this."

Peter shook his head and let out a short sigh as he dragged a finger across the car window. "You're lucky people hate reporters as much as politicians. If you get a fair shake, it's because the voters think the media is sticking it to you."

"I'll take that advantage if that's all we have. Now, speaking of fair shakes, let's go shake some hands."

"Fair enough," said Peter, continuing their play on words. "But please don't tell people you're pumping the flesh or we'll never hear the end of the sex jokes."

Three-dozen workers milled about the gated entrance smoking cigarettes and talking ballgames and kids before resigning themselves to punching in. They hardly paid attention when, an hour after dawn, a fifteen-year-old American car containing more steel than contemporary models pulled up outside the guardhouse. It was the kind of car many of them drove, and the rust spots along the passenger side gave it convincing character. They also didn't pay much attention to the long-haired figure with workman's hands making his way through the haze of cigarette smoke, exhaust, and environmentally underregulated fumes. If it hadn't been for the plain brown suit best suited for a lodge party or city-hall wedding, they might not have noticed him at all. For all they knew, he was some puffed-up, self-important government inspector who came here to make their lives hell despite having no real power to do so. They just didn't think he was important. Even after he introduced himself.

"Good morning. I'm Jesus Christ, and I'm running for the Senate against..."

"Yeah, good luck with that." And they kept talking.

Peter approached them from behind Jesus, his sharp suit raising a few eyebrows. This man was not here to apply for a position sifting scrap metal—and he made no pretensions otherwise. He had a blue-collar walk about him—forceful, shoulders pulled back by arms widened two inches further than necessary. He held his head high but not lofty, his jaw a flat ninety degrees from his neck. Still, there was no mistaking the stare that lasted a second too long. He eyed them as if he believed he did so in secret, faking a familiarity that indicated his smoldering contempt for them. He had worked his way out of the pits and had no intention of going back—and he wanted them to know it. Which only made them want to smear his suit. Or punch in his face. If only the guy in the brown suit wasn't so busy shaking their hands.

Andrew, the last to exit the car, held their attention the longest. He popped open the trunk and set up boxes of donuts and a portable coffee machine. Well, any candidate who brought coffee and donuts was worth a few minutes of their time. No reason to be rude, after all.

Jesus smiled as the men approached Andrew's makeshift café. Peter was right when he said, "The way to a voter's heart is through the stomach." And the worse the food, the better. That way, any indigestion could be blamed on the meal and not the message, meaning each box of donuts was worse than the last, from sprinkled and frosted to glazed and jelly-stuffed, to the final box containing deep-fried donuts wrapped in bacon and injected with mass-produced and artificially flavored crème. They finished that box first.

"Please, enjoy," said Jesus. "There's plenty more." The workers dug in, giving him the chance to talk with them individually and in small groups. Peter worked the line ten feet down, telling everyone to enjoy the free coffee and donuts but to be sure to grab some facetime with the candidate. He could help them if they gave him a chance.

"Let me get that," said Jesus, handing a cup of coffee to one of the men. "After all, I'm here to serve."

"Yeah, coffee and donuts," said someone at the table.

Tough room, thought Jesus, *if we were actually in a room.* Still, he admired their honesty. If every joke contained a grain of truth, these men were up to their eyeballs in integrity.

"Yeah, I saw that on the news," said another worker. "You really here to serve?"

"Absolutely."

"'Cause I got a sick kid—Mark…Little Mark—but my insurance don't pay his bills. My wife can't work much 'cause she's gotta care for him, and I can't see him 'cause I gotta put in the overtime."

Jesus shook his head, exuding sympathy. "Where is your son being treated?"

"Mercy Hospital for chemo and…other…" The man faltered.

"How many of you are worried about healthcare?"

Dozens of hands went up without hesitation.

"I promise that if you send me to the Senate, I will fight day and night for healthcare—yes, free healthcare for all. Healthcare is a right, not a privilege."

"How you gonna pay for that?" yelled someone in back.

Jesus launched into an ad hoc plan of tax hikes on the well-to-do, corporate incentives, price negotiations, tax breaks, and lower deductibles. "If religious organizations pay no taxes for healing our souls, hospitals should pay lower taxes for healing our bodies."

Behind Jesus, Peter scrambled to write this down. They had no healthcare plan on their website. For that matter, they barely had a website. He was going to have to get this up there as soon as possible in case someone checked. You couldn't just say "I have a great healthcare plan" and then put one thing—or nothing—on your website. Nobody would fall for that.

"But for you," Jesus went on, "it will be free. That's my promise. That's my belief." Jesus leaned forward and unexpectedly hugged the man worried about his son.

The man pushed back, a stern glare fixed on his face. Peter stepped in to stop any confrontation that could ruin this gathering, but the voters' short attention spans offered him the reprieve he needed as they yelled out their own issues and concerns.

"I can't put food on the table."

"Don't worry about food or drink. Seek righteousness. Overcome the rich and those things will be given to you. Elect me and let me fight for your justice."

The man stood there befuddled. Not the answer he expected. Or wanted. Jesus might as well have said, "Let them eat cake," except for the call to attack the rich. Righteousness wasn't about to put food on his table.

But the loud blast of a distant buzzer brought scores of heavily booted workers out of the factory, creating a surge of people in both directions.

"What can I do to help?"

"Ask and you shall receive, seek and you shall find. Spread the word. Let them know change is coming. Let the world know Herod is finished!"

His voice rose above the din, crossing the yard like a bullhorn. The third-shift employees gathered around this man too mild to be so boisterous, caught in the crossfire between a preaching politician and a stack of free donuts.

"You want to escape poverty?" said Jesus to one passerby. "Know yourself. If you do not know yourself, you will dwell in poverty and be that poverty."

"What the hell does that mean?"

"You are responsible for you, but I will set you on the path to riches and righteous prosperity."

"What about better wages?"

"The laborer is worthy of his reward."

"Huh?" said the man, raising an eyebrow before shrugging.

"You should get paid more. Wages should jump until workers are paid every penny they're worth."

"Got my vote."

The workers continued streaming by, more engaged than their morning counterparts.

"Why you?"

"Because I understand leadership. Whoever wants to lead must serve. I did that as a union rep, and I will do that in the Senate because I tell you that I come to serve and not be served."

"Hey," said a passerby, "I heard that on the news last night."

"That was me."

"Right! You're the Virgin Guy! Hey, it's the Virgin Guy!"

Jesus spoke over the snickers as the excited group swarmed around him like a celebrity sighting.

"It's good you remember me, but it was just a parable."

"Yeah, it was some kind of bull."

Jesus laughed along with them. This morning had all the good-natured-yet-cutting insults of a day on the worksite hefting boards and framing houses. But Peter couldn't let his

43

candidate be known as Virgin Guy. He darted between bodies, hoping to direct his candidate back to the issues. Then again, this was drawing a crowd. More people would listen to Virgin Guy than Unknown Candidate Guy. Virgin Guy had a hook.

Peter had to admit Jesus was right. The only way to combat this was to meet the people and win them over. They might realize that Virgin Guy, like many virgins, was a tad more experienced than they expected.

Jesus spoke for the next hour, though he could have gone another day if they let him. His voice bounced off the concrete slabs and buildings like the call of a wild man brought down from the mountains. The workers hung on his every word, huddling around him, sensing an exciting break in their routine. They could tell everyone they met Virgin Guy, and he was alright. Just your regular Joe. The kind of guy you could vote for if you wanted to shake up the system.

Only Peter tapping his shoulder quieted him.

"We have to go. You've got a big meeting back at the office."

"I do?"

"Yeah, you do."

"What about?"

"It's a surprise."

"I'd rather be here with the voters, my people..."

"It's time you lived by an old showbiz maxim: always leave 'em wanting more. If you satisfy them here, they won't visit your website and give us money."

Jesus nodded. Fire them up like a blast furnace and let the word spread like molten steel. The many he touched today could touch so many more tomorrow. He'd come back so they could hear him again, but for now, they'd heard enough.

As Jesus and Peter left the scene and the steelworkers headed home, one figure remained. Hades Steel's powerful CEO watched everything from his glass-plated perch high above the plant. He just had to meet this Jesus.

BLESS THOSE WHO
CURSE YOU

P eter and Jesus wound their way back to the car to find Andrew loading the coffee and donuts into the trunk. Peter helped him slide the folding table in, then told his brother to make good time getting back to headquarters.

"No," Jesus said. "Mercy Hospital."

"The hospital? Why?"

"There's a little boy I'd like to see."

"But we have to get back…"

"Nazareth can wait a little longer."

Peter wasn't sure how long he could keep his surprise in check. Probably most of the day if he applied pressure, but since most situations have more than one pressure point, he picked the one likely to provide the result he wanted. "How about we arrange to see him this afternoon? Makes it look less impromptu, which means less desperate."

Jesus knew Peter had some scheme up his tailored sleeve but let him have his way. He couldn't put him in charge of the campaign and not have him run it.

Andrew pulled away from the curb, rolling between the departing workers with care as if exiting a sold-out concert. He turned left onto 8th Ave. and headed north toward Nazareth. Peter sank into his seat, partly caused by his desire to relax and partly caused by the springs giving out. He was pleased with how the day was going, though he couldn't take all the credit.

The candidate had to get some of it, at least openly. Quick compliments are gold stars to a candidate.

"That went well," he said. "You're a natural with the working class."

"It's easy to give them hope," said Jesus, "because they need it the most."

"Yeah, but they're also in your backyard. We need to reach all of them throughout the state, and that won't be easy with the media piling on."

"I'll walk to every town if I have to."

Peter chuckled. "That's not a bad publicity stunt, but we'd never get you west of Ephrata before Election Day. We need to do what Herod's doing. We have to campaign without ceasing. It has to be like breathing. If you stop, you choke. We have to combine personal appearances with mass media. I mean, look at Herod. He's way ahead in the PR game. Before you know it, he'll be headed down the homestretch while we're still in the starting gate. He's grabbing the best headlines and landing the best interviews. It's amazing. He sits there dodging questions with his head up his ass while his hand-picked reporters sit there nodding like bobblehead dolls. They're not even lobbing softball questions. They stand three feet away tossing him foam balls like he's a two-year-old, and half the public eats it up."

"Yeah, but Herod works the camera better than anyone," said Andrew over his shoulder.

"That's because he has to be slick," replied Peter, who thought oily was a better word for it. "It's the only way to get people to vote for you while you're screwing them."

"Then that's how we beat him," said Jesus. "We hammer home his hypocrisy. If we attack him on the issues, the people will come to us. They'll have to."

Peter turned his head to look out the window as Route 22 came into view. They'd be in Nazareth in less than twenty minutes. That was enough time to make his point.

"Herod doesn't do issues. That's why he wins. We play one game while he plays another."

"We have to take the high road, Peter."

"The high road is the road to low expectations." He let that sink in for a second, but only a second, continuing on before Jesus could respond. "The high road always has less mud to sling, but Herod, for all his talk of clean campaigns, will get down and dirty. He'll crawl into the slop like a common pig and claim he sizzles like bacon. Both Herod and our porcine friends are happy wallowing in shit, and neither one thinks it's dirty. You can't nail Herod for hypocrisy because his supporters don't care. Want proof? Hey, Andrew, it's ten o'clock. Flip on the radio—any AM station will do."

Andrew raised an eyebrow in defeat. He hated AM radio this time of day, but orders were orders. He pushed the button on the dashboard and flipped to the first station offering a clear signal. A deep voice boomed from the speaker. He reached to turn down the volume, then realized it was almost at zero.

'It's *The Saul Tarsus Show* with your host, Saaaauuuulll Tarsus, author of *Saul Is Super, If I Ran the World,* and *Lying Liberal Losers of Loonytown.* The man the left can't stand and the right can't wrong—the superb superstar of it all, the man who counters the left by being right, Saaaauuuulll Tarsus!"

Jesus blanched at the sheer smugness of that introduction. God himself couldn't follow such a build-up. The man needed a dose of humility. A dose that could kill a horse. Or a horse's ass.

"Thanks for tuning in everyone, but then what else would you listen to? This is the best show ever. I'm your host, Saul Tarsus, the voice of sound reason. Your speakers bring you the sound, I bring you the reason. Yes, we're a team. I make this show possible; you make it profitable, and boy, are we gonna be cashin' in today. I guess you heard some pervert—sorry, lefty p.c.'ers—alleged pervert is running for Senate against our old friend, Herod Antipas. Did you catch that press conference? That hippie—that happy hippie—comes out there, long hair, tangled beard, and I'm guessing sandals over dirty feet and gnarled toenails, and offers, I don't know, what do you call it? Some kind of lovefest. Some kind of weird love-in. How many times did he say virgin? Ten, twenty, I don't know. Virgin this and virgin that, it was everywhere. Pure smut, that's what it was. Pure smut. Well, we don't need to talk about virgins on this show to get your attention."

Peter gave Jesus a crossways glance, but it was hardly subtle. Christ's political enemies were going to pound this home until everyone knew just enough about the story to not really know anything at all.

"Because we're a family show, we're not going to talk about virgins and whatever this Christ fellow was trying to get across, you know, about virgins. But why...why..."

Saul's pauses were long enough to get in a quick nap if it weren't for the punctuating words acting like a snooze alarm.

"...why ten virgins? He could have picked any number. Two would have done it. One hundred makes it unbelievable. Ten...ten...ten sounds like a fantasy. Like he's the pervert I say he is. Sorry, political cucksters—*alleged* pervert. Oh, look at that. The phone lines are lighting up. I know that's some of you calling in to back me on this, but I'm sure some are his mental midget supporters—and I only call them that not to offend the midgets out there—sorry, political chuckleheads—little people, but to point out that their brains have left their skulls for their backsides. Now, I know what they say: it's a parable. What the hell is a parable? That's one of those big words teachers use for fairy tales. Yeah, I said it. Fairy tales! His supporters will say this whole parable thing is not actually about virgins. Noooo, of course not. He only went back out there to talk about it some more. It's all about virgins! It's all about shock value! It's no parable. In fact, I'd drop the para part and say it's all bullsh..."

An air horn blasted through the radio speakers in place of the standard bleep. Jesus smiled, his lips barely turning upward, lest Peter see he was amused. Not by the content of Saul's message, which was horrid, but by the thought that no matter how effective the airhorn was at jarring his listeners, it should be the wakka wakka of a clown's horn. Jesus couldn't tell if Tarsus was a comedian or commentator but figured he was a little of both.

"...Sorry, political coppers—can't say what I really feel without you wanting me in free-speech jail. Para-b.s., that's what it is. Sorry to have gotten that off my chest first thing in the morning, but we have to talk about it. We have to broach the subject. We have to pop our cherry."

Saul gave that a long pause, possibly for dramatic effect or quite possibly to let the listener laugh and prove he was the comedian Jesus thought he was.

"We'll go to the phones right after these messages, so stay on the line. But remember—keep it clean. This is a family-friendly show that backs your family values."

The ads rolled through in quick succession, each carefully aimed at Saul's target demographic. Life insurance, followed by another ad for life insurance, then spots for a chain of funeral homes, a law firm that helped with living wills, more life insurance, a hair-growth product, and finally, a short ad for erectile dysfunction. Halfway through the ad, and not a moment too soon, Andrew parked the car outside campaign headquarters and turned off the radio as the commercial pitchman concluded the final ad with, "Life is hard, and you should be t..."

Click.

The trio climbed out of the car, whereupon Andrew held the office door open for Jesus and his brother. A second after their candidate ducked inside, Peter turned to their temporary doorman and said, "We have got to put a sign in that window. Anything to make us look like a legitimate campaign."

Andrew nodded and followed his brother inside. "I'll check the coffers. We should have a few bucks after last night."

Yeah, a few bucks, thought Peter, *which I hope is synonymous for a few million.* In some circles, it was.

Peter stopped just inside the office door. There sat the streetwalker from last night. *Looks like we not only gained a few dollars but a volunteer. She might not be top of the line, but beggars can't be choosers.* Except in politics, which was supposed to welcome every possible voter into the big tent but had to be choosy with donors because they came with baggage. And every bag containing a million dollars held a potential millstone. You couldn't align yourself with every donor no matter how much money they wanted to give you. Not if they gave money to a cause you couldn't support, or worse, made their money from a cause you couldn't support. Still, this woman could pass as long as no one knew her story. She ditched the miniskirt and stilettos for a pantsuit and espadrilles. She certainly cleaned up better than anyone else around here, but then there weren't many people around here to clean up.

Peter extended his hand cordially, not wanting to know her too well in case she was a political liability. "Peter Cephas, campaign manager. And you are?"

"Mary." Peter waited for more. He wasn't about to have anybody on board whose last name he didn't know. He'd never get a full background check on her without one. "Larnaca. Mary Larnaca."

"I knew you looked familiar!" Now, Mary raised an eyebrow. What sort of man knew a lady of the evening by her looks? Right. A cop. Or a politician. "You're Lazarus' sister. I volunteered on his campaign. Collected voter rolls and did targeted messaging. Shame what happened to him."

Mary smiled weakly. While she appreciated his concern, she didn't feel as comfortable around him as she did Jesus. She didn't want to tell Peter the shape her brother was in.

"Welcome to the campaign, Mary. We'll get you started in just a minute, but first, I have big news."

Peter turned the conference-room doorknob halfway before giving Jesus a cockeyed smile.

"Come see your surprise."

Peter spun the knob the rest of the way and pushed.

THE GREAT MUST SERVE

Peter swung open the door like he expected someone to yell, "Surprise!" Instead, nine stoic faces stared at Peter, Jesus, Andrew, and Mary as they entered the room. Peter greeted their silence with exuberance as he tapped Jesus in the stomach with the back of his hand.

"Meet your campaign team. I spent as much time as I could yesterday recruiting these guys. They're some of the best in the business, and after we got steamrolled over the last twenty-four hours, we need them."

"Peter, where did we get the money for this?"

"Don't worry about it. All campaigns run on debt." That answer didn't mollify the boss, who hated the idea of any contractor being shorted pay, so Peter gave him more detail. "They're working for deferred payment."

"If we promised to pay them, then we must pay them."

"Well, right now, they're being gracious and donating their time, but we will pay them. Some money was fronted to us last night by your somewhat wealthier supporters. It's enough to get us started, but before we do that…" Peter leaned around Jesus to address Mary. "Since you're the volunteer here, could you get us some coffee? Thanks."

Mary was insulted, but now was not the time to make a scene. At least she could get a cup for herself and a leftover donut or two from the boxes Andrew brought in. A day with a decent breakfast wasn't all bad.

"Peter, I promised Mary we'd pay her, too."

Mary stopped half a foot outside the door. Donuts and coffee could wait. The right deal today might mean a better breakfast tomorrow.

"Okay, we'll get her on the books first thing."

Mary pulled three donuts from the box and wrapped them in a napkin. This campaign was more broke than a drunk at closing time. "First thing" was never a sure thing.

Peter closed the door behind her, gesturing for Jesus and Andrew to take their seats while he took command of the room. Pointing to his left, to the upper corner of the rectangular table, he rattled off names and titles.

"You already know John. Everyone else, this is John Patmos, our speechwriter. Next to him is his brother, James. He's our advance man."

Jesus waited for Peter to elaborate.

"He'll head into town a day or two before you're scheduled to speak. He'll talk to the locals, find out what's important to them, relay it to John—bingo!—you got a speech. Next to him is Thomas Didymus, former copy editor and your fact-checker. The guy questions everything, which means everything that comes out of Herod's mouth. You get it right; Herod gets it wrong. On the corner is Simon Zelotes—Simon Z as I like to call him. He's on data analytics. He'll be crunching poll numbers and poring over demographics. If you need to pick it up somewhere, he'll let you know. At the end is Thaddeus Lebbaeus, good ol' Tad. He's your strategist. He'll help you stress kitchen-table issues. Watercooler issues. Sitting-on-the-toilet-thinking-to-yourself issues. Then there's a man you know, James Alphaeus…"

"Two Jameses?" said Jesus.

"We'll give one of them a nickname. Don't worry about it. Anyway, you two did some work in the carpenters union together, so he'll be our union liaison. We want to keep those guys on our side. Coming around the next corner is your rural liaison, Barnabas Antioch. We're calling him Barney because small towns love that downhome touch. Then there's my brother,

Andrew, who's our assistant campaign manager. You can't get a hold of me or Jesus, you reach out to Andrew and let him know what's up. Next is Philip Bethsaida, your event coordinator. He'll be booking your speaking venues. Now comes the underbelly of the beast. That's Bartholomew. No last name needed. Just call him Bart, as in Black Bart. He's one tough son of a bitch."

"Which means what?" said Jesus, grasping the edge of the table. He had no doubt a political team needed such a man. He, himself, had been called a tough son of a bitch during his union days, but they were fighting for the basic right to work, and sick pay and healthcare benefits. What did it mean here?

"Bart takes the heat for controversial ideas. He puts something out there to see how the public reacts. If they like it, it's your idea. If they don't, Bart says he was speaking for himself and not the campaign. You then offer a different position."

"Deceptive," said Jesus, a hint of disappointment in his voice.

"Not if you believe your new position," replied Peter, a haughty chuckle in his.

"And if I don't?"

"Offer the position you believe in." Peter didn't wait for Jesus to voice any further opposition. He admired idealism, as long as it included winning as ideal. "Our last team player, sitting right next to our candidate, is Judas Iscariot. Judas is our muckraker, our mudslinger, our dirty trickster. If Herod wants to play dirty pool, Judas makes sure his balls get knocked around."

The men in the room laughed. It was as good an analogy for campaigning as they'd heard in a while. Only Jesus kept a straight face, concern furrowing his brow.

"No more of that, Peter. We have to run a clean campaign. We can't use dirty tricks."

"They're not dirty tricks," said Peter. "It's opposition research."

The group laughed again, but that explanation didn't sit well with Jesus. It felt like heading south when your moral compass pointed north. He'd have to guide Judas to a better path.

"Now, before we kick around some ideas…"

Peter stopped as Mary entered the room carrying a drawer from her desk. Inside were twelve cups of coffee with assorted creamers and sugars on the side. Jesus beamed at her ingenuity. No wasted trips, no added costs, and everyone got what he wanted. The advisers made up their coffees with different amounts of cream and sugar, each reflective of his personality. Judas took his black without sweeteners of any kind.

How appropriate, thought Jesus. *What you take in is truly what you are.*

"Thank you, Mary," said Peter. "And guys, be sure to give Mary a tip on the way out. She's working gratis for now so you can work better."

"Hey, here's a tip," said Simon. "Buy low and sell high."

"Right," added Barney, going deep into his redneck character. "And don't count your chickens before they hatch."

"Or put all your eggs in one basket," said Philip, as everyone laughed along.

Mary frowned, gripping the desk drawer tighter, ready to chuck it at the next man who spoke. Her disappointment grew when Jesus stood up. She didn't expect him to join their boys club fun. Well, if she had to throw it at him, so be it. What could they do? Throw her back on the street?

"Mary," Jesus began, "I'd like to say something that goes for all of us. Whoever wants to be great must serve, and today, you have been great. Thank you."

Mary smiled, tears forming in the corners of her eyes. Those were the nicest words anyone had said to her in six years. Once again, on a different day, Jesus earned her loyalty. She nodded her head and ducked out the rear door, waiting until she was in the hallway to wipe away the creeping tears.

"We all must serve," continued Jesus. "Each other, as well as the people. Then, and only then, will we be great."

The men looked at the table, their frivolity over. They didn't dare question the boss. Not because he was the boss, but because they inherently understood he was right. What had been meant as good fun had become mean-spirited, and they had been appropriately chastised. Jesus returned to his seat, motioning for Peter to continue.

"So, let that be a lesson to all of us," Peter said. "We're on the same team." He paused a moment for no reason except to give his words the same gravitas as the boss's. They didn't, but with all eyes upon him and not the candidate, he felt the need to give it a shot. Having missed the net, the backboard, and possibly the floor with an airball, he picked up a blue marker from the whiteboard behind him and pointed to Simon. "Alright, what do you have for us?"

Simon spread several sheets in front of him, each one packed with lines of data and scribbled notes.

"According to overnight polling by SixSixSix, you and Herod are in a dead heat. He's up by three points, a statistical tie since it's within the margin of error. Here's where it gets interesting. Among people who've never heard of you, you're winning. That means they hate Herod so much, they'll vote for Candidate X. That's you."

"That's good," said Tad, conducting strategy on the fly. "We use that hatred for Herod while keeping you likable. You're a blank slate. If you follow this list of talking points…" Tad pulled a piece of paper from a stack in front of him and slid it across the table to Jesus. "…you'll stay that way. One: Veterans are heroes. Two: Children are the future. Three: We're studying that. Four: We're talking to experts. Five: Always say we. It allows you to spread the blame. Six…"

"There's nothing in here about policy," said Jesus.

"Sure there is. Eight: The middle class is overtaxed. Nine: My policies will lift people up. Ten: Our military is the best in the world. Eleven: First responders are heroes…"

"Is there anything specific?"

"No. We don't put out policy sheets until we see how it polls. Which is where Simon and Bart come in. See, we're already working like a well-oiled machine."

Jesus turned to Simon. "I don't want people liking some vague candidate. I want them to like me for who I am."

"Yeah," said Simon. "SixSixSix covered that. You're up by twenty points over Herod among people who've never seen a picture of you. The bad news is, you're down by twenty among people who have."

"I was getting to that," said Tad.

"Me, too," added Peter.

"What's wrong with the way I look?"

"Study the Senate yearbook," replied Tad. "It's a tribute to assimilation. Not a single member has a beard. Not one. I think one has a mustache, but you have to blow up his photo to find it. And no one has long hair. Even the women have bobs."

"I'm not getting a bob."

"You don't have to, but you need to look the part. If you want to be in the Senate, you have to look senatorial. People have to see you as a senator, not a hippie from a hemp shop."

"It's just not polling in the sticks," added Barney. "People hate it."

"I'm not changing who I am just to appeal to voters. This is who I am. This is my look. I've had it since high school."

"And that's just it," said Tad, drumming his fingers on the table, his frustration evident. "You're a high-schooler from the '70s. If I said draw me a picture of a teenage slacker, they'd draw you. We need to upgrade your image to something that says power and confidence…"

"Hey, how will I explain his sudden change in appearance?" asked James Patmos. "I'll have to address it in a press release or something."

"Great question," Tad said. "Hey, we should call you that. James the Great. I love it. Anyway, we explain it by saying that Mr. Christ has been so busy getting his campaign off the ground and caring for the great people of this state—saying the great people of this state is point number six by the way—that he hasn't had time to take care of himself, but now that the campaign is under control, he's gotten a shave and gone to a barber."

"I'm not changing my look!"

"Fine!" said Tad, throwing up his hands and pushing back his chair. "Maybe we can grab the youth vote and motivate some of the far left to swing our way to make up for those who pick Herod because he looks like a damned senator! That's the best I got."

Peter raised his hands, one palm toward Jesus and the other toward Thaddeus. "Alright, everyone calm down. Keep your look. You're the candidate. Tad, develop a strategy encouraging the underrepresented to show up at the polls. James, get some very flattering images of the candidate. Give him a glow. You know, a shine around his face. Maybe even a halo. Let people see him as we do, in the best light."

"Got it."

"Alright, anything else?"

The room stayed quiet. Everyone except Tad stared at Jesus. He fidgeted in his chair, overcome by the impossible task in front of him. The candidate picked the hardest path forward, making it that much harder to sell the middle-of-the-road message needed to win a statewide election.

Jesus thanked everyone for their hard work and said he looked forward to seeing their results. Peter told John and Andrew he wanted to see them in his office in half an hour, and for Judas and Bart to show up thirty minutes after that. As the meeting broke up and the staffers departed, Peter pulled his seat to the corner of the table nearest Jesus.

"Don't be too hard on Tad. He's got your back. He knows how to put together a winning strategy."

"I know, but we must not fall into temptation. The election is important, but I will not lose myself to win their praise."

"Okay, we'll figure it out. We'll just construct a series of campaign promises that reach the groups that support you. Remember what the legendary Tip Schlemiel said: 'All politics is local.'"

"No offense to Mr. Schlemiel, but all politics is not local. All politics is emotional. Inspired people vote. Social issues drive voters, not pocketbook issues. It's why the poor vote against their interests time and again. No, Peter, we must motivate them. We must bring people to the polls who might not otherwise vote. We will address the issues, but with an emotional plea. The key to winning is voter turnout. The greater the turnout, the better we do. If you touch the heart, you stir the feet."

Peter rubbed his chin. Jesus was right, of course, but it was a gamble. Relying on the unlikely to vote was almost as hard as getting party-line voters to give the other party a chance. That only happened once in a lifetime—when they aged out of the liberal party and into the conservative one.

"Alright, I'll talk to Tad. We'll develop a strategy for reaching your natural supporters—the poor, the disenfranchised, the overlooked. We'll get them to the polls even if they're kicking and screaming. And John and James will…"

A knock at the door interrupted Peter. He expected it to be Tad offering to make peace or pitch a new idea, but a concerned Mary opened the door.

"There's a phone call for Mr. Christ. It's the head of Hades Steel."

A MILLSTONE AROUND
YOUR NECK

Jesus put the conference-room phone on speaker so Peter could hear. Mr. Lucifer, the powerful CEO of Hades Steel and its seven subsidiaries, was more than cordial. He was endearing. He was glad to see someone taking on Herod and suggested they have a meeting sooner rather than later. He said it was possible he might throw his support behind Jesus if he liked what he heard.

Peter's eyes brightened like the morning sun. Lucifer carried weight with both the donor class and the working class. The right meeting could mean an insurmountable windfall pouring into their war chest.

Jesus was not so sure. Lucifer's support might put him at odds with those he cared most about: his union brethren. He had battled men like Lucifer his entire life and saw no reason to give up the struggle now. Still, he would hear him out.

"I'll be back in Bethlehem late this afternoon. Perhaps we could meet tonight."

Lucifer agreed, on one condition. "You must come alone. No campaign manager. This meeting is between the top dogs and no one else."

Peter was about to object. That had to be another rule of politics. Only meet a campaign donor in public. Alone in his office left you open to charges of graft and quid pro quo because if it wasn't your intent, it was certainly his.

But Jesus held up a finger to keep him quiet.

"How does eight o'clock sound?"

"I'll let security know you're coming."

Jesus entered the children's ward at Mercy Hospital and asked to see Mark. The nurse at the desk wondered if he was a family member, friend, or some stranger off the street in need of a good meal and a haircut. And maybe a suit that wasn't a decade old. She did not recognize him as a Senate candidate, but frequent double shifts at another underfunded hospital had that effect. It kept her in her own little world and not on top of the world outside. She admired that this man before her made lengthy eye contact, though. There was a softness to him, a gentility that spoke of a man of the cloth even if he looked like a man in need of conversion. His request convinced her that he was here to minister to the child rather than cause problems. And with the boy having no visitor restrictions, she pointed him down the hall to his room on the right.

Jesus told Peter to have a seat in the lounge. He'd only be a few minutes, and he was sure, he joked, that Peter would enjoy catching up on the news. There had to be more about the race.

Peter agreed. He viewed children as a waste of his time, but he could draw ideas from the talking heads on television.

Jesus disappeared down the hall and entered the room near the far end, two doors shy of the big window that let in the city lights.

The boy's father greeted Jesus the moment he walked through the open door. His wife, never letting go of her son's hands, looked up, believing this corduroy-clad man to be a co-worker. Her husband's tense shoulders and curt greeting said otherwise.

"What are you doing here?" he said with a growl that grew feral in the semi-lit room.

"I just want to make sure your son is alright. Your concern this afternoon touched me. I want him to get..."

"This isn't a campaign event."

"There are no cameras here. No one but us."

"So, you came alone?" The man's solid frame still blocked Jesus from entirely entering the room.

"My campaign manager is down the hall. This isn't for him."

"Can you really help my son?" came a desperate plea from deep in the room. The man half-turned to face his wife. It provided Jesus the opportunity to slip by, but he did not take it.

"I'm not a doctor, ma'am, but…"

"No, he's a politician."

"I know who he is. You're the…"

"Yes," said Jesus, not intending to interrupt her, just acknowledging what was coming. "I'm the Virgin Guy."

"No, the one trying to beat Herod."

Jesus smiled. He had to learn that not everyone would bring up the bad. Even in politics.

"I don't like Herod," the woman went on. "I voted against him twice, but he keeps winning." She fought back tears as she eyed her pallid son. Her thirty-year-old face was too young to know this sadness. Everything in the room, including her husband's protectiveness, made Jesus' heart ache more.

"The doctors…the doctors give him a year. Maybe less," Mark's mother said, a lone tear trickling down her cheek.

"Then it is up to us to give him a lifetime," said Jesus. "I will do everything in my power to make your son better. Better care, better insurance, better technology. Whatever can be done must be done, within the confines of morality."

"What the hell does that mean?" the man said, forcing his way back into the conversation. "Sounds like a damned politician."

"It means that we have a tremendous obligation to heal the sick so that no one suffers."

The man recognized the sincerity in Jesus' eyes but did not see what one senator in a hundred could do. What one inexperienced, unelected underdog of a politician could ever do. Not when he danced around his questions.

"May I approach your son?" Jesus asked.

"Yes," said Mark's mother.

"No," said the father, planting himself in front of Jesus, his elbows wide at his sides. He could give a straight answer. "Not until I see what you can get done for him. Prove yourself. Do that, and we'll see."

His wife lowered her eyes, sliding a frail hand over the peach fuzz clinging to her son's head.

"I'll pray for Mark," Jesus said, stepping back to leave the room.

"You gotta do a helluva lot more than that," said the man.

"Then I will see that your son gets the best care possible."

Jesus slipped away and headed left toward the lounge. A young man on his cell phone looked up as he entered the small, rectangular room, but there was no Peter. The news was on, if muted, but his ride was gone.

"Excuse me," Jesus said to the nurse at the station. "Do you know where my friend went?"

"He said he'd be in the lobby if you asked."

Jesus said thank you and took the elevator to the first floor. Knowing Peter, he was probably working the phones again, trying to find a few dozen donors with deep pockets or perhaps another event to join.

He reached the tiled lobby to find that Peter had been working the phones alright. And it didn't make him happy.

A woman approached Jesus with her cell phone extended. "Nicole Demus, *Bethlehem Star.* Care to say a few words about your visit here tonight?"

Jesus glared at Peter. This was exactly what Mark's father didn't want. His trip to the hospital had become a media event, no matter how minor.

"I understand you were visiting a sick child?" she continued. "Is that right?"

"Yes," Jesus said, speaking into the cell phone turned microphone. "He has cancer, and I wanted to wish him well and see what I can do about getting him better treatment."

"That's great," said the reporter as Jesus took a step toward the door. "Any luck?"

"It's too early to tell. I'm sure the staff here will do everything they can. I know I will."

Jesus made it all of three steps before the reporter spoke again. "Is this related to your position on healthcare?"

Peter put a hand on Jesus' forearm and whispered into his ear. "I know you hate this, but what better place to tell the world what you think of our healthcare system than a hospital?"

Jesus nodded his head and turned to face the reporter, not surprised to discover that she had never lowered her cell phone.

"My visit here has nothing to do with my position on healthcare. It's an act of compassion. We always hear love thy neighbor as thyself, and who is our neighbor? Everyone. That is what I am doing here: showing the greatest concern for a neighbor."

"That's great, but what are your thoughts on healthcare?"

Peter prodded Jesus from behind, urging him to expound in his usual, eloquent way.

"I support free healthcare for all. Period. Print that."

Oh, I will, Nicole thought, happy to get the candidate on record. Herod had danced around it for decades, his only on-the-record statement his vote against it.

"So, you support universal healthcare?"

"How can we watch children suffer and not help? I'll tell you this—whoever does not help the weakest and poorest among us—well, it would be better for him if a millstone were hanged around his neck and he were drowned in the sea. Because that is the sentence he is giving the sick and the dying. We must heal the sick, raise the dead, cleanse those with skin disease, and drive out the demons that afflict us. The system we have is corrupt and greedy, which makes it impossible to treat the poor and sick without driving them into bankruptcy. Why should despair and debt be the wages of disease? We must cleanse the body politic if we are to cleanse our bodies at all. We must help them as we expect to be helped—and we must do so free of charge. As we have received freely, we should give freely. I hope that clears things up."

The reporter stood there stunned. Such vehemence, such fire. Would others call it passion or insanity? Raise the dead? Drive out demons? Screw that other quote. She was running this one.

"Can we get a picture? A story isn't anything without a shot."

"I believe my campaign manager doesn't like the way I photograph." Jesus said it with a smile, but Peter took it as an oh-so-subtle dig about his candidate's appearance.

"Tell you what," said Peter. "Let's take it by the hospital sign along the wall. It's got a nice glow coming from it that will light you perfectly. Like an angel."

Peter, too, said it with a smile, but Jesus took it as an oh-so-subtle dig that Peter was proving he had his candidate's best interests—and image—at heart.

"Perfect," said Nicole, waiting for Jesus to get into position before snapping a shot with her cell phone. "And one more... perfect. Thank you so much. Now, where are you headed?"

Peter rushed Jesus toward the automatic doors. "You'll find out in the papers," he said, leaving the reporter with a wry smile. Jesus had no such smile, cross that Peter pushed him into violating his word. He had made the best of a bad situation, but it appeared to be a betrayal, the greatest sin Jesus could imagine.

For now, he was off to his own suffering. In twenty minutes, he had a meeting with Lucifer in the heart of Hades Steel.

LEAD US NOT INTO
TEMPTATION

The guards at the gate to Hades Steel waved Jesus through without hesitation, welcoming him to the compound with broad smiles. Peter parked the car in front of the main door of the always humming facility, its lights brimming white from the office tower and yellow from the factory windows, cutting a sharp, imposing presence in the dark of night.

Peter offered to join him inside, but Jesus said no. This was a summit meeting, campaign style. The two men at the top would have to work things out.

Jesus exited the elevator at the thirty-fourth floor, the penthouse, into a darkened hallway, the only light provided by recessed bulbs in the ceiling and fluorescent tubes along the walls, each placed above a poster showcasing the seven subsidiaries of Hades Steel, collectively known as the Seven Sisters.

The first poster featured a man with rippling muscles, his right arm bent to showcase his strength, while an equally well-built woman in tight shorts and sports bra placed a hand on the middle of his bare chest. The Body by Jove chain had spread nationwide, its catchy slogan repeated by would-be athletes everywhere: "Show off your Body by Jove."

The second poster focused on a man in a well-tailored pinstripe suit, his enormous wealth highlighted by a Rolex watch on his wrist and bags of money behind him in the ever-popular soft focus. It was never clear whether the man was a broker or client of Vulcan Investors, but it was clear he was living by their motto: "Have Money to Burn with Vulcan."

Jesus averted his eyes as he passed the third poster, but a mere glimpse meant you never forgot the image plastered on billboards, magazines, and subways everywhere. A lingerie-clad woman, nearly naked but for bits of lace in the appropriate places, looked into the camera with alluring doe eyes that did nothing to hide her intent. It was a common joke among teenage boys and puerile men that Venus Delicates spread more V.D. than a Roman whore. Their slogan was as enticing as their product: "Venus Delicates – The Next Best Thing to Nothing at All." And if she moved at all, viewers could make a direct comparison.

The next poster supported the ubiquitous Apollo-Mart, its smiling sun beaming down upon consumers as they passed, each unable to forget the easily recognizable yellow dot. Apollo-Mart long bragged that its low prices made it possible for everyone to keep up with the Jonahs, their ads telling rich and poor alike to visit their vast, splashy stores for groceries, clothes, home furnishings, TVs, office supplies, you name it. They did whatever they could to live up to their promise that you could "Own Everything Under the Sun" at Apollo-Mart. Even if you never needed it. If the Jonahs had it, they made sure you could get it, too.

The fifth advertisement showed Janus, the two-faced god and symbol for Famous Janus Bakery, where every package contained a baker's dozen of cookies or donuts or pastries or their specialty, devil cakes. The front face gorged on cookies, while the rear face, gaunt and sad, did as the ad suggested: "So good, your diet will look the other way."

The next poster represented the subsidiary Jesus hated most: Mars Defense Contractors. The Roman god rode his steeds, Fear and Terror, over whole armies as his right arm hurled a missile halfway across the globe. Cities lay in ruin and mushroom clouds rose on the horizon. Below this carnage stood the slogan this company too often proved: "Show Your Enemies the Wrath of the Gods."

The last advertisement captured a man sunk deep into a plush couch, his stocking feet resting on a perfectly placed Ottoman, the light from his TV glowing against his face. It was the perfect picture for Uranus Furniture and its unforgettable slogan, "So comfortable you'll never get off Uranus."

Jesus breathed a sigh of relief as he passed the final poster. These ads were placed with such hubris, such pride that one company derived nearly incalculable wealth (though their quarterly profit-and-loss statements proved they could, in fact, calculate it) from so many other companies. They blanketed human need, deriving power from frailty. Jesus stopped against his better judgment and turned to face the row of posters lining the length of the hall. He had to admit they had diversified their interests quite nicely. In fact, they had gotten rich through this diversity, much like the country had. He wondered if the powers that be understood how much the economy gained from inclusion. He'd have to make sure they did.

Unable to stall any longer, Jesus knocked on the ornate oak doors cast in shadows ten feet beyond the last light. The door clicked open at the press of a button. From the far side of the room, a confident baritone kept things simple.

"Welcome, Mr. Christ."

Lucifer rose from his desk, crossing the darkened room to shake his guest's hand. Jesus figured him to be no more than six feet tall but with a deceptively powerful build. His handshake confirmed it. It was not intentionally bone-crushing or jarring; there was no yanking back and forth like a lumberjack's saw, but it was firm and powerful and dictated that this man was comfortable in his element. And this tower, overlooking the plant and the city beyond, was his element. It was his place of power, and Jesus, like Daniel, walked in of his own accord.

But then, in recognizing a thief when he saw one, he did not need to accept this man's lies as truths and could relax, for as powerful as Lucifer was here, he was not powerful everywhere. Jesus believed he could confront him when necessary.

"Do you know why I invited you here, Mr. Christ?"

"No."

"Because I saw you out there today with my employees."

"Did that bother you?"

"Bother me? No!" Lucifer said with a sweep of his arm and a chuckle to follow. "You connected with them, Mr. Christ. You are a man of the people! An honest-to-goodness man of the people. So many politicians pretend to be while secretly contemptuous—men like Herod—but you...you are one of them. You share their roots and their language. You have no elitist education. No wealthy parents or donors. You worked your way up, and a man like that is worth my time." Lucifer walked toward a large cabinet embedded in the wall to the left of his desk. "A man like you I could make president."

"I don't want to be president."

"Are you without ambition, Mr. Christ?"

"I'm running for senator."

"Well said, Mr. Christ, well said. I do love that response. So honest and accurate. You have ambition, but you know its limits. You are a man of the moment." Lucifer chuckled harder than before, as if they were in a smoke-filled basement applying boiler-room tactics. When his chuckle subsided to a smile, he opened the cabinet door. "Care for a drink?"

"No thank you."

"Well, I hope you don't mind if I imbibe." He opened a bottle of whiskey and pulled out a silver shot glass, its metal surface keeping anyone from knowing just how much he drank.

"Bacchus Beverages. A company I've considered buying several times, but I'm happy with the seven we own. For now. Of course, we sell these spirits through Apollo-Mart, where legal." Lucifer carried the glass and the bottle to his desk and placed them in front of his chair, no doubt provided by Uranus Furniture. "You see, Mr. Christ, like you, I know the limits of my ambition."

Lucifer wheeled back his chair and took a seat, sipping from his silver chalice. "Please, sit down."

Jesus considered that request. One did not sit before a viper, but if snake handlers could take up serpents, he could face this deceiver in comfort.

He took a seat in front of Lucifer, unwilling to shy away.

"I am impressed, Mr. Christ, that you do not want to be president. That is precisely why you should hold the office."

"I'm afraid I don't understand."

"You don't have the ambition for it! That's what the people say they want—a man who'll leave the farm, serve his country, and return home. They say that. They don't, of course, but they always say they do. The people crave Cincinnatus, but they elect Caesar! That's why re-election rates in Congress are above ninety percent, and why the country is full of professional politicians. The people cry out for term limits but never send anyone there to pass them. And why would they? They don't really want them, either. Term limits kick out the experienced and replace them with dotards. Term limits don't remove politicians from office— they force them to seek higher office. Or land somewhere as lobbyists to practice politics in the shadows, away from the cameras. The only federal politician who has term limits in this country is the president because he can't go any higher. Your lack of ambition for glory and power makes you the perfect candidate. The only people who should serve in government are those willing to walk away from it—and they never run."

Lucifer poured himself another drink as Jesus leaned back in his chair. This man's tongue was as silver as his cup.

Jesus might take him up on that drink after all.

"You paint a very bleak picture of our democracy."

"Democracy, Mr. Christ? This is no democracy—it's a constituentocracy."

"A what?"

"A constituentocracy. A word I made up. It describes how politics works. In a democracy, you need majority rule, but in this country, you merely need to appease the right constituents in the right numbers to win. They don't even have to be rich. They just have to be motivated to vote. The candidate can be rich—as rich as Caesar!—and pay for every single campaign expense and still lose, but if he motivates the right people, the right powerbrokers, the right constituents, they forget about his wealth and elect him time and again." Lucifer downed another shot. "Are you sure you don't want a drink?"

"Perhaps I'll have a glass of wine."

"Of course. Bacchus makes a most delightful red wine, perfect for these evening hours. Allow me."

Lucifer rose from his chair and returned to his well-stocked liquor cabinet. He knew where the bottle was without looking. Crossing back to his desk, he poured a healthy portion of wine into a delicate, impossibly thin, etched crystal glass. Jesus' carpenter hands were not meant for such finery. Despite Lucifer's thirst for alcohol, Jesus believed this ritual to be too dapper for his upbringing and put down the glass without taking a sip.

"I know you have your doubts, Mr. Christ, but I assure you I'm right. One can become president while losing the popular vote. The majority of voters don't want him, but he appeals to the right constituents in the right districts and wins the election. That's not democracy. The majority of senators want a certain law passed, but the minority blocks them because they need to appeal to their constituents. Oh, not the voters back home, but the people they really answer to—gun owners, drug companies, civil rights groups, arms manufacturers, you name it."

"Steel companies."

Lucifer chuckled again. "Yes, steel companies, too. With the right senator, we are a very important constituency."

Lucifer poured himself another belt. "Please, drink up. It will make the message go down easier."

Jesus picked up the glass but still did not put it to his lips.

"So, to sum up, some of the people in Congress wouldn't be there if this were a true democracy. They appealed to the right constituents, convinced them to vote, and then reshaped the districts so they could hold onto power. They might lose a fair election in a balanced district, so they pack it with their constituents. That wouldn't happen in your precious democracy, but in my constituentocracy, it's de rigueur."

Jesus swirled the wine in his glass. It looked tempting.

"But it's more complicated than that. It doesn't just affect who lands in the nation's capital, it affects policies of every kind. The majority favor the basic right to abortion, but the politicians appeal to the pro-life movement, then chip away at it."

"And that is a position I support."

"But that's not a democracy, Mr. Christ! It is your right, I dare say, and I fully suggest you reach out to those pro-lifers if you want to win because that minority view will put you in power to fight the majority, but where's your precious democracy in that?"

Jesus took his first sip of wine.

"And on it goes, Mr. Christ. The vast majority of Americans favor gun control. The vast majority, mind you! But do they get it? No! Because the powers that be appeal to greater powers that be, and so the minority protects ownership of the most deadly weapons because it makes a certain constituency happy. It's the same story with dozens of other policies. The majority want universal healthcare, campaign finance reform, greater taxes on the rich, and so on, but in a constituentocracy they can't have them. That's only in a democracy, the one even you can't serve if you ever hope to win!"

Jesus took another sip of wine, upending the glass until the last drop ran out.

Lucifer handed him the bottle with a gracious smile.

"I should have left this here before. I'm not always the best host."

Jesus could not argue that point. A good host would not attack his guest's beliefs so vociferously. This was worse than

Thanksgiving dinner with a disgruntled uncle. At least the disgruntled uncle's argument fell apart after the third beer. Lucifer appeared to be capable of constructing a lucid argument regardless of how much liquor he consumed. And as if agreeing with Jesus, he returned to his seat and poured himself another round, but it took so long and was so slow, Jesus swore he poured himself a double. Maybe a triple.

"And the worst of it, Mr. Christ, is that the liars will prevail. They always do. They say exactly what their constituents want to hear. Not the voters, but their constituents because they are the ones who propel them to office. After all, there are always just enough supporters willing to believe their lies."

"There's nothing new in that observation," said Jesus.

Lucifer paused for a moment, not expecting to be challenged. He emptied his glass before continuing.

"You are right, of course. What is new is their willingness to lie openly, without any regard for the truth. You make your blunders, but your position is honest. Right now, we have a man in office who changes his story by the hour, the day, the week, whatever suits his fancy. He contradicts himself in the same interview and goes unchallenged."

"President Tiberius."

"Yes, Tiberius. He's an inveterate liar. A pathological prevaricator. A born spinmeister. His lies fit him better than his long ties and baggy tennis shorts. He lies without cause or reason. His entire life is a lie, a myth born of self-aggrandizement. He is a tremendous liar…and a very good friend of mine."

Lucifer downed another shot, then, almost without breathing, did it again, slamming his silver cup on the table like a college kid proud of his drinking prowess.

"What can I say, Mr. Christ? I helped put him in office. He gave me the tax cuts I wanted and threw business my way. As a result, our stocks bumped up. You see, Mr. Christ, even liars and cheats must keep a few promises to their friends. Or their…how should I put this? Constituents."

Jesus picked up his bottle of wine, not sure whether to drink straight from the source or mind his manners and pour himself a second glass. A half glass. No more than that. His host leaned forward, anticipating his choice. Jesus remembered his mother rapping his knuckles when he proved slovenly or ill-mannered. It was enough to bring him into line. He poured the wine into his goblet.

Lucifer leaned back, an arched eyebrow and downturned lip spreading disappointment across his face.

"Yes, Mr. Christ, Tiberius, our illustrious leader, is a natural-born liar. He's what I call a schizophresident."

"A what?"

"A schizophresident. Another word I made up. It's a politician who changes positions so many times you think he's two people. The really good ones look like four. Tiberius looks like eight. I mean he changes sides faster than the maid changes sheets and lies more than a whore on her wedding night. When you can do that and get away with it, they make you president."

Lucifer chugged straight from the bottle. When finished, he put it down on his desk with a thud, like the drunk at the bar demanding another. When no bartender materialized, he turned the bottle upside down and released the last drop. He looked into the opening and shrugged, then walked to his cabinet and removed an identical bottle.

"I'd offer you more wine, but it seems you haven't finished what you have."

"Yes," said Jesus, "I guess my cup runneth over."

Lucifer chuckled in his deep and caustic way. "Not yet, sir, but it will."

"Oh?"

"You are the antithesis to Tiberius, yes?"

"Yes."

"And Herod?"

"Of course."

"Then there's your answer."

73

Jesus took a sip of wine, mulling over his host's meaning. He thought he knew where Lucifer was headed but thought it best to ask. Make a man state his needs and his wants will appear.

"I'm afraid I don't understand."

Lucifer poured himself another shot of whiskey but did not return to his seat. He came around his desk and tapped the rim of his guest's glass, the nearly empty crystal ringing across the room. "Let's get down to business."

Gone was jovial Lucifer. In his place was a man as stern as the steel below them.

"I hear your coffers are empty. Your campaign barely has enough money to finish the week. You have no ground game; no grassroots support. Your campaign, Mr. Christ, is broke, which means broken. Even the contributions of Magdalene and her hordes can't keep you afloat. No, you need real funds. Millions, in fact. Now, I won't even notice the money is gone. My friends and I can contribute to your campaign and the various PACs we run. Hell, we put the 'super' in super PAC. You'll have so much bread you'll think you opened a bakery."

Lucifer tipped his glass toward Jesus and following a nod of his head, downed another shot.

"Man does not live by bread alone," said Jesus. "I support campaign finance reform and won't renege on it now. If you want to contribute to my campaign, I won't stop you, but all your cash buys you nothing. The Supreme Court was wrong."

"Is that so?" said Lucifer, filling his glass before swirling the liquor inside, as if barely listening.

"Yes. Money is not free speech. It is influential, but it will not influence me because your corporation is no more human than that desk over there."

Lucifer drew in his cheeks, his back stiff. He admired a man with backbone—unless he used it to stand up for himself. He had not expected this to be easy, but that's why cheating was invented.

He had another card up his sleeve.

"Then forget the money. How about a phone call?"

"To whom?"

"The press! I have contacts beyond your wildest imagination. Enough to make you a mountain on the media landscape. They all owe me favors, if only to keep an advertiser happy. I could have you on a handful of shows before Sunday. I can put that campaign manager of yours on the air, too, along with that young speechwriter. I can get your message delivered to every voter in the state. You'll be so famous, you'll be instantly viable because famous people always are. I can't promise you'll win, but if you do, you go to the Senate. If you don't, the media beats down your door to land you as a pundit. Hell, they might even give you your own show! Think about it. Support some of my policies, and you'll get to wax politic on the air forever."

Jesus had to admit it was tempting to preach to the masses without the struggles he faced. The chance to reach the voters directly was too good to be true. But that's because it was. It came with a catch. Lucifer would attempt to dictate programming. Call in favors. Money would become the message whenever possible.

"No," said Jesus, "I will not tempt the system. What I say will be my words done my way without your interference. The cost of your assistance is far too great."

Lucifer offered a terse chuckle, short, like a burst of static.

"Is it the cost, Mr. Christ, or the reward? Come with me."

Jesus stood, glad he limited himself to a glass and a half of wine. Lucifer placed an arm around his shoulder and led him to the long glass wall overlooking Bethlehem. The lights sparkled across the streets, the dirt and grime covered by nightfall. The glow dwindled in the distance, growing dimmer throughout the suburbs before disappearing in the countryside. It was the stages of civilization in miniature, from urban to rural, rundown to glitzy, all captured in a single picture.

"It's a spectacular view from up here, don't you think?" said Lucifer. "But it's only a small portion of the world."

"Yes, it is," replied Jesus, his eyes drifting upward, "but the stars are blocked by your pollutants."

Lucifer kept his low chuckle in check. "Indeed they are, Mr. Christ, but then I cannot give you the universe. I can, however, give you the world."

Lucifer took a long draught from his whiskey bottle, though it hardly kept him from his next point. "Herod's days are numbered. I said that a man like you could be president, but for now I will hand you the Senate. I am a powerful ally. My connections can make you a senator. Stay for just twelve years—when you will be a vibrant man in your mid-forties—and I will hand you the White House. You'll be able to shape this country anyway you want. Hell, you can shape the world because I promise you, you'll be the most powerful person in it."

Jesus had to acknowledge that such an offer—a chance to implement policies that would enrich the poor and strengthen the infirm—was nearly irresistible. He envisioned laborers receiving a living wage and doctors treating the ill around the clock. Healthcare for all and poverty for none. But this dream would have to wait because Lucifer did not understand that Jesus told him the truth the first time. It was not that Lucifer's offer was too low, it's that his price was too high.

"I cannot serve you. I serve the voters and my conscience. A man cannot serve two masters, and I have chosen mine."

"Then you're a fool! You'll never get what you want!" Lucifer stepped back from the window to hide his fury. How he craved another quick shot to calm his rage, but the bottle taunted him from his desk. "I told you I am a powerful ally. I am also a powerful foe."

"And I have a powerful message."

Lucifer finally released his full roar as laughter, every emotion unleashed. "Yes, you do, which is why I approached you. But you heard nothing that I said. Your message will never reach the right constituents. Your message will wither and die like grapes on the vine. Your grassroots movement will provide no seeds for they shall be plowed under."

Jesus came around a bank of chairs placed before the window and headed for the exit.

"Then, like Solomon, I shall cast my bread upon the water."

"And so you should, Mr. Christ, for I know what evil is coming. Would that you were as wise." The words were harsh, and Lucifer attempted to soften them, but that was beyond his ability. "Finish your wine before you leave. It may be the sweetest thing you taste for a while."

Jesus opened the door but gave his host one parting shot before leaving. "Even water can be wine sometimes."

Not to Lucifer. In his mind, even the weakest wine surpassed the purest water. "So, you are a fool. Goodbye, Mr. Christ."

As the door closed behind his guest, Lucifer took his last swallow of whiskey for the night. He slammed down his glass as the final bitter drop trickled down his throat. He regretted that he had not gotten through to his guest. That he had not gotten to call him Jesus, or some other informal, friendly name. That would have put them on the same team. Now that they were opponents, Lucifer needed more players.

He spun the empty bottle of whiskey ever faster, the thick glass whirling round and round until his fingers could not keep up. Letting go, the impromptu centrifuge spun hypnotically until slowing, lolling from side to side as it stopped. No, this was too important a decision to leave to chance. What Lucifer never liked to admit, and only would under duress, was that he didn't own the media. There was still a vast, liberal, mainstream consort that was all too fair. And fair was rarely good for the candidates he backed.

He needed a man who didn't do journalism by the rules.

A familiar voice picked up on the first ring.

"Hello, Caiaphas, it's me."

UTTER NO SLANDER

While madmen spend their nights sowing chaos and imploring the world to follow them, powerful men spend their days at the crack of dawn ordering it about. Joseph Caiaphas was such a man. He had a vast media empire, owning a dozen newspapers throughout the state, as well as a string of local TV and radio stations from one side of Pennsylvania to the other. He even owned a billboard company to place messages and appropriate ads wherever he wanted. But his pride and joy was the cable news station he ran that appeared on every local cable outlet under his control, from the two major cities at the antipodes to the heartland that separated them. If you wanted a message shouted from a mountaintop and heard in the valleys, Caiaphas was your man.

"Morning team, you're up in an hour. Look at your production notes. I want you to hit those points early and often. The writers have thrown together a few good phrases, and we'll get some longer pieces out there for you to read, but the big takeaway is this: From now on, we attack this Christ character. Got it?"

Everyone on the team nodded. They had expected to go on the offensive any day now. That day had come.

"Investigative team, you're up all day. I want so much dirt on this Jesus joker that molehills look like mountains. Pull up his records. Hit the streets. Talk to people. I want Jesus to fear the truth, so dig, dig, dig!"

The investigative reporters were scrambling before Caiaphas got to the third "dig." They didn't have cushy jobs like the anchors.

They could be gone before the people in payroll learned to spell their names right.

Caiaphas then instructed the primetime hosts to "shape the news to their individual personalities" but to abide by their audience's preferences. Instant polling would guide them toward what the viewers and sponsors liked. After dismissing everyone with a curt, "Now get," Caiaphas sipped his coffee, black as a bad news day. Black as printer's ink before the public demanded front pages as colorful as the comics. That thought made him smile. Maybe he should have put a little cream in his coffee because his mood was light. Lucifer agreed to buy another million dollars' worth of advertising last night, and he intended to make sure his biggest advertiser got his money's worth.

Within the hour, the morning team took to the air, raring to go with their usual good humor and bombast.

"Good morning, viewers. Welcome to cable TV's number one morning show, *Faust & Friends.* I'm Steve Doozy, here, as always, with my always congenial co-hosts…" The names of the two men on the ends of the couch covered in a pure white sheen flashed across the screen, but the woman in the middle had no such luck as the tech guy in the booth didn't know her name. She looked like every other on-air blonde in a short skirt. Besides, he figured she might be gone before the first break if she didn't show enough leg. The female anchors changed faster than several of the reporters' mistresses.

"I am so excited for today's show," Doozy said, "because we'll be talking about the big race on everyone's lips. No, it's not a marathon…"

"Or a sprint," said the dark-haired guy.

"Or any other kind of 'race' you might be thinking of," said the blonde, producing the sort of snicker you'd expect from an inappropriate joke.

"We're talking about the race for U.S. senator right here in our beloved commonwealth. Have you seen this Jesus guy? This Jesus…"

"…Christ," said the dark-haired guy.

"Right, that's the guy. Jesus Christ."

"He's the one who's been talking about virgins," said the blonde, introducing the topic while hoping that word would hold the attention of viewers so old they lost their virginity when the word virgin still had other meanings.

"Right, he's been talking about virgins. Lots and lots of virgins. Now, what's that all about? I mean, it sounded like he was getting ten virgins…"

"I don't think he was getting ten virgins," said dark-haired guy.

"I'm not saying he was, but that's what it sounded like. Now, I'm not saying he's a terrorist…"

"I don't think he's a terrorist," said dark-haired guy, doing as the lawyers suggested and covering their legal backsides, which he thought was a very good idea.

"I'm not saying he is because he's only getting ten virgins, sixty-two less than terrorists. Which means he's not one of them. So, I'm guessing he wants to do less damage to the country than terrorists. But he will damage this country. You know, just less than terrorists. Which is a really high bar."

"Or high Akbar," said the blonde, producing another round of laughter, albeit a quick one so the host could get on with his point.

"So, no, I'm not saying he's a terrorist," said the host, emphasizing the word like a president on the campaign trail.

"He isn't," said dark-haired guy.

"But who knows? Maybe he is, maybe he isn't. Should we take that chance? We don't even know if he was born in Pennsylvania."

"You don't have to be born in this state to be our senator," said dark-haired guy.

"You don't?" said the blonde. "That's a stupid law."

"It is," agreed the host, "but stupid or not, it's the law. But wouldn't you like your senator to be from your state?"

"Of course," said the other two, knowing their cue when they heard it.

"Me, too," said the host. "And we know Herod Antipas was born and bred here because his father was from here."

"Didn't he go to college out of state, though?" asked dark-haired guy, who thought if he didn't bring it up, the other side would. Besides, it was on the teleprompter.

"Yes, he did, but he came right back here as soon as he graduated. And that's something the voters should consider. Remember just how much Herod loves this state when you go into that booth."

He sat back for two seconds, the appropriate time for a dramatic pause. He looked at his co-hosts as if he'd just won a case before the Supreme Court or got his client off for murder. No, wait, he wanted murderers executed. Like he'd just gotten his client off on a white-collar charge of defrauding people of billions. Yeah, that sounded better.

His pause done and his message sunk in, the host stared deep into the camera lens. "We'll be right back with our first guest, another man we know was born right here in Pennsylvania. And boy, does he have a story to tell about Jesus Christ. You won't want to miss it."

The program cut away seconds after the channel's famed bumper *Phobos News: Fear & Bias* scrawled across the screen. Several commercials played in quick, attention-numbing succession, starting with a workout spot for Body by Jove and finishing with ads for Famous Janus and Uranus Furniture.

The three smiling hosts' faces lit up the screen as the news crawl rolled beneath them: *Dow Jonas futures up; Phobos poll says Herod up by ten; Crude Senate candidate Christ talks virgins...*

"Welcome back to the program, and have we got something special for you. We're going to continue with our subject du jour, the campaign of Jesus Christ. And the reason I say du jour..."

"That's French," the blonde said with a twinkle in her eye and a knowing smile.

"It is French," said the primary host. "And the reason I say du jour is that I can't see his campaign lasting du week, du month…"

"And certainly not du election," said dark-haired guy.

"Absolutely. Not after our first guest gets through with him." Doozy gave his little pause that pulled in the viewer. It was effective because everyone wanted to know what was coming. The man certainly knew television. He knew it well enough to know that you kept talking when you should be introducing someone, though he did finally surrender the spotlight. "We're joined by an employee of our friends at Hades Steel. His son… well, I'll let our guest tell you. I just…I can't get over it. Welcome to the program."

The screen split, the hosts sliding left as Little Mark's father, dressed in a carefully chosen plaid shirt and superfluous construction hat, popped up on the right. His name and the fact that he joined them from an affiliate in Bethlehem appeared below.

"Mr. Lystra…Timothy…may I call you Tim?" Doozy asked.

"Sure," Tim said, displaying a slow drawl in front of the cameras, perhaps a bit unsure of himself under this sudden media glare.

"Okay, Tim, now, you're a hardworking man…"

"Yeah, I work the pig machine where we take molten iron…"

"Sounds fascinating," said the blonde, almost cooing.

"It does," added Doozy, "but we don't want to get off-track here. How did you manage to get the day off from work, Tim?"

"After what that Christ fellow did to me and my family, I was mad. I was fuming. I was…" The engineer in the sound booth went for the dump button to bleep out whatever followed. "…well, I was a word you can't say on TV. He showed up…"

"Before we get into what Jesus Christ did—and I still can't believe he did it—why don't you finish telling us how you got the day off from work," Doozy said, redirecting the interview to the needed talking points.

"Like I said, I was so mad, I went to my boss and told him about it. I guess he told his boss because I got called into his office and was told to call your show. They said you'd be interested and gave me the day off—with pay—to do it."

"Well, we're certainly glad you did. And it sounds very generous of our friends at Hades Steel. So, let's get down to it. What did Jesus Christ do that made you so mad?"

"Did he offer you a virgin?" said the blonde with a laugh.

"No, but if he had, that would have made me mad, too. I'd never do that to my wife."

"So, what did he do?" asked the host, nodding almost imperceptibly to the director telling him he'd speed things up. They'd made the audience wait long enough.

"He came to the plant yesterday morning. Brought coffee and donuts and all that, you know, I guess trying to buy our votes or something. So, a couple of us got into talking with him. Our big concern is wages and healthcare."

"Like any working man," said the dark-haired guy, just breaking up the conversation because one man talking on screen was an invitation to turn the channel.

"Right. Of course, I got another reason. My son..."

"Mark," said the blonde.

"Right. Mark. Mark is sick. He's got leukemia..."

"And how old is Little Mark?" asked Doozy.

"He's six. So, I'm worried sick about the cost of health insurance and medicine, and this Jesus takes a real interest in my son. Asking me all these questions about him, like what hospital he's at and all that. Then, last night, he shows up at the hospital. Walks right into the room where Mark, me, and my wife were. I'm mad right away because I think he's using this as a gimmick, you know?"

Tim's anger was apparent, growing right before the viewers' eyes. And that overpowering emotion made his story compelling. He was at last comfortable, forgetting the camera as if talking to old friends. For the first time, his story flowed.

"But he promised me he wasn't. This was personal, and that he really cared about my son. And then what do I see this morning?" Tim held up a copy of *The Bethlehem Star* at the same time as Steve Doozy. The director threw up an enlarged copy across the screen so viewers could see what they had. "He's right there in the paper! There's a picture of him standing next to the hospital sign with all these quotes about his healthcare plan. He used my son as a photo op! He used my son as a prop! He…"

"And that's all the time we have right now. Thanks for joining us, Tim, on *Faust & Friends*." Timothy Lystra, distraught and angry father, was swiped right as the three hosts took centerscreen.

"We hope your son gets better soon, and we'll be sure to discuss all the other despicable things Jesus Christ did yesterday when we come back. Stay tuned."

Jesus' lips grew thin and firm as he turned to face Peter in the back seat of their beat-up car. His campaign manager slipped his phone into his jacket pocket.

"That's what I didn't want to happen," Jesus said. "A tender moment with a scared family should have stayed that way."

"I'm sorry, I didn't know you told them no press. If I had, she would have been gone."

"But you knew I didn't like it."

"Yeah, well, we have to get your message out there. We're getting killed in the news cycle."

Jesus rubbed his beard. "The news cycle?"

"Yeah. Every twenty-four hours the news needs another big story. Something that grabs viewers. They pounce on it, keeping ratings up. It's the media's version of Whac-a-Mole. People don't want to admit it, but they want the news to be as unpredictable as the weather. Herod is dominating the news cycle, but if today's event goes well and you knock it out of the park, we push this cancer-boy story off the front page and put you back on solid ground."

Jesus noticed Peter spoke in clichés when searching for a way to spin bad news. He wondered if that was every campaign manager or just a personal quirk.

"Besides," said Peter, opening his briefcase, "the only people paying attention to this right now are all Phobos News' viewers. They weren't voting for you anyway."

"Maybe," said Jesus, "but we can't afford to lose the blue-collar vote."

"And we won't. That's your bread and butter."

Jesus sighed. Another cliché.

"Alright, maybe we lose a few," Peter conceded, "but you'll get them back with your tax policy. I mean plan. Your tax plan. Never call it a policy. Policy is what you have after it's passed. Until then, you have a plan. People like plans. Plans show direction. Plans have hope. And if it doesn't work, you can always say, 'We're changing the plan' or 'It was just a plan.'"

"Twenty minutes to Center City," said Andrew from the driver's seat.

"Perfect," said Peter. "Plenty of time to go over your tax *plan*."

He handed Jesus a cheat sheet of half-fledged ideas, promising that too many details on tax policy bored people and gave critics too much ammo to shoot holes in it. After reciting a slew of facts about the wealth gap, pay gap, income gap, investment gap, property gap, gender pay gap, racial pay gap, tax gap, and just about any other gap that could convince the public taxes were too high and benefits too low, Peter looked at his watch.

"Hey, Andrew…"

"I'm on it, boss."

At ten o'clock on the dot, Andrew flipped on the radio, once again randomly picking an AM station. The booming intro of *The Saul Tarsus Show* rattled the windows, and Andrew swung his hand forward, lowering the volume to a manageable level. The rock 'n' roll he played last night didn't make his ears bleed like this.

"Welcome, dear listeners, to the best three hours on radio. Ah, let's face it—the best three hours anywhere, right? Because I get to discuss the election with the smartest people in the world: you! And how do I know you're that smart? Because you listen to me!"

Tarsus clicked on the computer screen in front of him and played a pre-recorded effect of a thousand people yelling, "Saul is super!" which was really twenty people dubbed over fifty times to give it volume and prestige.

"So, tell me, astute listener, what was that shtick the sick Christ pulled yesterday? Did you hear him? Free healthcare. Hey, fine, you want free healthcare, good for you, but how are we going to pay for it? Yeah, these hippies never have a plan for that. It's all gimme, gimme, gimme. The only plan they have is to bleed you dry—so that you need a doctor. Ha! That's what liberals do. Spend, spend, spend your money! Well, let me tell you something— health insurance is just that: insurance. If you use it, you pay more. Get sick, you pay more. Why should my rates go up just because you get sick? If I have an accident, do your rates go up? No! If my house catches fire, do your rates go up? No!"

Tarsus paused, though it was less for effect and more because he couldn't think of another type of insurance.

"Oh, look at that, the phones lit up." Saved by the red light on the phone bank. The one light that indicated one caller. Well, a fight with an opponent or accolades from a fan were enough to get him out of his strained analogy. "You're speaking to Saul. What's on your mind?"

"Hi, Saul. Love the show. Catch you every day."

"Thanks. Love to hear it."

"But actually, your insurance rates can go up if enough of your neighbors have an accident, or get sick, or their homes burn down because the risk is spread out over a pool. All costs go up to cover the increased risk. It's a basic approach to protect against calculable loss..."

"Listen, knucklehead," Saul said as the line went mute, "don't call up my show telling me you know how insurance works when the math is way too hard for anyone to do. If I stay healthy, I stay in a healthy pool with low premiums. You get sick, you go in a sick pool with high premiums. Insurance targets you and only you. That's the way it works because that's the way it's always worked. Now get off my phone. Don't call me until you've done your homework! Are you there, caller? Are you?"

Of course he was, screaming back into the phone about how insurance actually worked, but Saul had put the line on mute. In a minute the caller would hang up. If anybody ever checked, Saul could always say that he had nothing to do with it. 'Hey, the callers hang up, not me. And you know why they hang up? Because they're losers.' That's what he always said.

"I didn't think so," Saul went on. "You know, folks, don't call up this program if you don't know spit. I'll bury you."

Jesus looked out the window of the car, doing his best to ignore the rant coming over the airwaves. It was a three-hour harangue of callers based on convoluted logic and half-thought-out positions.

At least he hadn't brought up the really bad stuff, yet. The really damaging quotes.

"And what was that thing Christ said about 'raise the dead' and 'drive out the demons'?"

Then again…

"And that thing about the body politic. Huh? I'd read you the quotes, but I don't speak gibberish. He's got some kind of tick, alright. Ble-ble-ble-ble-ble-ble-free healthcare. He should see a doctor for that."

"Why do we have to listen to this?" Jesus asked, wishing Andrew would just pull over somewhere so he could walk the rest of the way.

"Because you have to know what you're up against."

Jesus knew what he was up against. Corruption, complicity, and conspiracies that created an angry public dug so deep into their positions that any new information became a lie.

His chance to turn that around was here. Andrew parked in front of the Philadelphia tax office where picketers carried signs showing an anger that dwarfed Saul's ever-present rage.

GIVE UNTO CAESAR

Protesters formed a semi-circle around Jesus and Peter the moment they stepped from the car. Their signs made clear what their various chants, indistinguishably muddled together, could not.

Taxes are too damned high.

Pay your share.

Overtaxed and underpaid.

Our tax $$$ make no ¢ents.

Peter placed a hand on Jesus' shoulder as he guided him through the dozen-and-a-half protesters pressed together like a rugby scrum. Behind them, the additionally aggrieved marched relentlessly, their circle gaining little attention and even less progress. Jesus knew that their anger, while in earnest, only made a difference to the tax collectors when they dodged them on their way in and out of the office. Policymakers in the nation's capital saw them as a foul-mouthed rabble incapable of understanding advanced economic principles. They were probably right. But these people understood fairness. They understood poverty and corruption and an inability to make ends meet, which the policymakers did not. The problem with eating out all the time is that you never discuss kitchen-table issues.

Peter leaned toward Jesus, shouting above the din. "We have to win these people over. They vote!"

Jesus nodded as they reached the door. Once inside, they walked through a sterile, red-marbled lobby dotted with black furniture and impersonal chrome artwork. The two guards behind the three-inch-thick Plexiglas refused to believe they were there to meet the regional tax director. They shook their heads several times and asked for ID, convinced Jesus was just a protester who lost his sign or couldn't write well enough to make one, and that the much-better dressed Peter was a publicity-seeking lawyer here to bail him out as soon as the trouble started. After calling upstairs and confirming that, indeed, these men had an appointment, the shorter guard handed them temporary badges and escorted them upstairs. He didn't have to, but he still wasn't convinced they weren't troublemakers. He was half-tempted to frisk them for spray-paint cans, tomatoes, weapons, or the worst thing of all, subpoenas for some public official's tax records.

A tall, clean-shaven man solidly in his middle years but looking older under the stress of his job addressed Jesus without taking his hand. "Mr. Christ, I'm Levi Matthews, regional director. I'm not sure what you want from me, but I understand you are running for senator. I am at your disposal for the next," he looked at his watch, "thirty-seven minutes."

"It's a pleasure to meet you, Levi," said Jesus, who always preferred the informal approach, particularly if it meant making someone an ally. He had a feeling that a stressed-out, routinely under-assault tax collector needed a friend. "And what you can do for me is come outside and meet the protesters."

A noticeable sweat broke out over the man's left eyebrow. "Oh, no, no, I couldn't do that. I spend most of my day inside trying to avoid them. I don't go outside until it's time to go home. I…I prefer numbers. They don't get angry. They just add up."

"You have ample security, plus the media will be here any minute, right, Peter?"

"That's what they said."

"Which means we'll address their concerns. All you have to do is listen."

"Oh, we have customer service for that. That way, I don't have to listen." This argument relieved Levi. As long as others were taking personal responsibility for things, he didn't have to.

"Levi, if you don't go out there," Jesus said, clapping a hand on the tax collector's shoulder, which made the man wince and step forward, "I'll tell them that you're too scared to face them. How would it look if the man charged with taking their money is too afraid to confront them in person?"

"Better too scared than too dead," said Levi.

Peter saw fear in the man's weak smile, but Jesus saw something else.

"A man brave enough to do our dirtiest deed—collect taxes— is a brave man indeed. Brave enough to stand up for himself and stand up to others. You're that man, Levi. You are brave indeed. Now come, follow me."

Jesus turned toward the elevator while Levi scanned the beige carpet. It was dirty and threadbare with thin black streaks on the most tread-upon spots. It lay trapped between eggshell- colored walls in need of paint. It had been twelve years since they were last refreshed. Fourteen years for the carpet. *Why was this area so dirty and downstairs so imposing?* he wondered. *No one has to be intimidated up here because no one ever comes up here. Not since security tripled after that person snuck in six years ago. Two security guards at each door, each with nine bullets in his gun...*

Jesus spun toward Levi after realizing he wasn't following but was deep in thought. Believing it best to interrupt the tax collector since he only had thirty-odd minutes of his time, Jesus said, "Levi, walk with me. Tell me some facts about taxes."

Levi lifted his eyes from the carpet and nodded. He was the host and therefore had no choice. He had to accompany his guests around the office.

Peter, slightly amused, crinkled his brow, impressed by how easily Jesus manipulated this man with kindness. He shrugged his shoulders and joined this tour group of two at the elevators.

Levi prattled on about taxation a full minute before the elevators opened up. To Peter, it was a run-on supply of facts, many of which were in the papers he showed Jesus in the car, but to Jesus, they revealed something significant about the man. Something he could use later.

"Trickle-down is exactly what it promises. It's sold to the public as a deluge for the working class, but it's really just a trickle. The name is appropriate. It's also a trick played on them, so that works like a joke. The rich who already have money to invest because they have large sums of capital and access to credit are given more money to create jobs. Sometimes they do, but most invest the money in companies who give it back to the investors as stock prices go up thanks to increased investment. Very little of the tax windfall is reinvested in jobs or used to begin new companies. The money is invested in places where it gets the best return: the stock market, government bonds, and overseas markets where labor, land, and resources are cheap. A small percentage finds its way into improving our country's economic position. Is this boring?"

That last line jarred Peter, who realized after a moment's silence that it was directed at him because he'd been looking at his watch. "No, I was just wondering how long before the elevator gets here."

"You can't tell by looking at your watch," said Levi. "You have to look at the floor numbers. It's five floors away, so ten seconds if it doesn't stop."

"Thanks," said Peter, who had another reason to look at his watch to see if it really took ten seconds.

"Most of the new jobs in America are service jobs created by middle-class people running start-ups, franchises, or freelance businesses. They need tax cuts to ensure those businesses succeed while paying their employees a living wage."

Ding!

Peter had to smile. Ten seconds on the dot. The elevator door slid open and Jesus motioned for Levi to enter first, but he stayed put. "No, I have to go last." Jesus nodded as he and Peter crossed the threshold, but Levi felt the need to explain his actions in a rational fashion. "I'm the host. You have to go first."

"Thank you," said Jesus. He stepped to one side as Peter pushed the button for the ground floor. Levi stepped to the rear corner opposite Jesus and behind his companion.

"The people who need the money most to help the economy don't get it. They get peed on. It should be called tinkle-down economics." Jesus and Peter offered sly smiles at the unexpected term. "That's also a joke."

"And a very honest one," said Jesus, remaining civil despite knowing he could never use the term himself. But a tax collector calling it that? The people would love it. "What else can you tell us about taxes?"

Levi rattled off facts in a non-sequential stream until they departed the elevator, passed through the lobby, and stood outside before the protesters. Most of what he said concerned how unfair the tax system was. How the ultrarich used tax shelters as a tax dodge, didn't pay enough into Social Security, and paid a lower tax rate than the regular rich since there was no ultrawealthy tax bracket. He concluded with a simple observation. "Taxes, like comfort, are relative."

Jesus was captivated. Everything Levi recited was more elucidating than all of Peter's dense paperwork because this hated tax collector put a human spin on the working man's toil. He understood the failure of the system because he enforced the system.

"Thank you, Levi, but you can stop now. We're here."

Peter expected the man to bolt in the face of the protesters, but he stayed calm. Perhaps he didn't perceive the danger he was in, or perhaps he expected an opportunity to race through facts and figures as if the protesters were budding accountants.

Jesus raised his hands before the protesters, who eyed him with a mix of curiosity and skepticism. None of them lowered their signs. None of them paid any attention to Levi, either, because they had no idea who he was.

"My name is Jesus Christ, and I am running for the Senate against Herod Antipas."

A light chorus of boos ensued. Jesus assumed they were aimed at his opponent, but they could have just as easily been for all politicians.

"Next to me is Levi Matthews, regional director of the IRS."

A much louder chorus of boos followed. Those were definitely for all tax collectors.

"I appreciate your disdain for this institution and the policies it enforces. As a poor carpenter forced to make a living by taking side jobs and temporary assignments, I know the sting of taxation. I know what it's like to wish you had that extra ten dollars, or twenty, or fifty in your pocket and not Uncle Sam's. I know your anger when you learn that rich men cheat the system by changing the system to make their cheating legal!"

The booing stopped. The signs came down. They were enthralled. They were ready to be led if this man could simply bang the drum this loud in Congress.

"We must tax the rich to feed the poor. They say you can't take it with you, but common wisdom is not their wisdom. They will try to horde it for themselves and their offspring, but I tell you it is easier for a rich man to pass through the eye of a needle than to enjoy their riches in the afterlife. How much does a man need? Simple. No more than his neighbor. So what do they do? They surround themselves with rich neighbors! They wall themselves off in towns so rich the poor can't even visit. Enough! We must tax the few to save the many!"

The television cameras and newspaper photographers turned their attention to the crowd, now doubled in size and no longer consisting solely of protesters—the definite voters—but inquisitive, potential voters. People who could make a difference against Herod and swing the election.

The energized gathering took up the chant, "Tax the rich! Tax the rich!"

Behind Jesus, two feet to his left, Levi mumbled, "Tax the rich. Tax the rich," in perfect syncopation with the once-feared protesters.

A reporter, having sneaked along the massive marbled wall, leaned toward Peter, her only chance to be heard over the din. "Hey, does your candidate pay taxes?"

"Of course," said Peter, still marveling at the crowd, hoping any minute they'd change their chant to "Jesus! Jesus!"

"Has he released them?" the reporter shot back.

"Not yet," said Peter, who realized he walked into a trap with fewer loopholes than the millionaire's tax code. Only one answer would do. "But he will."

"When?"

"As soon as he's rich enough to afford an accountant." Peter hoped that his mildly humorous dodge proclaiming Jesus a frustrated, last-minute taxpayer would send the reporter on her way. She should be hounding Herod, who had a team of accountants and had yet to release his taxes under the guise that he was being audited and that his taxes were too complicated for anyone in the media to understand. As if the press couldn't find their own hotshot Wall Street accountants to review them.

The reporter handed Peter her card. "When he does, call me."

As the reporter pulled herself away from this spectacle, a handful of tax collectors gathered on one side to see what the hubbub was about. Pay no taxes? The outrage! The sacrilege to capitalism and the American way. There was an audit in store for these people if they could ever figure out who they were. But there was one name they knew, and they were busy texting that to their supervisors upstairs. Jesus Christ. He was getting an audit as soon as possible. Which Peter secretly hoped for so Jesus wouldn't have to release his taxes. If everybody found out how poor he really was, nobody would ever vote for him.

"Yes, we must tax the rich," said Jesus, hoping to calm them down. Firing them up was one thing, but encouraging a full-scale riot was never good press. Well, except among the anarchists, and their platform was never to vote. "But we must not shirk our duties. We must pay our taxes to show the rich the way."

The crowd fell silent, the only noise the occasional car passing and the revving engine of a bus across the street.

"Tax the rich! Tax the rich!" two people called out like concertgoers yelling out requests to the band. They couldn't carry the momentum, though, even as Peter joined them. Nothing kills an anti-tax rally like telling people to pay their taxes.

"So, people should pay taxes?" yelled one of the reporters.

"Take out some money," Jesus replied. "Any amount."

The reporter did, willing to play along. Several of the gathered protesters did the same.

"Whose picture do you see?"

"Dead presidents!" people yelled, interspersed by ex-presidents, specific names, and one cry of "Old white men!"

"And what do you see on the back?" asked Jesus.

The people called out the names of various national monuments.

"Then give to the government what is the government's."

The grumbling of protesters betrayed was immediate. Their sudden leader, this man raised up through the dung heap like them, had turned traitor. Only rich men should tell them to pay taxes, and they always ran on the platform of cutting taxes. Theirs first, and eventually yours.

"But I tell you this," said Jesus, cutting off the irritated before the microphones broadcast their griping. "We pay taxes for a reason. And what is that reason? For services. And who serves us? The authorities. If they fail to serve us, replace them with those who will!"

Applause broke out, though it would have been more effusive had the crowd not known Jesus was talking about himself. Or if he hadn't told them to pay taxes. That had killed the mood and the movement.

"And so I leave you with this: don't complain about paying taxes. If you owe tax, pay it. If you owe respect, pay it. If you owe honor, pay it. But make sure that your leaders pay it back because they owe you, too!"

The audience applauded again, except for those who were booing. The reaction was a muddled morass defined by confusion.

Pay taxes. Don't pay taxes. The cattle had been whipped into a stampede and then left to wander without direction. The group broke up. Most dropped their signs on the pavement, while a few dragged them behind like security blankets, the wood and paper scraping the sidewalk, forgotten weapons in a one-sided war.

"Let's get out of here," Jesus said.

"Agreed," said Peter.

Levi, much like the mob, stepped from side to side, not sure what to do. Jesus put a hand on his arm, but this time, the regional director did not flinch.

"Levi, how would you like to work for us?"

"Um…um…give me a minute."

Levi rushed into the building and past the security guards who didn't dare stop him. Outside his office, Levi handed his badge to his assistant and said in his loudest voice, "I quit!"

She had no idea why he was telling her, but she appreciated the heads up in case anyone asked. And people certainly would. Half the heads on the fifteenth floor looked his way.

He said nothing else until he was outside one minute and seventeen seconds later.

"Shotgun," he said as Jesus and Peter waited by the car.

"Of course," said Jesus as Peter climbed into his usual spot in the back seat where he hoped to configure Levi's new duties—as soon as Jesus told him what they were. At least one of them, however, would be assembling Jesus' taxes for swift and immediate release.

But they should have been paying more attention to the one photographer who stayed behind to snap a quick pic of Jesus holding the car door for Levi the tax collector.

A VOICE IN THE
WILDERNESS

The four men clambered into their lone campaign car, Andrew and Levi in front, the candidate and his manager in back. Peter gave a head nod toward the accountant in the passenger's seat, his curious eyes asking, "Why did you ask him to join our team?"

Jesus held up a finger and gave a slight nod, as much with his eyebrows as with his chin, telling Peter to be patient. Everything would be answered in time.

Peter pulled out his cell phone to check his messages. Before he could punch in his password, Jesus spoke. They hadn't made it to the end of the block. Even Peter could have waited that long.

"Levi, do you know why I asked you to join us?"

Levi turned around. He expected a question involving numbers, so this was a pleasant surprise.

"Because you need an accountant to figure out your books and make sure they comply with federal campaign finance laws."

Nailed it, thought Levi, who was more accustomed to being right than wrong.

"No," said Jesus, "although we need help there, too. No, the reason I asked you to join us is because when I asked you to tell me about taxation, you didn't give me dull facts about tax brackets and revenue streams and unclaimed refunds. You talked about how taxes affect people—poor people, the working class. You showed sympathy for them."

"I did?"

"Yes, and that impressed me. You care about people as much as anyone on this team, even though you sometimes bury it beneath rules and regulations."

"And do you know why I said yes?" asked Levi, turning half his body to face Jesus. The man was barely able to contain his smile, one Jesus felt compelled to return.

"No, why?"

"Because I'm free!" Levi threw his hands in the air and spun around to slam them on the dashboard. "I'm free! The burden is gone. The guilt I felt for taking other people's money is gone. The burden has been lifted. I have a chance to be a new man. I'm not Levi the tax collector, I'm…Levi the tax connoisseur!"

Jesus laughed wholeheartedly. This sinner had been lifted out of his despair to bring joy to others. "Tax connoisseur. I like that. We'll have to use it. What do you think, Peter?"

"Hmm? Oh, yeah, yeah, tax connoisseur. I like it. We'll put it on the website. Put out a press release or something."

Peter did not tear his eyes away from his phone. Though his face held more of a smirk than a smile, it was as sincere as Levi's. Peter, the harbinger of bad news, the cheerleader with little to celebrate, was ebullient. Well, for him anyway. He stopped scrolling, mesmerized by the words in front of him.

"What is it, Peter? What has you so distracted?"

"Tad sent me a link. You finally got some good press! I mean outside John's article in *The Star*."

Jesus took the news with reservations, waiting for more information before committing himself. He leaned closer to Peter's phone in an open effort to glean some information before asking directly, "So, who's giving us good press?"

Peter finally looked up from his phone.

"Some vlogger I've never heard of. Looks like the guy's been posting videos for about a year and a half. Few hundred subscribers, but they look committed. The thread is filled with comments."

"That's good," said Jesus, but he wondered what Simon would say when he crunched the numbers. How many were trolls out to pick a fight? How many were bots that couldn't vote? A hundred comments might mean ten people. "What's it called?"

"*The Political Messenger.*"

"Oh," said Jesus with a noncommittal shrug of his shoulders.

"You don't seem impressed. Look, it's not one of the big stations, but we can work with it. This guy's got thousands of posts up. Man, he's prolific. I wonder if he ever sleeps."

"He doesn't," said Jesus, recognizing the symptoms of a fellow insomniac.

"Yeah, I can believe that. Look at this guy."

A man in his mid-thirties stopped four or five feet from the camera, his wild hair flitting about as if he'd been pulling at it all night. His beard was beaded along each cheek in red, yellow, and blue, apparently accessorized to match his soft, flexible hemp hoodie. Then, this hippie who appeared lulled into the depths of a marijuana stasis burst forth like an angst-ridden comic releasing a lifetime of frustration in a matter of seconds.

"For months I have spread the word about he who is coming to cleanse the system. To save us from the infested body politic and its festering boils of corruption and corporate complicity. I have warned you that one man shall come, and today he is risen! He is here to cut out the rot and decay that plagues our system from top to bottom, from Herod the Heretic to the political machines whose machinations distort our votes and deny our democracy. This man wields a sword—no, no, an ax! An ax cutting through the overgrown weeds of our discontent. And indeed, if you have been paying attention, his ax is already laid at the root of those trees, so that every tree that does not bear good fruit will be cut away and thrown into the fire. This man will burn it down! He will burn the system down!"

"What the hell was Tad thinking?" Peter said, pushing the stop button with his thumb. "We can't use this."

"Play it anyway," Jesus said, putting his hand over his manager's thumb. "Let's hear him out."

Levi spun around in his seat again, wide-eyed concern splayed across his face. Andrew made eye contact in the rearview, waiting to see what his boss would do. Peter sighed and did as he was asked. After all, he had a boss, too.

"Repent of your past political sins, dear viewer, and join his camp. Shake off your apathy like chaff from wheat. Know that I have baptized his campaign with my blessing. For I tell you that though I baptize with water, he shall baptize with fire! Believe in him. Rise up as he has risen! Embrace the blazing sun that is Jesus Christ!"

"Okay," said Peter, "if we can't use the video, maybe we can use that quote as an endorsement. This guy will never play to the opposition."

"He doesn't have to," Jesus said, recalling Lucifer's summation of American politics. "He only has to motivate the base."

"Well then, I hope your base isn't women and children because this guy will scare them away."

"Probably," said Jesus, a smirk spreading across his face. "But let him finish."

"In the days of old, they silenced critics with a taste of hemlock. The powers that be, these men of *righteous* might, charged that their victims were at fault—the same victims whose blood they spilled. Yes, these men blamed the victims for their own destruction. *Moral* men of greed and vice twisted others' actions into political suicide, but we…we Christians know the truth! We keepers of the vipers, we Bohemians of eternal vigilance, know that the righteous cannot be defeated even in the face of death. An irreplaceable man has come to save us, and we must battle by his side! Face your fears and fall in. Though he looks like a lamb, he has the claws of a lion! Now, you, like our enemies, have been warned! You are either with him or against him. Spread the word. March. Move. Write. Descend upon Herod like locusts!"

And the madman fell completely silent as a pre-recorded voiceover added, "If you like what I've said, please subscribe, leave a comment, click the Like button, and retwit the link to friends." It was a bit anticlimactic, but a business necessity, even for a self-proclaimed Bohemian.

"All right," said Peter, exasperated that he had watched the whole thing and could use almost none of it. "We'll pull some clips from it. That Christian thing was damned good, and maybe that bit about you being like the blazing sun, but he practically called for an uprising. If you want to lose the man on the street, call for a street riot. That guy's crazy."

"You don't have to call him crazy," said Jesus. "His name is Jean Baptiste."

"You know him?" Peter asked, rather incredulous. He was afraid to ask how his candidate, a man of little political experience, knew about an obscure, radical channel. "Is he a carpenter, too?"

"No, he's my cousin. He's the one who convinced me to run. Started working on me six months ago, and it finally took hold."

Peter did not expect to be blindsided in that fashion. He flipped his phone in the air and let it spin end over end until it landed on a manila folder and slid onto the cushion.

"When was the last time you saw him?"

"Couple weeks ago."

Peter bit his bottom lip. He wondered how much more his candidate failed to tell him about his past. Now, he couldn't use any of the quotes. If the only positive review came from a cousin, no one would take it seriously. The press would denounce it as fraudulent favoritism. All the added headlines would send the guy's pageviews through the roof out of curiosity. That was the problem with loudmouths. They got more money for pandering to the hardcore, can't-get-enough fringe ideas, and the middle-of-the-road moderates abandoned you for aligning yourself with a lunatic. There was no winning if he tried to use any quote from this Jean Baptiste.

"So, uh…why didn't you tell me you had a cousin in the media?" asked Peter. "Maybe we could have gotten him to tone it down a bit and landed you some usable footage."

"Because it's nepotism."

"Nepotism?" Peter could no longer restrain his long-simmering incredulity. "My brother is driving the car! John and James are brothers. Our campaign is filled with nepotism, and so is theirs! Hell, Herod got the job from his father, and half his family either works in his office or runs his companies. I don't think a cousin with a working camera is too much to ask!"

Peter turned his head to the window. He should have controlled his anger. An outburst like that in front of a brand-new recruit was unprofessional, but he couldn't help himself. The campaign needed good news, yet every time they got close, it slipped through his fingers like a flipping carp.

Levi, still facing his new colleagues, broke the silence. "Did you say his name was Jean Baptiste?"

"Yes," said Jesus. "Why?"

Peter turned back to the conversation. He doubted this was information he could use, but he had to know. Better to find out now than later, when it was sure to do more damage. Just once he'd like to be in front of a story when it ran him over.

"Three-and-a-half weeks ago we got an anonymous letter requesting we audit his taxes. The letter was full of legalese and inside information. We gave it a quick look and determined that his income made him poor enough for us to audit since it would be an easy job. The audit found nothing irregular. He makes too little to hide anything at all, so we closed the case."

"Now, why would someone want to investigate a smalltime vlogger who looks like he sleeps in an alley?" said Peter.

"And why would they do it before I declared my candidacy?" replied Jesus.

The two men mulled over their questions, compiling a list of possibilities and considering each implausible. Was someone out for revenge against Baptiste, or did this have something to do with the candidate himself?

Once again, Levi broke the silence.

"Who's up for some lunch? My treat." He flashed that same infectious smile he gave when they climbed in the car. Jesus realized Levi was right. He was free. Levi the tax collector, now tax connoisseur, was a different man.

"Who can say no to a treat?" said Jesus.

Peter bit his tongue. He almost said they might as well get a bite to eat because it could be the only good thing to happen to them today, though all he said was, "Sounds good. Andy, pull into the next diner you see."

Peter picked up his phone and quickly dialed the office. He told Mary they'd be back as soon as possible, then added, "Tell the boys there will be another meeting. Oh, and keep the coffee warm. We're going to need it."

It was all Mary could do not to slam the phone in his ear.

SALT OF THE EARTH

Andrew turned the car into David's Key Diner just inside the Philadelphia city line. The structure was classically prefab and decades old, a shiny cigar tube marked by polished steel and sparkling windows subject to a daily scrubbing. As inviting as the outside was, the inside showed its age, with occasional rips in the vinyl seats and sporadic cracks breaking up the tiled floor. The chalkboard just inside the door boasted of daily specials, with today's top choice two poached eggs on toast. Signs throughout bragged of home cooking and delicious dinners, including such delicacies as gyros, corned beef, and omelets of any kind. Every serving came in Goliath portions, and the ample girth of half the patrons proved it.

Two dozen customers kept the place a little more than half full, a moderate midday rush, and the four men, led by Peter, found a corner table to the left of the door. It gave them a view of the entire diner, including the swinging metal doors behind the speckled Formica counter. Their waitress, one table over, departed her apparent regulars with a cackle she hoped was taken as a laugh but had all the appeal of a pealing bell if you were strapped to it inside the tower.

Although Levi told his companions to order whatever they wanted—this was, after all, his treat—Jesus reminded them of the need for austerity. Not just because the campaign struggled financially, but because their hunger would only be satisfied by justice. The message sank in and each man ordered the daily special and a glass of water, Peter's with no ice, or as their server said, "Four Adam and Eves on a raft, four Adam's ales, one hold the hail. Got it."

"Does anyone know what she just said?" asked Andrew.

"I think that was our order," said Levi.

Peter chuckled, looking up from the local business ads that formed a collage on the paper mat in front of him. Turning his head toward Jesus, he added, "It was our order, alright, but it was about as clear as one of your parables."

When the waitress, who heard everything in this diner, heard the word parable—which had been in the news a lot lately—she backed up two steps and looked more closely at the bearded man in booth number seven.

"It's you! Everybody...everybody...stop eating. We have the guy running against Herod!"

The diner fell quiet, the ping of stainless-steel forks switching from plate to table to silence. Even the groaning vinyl seats hushed while everyone had their stare.

Peter handed the server a business card. "We sure would appreciate your vote on..."

Jesus motioned for Peter to end his pitch so he could try his. "If there's anything I can do for you, please let us know. If you have any questions, just ask." He motioned Levi to stand up so he could slide out of the booth. "We'll take our lunch at the counter, if you don't mind. It will be easier for people to get their answers."

"No...no, I don't mind."

Jesus took a seat at the counter and spun on the stool, resting his elbows on the Formica to address the diners. The Q&A Peter expected never materialized. The customers had questions, but they were no gaggle of reporters intent on policy nuance. Their questions were more basic. Why should I vote for you? How can you fix low wages? How can you fix high rent?

Jesus fielded every question with ease, comfort sliding off his tongue like melting ice chips across a table.

"The pain you feel can't compare to the joy that's coming... Seek, and you shall find...Love one another...Beware those who flaunt their power…Beware false prophets who come in sheep's clothing but are ferocious wolves…" Picking up a shaker of salt, Jesus addressed them again. "You are like the salt in this shaker. You are the salt of the earth, but if you lose your flavor, you will be thrown out. Do not lose your flavor. Be as valuable tomorrow as you are today."

It went on like that for more than thirty minutes, simulating the ebb and flow of the summer tides. And it might have lasted for the same eternity had Peter not stepped in to remind Jesus they had to get back to the office for an important meeting.

Jesus thanked everyone for their time and shook their hands, always going to them and not the other way around. Behind him, Levi handed the waitress his credit card, whispering into her ear that he was paying for every single customer in the diner. He even threw in a generous tip. Free from the office, he felt free from his money.

In the diner's vestibule, Peter pinned a business card to the corkboard. Today's visit might draw some much-needed support for his candidate, but a little reminder didn't hurt.

In the car, Peter was his renewed self. "That was beautiful!"

"They made it easy."

"Everything you said in there was inspirational and positive and told them of a great future, and it was absolute drivel. Those phrases mean nothing on their own, but they loved it. They ate it up like salt on corn because you made them feel good about themselves. You're right: politics isn't local, it's emotional. We need more of that. Lots more of that."

Jesus remained silent. Peter conflated his two positions. His "drivel" was significant because it was inspirational, and if there was one thing he learned from watching Herod, inspirational drivel was the key to winning elections.

RAISING THE DEAD

Upon walking into the office, Peter ordered up some coffee and called a general staff meeting for anyone in the building. Everyone but James "The Great" Patmos and Barney—and Mary, of course, who only appeared to fill their cups—took their seats in the conference room. Peter gave a quick introduction for Levi, explaining he was the new bookkeeper.

"If you have any expenses, check with him first. He'll also aid in fundraising..."

"Oh, I'd prefer not to," said Levi. "I've never been very good on the phone. I'm better with numbers."

"Alright, we'll find people to work the phones. You just make sure the campaign is in the black."

Levi reached into his pocket and pulled out his checkbook. The meeting ground to a halt as everyone waited for him to write in an amount and sign his name.

"It's made out for the maximum amount allowed by law."

This did not make Peter smile. He was sure Levi's check was made out to the number. There would be no PAC funding here.

Jesus, however, gave his newest adviser a broad grin. "It's better to give than receive, eh, Levi?"

"It certainly is. I wish I could give more."

"Well, there you have it," said Peter. "A man setting an example for all of us. Give till it hurts."

"It already hurts," joked Judas Iscariot, his voice as sardonic as the statement itself. "We're volunteers."

The room laughed because they understood Judas' criticism, though Christ remained calm, his bright eyes declaring his appreciation for them all. "But you have invested yourself in this campaign, and for that I am eternally grateful."

Judas mumbled something about not being able to eat gratitude, but Jesus did not pursue it. Instead, he instructed Levi to remedy this situation as soon as possible. "Judas is right. Find a way to pay each according to his labor. A man, no matter how invested, does not work well on an empty stomach."

Slight applause broke out throughout the room, particularly among those like Judas and John who struggled to meet even their basic necessities.

Peter took control of the meeting again and said, "Alright, now that that's wrapped up, let's get down to business. Tad, what have you got?"

Tad explained that he and Mary had put up posters and handed out the campaign's newly minted pamphlets featuring a smiling Mary Magdalene on the front fold. The pamphlets went quickly, and he suggested they print up more if they wanted to continue building a buzz.

"Alright, we'll do it. John, what do you have for us?"

"Good news—the first edition of our e-newsletter, *The Good News*, went out this morning. I suggest you all read it so we're on the same page. Also, I've finished the early drafts of what I think is a tremendous speech for this weekend's Pocono event."

"The Poconos?" said Jesus. "What's in the Poconos?"

"That's where James and Barney are. They're setting up an event for you this weekend. Don't worry, it's going to feel just like the diner."

Jesus nodded his head, hoping it went better than the steel plant, the hospital, and the tax building.

"Okay, Simon Z, what do you have?"

"Latest polls are in. This 'raise the dead' thing is killing us. You're down twelve points to Herod. The right is portraying you as insane." He explained that memes had popped up everywhere showing Jesus leading an army of zombies, frequently depicting his supporters as mindless, disheveled, welfare-saddled eating machines. Critics further joked that Jesus was just trying to add names to the voter rolls, with one late-night host saying the dead had already elected him mayor of Chicago.

Peter sought suggestions on how to explain away the comment, only stopping for a second to ask Jesus what it meant. "Never mind. John, put out a statement saying the candidate misspoke. He meant saving people on the operating table or in hospice care. Getting everyone better treatment. He was raising the metaphorical dead, not the actual dead."

John jumped on the assignment, though Judas suggested a meme of their own—Jesus raising Herod's father from the dead to call him a loser. Jesus put the kibosh on that quicker than he answered Peter's question. He wasn't dragging Herod's family into this. Not when he was desperate to keep his own out of it.

"Look," said Tad, "the reason the right can call our candidate insane is because he looks insane. Look at that hair. He looks like he should be on stage biting the heads off bats. If we make him look respectable, that will change, I promise you."

"Well, before we change my image," said Jesus, who didn't like a word of Tad's idea, "let's hear what else Simon has to say."

"Tad's right. You have an image problem. You're still doing terrible with people who've seen your picture. Our focus group said you look lazy, unprofessional, and smell bad."

"That's it," said Tad. "Shave and a haircut. Now."

"No," said Jesus.

"We'll come up with another plan," said Peter. "Go on, Simon."

"So, we threw in a new question. You're going to love this. We asked people, 'Who would you vote for: Herod Antipas or Virgin Guy?' Virgin Guy won by eighteen points. Even people who said they don't know who Virgin Guy is prefer him to Herod."

Peter let out a howl as he smacked his forehead with the heel of his hand. "Of course! I should have thought of that!"

"Thought of what?" said Jesus, leery of any idea that got Peter this excited after hearing about virgins.

"We've been thinking of Virgin Guy all wrong. Sex isn't the negative it used to be. It's the new which-candidate-would-you-rather-have-a-beer-with question. Candidates have been caught having affairs, hiring prostitutes, you name it, and they keep getting elected."

"So, we ask them which candidate they'd rather sleep with?" said Jesus, ready to put the kibosh on that, too.

"No," said Peter.

"Could cost us the female vote," added Tad.

"We just need to play this right," Peter said as a hush crept across the crew. Jesus, who liked to know what people were thinking, remained glad he was not yet inside the mind of a campaign manager. They had to spin every straw-man issue into pure gold—and usually produced something akin to tarnished silver. The longer the campaign lasted, the faster the manager spun. And yet, as far as Jesus could tell, the campaign manager was less whirling dervish and more bumbling devil. Everything got twisted to their advantage. Everything. The campaign manager was a contortionist of language, logic, and legality.

So, Jesus guessed this should be interesting.

"The press keeps presenting you as some sort of pervert obsessed with virgins, right? What if we go the other way and make you the virgin?"

"Peter, I'm not a…"

"You're not linked to any women, right?"

"No, but…"

"And I'm not saying an actual virgin. It's another metaphor."

"For what?"

"For purity. For innocence. For…incorruptibility!"

"Metaphors don't work in campaigns," said Tad.

Peter sipped his coffee. He had to admit Mary made a damned good brew. "Alright, point taken. The voters don't do subtlety. But we reinforce the concept with an image change. Your long hair and beard make you look like a high-school metalhead but throw you in a pair of glasses and a ponytail, boom! You're a sensitive folk singer. A more innocent you becomes the virgin."

"Peter, the virgins represent the voters..."

"And nobody remembers that. Besides, they don't want to be virgins. They think they're all cynical even when falling for childish gimmicks. We make this work by flipping the tables."

Jesus drummed his index fingers on his coffee cup. Arguing with Peter was like arguing with a rock. He was steadfast to the point of being obstructive, yet he never truly forced his views on Jesus. He always caved when his ideas were reduced to rubble, so Jesus couldn't back down. In the right light, Peter would see things his way.

"Look," Peter said, "people love a goof. It's all the rage in politics. Characters! Congress is littered with them. Now, we can't make you a goof in Gucci like Herod, but we change you up a bit. Give you a catchphrase: 'You're hired,' 'You're fired,' 'Make America Rich Again,' whatever. Something people can latch onto. People don't want a politician—they want a meme with legs. After all, they view politics as a circus, so you might as well send in the clowns. A clown who can laugh through their tears. So, sit in a firetruck and make a siren sound. Sit in a big rig and pretend to pull the horn. Hug a flag. Wear a ballcap. Ride a bike. Ride a tank. Eat a burger. Chop wood. Choke on a pretzel. We need to humanize you."

"I refuse to debase myself for this office." Jesus hoped that would sink in, even though he realized the office of senator was sometimes debasing. It didn't. The problem with managers is they like to manage.

"You're not debasing yourself, you're connecting with people. You're simplifying your message so that people can take it home and digest it with their evening meal."

Jesus ran his finger around the rim of his coffee mug, an empty gesture. He knew his mind. "No. The goals aren't worth pursuing if the personal cost is too great. And this comes at great personal cost. It's deceptive. I can't do it."

111

"It's not deceptive, it's slick. And it's necessary if you want to win because we can't get ahead of any story as long as the media narrative works against us. We need people to get behind us. Basically, we need to fool enough of the people, and the right people, to win the election."

"A constituentocracy," mumbled Jesus.

"A what?" said Peter.

"Nothing. A word I picked up."

Before Peter could pursue it further, Levi raised his hand. No one ever raised their hands in one of these meetings because it wasn't school, but Peter did like any teacher. He called on Levi.

Their new numbers-cruncher turned a piece of paper around and said, "I did a quick cost-benefit analysis on goals versus personal cost. Mr. Christ is right. It's not worth it."

Peter examined the chart for a fleeting second. How Levi did it that fast he'd never know. Some kind of mathematical genius. But Peter was a political genius, and he spotted the flaw right away. Or rather something he could sell as a flaw.

"The problem with your chart is that you've undervalued goals. People sell their souls for this job. If you want it bad enough, the value goes up and the cost goes down."

Levi adjusted goals on the y-axis and nodded with his lower lip jutting out. "Oh, yeah. Never mind. Peter's right."

Another victory, thought Peter.

At last Thaddeus jumped in, looking to make peace. He proposed John come up with a slogan for the event in the Poconos. He then urged Jesus to meet with the people in those professions—firefighters, truck drivers, and the like—without Jesus acting like a preschooler. The meeting ended with everyone agreeing to take the middle path while grabbing as much attention for the candidate as possible. They would push issues over personality, but where possible, blend the two.

As everyone departed, Mary stuck her head in the door. "Mr. Christ, you have a phone call."

"Who is it? The press?" asked Peter.

"No," said Mary, since the press rarely called here, and when they did, it was only for a comment on a negative story they were running. Those calls always went to Peter. "It's a doctor. He asked for you specifically."

Jesus shrugged his shoulders and rose from his seat to take the call. Before he reached the door at the far end of the room, Peter threw back his head and yelled (officially at the ceiling but technically far beyond), "For the love of God can't we get a break?"

HEAL THYSELF

J esus took his hand off the conference-room door to address Peter. His campaign manager had his own hands to the sky imploring God for a favor, but when he noticed his boss looking at him, he lowered them, placing them in front of his chest, each hand twitching incrementally as if he were an offensive lineman stopping a charging tackle. His frustration mounted, looking for a way out, as he tapped the ball of his palm against the edge of the table.

"You going to be alright?"

"Yeah, yeah, just another banner day. Take your call. I'll fill you in later."

"Okay. Just don't do anything rash."

"Who me? Cool as a cucumber," Peter said, which denied everything he was thinking. The candidate was the one who did rash things. Who did the unexpected. Jesus should have been a pitcher. His curveball always had Peter swinging and missing. At least he could give Jesus the bad news after he hung up with the doctor because this news was sure to make any symptom worse. It had already spiked Peter's blood pressure.

Jesus picked up the phone in his office. It took a second to remember how to take a call off hold, but three tries later, he pushed through.

"Hi, this is Jesus. Can I help you?"

114

"Hello, Mr. Christ, my name is Dr. Luke, and I'm calling from Lebanon Medical Center. I'm sure a man of your importance is quite busy, so I'll…"

"I'm not important yet, Doctor. Unless you know a way to get me into the Senate."

The doctor's brief chuckle gave way to a more serious sigh. "I'm afraid not, unless what I'm proposing helps you. I would love to see you beat Herod."

Jesus wasn't sure how a medical man could boost his poll numbers, but he would listen to an entire thesis if it put him ahead. It would be nice to go back to Peter with good news if all Peter ever had was bad.

"What can I do for you, Doctor?"

"As you know, we have a great system—we insure the healthy and deny the sick to keep rates down. Well, here at Lebanon Medical we treat patients at no cost to them, even when politicians cut our grant money or prevent the poor from getting healthcare."

Jesus detected the doctor's initial sarcasm but ignored it to keep the conversation upbeat. Best to take his medicine with a spoonful of sugar. He'd save the Herod beatdown for the left-leaning press and the boys down the hall. "All patients should be treated for free."

"I completely agree. I've worked on people who've been to a dozen doctors to no avail. We've treated edema, paralysis, leprosy, even a woman who had a twelve-year menstrual flow—all free of charge. Our treatment isn't disease-driven or medicine-driven—it's patient-driven because patients are people first. Always have been, always will be."

Physician, heal thyself! Jesus could have used a smaller sales pitch. He had a person of his own having a nervous breakdown one room over.

"That's terrific, Doctor, but what can I do for you?" The stress in Jesus' voice indicated his patience had waned.

"Sticking to your motto of coming to serve. That's beautiful. And serving others is exactly why I'm calling. I heard about the little boy you visited at Mercy. It's a touching story. Now, I have no doubt he'll get good treatment there, but he'll get world-class treatment here. For free, of course."

"Is that so?"

"Yes, sir. We currently have one of the best pediatric oncologists in the world on loan to us for six months. Truly one of the best. We'd like you to convince the family to let us treat Little Mark."

Jesus rubbed his left eye with the tips of his fingers. He thought the doctor wanted to offer advice on healthcare or ways to improve the system, but he was calling with much better news. If only Jesus could fulfill his request.

"I'm not sure the family wants to hear from me right now," said Jesus, his honesty tinged with sadness.

"I know, I saw that, too. But this could be a real win-win. The patient gets top-flight care at the best price available—nothing—while we get the credit for treating him, which will increase the amount donors give us. Treating someone in the news is always good for the bottom line."

Jesus finally understood what this was all about. Medicine be damned because money was at stake. The hospital relied almost exclusively on donations to survive because the system could not provide for it. Doctor Luke's sarcasm about the sick being denied cut as deep as a scalpel. Little Mark would get the best care but at a price—the price that he become the poster child his parents didn't want him to be. The best way Jesus could rationalize this was to say that the boy would survive leukemia and the hospital would survive its funding drought, both of which outranked the parents' outrage. It was a terrible choice to make, but the good of the many outweighed the good of the few. Jesus put aside his better nature and agreed.

"I'll do it, Doctor, but I can't promise anything."

"That's all we can ask for, Mr. Christ, but if you pull this off, you definitely have my vote."

The two men said goodbye, although Jesus did not hang up right away. He placed the receiver against his forehead. This was a hell of a way to earn a single vote. Medicine be damned? Integrity be damned. He was twice violating the promise he made to the boy's father, and all so he might win a seat to maybe do some good in an august body that moved at a snail's pace. The whole event turned the bad taste in his mouth to acrid smoke.

And with that, he got up to find out what left such a bitter taste in Peter's mouth.

SUBMIT TO AUTHORITY

Jesus entered the conference room to find Peter working the phone in sound bites.

"...the candidate believes in higher taxes on the rich and only the rich...When he said pay your taxes he was merely telling the rich to stop paying less than their fair share..."

Peter spun his laptop around to show Jesus a photograph of them climbing into the car with Levi just a few hours ago. He had to admit the photographer did a good job keeping Peter in the background, placing Jesus and Levi prominently in the foreground.

"Yes, he did leave with a tax collector, but that was only because after just ten minutes with our candidate, the tax collector QUIT HIS JOB...No, Mr. Christ does not like tax collectors the way he likes virgins...No, wait, that didn't come out right..."

Click.

The line went dead. The reporter knew he'd never get a better quote than that one.

"Damn it. Alright, I'll call him back in a minute."

"What's this?" said Jesus, pointing to the computer screen. He knew what it was, of course, but he wondered what spin Peter would give it.

"That's you leaving with a tax collector. That's why we can't have surprises. Everything has to be planned or you leave yourself open to attack."

Jesus read the caption beneath the photo. *Senate candidate Jesus Christ loves tax collectors more than he likes those protesting* high taxes. *Here the inexperienced candidate leaves the regional tax bureau in Philadelphia with his new best friend, head tax collector Levi Matthews.*

"It's running online in *The Morning Star.*"

"Is that who you were on the phone with?"

"No, that was *The Bethlehem Star.* Can you believe the questions they ask? And they're on our side. At least they'll quote us. *The Morning Star* said the reporter will call back—probably tomorrow morning, which lets their version simmer for another day." Peter spun his laptop around to face him again. "In the meantime, John and Tad are drafting releases about Levi calling it a corrupt system. We'll get our side out, but it won't get much traffic."

"Why?"

Peter just about yelled at Jesus but kept his cool lest his candidate yell back. He still had hope for turning things around. Getting off on a bad foot wasn't as bad as finishing on a bad foot, or not finishing at all. Peter closed his laptop, scooped it into his arms, and stood up.

"Because the most shocking thing about his is that you left with a tax collector. Saying taxes are too high on the poor is dog bites man. Leaving with a tax collector is man bites dog. Welcome to being the man."

Jesus scanned the list of press calls on Peter's desk, picked up the phone, and dialed the first one that hadn't been crossed out.

"Who are you calling?" Peter asked, ready to rip the phone out of his candidate's hand if he didn't like the answer.

"A friend."

Peter was unsure about that answer. A friend would be good, if they actually had one. He knew there weren't any listed on the scraps of paper littering his desk, which meant Jesus was not calling a friend at all. Peter lunged for the phone but came up short as Jesus turned and started speaking.

"Hi, Nicole Demus, please...It's Jesus Christ." Jesus waited a few seconds while the receptionist transferred the call. It gave him enough time to wonder if she was, in fact, a friend of the campaign or an honest reporter who couldn't be trusted. He was about to hang up when her voice came on the line.

"Hi, Ms. Demus. How'd you like to take my statement on this tax-collector story? …Well, I know you're not working on it, but I'm sure you'd like to get a statement direct from the candidate's mouth. No one else has." Jesus smiled at Peter. It was not a matter of manipulating a person's greed so much as knowing what she wanted. People who weren't predictable personally were often predictable professionally. For a reporter, it was an exclusive.

"For the record, I do not like tax collectors—I feel sorry for them. Everybody blames the tax collector for their taxes, but they're only collecting what they're ordered to. The problem is, they're enforcing bad policy. They didn't create it. Congress did. And we did by voting for them. Well, let's change that by changing the people who make policy. Vote for me and I will make our taxes fair…Did you get that? Thanks. I knew I could… what's that? Why did I say people should pay their taxes?"

Peter swung his hands up, violently swiping them across each other, the clear sign in any language to hang up and never answer that question. If only his candidate spoke one of those languages.

"I told people to pay their taxes because I don't want them breaking the law on my account. Submit to authority on this and avoid jail at all cost…Alright, Ms. Demus, thanks. I'll talk to you later."

Jesus turned around to find Peter hanging his head. That wasn't the response he would have scripted. Or improvised. Or said with a gun to his head. Once again, the candidate was off-message. How far off they'd find out tomorrow.

Peter's concerns for tomorrow were optimistic. Within minutes of the phrase "submit to authority" landing on *The Bethlehem Star's* homepage, the far left and right had full-scale meltdowns while the middle developed symptoms of a nervous tick. For the left's outer reaches, this was an ideological position, in as much as anarchists never want to submit to any authority. The worst of the left took to vandalism and looting, if only to prove they were not submitting. For the fringe right, it was their greatest fear and fantasy come to life—submitting to authority over taxes while desperately craving an authoritarian leader they could follow without question. Small groups grabbed semiautomatic rifles and stormed local town halls, shouting out all the things they wanted, including jobs, haircuts, and the right to peacefully assemble. They dutifully departed when the police with bigger guns showed up. All the middle heard was "pay your taxes" and they started gasping for air.

Saul Tarsus jumped on the story almost before his pre-recorded intro belted out his name. "I'll tell ya something, this Jesus Christ fellow is putting the tax in tax and spend, that's for sure. Need proof he's a commie? There it is. Taxes! Taxes! Taxes! And I'll bet a year's worth of his tax money Jesus doesn't even pay taxes. Know how I know? The poor never do. They just get other people—rich people—to pay it for them. They think the rich are just some cash cow they can milk. Which is why Herod doesn't have to release his taxes. He's rich, so we know he pays. But Jesus? I bet he doesn't pay a dime, which is why he expects you to. Prove me wrong, Jesus, prove me wrong! Release your taxes! Release your taxes!"

Saul faded off into a hypnotic chant as an overdubbed audio track that sounded like thousands demanded, "Release your taxes! Release your taxes!" until half the listeners joined in, believing they were part of a nationwide rally without ever having to leave their homes.

Before the day was done, Jesus held a press conference to apologize for being a tax apologist. Levi handed out copies of the candidate's tax returns—which took longer to print than compile—to the assembled reporters. There were no complicated forms, deductions, or…income, really. Jesus was solidly lower-middle class and a man of few worldly goods.

Which was the first thing Herod's campaign attacked. They called him a loser and a failure and pointed out that each of Herod's hotels made more in a year than Jesus made in a decade. This, like a diabolical tax policy that expects those with more to pay more, balanced out the poll numbers between the classes. Jesus' numbers shot up among the working poor and middle class who saw themselves as poor while plummeting among the rich and upper-middle-class who thought they'd someday be rich. The middle-middle class remained evenly split, although one poll suggested that if Jesus won the election and earned a senator's salary, they would like him more because he'd be more like them.

The staff at Phobos News spent the next few hours poring over the returns. By the time the *Faust & Friends* team hit the air, they had Christ in their crosshairs.

"Can you believe," Doozy began, "that this man gives ten percent of his income to charity? Ten percent!"

"I think that's called tithing," dark-haired guy said.

"It's also called stupid," said the blonde.

"All I know," added Doozy, "is that if he's giving away his money like that, you know what he's going to do with yours."

"Give it away," said the blonde.

"Yep," said Doozy. "I mean, I just can't get over these taxes," he added, holding them up as if the home audience was playing along. "No tax deductions. Nothing. Not even the ones he could take. Tools. Work clothes. Union dues. Mileage. Nothing."

"And you know if he's not taking them, he's going to push to make sure others can't take them," said dark-haired guy. "He's going to hit his union brothers hard."

"I bet he takes away the mortgage deduction," said the blonde. "People will end up homeless!"

They ascribed power to a single senator like he alone could make these ideas law. But creating fear requires no more logic than being afraid.

"And you know a man who lives in debt like this can't understand billion-dollar budgets and trillion-dollar deficits. You know he'll spend another trillion like it's nothing."

"Actually," dark-haired guy said, "he has no debts."

"Then he'll crush American business," said Doozy. "Companies rely on government spending to stay in business. He'll destroy the American economy!"

"Don't you know it," said the dark-haired guy, who understood that a good salesman could say the exact opposite thing about an item if it was what the consumer wanted to hear. And the Phobos viewers wanted to hear it.

But despite the media bashing and a drop in the polls, Jesus was up among one group: the group unlikely to vote. He took that as good news because it was the only good news they had. The bad news was that his taxes and the Levi story would soon look positively quaint.

NO ROOM AT THE INN

A local reporter stood in front of a rundown motel, the sort of mom-and-pop operation that still listed Color TV as a benefit. The only part of the sign that lit up was the neon No Vacancy, and that only said "N Vac ncy." The parking lot sprouted weeds through a road map of cracks, and the stained blinds over the office window were pulled down despite the sign saying "Open." Eight rooms stretched off to the right, each with a brass digit nailed to a burnt orange door, the number six dangling upside down in an apparent attempt to confuse anyone who had not counted up from one.

"We're standing in front of The Inn here on the edge of Bethlehem to bring you a remarkable story. What we learned will shock you."

The feed switched to pre-recorded video sweeping across the building behind him, showing it in greater detail.

"This is the birthplace of Senate candidate Jesus Christ. Although it may surprise you that he was not born in a hospital, that is the least shocking part of this story. Christ's father, Joseph, was a forty-one-year-old carpenter, and his mother, a fourteen-year-old bride. The couple traveled here from Nazareth in late December thirty-three years ago with fourteen-year-old Mary nine months pregnant. Why they were traveling so late in her pregnancy has yet to be determined, but we have spoken with several people familiar with this story."

The video switched to a grizzled man in his late sixties or early seventies listed as the owner of The Inn.

124

"Yeah, I remember them. You don't forget a night like that. This man and this girl came knocking on our window asking for a room. We told them we were full-up, but she was about to pop. Well, I couldn't clear out a room for them, but we got this tool shed out back, so I set up some cots and cleaned it up real fast, and they slept out in the cold next to the lawnmowers and shovels."

"Were you shocked by the girl's age?" asked the reporter, placing the microphone an inch closer to the man's face.

"Yeah, but we sometimes got teenagers in here back then, so maybe she was eighteen, though she looked younger. We run a real respectable operation, so we were concerned but thought maybe he was her father or something. Anyway..."

"Then what happened?" asked the reporter, injecting a question to keep the biggest story of his life from becoming the most boring story of his life.

"They weren't here a couple hours before she started screaming. Me and the guests came running, but they wouldn't let us call a doctor. The woman screamed 'No,' so my wife..." The camera panned left to show a dour woman in peach sweatpants for a mere second before swinging back to the man. "...pitched in and helped deliver the baby. I went and got some towels and we wrapped him up. They stayed out in that shed for twelve days before they headed home."

The video switched back to the reporter once again giving his live report in front of the motel.

"We tracked down several neighbors of the Christ family from thirty years ago, who gave us their thoughts on the situation."

The screen returned to a montage of pre-recorded interviews, listing all the participants as current or former Nazarenes.

"There were all sorts of rumors about them. The way I heard it was somebody else got Mary pregnant but he took off and Joe raised the baby as his own," said one woman.

Another woman added, "There was one story that the baby belonged to one of Joe's other kids, and Joe was worried it would ruin his son's life, so he took care of the baby."

125

"I don't know what their story was," said a man. "They were gone for a couple weeks, and when they came back, they had a baby. I heard they adopted, but I never asked."

"Did their age difference bother you?" asked the reporter.

"Yeah," the man said. "Always did. They were good neighbors, though. Quiet. But him marrying a teenager like that? I never hired him for a carpentry job. Not even an odd job around the house. The whole thing was wrong."

The feed once again switched back to the reporter ready for his wrap-up.

"Everyone we spoke to expressed concern about his parents' age difference, with most of them saying they would not allow Joseph around their own children, particularly their daughters. We have contacted the Christ campaign for comment, but as of this broadcast have not heard back. When we get a reply, we'll update this story."

"Thanks, Gabriel. Have a safe trip back," said the graying male anchor alongside a pretty, just barely thirtysomething co-anchor. "To repeat—our top story tonight: Joseph Christ, father of Senate candidate Jesus Christ, was forty-one, and his mother, Mary, fourteen. Coming up—weather, sports, and an in-depth look at words that sound dirty but are okay for your kids to say."

Jesus turned off the TV in his office. He had hoped to keep his parents' relationship out of this campaign, but he should have known the press would find out. As much as he wanted to focus on the present and the future, the press and the public never let go of the past.

That didn't mean his campaign manager wouldn't try. Peter appeared in the doorway with one simple statement: "We gotta distance ourselves from this."

Jesus wasn't sure how he could distance himself from the people who brought him into this world. He certainly couldn't say he barely knew them, but within the hour, he took to the cameras to address the scandal directly. He condemned his parents' actions three decades ago, saying that his family had acted "inappropriately." He then put the sort of spin on it that Peter loved to see and wished he constructed. Jesus rhetorically asked, "Who is my mother? My family? The people of this state are my family. The voters are my brothers and sisters, and when I get to Congress, I will never forget that."

It was a strong statement, but it failed to blunt the impact of a story this powerful. The local TV report swept the state and crept into the national headlines. Phobos News ran the piece with their own commentary and field reporting on a loop day and night. *The Morning Star* blared the headline *Pedophile Parent Raises Senate Candidate*, and Saul Tarsus conducted his usual rant containing anger, innuendo, and a touch of sophomoric humor.

"His father was forty-one and his mother was fourteen! What, was his father dyslexic? Even if she said she was forty-one like him and juxtaposed those numbers—and I doubt it—her sweet, young, innocent, teenage face should have told him otherwise. Look at that photo our friends at Phobos found of her in eighth grade. Eighth grade! So sweet and innocent, but did that bearded pervert care? No, of course not. Now, hey, I'm as glad as the next conservative because, and I say this with pride, I am compassionate, so, I'm glad they carried the baby to term unlike a lot of those hippie parents who use abortion as birth control, but..." And here came another long pause that could have held a commercial but held the listener's interest instead. "...but I'm sure that them carrying the baby full-term had more to do with her age than anything. When you get a fourteen-year-old pregnant, you hide it. You hide the evidence! You hide your shame! They could have gone to some back-alley butcher shop, but they didn't. Well, good for them. And good for the system shutting down places like that and keeping teenagers who get molested from getting abortions. Now, hey, I'm not crazy, folks—you can't blame the baby, but you can sure look at the way it was raised. Pedophiles raise pedophiles. Child abusers raise child abusers. Is that the kind of man you want in the Senate? No! Remember that when you go to the polls. 'Cause those aren't the sort of poles pedophiles like..."

Tarsus then threw to a series of commercials that led off with a live promo. "I know you don't have problems getting up for this program but maybe you have problems getting up elsewhere." He finished reading this copy for erectile dysfunction before switching to pre-recorded spots for Body by Jove and opposition to HPV shots for teenage girls. The break finished with an ad that was pro Herod only in as much it was anti-Jesus. A strong narrator questioned various actors pretending to be your average citizen-about-town.

"Are you for government-run medicine?"

"No, that's a communist thing," said an indignant woman.

"Do you want the government taking your guns?"

"No," said an angry man, "that's a commie thing."

"Do you want government telling Wall Street what to do?"

"No," said another woman, "that's a communist thing."

"Higher taxes? Poor roads? Standardized tests for your children?"

"No," cried a multitude of voices. "That's a commie thing!"

"You know who does support commie things?" the narrator continued. "Jesus Christ. Vote Herod on Election Day."

The narrator delivered his final lines a half-octave higher and three speeds faster. "Paid for by Concerned Citizens Against Communism. Not affiliated with the Herod for Senate campaign."

Jesus and Paul, for the first time since the campaign began, heard none of Saul Tarsus' open-mic routine. Not an ad, not a criticism, not a joke. Instead, a photographer streamed ethereal tunes, instructing Jesus to turn this way and that. He constantly moved the light behind his subject, creating a halo around Jesus' head and a glow upon his cheeks. His hair flowed like a romance cover model; his beard trimmed and neat, adding gravitas to his profile. For a moment, Peter believed they might actually land a candidate in the Senate with intentional facial hair.

Still, he couldn't quite overcome the feeling that something was missing.

"Come on, try the glasses," he said, holding up several prop pairs, from nerdy black frames to thin wire rims, all with no lenses. "It's for your image."

"No," said Jesus, "it's for the image you want me to have."

The photographer held off shooting for a second, pretending to check the lights while his clients argued over artistic differences.

"Glasses will give you an intellectual look," Peter said. "An academic look. Isn't that what you want?"

"I want my look," replied Jesus. "My policies are what make me thoughtful." He looked at the photographer for confirmation, but the photographer only shrugged. Glasses, no glasses...as long as the check cleared, he could wear a clown nose, powdered wig, and tiara. Hell, these days, that might make him look presidential. Anything worked if you said the right things.

"Come on, just one shot," said Peter, attempting to put the glasses over Jesus' ears, which wasn't easy given the perfectly coiffed and sprayed-into-place hair. "If you don't like it, we won't take another."

"No," said Jesus. "If I let you take even one photo, that's the one you'll use."

Jesus, for all his naiveté about political imaging, was starting to catch on. If he wanted to control his image, he would have to control the people imagining it.

"Look, they're hitting you with the pervert charge right now. Phobos has been running with it since last night. Glasses make you look innocent."

"If glasses are all it takes to proclaim innocence, defendants should give up lawyers."

"Not that kind of innocence," said Peter. "Purity."

"I'm sure the lights and airbrushing will take care of that."

Peter almost jumped through his skin with excitement. Airbrushing! Right—change the image. Shop in some glasses, like models miraculously losing weight or...limbs. Photo alterations shouldn't just be of the other guy. Change your own image with a little digital magic.

"Fine," said Peter, hoping he managed to mask his exuberance. "Let's finish up here, choose the shots we want, and get your new face out there. I have a surprise for you."

Jesus held in a sigh. So much for controlling the people around him. Still, that didn't mean he had to do it, whatever it was. Not if he didn't like it.

The photographer snapped a few more images before bringing up forty shots on his computer screen. After some wrangling, they chose a right-side profile that presented Jesus as a god. It said compassion and love, his eyes focused in the distance as if looking to the future or on something beyond human understanding. The angle kept his nose slim, his hair curled around the base of his neck, the light casting shadows away from his face, creating the impression that darkness itself could not touch him. The photographer smiled at its mastery. It looked nothing like the candidate, which was the best way to sell him. In fact, he found it was the best way to sell anyone. He recalled the saying that "Politics is show business for ugly people." It was why it was filled with so many character actors and so few leading men. And given the impossible standard for ingénue, even fewer leading women.

He hit send and emailed these aspiring politicians the shot, along with a few others that, while impressive, didn't quite stand up. As they left, he decided to put the best one on the wall of his studio near the entrance. He'd tell everyone, "If I can make a politician look that good, imagine what I can do for you."

As Peter led Jesus back to the car, he called the office, telling Mary to forward the incoming high-res image to their media team and have them mock-up a poster. After hanging up, Peter leaned into the driver's side window to say something to Andrew, who had only gotten back seconds before after a burger run down the street. Andrew nodded, and with his passengers inside, took off in the opposite direction of campaign headquarters.

Andrew drove over unused railroad tracks into what Jesus' mother called "the sketchy" part of town. It was, in her mind, the politest thing to call this section of Bethlehem. It wasn't the stark ghetto of larger cities, but it was subtly different than the upscale neighborhoods, the McMansions and trimmed lawns giving way to cracked facades, both of buildings and people. The chipped sidewalks buckled upward, seemingly driven by seismic shifts in fortune, from once middle-class abodes to working-class barracks. The signs that should have meant nothing but always meant poor—the lone shopping cart against a withering tree; sneakers strung over telephone wire; young children playing in the street and older children on street corners—drifted by the window as Andrew scoured addresses between the check-cashing storefronts, pawnshops, and mini-marts turned gated bodegas offering fatty, salted goods at inflated prices, a food desert responsible for both malnourishment and obesity. Jesus wondered why, as a young man, he disappeared into the mountains to meditate and fast when he could have done so here, sure to have been hungry and forgotten, whether by the government, society, or his neighbors.

"It's two blocks on the left," Jesus said.

"You know where we're going?" Peter asked.

"There are many reasons to come here," Jesus replied, "but only one that concerns you."

The three men entered a dilapidated brownstone without knocking, the security buzzer hanging by a single, stripped wire. Jesus took the lead as they headed up three flights of stairs, each marked by a different tile floor but the same cracks, peeling paint, and occasional hole in the wall that exposed wooden slats beneath crumbling plaster. It was a building inspector's dream, which was the best reason not to condemn the place. As long as it stood, the dream stayed alive. There would be time to close it and crush it when either the public found out or the owner got a better offer for the land.

Jesus rapped his knuckles on a white door at the end of the hall in desperate need of fresh paint. No one asked "Who's there?" or barked "Go away!" or fell into forced silence until the intruder disappeared. Instead, the door flung open and a wild man with unkempt hair and unclean clothes burst forward with arms wide open. A gambler would bet even money that a stranger would flee in horror or settle in for a muddy cup of coffee.

"Cousin! People I don't know! Welcome! Come in!"

Jean Baptiste rushed back into his one-bedroom sty, waving for them to follow with an energy they could not match. He scooped up a mug, downed whatever contents were left, and poured himself a refill from the dregs of the pot.

"Anyone care for some coffee? I can make more!"

"Uh, no," said Peter, taking a courteous second to consider his companions. "We're good. I assume you know why we're here."

"Of course! Make yourselves comfortable. Sorry I don't have chairs for everyone, but make yourselves at home on the edge of my bed. Very springy."

Andrew examined the rumpled sheets, flattened Tic Tacs for pillows, and an open bag of chips on the nightstand. The opening, pointed toward the mattress, and the trail of crumbs in the folds of the sheets, convinced him to stand.

"When can we start?" asked Peter, sticking to business in the hopes he could get back to more savory business after this.

"In a moment. I upload several videos a day. That's how I make my living. I made a dollar forty-seven in royalties yesterday, and I've already donated it to your campaign."

"Thank you," said Jesus. He thought his cousin would be better served putting it toward a hamburger or cleaning supplies, but he knew enough to appreciate generosity. The rich gave for influence, the poor for reward, but Baptiste embodied the cheerful giver. He gave because he believed in his cousin's cause more than any campaign manager ever could. Jesus understood that he would build his campaign on Peter's shoulders but spread it through Jean Baptiste's mouth.

"Okay, I'm going to shoot one video before we get to yours. Sit back. This is gonna be a blast!"

Baptiste poured a shot of wine into his coffee cup, downed the revolting mix in a single swallow, and stepped back, hands on either side of his nose, index fingers jabbed into the corners of his eyes. He stood motionless, the focused actor about to originate some brilliant improv or a minister about to confess his sins to God.

He brought his hands down in a swift chop, the words flowing from his mouth as if completing an unfinished conversation.

"Oh, Herod, I have heard your minions in the media attack Joseph and Mary for their marriage—a marriage I swear to you was based on love. But reporters who extol the worst of mankind suddenly find themselves appalled by this story. Their faux outrage is brought to us as caustic comedy, but it is we who laugh at them, for they follow the age-old rule of politics that we here must tear asunder: condemn in your foes what you accept in your allies. If they have turned a blind eye to your faults, it is because they have gone blind from pleasing themselves!"

Jesus turned his head at this reference to politics as self-pleasure. Peter was just glad he hadn't taken that cup of coffee or he would have choked on it by now. Perhaps it was not too late to pull his candidate, family or not.

"They would have us forget your foibles, your many affairs of the heart and loins. It was just three years ago that you married your sister-in-law. Yes, your brother's wife, but if that were not enough, she was also your niece! Inbred tempter! Incestuous whore! That is who you are, Herod, and like the leopard that cannot change its spots, a politician cannot change his peccadilloes! Who is your whore now, Herod? Show her to us! Parade your mistress like you parade your niece. Oh, you preach of family values in others because you do not have them in yourself. You speak of the nuclear family while you explode the concept. Well, you shall not do that to us, dear Herod! No, we shall stand strong beside Jesus Christ for he is a man of great value. His parents loved each other while you love only yourself! We know you, Herod—Herod the Lesser, forever in your father's shadow! You are a lesser man than he, and he a lesser man than Jesus. Jesus understands fidelity, but you…you understand none of it. You have not changed, Herod, and you never will. You were no bastard son, but you are a bastard now! Show us your whore…show us your whore!"

Jean then leaned into the camera and said as sweet as a day spent rowing across calm waters, "If you like what I've said, please subscribe, comment, like, and retwit."

His promotional obligation done, he turned off the camera and hit Upload. In twenty seconds, his latest screed would be live to the world.

"Aren't you going to edit?" asked Peter.

"I never edit!" declared Baptiste with a dismissive wave. "I rant. I rail. I rave. The three Rs of making money on the Internet. I say something outrageous but something I deeply believe, and the clicks, like cash, come pouring in."

Peter examined the shabby apartment and wasn't sure 'pouring in' was the right phrase, but given the spreading water spot above the bed, it seemed oddly accurate.

"Aren't you afraid of being sued?" asked Andrew.

"No," said Baptiste. "If Herod did that, he'd have to testify under oath. Too big a risk of perjury because you can be damned sure he has a mistress somewhere. He'll bitch, but he'll never sue. He's not going to jail over some weirdo on the Internet." Baptiste laughed, directing both thumbs to his chest. "Me!"

Peter nodded with appreciation. He admired Baptiste's confidence, but there was a strategic advantage to being here. He only booked Jesus because his cousin had a camera and a small but devoted following. He could call it a following on the Internet, but if anyone raged like this in person it would be a cult. Christ had tied Judas Iscariot's hands from slinging mud at Herod, but in Baptiste, Peter had an ally who could sling mud like a monster truck at a county fair.

"Look at that!" said Jean Baptiste. "Thirty views already. This will easily hit a few thousand. Probably be one of my all-time best. It's the headline, you know. *Herod Antipas likes whores.* Catchy, but sex sells, even on a video site that doesn't allow it."

Peter realized that by Baptiste taking the low road, Jesus was automatically on the high road. He appreciated his own genius in putting his candidate on this show.

"Alright, let's get this interview done," said Baptiste, taking a swig of wine right from the bottle. "Cousin, you sit there, and we'll show your brilliance to the world."

But what Jean Baptiste, for all his confidence, did not know, was that a man would do for lust what he would not do for love. Herod and his intern watched the video in his office. He was prepared to dismiss it, but she would not let it go.

"I want his head on a platter." Venom dripped from Salome's lips. No man could call her a whore, and Herod's consoling, even unctuous nods would never satisfy her need for vengeance. "You said you would give me anything I want. I want his head!"

Herod nodded one last time, but not in agreement. He recalled making that promise, but he was simply seducing her. If only she hadn't looked so good at the office party. The music, the wine, the palpitations the old man initially took for a heart attack. He did promise her anything. It's what men of power do to get women a third their age—and now it was what he had to do to keep her.

He picked up the phone to call his usual cohorts. Baptiste wouldn't know what hit him.

SERMON ON THE MOUNT

Jesus was twenty minutes away from his speaking engagement in the northern end of the Pocono Mountains. His interview with Jean Baptiste hit the web twenty-four hours ago, and so far had no repercussions. Peter was right to order it released late on a Friday afternoon. It gave social media addicts, who never slept, time to view it and comment on it and forward it, but held no real interest for the traditional media who saw viewership drop on weekends.

And the video, despite Baptiste's antics, was boring. "Downright banal," according to Peter. Although that was not his general preference—after all, he wanted everything to garner attention and drum up support—but after a week of news bashing, he could use something quiet.

Jesus gave him that. Baptiste spoke of how proud he was to witness his cousin's campaign. How thrilled he was to prepare people for it. Yet, Baptiste avoided any controversial topics so as to avoid digging Jesus too deep a hole. He knew the time would come for the candidate to be abrasive. In a constituentocracy, you can't afford to offend anyone until you have an unmoving base willing to vote for you no matter what. Well, if not you, then your party or platform. Once your base was secure, you could offend anyone else you wanted. That made your base more devoted to you because they wanted to insult them, too.

The only challenge his cousin offered in the ten-minute interview was his attacks on Herod. Baptiste temporarily unloaded on him, hinting at the accusations in his previous video, before finding a calming hand in Jesus. He returned to his reined-in form, though he did tell Jesus to strike back at his opponent. Jesus noted that Herod had said nothing negative about him. It was all underlings, the media, PACs, and super PACs—which was the nature of the system. Fight dirty by letting other people talk trash. Jesus said that wasn't his approach, adding, "I will hold my peace and remain at rest because, and I mean this: blessed are the peacemakers."

That single line became the impetus for today's entire speech.

Once at their destination, Jesus stretched, refreshed by the miles of tranquil woodland and speckled farmland that took his mind off politics for minutes at a time. Today's crowd might be small, but they had a raw energy that inspired him. Fifty people and a few of their children sat in folding chairs on the edge of a ballfield facing a wooden grandstand draped in red, white, and blue streamers. The people—the usual assortment to be found in a town this size, which was to say a blip on the map between bigger boroughs—made Jesus smile, unlike the poster hanging behind the podium. Peter had Photoshopped in glasses, its thin-wire frame giving Jesus a near-sighted squint that kept him from looking like a man of great vision. Or any kind of vision. It was Jesus' face alright, warm and friendly but no longer sage. The words splayed above with his name below, all against a blue field, said *Vote for Jesus*. All in all, you couldn't get more bland than this. It told the people nothing. It was merely a command to vote for a person whose face you liked. With any luck, he also represented your values.

Jesus sought out Peter to protest the display, but there was no time. Organizers raced about rounding up the few stragglers still getting free donuts and coffee from a folding table to the right of the makeshift stage. Finally, a woman dressed in what could best be described as the female version of the leisure suit, although she made it look smart, introduced him with the standard, and therefore almost comical and rarely right, "The next senator from the great state of Pennsylvania..."

Jesus took the stage to a solid round of applause, though it was hard to tell in this outdoor event. The sound carried upward and away, making it difficult to hear more than a smattering. He only hoped his speech carried better.

"Ladies and gentlemen, thank you for joining me on this beautiful spring day. I'm thrilled to be here in Canaan, a town that represents the heartland even if it's not located in the heart of this state. You signify the best of what we are and what we have. That is why I know that you, like me, are blessed."

That line gathered both staunch applause and awkward glances. Those hanging on the edge of the economy, surviving in a town on the margins of importance, didn't feel blessed.

"You are blessed because you are the sort of folks the government should look after." John had added the word 'folks' to make Jesus more folksy.

"Blessed are the poor in spirit. Blessed are those who mourn, for they will be comforted. Blessed are the meek..."

"Tell that to the inmates!" yelled a heavily bearded man seated near the front row, jerking his thumb over his shoulder toward a large federal prison looming in the distance. The gathering laughed, but Jesus, whose innate empathy told him to laugh along with them, found himself sympathizing with those inside.

"And so I shall, for you have proven my point. Why are they there? Because they preyed upon the weak. We rightfully blame the perpetrator, not the victim. Their show of strength means those prisoners are no longer blessed. Their only hope for a blessing comes from being inside where they are meek and we are strong. We have power over them because we decide their fate. Keep them locked up? Offer them parole? Commute their sentence? Whatever their fate, we are stronger than them. They may not be blessed today, but they may be tomorrow if they accept their meekness."

The man thought he followed the logic. At least he didn't rebut the argument. No one did.

Peter hoped that a tangent like that might produce some applause, but it produced the empty stares Jesus often got when speaking at length. They didn't feel blessed by their meekness. In fact, they would trade it for power any day. Today preferably. It sure beat being victimized by debt and taxes. They were free, but to what end? A lifetime of servitude to the almighty dollar and the powerful who abused their labor to earn a thousand times more? Like the men behind the razor-wire, they were meek, and it sure didn't come across as a blessing. But before anyone could make a cogent argument, Jesus moved on.

"Blessed are those who hunger and thirst for righteousness, for they will be filled. Blessed are the merciful, for they will be shown mercy. Blessed are the pure at heart, for they will know love. Blessed are the peacemakers, for they will bring peace. Blessed are the persecuted, for they shall know justice."

Jesus hit the word justice hard, letting it ring out across the open air. It earned him applause, much of it an expected reaction to merely hearing the word justice.

"If they accuse you of lies—and Herod's supporters will—then accuse them of evil. Do not let them judge you. Celebrate your freedoms. Rejoice and be glad. Fight the powerbrokers and reap your rewards. As they persecuted your ancestors, they will persecute you and you will survive!"

The audience burst into applause. He was silver-tongued alright, but with a heart of gold. Peter, standing off to the side, patted Barnabas on the shoulder. Jesus had done it. This speech worked for everyone, from the persecuted minority to the majority believing itself to be the persecuted minority. It was so vague that everyone could see themselves in it. Jesus roused them simply by not giving them details to dispute. He set up an us-versus-them paradigm they could carry forward. Rich versus poor. Givers and takers. The haves and the have-nots.

Peter wiped a tear from his eye. He couldn't believe it. Jesus was a populist.

"But woe to you who are rich, for you have received your comfort. Woe to you who are well-fed, for you will go hungry. Woe to you who laugh now, for you will weep. And woe to you of whom everyone speaks well, for you will be demeaned. We will see the rich taxed and the poor fed—and the powerful will laugh no more, for they will provide it!"

This got a smaller round of applause since it seemed less impassioned than his impromptu attack on the well-to-do, but at least it earned some recognition. When John and Jesus first conceived it, it felt powerful, but then it was never meant to follow a commanding attack on the elite. Peter made a note to have Jesus be more spontaneous and less controlled, unless, of course, he went back to saying foolish things that didn't poll well. But for now, he was all for letting Jesus wing it.

"Of course, these things take time."

Peter hung his head. Damn it! So much for winging it. He was going to demand Jesus stick to the script. 'Things take time' was an excuse, not a campaign promise. You say, 'And I will do these things on day one,' or even the weaker, 'I will introduce legislation on day one,' and then when things didn't happen, you say, 'These things take time.' You could always say it wasn't a broken campaign promise because you've been working on it since day one, but you've run into unexpected opposition—you know, the other party. The president. Lack of money. Common sense. Anything but it being your fault. By putting it out there now, he'd have to say Jesus was being pragmatic, unlike his "dreamy-eyed opponent." Which didn't sound like Herod at all.

"How many farmers do we have here?"

Three hands went up.

"A few. Well, let me explain things with a parable."

Peter almost bolted out of his shoes. He might have if James hadn't put a hand on him. Not another parable! He'd wring his neck if he could find it under that god-awful beard.

"A wealthy landowner had a fig tree."

"We don't grow figs," yelled one of the farmers. "We grow pigs!"

The audience laughed, and this time Jesus joined in. "An apple tree, then. Any kind of tree. It doesn't change the story. Now, this landowner noticed the tree hadn't produced any figs for three years, so he went to the farmer who worked the land and told him to chop it down. The farmer said, 'Give it one more year. If it doesn't produce figs, I will.' The next year, the tree produced figs."

There was a murmur among the crowd, which, had it been mic'd, would have been broadcast as, "What the hell?"

Peter moved his left hand in a circle near his chest, urging Jesus to explain what he meant. This wouldn't be a repeat of the Ten Virgins parable, but he still didn't want to run out there and interpret it.

"The landowner represents the public, I am the farmer, and the fig tree is the legislative process. People expect things to be done quickly, but the wheels of government turn slowly."

Jesus turned his head just enough to catch Peter out of the corner of his eye. His campaign manager gave him the okay sign. He was happy with that explanation.

"Thank you all for coming out today. There are a lot more donuts and a few tchotchkes you can purchase to help our campaign. I'll be over there serving coffee, happy to meet every last one of you."

Half the crowd got up to leave and half walked toward the baked goods. Peter raced toward the exit, waving freshly printed pamphlets, Mary Magdalene's captivating eyes calling out to anyone trying to go. Jesus handed out donuts, glad-handed scores of voters, and even held a few babies. Along the way, he autographed dozens of the campaign's official—and doctored—mages. The one without glasses he signed with his name, and those with he was always asked to sign as Virgin Guy. Despite his deep displeasure he played along, his top priority to keep these voters happy. And James snapped photos of it all, knowing a smiling candidate with smiling constituents made great public relations. If a picture was worth a thousand words, it was also a way to erase them. A good image could make people forget bad words like tax collector, virgin, and politician.

At least Jesus could hope it did.

KEEP YOUR TONGUE FROM EVIL

The video of Jesus calling out the persecution of the poor and the marginalized got little press beyond the local press, but its online life was just short of viral. James posted the entire speech, as well as the one-minute edition of its most brilliant moment, on their website and social media pages. Within hours, it had been liked hundreds of times, twitted and retwitted hundreds more, and provided a slight bump in overnight polling. It was generally believed he would have gotten a bigger bump if the right wasn't busy attacking him for lacking family values for denying his mother. It turned out they believed insulting his mother was their prerogative, not the candidate's.

With the major media shut down for the weekend, or rather, using second-tier anchors and correspondents, the Sunday morning shows picked up the slack. And none was more popular than *Punch/Counterpunch*.

The host, who served as a middle-aged referee after having been a punching bag in real life, introduced the program before introducing the pugilists he preferred to call pundits. "It's Puuuuuuunch/Counterpunch!" at which point the immaculately styled man sitting on the right said, "I'll hit 'em with a right cross!" while the man next to him, hair neatly parted in the middle, replied, "And I'll hit 'em with a left!"

The moderator, sitting in the middle, looked into the camera and said, "And I'm here to see that it's a good, clean fight." Which wasn't his job at all. It was to ensure a bloody knockdown, a brawl of epic proportions. The kind of fight that kept the ratings high and viewers saying, 'Shouldn't the ref stop this?' while simultaneously turning up the volume and throwing jabs of their own.

"Alright, gentleman, big week this week. Your thoughts on the Senate race…Righty?"

"This Jesus Christ is a lefty loon. His policies say he's a lefty, and he's a loon for thinking he can beat Herod."

The actual Lefty jumped in quickly. "A lefty loon isn't pro-life. Christ said he was pro-life at his first press conference. He's a moderate who can appeal to the average voter."

"No way. This guy's only pro-life because it's the right thing to do. Even he knows our position can't be touched, no matter how much you protest. But everything else? Lefty loon. Higher taxes, increased welfare, free healthcare, fewer guns…This guy's so far left, he's left alone. No one's backing him. Politicians aren't standing up for him, and his campaign is broke."

Lefty wasn't buying it. "He's offering common-sense solutions for the average citizen. He wants to get things done. He's liberal on some things and conservative on others."

"That's right. His policies are all over the road like a woman driver."

Lefty's jaw dropped open as his right hand went to his forehead. "This is why women don't vote for your side."

Righty, however, knew the facts. "Forty percent of women voted for us in the last election—the ones that can drive!"

"Alright, back to your corners," said the host, his punchy sentence resembling a bellowing sideshow barker with a smidge less subtlety. "Next question: Christ made his first media appearance this week. Thoughts…Lefty!"

"He looked good. He stayed calm, answered the questions, stuck to the talking points…He didn't make any major gaffes."

"No, he saves those for his live appearances," said Righty. "Look, I don't want to bring any attention to this Jean Baptiste fellow—Lord knows he does enough of that with his hair—but

Christ looked awful. Substandard equipment, bad lighting, no make-up…it looked like a high-school production of *The Manchurian Candidate*."

"This is just like the right," came the reply. "They only care about the optics and not the substance. You can say outrageous things as long as you look good doing it."

"Yeah," said Righty, "and it's been that way for decades. It's called television. This Baptiste guy is no Phobos. Print has more reach. Look, you need to look good—not like some long-haired hippie making home movies while high…"

"That's slander," said Lefty.

"Hey, I'm not saying he was high, just that he looked like it. To me."

Lefty tensed up. Righty was pulling the typical pundit move. Say something outrageous, walk it back a half-step, and then cop out by creating the defensible, 'that's what it looked like' or 'that's what I heard.' It was news analysis by defensive briefing, or the pundit's version of the sucker punch. Make it clear it was an opinion or a rumor. The public would only remember the claim, not the aside. Lefty never learned how to do that in journalism school. Or after ten years on the air.

"Look," Righty continued, "playing the media is a game. And if you want to play their game, follow their rules. Have good sets, attractive hosts, and sensible questions. Don't hire your Uncle Dave to use a handheld in a horror film."

"Solid body shot from the right," said the host, jumping in to redirect the conversation. "You brought it up, so let's pursue it. What do you think of his speaking style? What would you call his speeches?"

"Lies," said Righty.

"An elegy," said Lefty.

"See, there you go again. Using big words," came Righty with a verbal jab.

"That's because we respect voters' intelligence."

"So do we. That's why we don't feed them crap."

"Hey, we tell the truth *and* respect their intelligence."

Righty chuffed. While you could do both, it was always better to pick one or the other. Too many people found it easy to have their truths twisted by big words. Lawyers and politicians did it all the time. Keeping things simple made sense. And it made sense in the best way possible: the common-sense way. Common sense was easy to follow, even when it was a complete lie.

"What are those things he uses in his speech? Those stories? Metaphors?"

"Parables," Lefty said, proud of himself for knowing such a term.

"That's because it takes a pair of balls to tell them," said Righty, who knew the word and had prepared a line to prove it, though he wasn't going to show his intellect to his fan base.

"Low blow!" called the host, "but I'll allow it!"

"They are reflective allegories for our times," said Lefty, holding on to his position with all the verve of a one-armed man in a tug-of-war.

Righty continued. "Your side has got people running to the dictionary to look up words like parable and allegory."

"And your side has them looking up emoluments and collusion," replied Lefty, getting in his first blow of the program. It always took him until the later rounds to get fired up.

Righty leaned forward, less than a foot from his opponent's face. He was about to demonstrate a play from the second page of the political handbook. Change the topic and resort to name-calling when your arguments aren't working. "Jesus Christ is an elitist!"

"He's an everyman!" came the passionate rejoinder.

"Break!" yelled the host, and every regular viewer knew what was coming. Three minutes of commercials followed by the lightning round. The first commercial was already getting plenty of airtime: the so-called Commie Christ ad. Herod's favorite PAC knew the show would address the election and bought airtime. The last commercial in the bloc was an official, clean-cut ad featuring a smiling Herod amid average Pennsylvanians shaking his hand, eating hot dogs, riding horses, mowing the grass, wearing hard hats, attending ballgames—everyday activities that played well everywhere. Then came quick images of Herod discussing policy with President Tiberius, all while a smooth narrator told everyone the obvious: Herod supported tax cuts, bringing big business to Pennsylvania, helping small businesses grow, more tax cuts, keeping drug costs down, and more tax cuts. The only specific detail in the entire spot was, "I'm Herod Antipas, and I approve this message."

Of course, there wasn't much to approve of. The ad said nothing of substance and was largely contradictory. Bringing big business in would surely kill small businesses, but Herod never let truth get in the way of a slick commercial. That just wasn't common sense.

Punch/Counterpunch came back, the ever-tough-but-somehow-jovial host talking over the brassy music. "Time for the Knock-Out Round. Quick questions, quick answers, and someone's coming out bloody."

The host snapped the index card in his hands with a loud pop, an attention-grabbing trick that was all for show. He didn't need the cards—they just made him look smarter, like wearing glasses or a sportscoat. The cards were his mortarboard, an academic rite toward viewer acceptance. They weren't blank but were unnecessary since the questions rolled rapid-fire down the teleprompter in front of him.

"Alright, we just saw the Commie Christ ad. What nickname would you give Jesus?"

Righty jumped in first. "I'll stick with Commie Christ."

"Compassionate Christ," said his counterpart.

"Compassionate Christ is more accurate," said the host, pointing to Lefty before swinging his index finger the other way, "but Commie Christ will stick. Point to the right!"

Both sides agreed with that. Commie Christ was just more memorable.

"A nickname for Herod?" said the host in his usual bombast.

"Hammerin' Herod," said Righty.

"Herod the Lesser," said Lefty.

"Herod the Lesser has been done and hasn't stuck," said the host. "Point to the right! Does Jesus Christ connect with the common man?"

"No. He may be a carpenter, but his platform is full of holes," said Righty with a wry smile.

"Yes. His platform is strong."

"He should, but he doesn't. Point to the right!" barked the host. "Does Herod connect with the common man?"

"Yes," said Righty. "He's a native."

"Not with that silver spoon in his mouth," said Lefty.

"He could be better, but he's better than Christ. Point to the right!"

Lefty was feeling battered and bruised, unable to get in a point against the always right-leaning host. If this were a real fight, he'd be guarding his ribs in exchange for a concussion. He should be used to such a beatdown, but it felt fresh every time. Maybe if it didn't, he would come in sooner with guns blazing. Or at least his fists up. Every question was just another shot to the jaw. If this kept up, he'd be unable to speak before the next commercial break.

"Does Herod debate him?"

"Yes," said Righty. "He's not afraid."

"Yes," said Lefty, "but only after making some crazy demands."

"Yes…" agreed the host, who drew out his reasoning for dramatic effect, "…but only after crazy demands. Point to the left! Does Jesus manage to raise money?"

"Yes," said Lefty, who had earned the right to go first by picking up a point. "There are plenty of rich liberals looking for a candidate like him."

"The rich won't come through. He'll be doing bake sales before long."

"Yes," called out the host. "Liberal donors will get desperate, but until then—bake sales! Point to the right! Where does Jesus do better? Left or right?"

"Left," said Righty, having earned the right to go first again.

147

"Middle," said Lefty.

"Left!" yelled the host, almost angry that someone made a choice he hadn't offered. The middle was shrinking so much in a polarized electorate that they were only worth playing to in a close election, and this was not shaping up to be close. "Does Christ stay in until Election Day?"

"No," said Righty. "He'll be twenty points down in the polls and be out in two weeks."

"Yes," said Lefty.

"Yes!" called the host, cutting him off before he could give a reason. The clock was winding down. If he wanted to get all his questions in and get to the all-mighty commercial, he had to hurry things up. "Let's hit the speed bag, boys. Does Christ win?"

"No," said Lefty, "but he does better than expected."

"No," said Righty.

"No," said the host. "Loses by eight-to-ten, which might be better than expected. Point to the left! And finally, what does Christ do after he loses?"

"Becomes an activist working for the people," said Lefty.

"He won't even get elected dogcatcher," replied Righty in his most snide tone of the morning.

"He stays a carpenter," said the host, "because he can't get elected dogcatcher! That's it. The winner by knock-out and a devastating right cross is Righty!"

That came as no surprise to Lefty, who left this show more than once flat on his back. And yet, he'd be back next week even if his glass jaw was wired shut.

The host turned toward the camera, thanked the pundits for joining him, and thanked the audience for watching, closing out with his famous tagline, "Tune in next week when we deal another body blow to the body politic. Bye-bye!"

WISDOM IS BETTER
THAN GOLD

Monday morning brought a flurry of activity around Christ campaign headquarters. John and James sent out emails with *The Good News* embedded below. Peter and Tad worked the phones, making call after call to party loyalists. Everyone had one goal: raise money masked as spreading the word. Every call and email had some version of "We're gaining ground…" "If you care about this country, you can't let Herod win…" "Your money is your voice. The more you give, the louder you sound."

Donor after donor, however—and that was only the one percent of callers who picked up the phone—declined or said they'd give later. Each one was worried about throwing good money after bad news. Negative stories stuck to this candidate. Peter and Tad tried to explain that their money could combat that. If they could just see their way to giving a thousand dollars…okay, five hundred…for one hundred dollars… anything at all…it was an auction in reverse in which the price never went back up. The only one who succeeded was someone who wasn't in the office at all. Mary Magdalene called a few friends who called in to donate. When she ran out of friends, the calls stopped. Although, in another way, they did get a handful of smaller donations thanks to Mary. Several men sent money after clicking on her smoky-eyed image on the website. At least one said he'd cut a check if she agreed to a date, and another thought she was the candidate and couldn't wait to see her on the news.

That made Tad smile. He tapped the table with a knuckle and called the one person who could convince Jesus of his follies and finally sell himself the right way—like Magdalene.

Two hours later and a little before lunch, Mary Larnaca stepped into Jesus' office with a visitor.

"Mr. Christ, may I present my brother, Lazarus."

Jesus stood up to shake his predecessor's hand, but this Lazarus bore no resemblance to the confident candidate who lost in a landslide to Herod. He was meeker, humbler, his first step shorter, the physical form of a stutter. He offered his hand in return, but it no longer burst forward with arm locked, asking to be gripped. It was crooked at the elbow, creating deep wrinkles in his polyester-blend jacket.

"It's a pleasure to meet you, Mr. Larnaca. Please, have a seat."

Lazarus sat in one of the two stubby brown lounge chairs with the bolts near the legs popping loose. Used furniture to be sure, but it was exactly how his office looked back then. Once comfortable, he looked at the Vote for Jesus poster hanging in the middle of the wall to his right. "Nice poster. The dove flying through the 'o' in vote gets across your position on peace while reminding people to vote. It's subtle without taking away from your face, which is the centerpiece of the whole thing. That's a solid design. Ditch the glasses, though. Makes it look like you're trying too hard.

"Thanks. The dove was a last-minute suggestion from my campaign manager. So were the glasses."

Neither man noticed Mary fuming by the door. *The bird was my idea!* Peter never told Jesus she suggested the bird. No one ever gave the coffee girl credit—only blame. The position had become a political punchline. Something goes wrong and the person immediately became the person who got the coffee no matter how close they were to the candidate.

"Well, I hope it draws more voters to your campaign than my poster did. I'm here...I'm here to tell you what you're up against."

Mary opened the door a sliver, enough to slide her slender body through. Jesus caught her a second before she could close the door. "Mary, could you send Peter in? I think he could benefit from your brother's wisdom. Thank you."

Mary wanted to scream, *He could benefit from my wisdom, too! You all could. I was part of that campaign. I was up to my elbows in muck!* But all that came out was, "Right away."

Peter joined them inside a minute, going straight to Lazarus to embrace his old boss. Lazarus tensed up during the hug as if it brought back uncomfortable memories of his loss. Peter could not give up the slick affection of political showbiz, the loss not affecting him as deeply as it did the man whose name was on the ballot. Peter poured on the compliments about how great it was to see him again and how serving in his campaign was among the greatest honors of his life, defeat or not.

Lazarus took the compliments graciously, though Jesus sensed he was eager to get down to business. Or perhaps, better put, to get this out of the way. What he had to say could not be easy because he'd have to rehash his mistakes on the grand political stage. Jesus, hoping to make this easier, instructed Peter to have a seat before encouraging Lazarus to share his experiences.

"What you have to understand," Lazarus began, "is that Herod buried me. He raised three times as much money, cost me my entire fortune, and smeared my name and my reputation all over the press. He attacked my family, my friends, my business. Nothing was off-limits. He will come after you with everything he has."

"We're aware of that," Peter said, "but we're holding our own. We're only down eight points."

"And we're doing rather well in name recognition. Fifty percent of the voters know my name."

"And fifty percent know you as Virgin Guy," said Lazarus. "And Herod will do everything to keep it that way because some voters are dumb enough to look for that name on the ballot."

"We have a strategy for that. We're going to embrace it."

"Then you'll get a new nickname, and it will be something worse. Maybe something that doesn't make sense. He'll hang a nickname on you like a child naming a pet. It will be cute and insulting at the same time. He hit me with Lazy Lazarus, then Lyin' Lazarus and Low-down Lazarus. He'd have called me Lascivious Lazarus if he knew what the word meant. And it didn't just apply to politics. People thought I ran my business that way. My clients abandoned me. It never ends. Six years later and he still brags about beating me. Be careful he doesn't ruin you, too."

"What do you suggest?" Jesus asked.

"Fight fire with fire or you'll spend all your time putting them out. And while you're putting out one fire, his team is throwing kerosene on three more. You need to keep him fighting the fires you set."

"We need to run on the issues," Jesus said. "For the most part, the public agrees with our policies and positions, sometimes overwhelmingly."

"Go ahead, try it. Your base will form an echo chamber. Your strategy only works in a democracy. This is a constituentocracy!"

Jesus knew the moment Lazarus used that word he met with Lucifer. He also knew that the attacks by the conservative media meant Lazarus turned down his offer for money and power. It was why he lost. Idealism rarely won elections. Or friends. Or a future.

"So, who's your dirty trickster?" Lazarus asked.

"Judas," said Peter.

"Iscariot? Oh, he's a real zealot. He can run with the best of them. Fake leaflets, fake news, fake social media accounts, fake poll numbers, you name it. He can make you look good and the other guy look like a tricky-dick grifter with a love for underage goats—if you let him loose."

"We just might," said Peter, knowing that 'might' was the political equivalent of 'yes,' and the legal equivalent of 'but we can't.'

Jesus took the slightly softer, "We'll see," which was the political equivalent of 'we'll consider it until something pushes us over the edge and we have no choice.'

"I tried to run a clean campaign, too," Lazarus said, unable to finish his thought as Tad came through the door.

"Sorry to interrupt," he said, which was in no way true, "but Herod just filed paperwork accusing us of campaign violations. The news is all over it."

As the three men stood to follow Tad down the hall, Lazarus forced out a sign filled with recognition. "It looks like Herod brought more kerosene."

CONCEIVING MISCHIEF

Peter entered the conference room, followed by Lazarus and Jesus. Half the staff sat around the table, each on their cell phone, watching different stations cover the same story. Not surprisingly, the story had broken on Phobos first, likely tipped off by the Herod campaign before they filed. The other networks and online outlets jumped on board within minutes, offering a version of the same narrative because they had yet to get their own sources on the air. What they couldn't confirm, they copied—with the caveat "according to..."

Only Jean Baptiste, in his lonely garret, fired off missives without restraint. "We have a system that bans a few hundred dollars to feed the working class, yet five-thousand-dollar-a-plate dinners to enrich wealthy candidates gets the government's stamp of approval. It is no surprise when beneficiaries write laws to benefit themselves! Why when money flows downstream is it a trickle, but when it flows upstream it is a flood?"

"Turn that down," Peter said to Thomas. "Alright, what do we know?"

Levi started to speak, but he was no more than two words in when Tad cut him off. "You know that stunt Levi pulled paying for people's lunch in some diner? Herod says we attempted to buy votes."

"I didn't know," said Levi. "I'm an accountant, not a campaign finance..."

"Let me think, Levi!" snapped Peter. A week of bad news he could handle, but law-breaking was tougher to spin.

"That's the sort of stunt Herod pulled on us," Lazarus said. "He's hitting you with a legal argument. Even if it fails, the public will think you're running a dirty campaign."

Judas raised an eyebrow, surprised to see his one-time benefactor amid this brain trust. The man who had eschewed government forever had joined the fight. Judas gave him a nod, but Lazarus didn't respond. And Judas didn't blame him. It was okay to keep a trickster on staff, but you kept your distance as a means of plausible deniability. That didn't end when the campaign did. No, politics was ongoing. Everlasting. It was as sure as death and taxes. If Lazarus ever got back into the game, he might need Judas' special talents but never his friendship.

"I got it!" said Peter. "Levi wasn't an employee of the campaign. Therefore, he couldn't represent us at the diner."

"But I already asked him to join the campaign," said Jesus, knowing the press would bring that up in their both-sides-of-the-story counterargument.

"Had he been paid?" asked Lazarus.

"No," replied Jesus.

"Did he sign anything?" Lazarus said, continuing his inquiry like the lawyer every politician needs to be.

"No."

"Did you discuss his joining the campaign at the diner?"

"No. The waitress recognized me, and we got into talking with the customers before I ever had a chance." Jesus scratched his head and looked to Peter for confirmation. His campaign manager nodded.

"And he paid with his own money," Peter concluded, "which means he did so of his own volition and not as a member of this campaign. John, you and James run with that. Put it out everywhere. Get ready to go on camera, if necessary."

"Hold on," said Lazarus. "It's not enough. It's a defense. You need something positive."

"You're right," said Peter, rubbing the back of his neck, disappointed by his impulsiveness. That was a candidate thing. At least in this campaign.

155

"Simple," said Jesus, all eyes turning toward him. "We were so touched by his generosity that we made it official. He became part of the campaign for demonstrating kindness to strangers. He treats others as he wants to be treated. He understands that the love of money is the root of all evil, and he rose above it. Something along those lines."

John nodded and stood up, disappearing through the closest door with James in tow.

"Herod's not pulling punches," Lazarus said. "This is all part of a coordinated campaign to drain your resources on lawyers. If your strategy convinces the feds not to investigate, you're in good shape, but don't think he'll stop there. He'll look for other legal loopholes. It's the political form of capping the knees."

"It's not a legal loophole if we did it," said Jesus.

Lazarus gave him a serious look, his legal mind working overtime. "It's all legal loopholes if one side gets away with it when another can't. So, dot your i's and cross your t's because Herod can get away with it."

Jesus admired Lazarus' courage. His formidable mind and backbone should have been enough to defeat Herod, but elections weren't won by one approach alone. Herod not only covered all the bases, he brought the ball, the bats, the gloves, paid off the umpires, hired the scorekeeper, and packed the stadium with fans pulling for the home team. No matter how much talent you had, winning was a long shot. If you pulled it off, they called it a miracle. If you lost, they said it was expected.

Lazarus had expected to lose.

Jesus expected a miracle.

But he understood why Lazarus expected to lose. The odds were stacked against him. His courage came in taking the field at all.

"Peter, put on your best suit because you're doing the interviews. The press doesn't want this old hippie right now."

Peter nodded his head as Jesus left the room, happy to be taking the lead and sure he was the only person who could present the argument effectively. He tapped Judas on the shoulder on his way out and said, "My office. Now," then stopped next to Lazarus. "Care to join us?"

Lazarus shook his head. "I've done enough for today," though he was sure Herod's campaign style would have him back here within the week. He patted Peter on the shoulder, letting Judas slip by untouched. "Good luck. You'll need it."

Peter thanked him and turned toward his office. Halfway down the hall, he put on the brakes so hard Judas came within inches of rear-ending him. Jesus was exiting through the front door. Peter could only hope he was going home or out for a cup of coffee because he did not have enough resources or patience to clean up another mess.

Which meant another had to be coming.

WHOEVER WOULD SAVE HIS LIFE

Mark's father knew the knock at the door was no nurse. He'd been here too many months not to recognize their quick knock followed by an even quicker entrance whether you responded or stayed silent. This person waited. That could be good, but it was most likely bad.

It was bad.

His eyes drew narrow and his jaw firmed up. Coming off an overnight shift so he could see his son in the daylight kept him cranky and ready for a brawl.

"What do you want?"

"I came to check on your son."

"That's none of your business." Mark's father grabbed the edge of the door to swing it closed but stopped when Jesus pulled a scrap of paper from his corduroy jacket.

"You're right. You don't have to tell me anything. Just take this."

Jesus' eyes implored him to take it. Against his better judgment, Mark's father complied, studying the words. Lebanon Medical. He was impressed but skeptical. Too many doctor dodges had made him that way. "Is this legit?"

"Yes. They have a world-famous oncologist there willing to treat Mark for free. Ask for Dr. Luke."

Jesus turned to head back down the hall. No sense in waiting for a thank you he didn't deserve. Not after what happened the last time he was here. But before he could take a full step, Mark's mother was at the door, pulling it out of her husband's grasp.

"Why are you doing this?"

"We must care for each other. My office had the chance to do that for you."

Mark's mother waved her hand frantically, gesturing Jesus forward. "Come in, come in, get out of the hallway," she said in a voice a mere breath above a whisper. It was the only way to keep her voice from cracking. Although Jesus was unsure, he entered anyway, into her embrace.

"Thank you, thank you! Do you really think they can help?"

"Yes," Jesus said. He didn't want to give false assurances, but hope was always real. If that was what they needed to take action, he would offer it by the bushel.

"Where's your reporter friend?" said Mark's father, a foot away from Jesus after closing the door.

"There's no press here. No cameras, no reporters. Not even my campaign manager. That was a mistake. I was ambushed and talked into something I shouldn't have done. I'm new at politics, but that's no excuse. Your son is not a political prop. I broke my word to you, and I'm sorry."

Jesus extended his hand, his eyes offering a steadfast and sincere apology. Mark's father knew how hard it was for a politician and a working-class man to say he was sorry and figured it must be twice as hard for a working-class politician. He took Christ's hand and shook it, the past between them buried. He wouldn't give him a second chance to screw up, but he could forgive a first offense.

Mark's mother invited Jesus to the back of the room. Mark had grown paler and thinner yet retained the dark circles under his eyes. The tubes in his arms had doubled in just a few days, making it difficult to tell whether they kept the young man alive or strapped him to his deathbed.

Mark's father took his son's fragile hand and commented on how far away Lebanon Medical was and how he would see his son even less.

Jesus said, "Better to separate from your son for a day than to lose him forever."

Mark's father grimaced at that reality but knew that providing for your family meant having a family to provide for.

Jesus tried to console him, aware that it might sound like a pitch to vote, but he proceeded, if only to show them the pain this system caused. "If it were up to me, you'd have family leave to see your son. Everyone would. And when I'm in the Senate, I will work tirelessly to see that it passes."

Jesus was about to add "Believe me," but that used-car-salesman approach sounded empty. Unrealistic in the current political climate. Voters might believe the same broken promises again and again, but that was no reason for an honest politician to make them. And that was the problem. An honest politician wouldn't, which meant the other ninety-nine percent would.

A few minutes later, Jesus wished them luck and begged them to call Dr. Luke as soon as possible. The parents thanked him again, Mark's mother asking as Jesus reached the door, "What can we do to repay you?"

Jesus patted her on the shoulder with a hand as gentle as his smile. "Spread the word. Tell your friends and family to vote for me. Word of mouth from trusted friends like you is more effective than any ad can ever be."

THE LEAST OF MY BROTHERS

Jesus left the hospital without a plan to strike back at Herod, though he realized one thing: he might be different than his opponent, but he'd yet to convey that to the public. Herod's shell game and the media's obsession with slip-ups kept him on the defensive. He needed to visually demonstrate those differences, and today was the perfect day to do so.

He picked up his cell phone and told Peter to meet him in Bethlehem—and to bring a camera, which was his way of saying, "Have Andrew drive."

Thirty minutes later, the two men met outside a once-majestic building that, like the people inside, had seen better times.

"Alright," said Peter, "I'll bite. What are we doing outside a homeless shelter?"

"It's a meal center," said Jesus. "And we need it for the optics."

Peter raised an eyebrow. Not because this wasn't a good idea but because he didn't believe Jesus would use these hard-hit people as a stunt. The candidate would concede to his conscience and turn off the camera because doing the right thing served as its own reward and did not require proof. Doing the wrong thing also required no proof because people would readily believe it.

At least that's what he told Judas this morning.

"Okay," said Peter, granting the point so he could make his ubiquitous "but" argument. "But this is your one-time soup-kitchen appearance."

"Peter, please, it's a meal center," replied Jesus as a handful of people filed into the building. "And we're doing this to separate ourselves from Herod. He wouldn't be caught dead in a place like this."

"Of course not. It's not good for his campaign."

Peter pulled Jesus aside, away from unfortunate families forced to go inside. "Look, I'm not saying you don't care about people. You do. We both do, and Herod doesn't. But he understands 'optics' better than you. People want to see success. They see themselves in the people that surround you, which means they want to see successful, happy, people. That way they think that if they follow you, they'll succeed, too."

"That's ridiculous."

"No, it's Political Science 101. Or Campaigning for Dummies. Or maybe Campaigning to Dummies. Politicians visit the working class all the time, but they always do so at their work, where they have a job. They visit them at factories. They visit them at restaurants where people still have money to buy food. They shake hands at ballgames and Fourth of July picnics where everybody appears happy and healthy...and *successful*. Whenever they show people down on their luck, it's stock footage to make a point about how hard people have it. Politicians never appear in those shots. They never appear when people get turned down for a loan or lose their home or get their car repossessed. They're never there when they get laid off, and they're sure as hell never at a soup kitchen! Err, meal center. Except once, to show they care. People associate that with failure, and politicians don't want that associated with them. Project success, and people associate success with you."

"People want a happy ending."

"Of course they do. People also want their lives to be rom-coms where everyone has good jobs, nice clothes, and great hair. Politics is showbiz because it offers escapism. That's why it offers you a chicken in every pot and two cars in every garage. You want to give the public a happy ending? Fine. But cut to the chase. Find someone who pulled himself up by his bootstraps and made something of himself. Make people think they can, too. And you do that by taking someone's entire life and cutting it down to a thirty-second ad. We don't need the full three acts. And appearing at a soup kitchen isn't the happy ending. It's the prologue. Let's get some footage and get out of here."

Jesus reminded himself that Peter's cynicism and insights were born out of losing alongside Lazarus. The tactics he proposed presented a traditional campaign, but candidate after candidate had tried that against Herod and lost. They probably tried it against his father and lost. Jesus wasn't about to dismiss Peter from the campaign, but he had to convince him to be bold.

"Okay, we go inside, serve food for half an hour, maybe an hour. Get some footage of me talking with them. Nothing much, but we must promise to help them."

Peter smiled, thinking Jesus had moved partway to seeing things his way. "I would expect nothing less."

The two men went inside, ahead of cameraman Andrew. He caught everything the candidate did, editing good shots in his head to tell a gripping story. Jesus donned an apron and served fish and bread to the masses, who grasped his hands in appreciation, surprised at being allowed to come back for seconds as more fish and bread appeared from the kitchen. They wished him luck and cursed the name Herod for voting year after year to cut their benefits.

When the last of the food was served and the volunteers were cleaning up, Jesus took a moment to address those assembled. He had no microphone or makeshift stage, no soapbox or teleprompter. Still wearing his apron, he spoke from the heart in an impromptu manner that filled the hall like the bread had filled their bellies.

"Tonight, you have been magnificent. I often tell my staff that as you do unto the least of my brothers, you do unto me, and I consider each of you my brothers and sisters. I have shared your table and will always treat you like family. I know that if our situations were reversed, you would help me, and so I must do the same for you, whether it is here in this kitchen or in the halls of Congress. When the time comes, I hope I can count on your vote so that we may remove Herod from office and help the least of us!"

That line received a smattering of applause, but also a few tears. Tears of frustration and desperation, but underneath it all, tears of joy. Someone so close to power cared about them.

Only Peter remained unmoved. Few people in this room were registered to vote. Many of them had no district to call home. For all the beauty of his words, his candidate had done himself no good. Despite their vast numbers and ability to swing an election, the poor almost never did. Herod, meanwhile, was addressing thousands at a stadium in Philadelphia. Voters ready to take up his cause because he would take up theirs: he would stop the poor from taking a larger share of the pie. Herod understood Economics 101. Keep the middle class secure by keeping the poor from joining them. Keep their wages depressed and their benefits slight so that there is always a lower class because once there is no lower class, the middle becomes the bottom.

Herod took the stage in front of three twenty-foot screens angled so that every last one of the more than ten thousand people in this packed stadium could see him speak. And he was ready. He had rehearsed his applause lines for hours, knowing when to hit hard and when to hit harder. He let them chant "Herod! Herod! Herod!" for a full minute before he dared speak. The blended applause and chants were thunderous, the flashbulbs sparking like downed powerlines. He smiled and waved, then turned and repeated himself. He pointed at real people in the front row and no people if the camera angle was just right. He saluted soldiers who weren't there and supporters who were. He hugged the flag and did soft-shoe and a golf swing with a poor follow-through. He did everything but pirouette on his way to the podium, and that was only because his spindly legs could never support it.

"Good evening, Philadelphiaaaaaaaaa!" Herod boomed into the bevy of microphones in front of him. He understood the subliminal. Act like a rock star and you'll be treated like a rock star. The crowds cheer, the women want you, and the money flows in for tickets and memorabilia meant to advertise your presence years after you've gone.

"Oh, that sounds so beautiful," Herod said, the grin on his face growing larger, telegraphing the approach of a self-serving joke. "There are no virgins here. No...they're all at that other guy's campaign." He timed his words between the whistles and the chuckles. "How stupid was that? Does anybody know what the hell he was talking about? I mean ever? Does anyone ever know what the hell he's talking about?"

He paused for the laughs driven by his stage persona. He never had punchlines, just set-ups that worked with his fanbase. It was like getting laughs just for saying, "Did you ever notice?" He might as well have said, "What's up with Jesus?" taken a bow, and never delivered an actual bit. Herod could have easily starred in an inane sitcom on low-rent cable instead of the hallowed U.S. Senate.

Except when he got serious.

"Did you catch that speech last weekend? I mean, what the hell was that all about? Blessed are the meek? Yeah, blessed are the meek because we'll be beating the crap out of them while taking their stuff."

Sure, the line didn't make any sense, but his bombast was enough to get a laugh. It was all in the attitude. Just plow through. Grab 'em by the throat and don't let go.

"Are you meek?"

"No!" came ten thousand towering voices.

"Are you persecuted?"

"No!"

"Are you peacemakers?"

"No!"

"Will you vote for Jesus?"

"No!"

"Because you're sick and tired of Jesus, right? Am I right?"

The audience again burst into laughter, egged on by the supplicating "Am I right?", the comic pleading to be liked.

"You hunger for justice, right?"

"Right!"

The crowd had shifted gears. Herod could have told them they were cockroaches and they would have agreed so long as he gave them their cue.

"He says woe to the rich. Woe to the well-fed. Woe to those who laugh. Well, I tell you, I'm rich and well-fed and I'm laughing right now. Laughing at him. Aren't you?" Herod paused for a quick laugh but didn't milk it because he didn't want to interrupt his own roll as he moved toward his closing bit.

"He says people like me will be insulted and demeaned. Just put him on that debate stage and he'll find out who gets insulted." The audience waited for the answer, though it seemed a few of the more astute had already guessed. "Him!"

The audience, having its cue to laugh and cheer again, obliged. Their rock-star comic had delivered something close to a punchline, and that was enough.

"But I don't want to make tonight all about Jesus. We've had some fun at his expense, but it's a cheap laugh. As cheap as his suits." A few chuckles, including one from Herod himself. "Or the freeloaders who support him." A few cheers and a self-satisfying smirk from Herod. "It's time to talk about someone important: me! No, I can't do that. I could do it all day, but I can't do that. Should I?" He ignored the sparse chants of "Do it!" and the laughter that encouraged him. "No, I can't. I could, but I won't. I'm going to let someone else do it! Someone you know and love because you listen to him every day. Please welcome your good friend and mine, Saul Tarsus!"

Herod waved his arm like a comic bringing up the next act. He placed a palm on the radio host's shoulder and shared the spotlight with him for a minute, at one point holding up his guest's arm like a prizefighter, encouraging the audience to cheer some more. But in reality, it was still about Herod. He controlled the situation. He decided when he would step aside, and he never ceded the stage. He stood three feet away so that he never fully left the spotlight. In fact, there was no doubt that should Herod step away, the spotlight would follow him into the wings. The tech crew wasn't getting fired because Herod was unhappy.

Once the applause died to a dull roar, Tarsus stepped into the bed of microphones, talking to this crowd with the familiarity of his listeners. "Thank you, Senator. Thank you for the honor of letting me be here tonight. One of my best-selling books, and I've had many, is *Saul Is Super!*, and I want you to know that I'm super again. I predicted last week that Jesus Christ will lose this election and Herod will win—and I guarantee it!"

The arena erupted once more in mighty applause as if Tarsus had taken Herod's dog whistle.

"And to help with that, we have a little surprise tonight. A brand-new, world-premiere television commercial that I know you're gonna love."

Tarsus stepped back as the stage went dark and the three screens went bright. Jesus appeared, his eyes squinted and glazed over, a joint dangling from lips parted in a stupid grin. Rapid-fire words descended upon him.

Higher Taxes
No Guns
Open Borders
Welfare
Drugs
Tax and Spend
Anti-Military
Anti-Business
Big Government
Big Debts
Big Dummy
Happy Hippy

A narrator's baritone kicked in as the words swirled at a snail's pace around the screen, picking up speed as he spoke. "Is this the man you want in the Senate? Vote Herod."

And as the narrator said the candidate's name, the words exploded in a flaming bonfire, collapsing to show a full-color picture of a confident Herod Antipas.

The narrator's voice then rushed through the legalese in a voice just below chipmunk, so fast and high it was hard to comprehend. "Paid for by Citizens for a Bathtub Government. Photo not actually Jesus smoking pot. Not endorsed by candidate. Vote Herod."

The place erupted once again as Herod grabbed Tarsus by the hand and raised it high in the air. Although the ad was not endorsed by the senator, you'd never know it from their show of unity. He gestured the shock jock offstage, followed by a long, loving wave to the audience as they chanted his name, "Herod! Herod! Herod!"

DON'T LET THE
POWERFUL BOAST

The next morning, *Faust & Friends* discussed Herod's rally, laughing along with his best lines and reveling in the loudest cheers. The program opened with a ten-minute segment on the rally and closed with a five-minute review. They aired the Happy Hippy commercial several times during the breaks and twice during the program so they could discuss it at length, calling it "funny" and "accurate." To show they were fair, however, they included a minute-and-a-half conversation on Jesus at the "soup kitchen" shortly before the program wrapped when viewership waned. In between these segments, they addressed fear by interviewing Herod live on the phone.

"Just a great rally last night," said Steve Doozy. "You had them eating out of the palm of your hand."

"Yeah, they were a great crowd. You do those things to find out what the people want. That's why you meet them. They were a great crowd. Great crowd."

In those few sentences, Herod said nothing but complimented his diehard supporters and never offered any evidence that he met the people. None of which stopped the *Faust* team from asking a hard-hitting follow-up.

"So, are you doing another one?"

"We'll see. I love doing them. The crowds are great. I'm sure we'll do one in Bethlehem or Lebanon or somewhere. Maybe right in my opponent's backyard in Nazareth. We're real popular there. More popular than he is, that's for sure."

The blonde jumped in with an actual journalistic question, although it was soft enough to float in like a beachball. "Senator, you said you learned things last night. What did you learn?"

"That's a great question." It wasn't, but Herod, like many politicians, was the master at complimenting any sycophant on his team. It was a reciprocal relationship that made it difficult to tell who was the parasite and who the host. "I learned that people are really worried about immigration. Illegal immigration. We're a nation of immigrants. People call us—not all people, but some people, people I've been talking to. Very smart people. The best people. They call us a melting pot, but you know, when you melt things, if you melt the wrong things, it comes out all black and brown and yucky. And that's the problem with the melting pot. So, we have to be careful about that. And people are very concerned about immigration, people coming across the border, so we're going to stop that."

"How, sir?" asked Doozy.

"I'm glad you asked," said Herod, who actually was, because while the public didn't know it, after thirty years in the Senate, he liked to discuss policy. What he couldn't do was discuss it in any detail because he had no details. "I'm going to suggest we build a wall along our southern border to keep the Samaritans out. You know, when Samaria sends its people, they're not sending their best. They're sending people with problems, and those people are bringing drugs. They're bringing crime. They're rapists. And some, I hear, are good people. But most of them are criminals. So, we're going to build a wall, either out of concrete, steel, plastic, glass, stone, sand, barbed wire, chain links, tin foil, or papier mâché. We haven't decided yet, but it will be medieval. Unless we use cameras or some kind of technology, like infrared or sonar or nuclear—which is very dangerous, by the way, not a lot of people know that—to stop them."

"Very good, sir," said Doozy, who thought that if he glossed over the word nuclear, viewers might, too. They interviewed

Herod for another minute, finally cutting away when he said his wall might involve a "pit filled with tigers or possibly a pack of chupacabras which, you know, are native to the area."

The hosts thanked Herod for his time and added, "Let's go to break on a happy note with one more look at the Happy Hippy."

By the time Jesus reached the office at seven in the morning, Peter was at his desk crafting responses to Herod's rally. He repeatedly remarked that it was the politics of personal attack. That the speech had no substance or insight. That the rally crossed the line by assailing a fellow candidate.

Those responses weren't what he was most proud of, however, as he waved his boss into the office.

"Check this out."

He spun his laptop around to reveal the opening frame of the Happy Hippy commercial, the bleary-eyed Jesus sucking hard on the prominent joint. The very thought of it made Jesus cringe.

"I've seen it."

"Not this one you haven't. Judas was up all night and sent it to me about an hour ago. Tad and I think it's terrific."

The ad started as before, the camera closing in on the face of Jesus the joint smoker. Jesus the drug fiend. It made him angry that his image had been misused this way, but he sat there taking this barb to its conclusion. And he was glad he did. The words descended in the same font but with new meaning.

Tax the rich
Feed the poor
Free medicine
Free college
Gun control
Prison reform
Border security
Job creation

Small business
Family farms
Fidelity

And just like the other ad, the phrases swirled in tight, concentric circles until the image itself exploded. The narrator's voice kicked in, Judas' powerful tenor taking up the screen. "Of course this hippie is happy. He's bringing you the good life. If you want to be happy—happy like this hippie—vote for Jesus. Be happy. Like a hippie."

The disingenuous image of the doctored photo twisted into the disingenuous image of Jesus in a glowing halo, his '70s rock-star hair draped about his shoulders. Even Jesus had to admit it was a good shot, a powerful picture that captured the man he wanted to be.

Then the legalese kicked in. "Not an actual photo of Jesus smoking pot. Visit VoteforJesus."

Peter looked up as the screen froze on the candidate's smiling face. "All we need you to do is add, 'I'm Jesus Christ, and I approve this message.'"

That was a tall order. It wasn't a message he had crafted and that, by definition, made it difficult for him to approve. He hoped that was true of any candidate but was sure it was not. They often supported messages created by staffers, lobbyists, activists, their committees, and occasionally foreign governments. If Jesus was going to stick his stamp of approval on this and give it his campaign's imprimatur, he needed more convincing. Any reason to say, "No, don't do that," was good enough for him.

Jesus leaned forward, placing both hands on the edge of Peter's desk. His chin jutted forward like a boxer daring him to hit it. "Why do you think it's a good idea?"

"More Poli Sci 101," said Peter before taking a sip from his third cup of coffee that morning. "Get ahead of a story by owning it. Don't run from the label. Embrace it. Show you have a sense of humor. Show you can take it. They can't use it against you because you're stealing it from them. You're saying, 'Go ahead, call me a hippie.' Accuse them of name-calling while you're talking about the issues, even if you're not. It's political gold."

"So, it's sticks and stones..."

"But this name can never hurt you," said Peter with a chuckle. Then he laughed a little harder when he realized he finished Jesus' sentence. Maybe a candidate and his campaign manager really did end up feeling married. "People are already calling you a hippie. Take away their ammunition."

Jesus liked that. It did sound like sound political strategy.

"Besides, we need to get on this. The overnight polling is in, and you're down 53-38. You have to pull in the entire undecided vote—and you won't—plus cover the spread on the margin of error just to manage a tie. We need to get aggressive."

Jesus put a hand over his stomach. His gut said do it. He promised himself he'd get aggressive, and this ad did it without attacking his opponent. It promoted his virtues instead. He could live with himself in the morning.

Jesus leaned into the computer's microphone and recorded his one and only line: "I'm Jesus Christ, and I approve this message."

He hoped he didn't regret it.

DESERVING OF THEIR WAGES

Jesus' version of the Happy Hippy ad was re-edited and out before lunch. The campaign had no funds to place it on TV, but Simon Z added it to their website and social media pages. It received little traction until *The Bethlehem Star, The Philadelphia Inquisition,* and several other papers placed it on their websites framed as news. Jean Baptiste jumped on it the moment it came out, rejoicing at its release the way *Faust & Friends* rejoiced at the original. Before the day's end, the video received several thousand views, two dozen Likes, two dozen Dislikes, several retwits, and three hundred comments from trolls looking to stir up trouble.

Jesus knew none of this. He spent the day in isolation rehearsing the biggest speech of his life. No matter how many speeches he might give, this one would remain the most significant.

He was going home.

He would be among friends. The most generous people he knew. The straightest trees in the forest, or should he say, the straightest planks in the lumberyard.

He was addressing his union brothers.

The head of the carpenters union called Jesus the day he announced his running. He said the union's endorsement was a foregone conclusion, but they wouldn't offer it until Jesus spoke to them. After all, if they gave an endorsement without the candidate addressing them, it would look like they had no power over the candidate. That might be good for the public and media to think, but it wasn't good for their members. So, Jesus agreed to speak to them as soon as he was formally asked.

He'd been on the other end, of course. For thirty years, going back to when his father was a carpenter, the union had asked Herod to speak to them. He, or rather his handlers, always said no, with the explanation that the senator was too busy. Except during election years. When staffers said no then, they did so by saying the senator supported their causes while ignoring the fact that he met with and took money from their opposition during the previous five years.

What Jesus knew, as a union rep caught between leadership and its members, was that half of them would vote for Herod anyway because they agreed with him on social issues or because they liked how tough he appeared when talking about foreigners. Not even foreign competition. Just foreigners in general.

Leadership hoped that Jesus, as one of them, could be the difference-maker and swing the majority of members to the candidate they supported.

The union hall looked exactly as Jesus remembered, rough-hewn beams bracing the walls and ceiling, the hardwood floor so smooth and flat a marble couldn't move without a gentle nudge. More than one hundred chairs—double the usual number—graced the front of the room. The cafeteria tables lining the back held a variety of dishes, both hot and cold and ready for consumption. A bar, not yet open lest members imbibe too much before the speech, nonetheless appeared ready to open at a moment's notice. Jesus loved this place. It was part lodge, part grange, and all camaraderie.

It was why he loved these people, too.

He greeted dozens of them by name, shaking hands and slapping shoulders. The prodigal son had returned.

Jesus took the stage, and after waiting out a long round of humbling but appreciated applause, he began the way he often did not: with a joke.

"Thank you so much. I was tempted to come out here in overalls and a toolbelt, but you made me feel right at home without them."

The line got a chuckle, but the applause that followed touched Jesus the most. It was probably why he didn't tell more jokes. They just weren't as sincere as he wanted.

"When I first put on that toolbelt, people asked why I became a carpenter. Saying my father was a carpenter was the easy answer, but it wasn't the whole answer. It took me several years to figure it out. Several years working and sweating beside you to realize that when you work with your hands, you walk upright. You walk with pride because you are dependent on no one. You do for yourself. And when, on that rare occasion you are knocked down, you never stay down. That's why I'm proud to call myself a carpenter."

Jesus paused for the applause he knew was sure to come, and his union brothers did not disappoint.

"The soul of the sluggard desires everything and gets nothing, while the soul of the industrious is rich and deserving. But rewarding your soul is not the same as rewarding your wallet. Those who back my opponent like he backs them want you to work for slave wages. Herod supports their policies because they support his coffers, but I'll take it further—he writes their policies because they write him checks!"

Most of the members applauded again. They accepted as truth that all politicians support those who put money in their pockets. If they gave money to Jesus and he voted for them, it was better than giving money to Herod and having him vote against them.

"You're never lazy. You work hard and do your jobs enthusiastically. You deserve your wages. Every worker does. But it cannot be wages alone—they must be just wages. You must put food on the table and clothes on your children. It is more than fair to ask for your share. When the one percent lord their wealth over you for work you have done, you must rise up and demand fair pay. Do not let them short you! Do not let them pay you less than you deserve. Do not finish a job and settle for something because it is better than nothing. Rise up! Take what is yours!"

Nearly every member joined in the applause. Whether voting for Herod or Jesus, they could support getting more money. And so could the bartender. He smiled behind the bar. These people could drink if they were happy or depressed, but they tipped better when happy, and he was all for getting better wages, too.

"If I am elected, I promise to make it my mission to see that you are paid fairly. Employers must pay the price agreed upon at the beginning of a job. They can't decide to pay you less and then tell you to take it or leave it. Hourly wages will be established that allow you to eat. No longer will work be a race to the bottom because that is a race you cannot win. But I need your help to make that happen. You see, the pundits say there is a race I can't win, either—the one for U.S. Senate. But I have seen the people in this room overcome tremendous odds and come out winners. Together, we can do it! Vote for me and send Herod packing!"

The carpenters stood and gave Brother Jesus a unanimous round of applause. The union president smiled, knowing he had finally found a candidate who could unite the members. And in the back, the bartender opened up shop because, like the carpenters, he was ready to make his money now.

But first, Jesus opened the floor to questions. His friends were quick to respond.

"What do you think of foreign competition? We can't compete with cheap labor."

As a man of little means, Jesus often found himself tempted by the cheap cost of foreign goods. As a consumer, he often found himself trapped by the inability to buy anything but foreign goods.

"Whenever possible, support your fellow workers. We call upon the workers of the world to unite against their oppressors. Well, our oppressors are here. A hundred years ago, carmakers paid their workers enough to buy their cars, and those workers did. Now, retailers pay their employees just enough, and give them so few hours, that they have no choice but to shop for cheap, foreign goods, which just happen to be sold in the very store that pays them. Apollo-Mart is the new company town. You can get almost anything you need without leaving the store, forcing you to give back the money they just gave you. There are those who cannot afford anything but those cheap goods, and so it starts with you. Buy American whenever you can. Support American workers!"

"What do you think of Herod's wall?"

To be honest, Jesus hadn't thought much about it, but he knew a chance to inspire when he heard it. "If Herod builds that wall, it will come tumbling down like the walls of Jericho."

The crowd took to grumbling. They weren't happy about this. They supported the wall. Only a strong voice silenced them.

"What do you think about Herod saying the Samaritans are rapists and thieves?"

Jesus looked into the glare of the stage lights. He knew that voice. It wasn't one of the carpenters. No, it was far more familiar than that. Peter had slipped in the back to throw him a softball on an issue this audience cared about.

Jesus smiled. "The only Samaritans Herod knows are the ones he hires to work in his hotels."

The audience chuckled. It was a good line, but the earlier grumbling grew louder. Apparently a few of the carpenters thought the Samaritans were criminals, too.

"Everyone in this room has worked with a Samaritan at some point, whether documented or undocumented. Every one of us. Was there a problem? Did they bring drugs with them? Follow you home to rape your wives or daughters? Herod is scoring cheap political points, and I refuse to do that."

Jesus took a few more questions before saying goodnight and joining his comrades in carpentry at the food tables and bar. He wasn't sure he had convinced everyone to support him, but he hoped that a few more hours in the place he loved best among the people he loved most would win them over.

And that's also what Peter hoped, strategically maneuvering himself among this brotherhood. As the bartender raked in money and the alcohol set extra cash flowing, Peter stepped in to legally lighten a few wallets. The campaign was working for tips now, but that got them prompt service from Peter. The union threw its support behind Jesus and with it, thousands of dollars to take on a billionaire.

PATIENCE CALMS A QUARREL

Over the next few days, the polls didn't budge, at least not statistically. Jesus went up a mere two points after getting a series of favorable stories in quick succession. First, the carpenters union endorsed him, an action followed by a half-dozen like-minded organizations. The next day, the election committee announced it was not pursuing charges against the campaign or Levi. Although everyone thought Levi was guilty, they were caught on a technicality. Levi had not signed anything saying he was joining the campaign. That didn't come until a few hours after the diner payment. He was still a private citizen free to spend money as he wished. It was his First Amendment right of free speech, at least according to the courts, which allowed unlimited amounts of cash to pour in as long as it didn't go directly to the campaign. It didn't. It went to a restaurateur and his customers. Perfectly legal, since private cash equaled personal opinion. The pundits at Phobos derided the decision but didn't dwell on it because it was good news for the Christ campaign, and they weren't in the business of spreading his good news.

They did, however, cover Herod's threat to sue Jesus quite extensively. Herod said Christ's claim he wrote policies favoring corporations because they wrote him checks was pure slander. There was no quid pro quo. Herod even made sure his public relations people included the phrase "quid pro quo" because he wanted to show off his expensive education (without mentioning that the schools let him in because his father gave them money). Jesus countered that he was a political outsider and didn't know how the system worked—only that it looked as if there was mutual back-scratching going on. Peter insisted on the phrase "mutual back-scratching" to show that Jesus didn't rely on fancy legal terms because his father had no money.

Herod ramped up his charge that Jesus should know how the system worked if he wanted the job and attacked him for his inexperience, saying he guessed his opponent's Virgin Guy persona had less to do with sex and more to do with political innocence. Baptiste got in the best shot when he said Herod's campaign had taken so much corporate money the checks should come with an Employer Identification Number. Herod's lawyers, fearing a First Amendment fight they could not win, talked their client off the legal ledge when he threatened to sue not only Jesus but this upstart journalist. His advisers agreed, telling Herod to stay above the fray.

The Christ campaign turned to thwarting Herod's negative ads. The union money allowed them to place their version of the Happy Hippy on TV. Some stations even ran the ads back-to-back. It turned out to be a great hit, earning laughs across the state. It dented Jesus' numbers in the central part of Pennsylvania but didn't hurt him much on the vertical borders.

The fight, though ugly, was no longer a one-sided bloodbath. The sides had chosen their corners, and by punching back, Jesus put the champ on defense. Ironically, the ugliest part was also the most beautiful.

Salacious photos of Herod and several young women, none of whom were his first or second wife, popped up on social media. Several were decades old and could be forgiven had Herod not been married at the time. There was Herod on a yacht with a young blonde from twenty years ago. Herod holding hands with a young brunette twelve years ago. Herod's hand on the backside of a slender redhead four years ago. And a video of Herod winking at his wife at his recent campaign rally, then, in the same speech, winking at an intern. Someone also turned over a snapshot of Herod hugging the intern later that night.

The only thing that saved Herod's campaign from self-destructing was America's indifference to sex scandals for people who had prior scandals. It made for great headlines. TV ratings shot up, newspapers flew off the shelves, and web traffic soared, but Herod's camp suggested this was proof their candidate was the best man for the job since it proved he was all man. His first marriage may have been marred by infidelity but he now embraced family values so deeply that he knew Jesus did not have them. They also claimed that Herod's philandering had already been addressed. Jesus' sexuality, they argued, was still fair game since "Jesus Christ has never been linked to a woman. Not one. Not now, not ever. Is that the sort of man you want in the Senate?"

The implication that Jesus was gay was not as subtle as his campaign manager thought. More than just his base picked up on the charge. The press sought proof that Jesus was gay. After all, Herod was right. They'd covered his wandering eye ad nauseam. It wouldn't hurt him with his base. But Jesus was fresh meat, and they wanted a taste.

Peter popped into Jesus' office within seconds of the Herod camp release. They knew it was coming and had already drafted a preliminary response. They just wanted Jesus to sign off on it.

"I appreciate that it says I like women, but we should go further," said Jesus. "I'm not comfortable with homosexuality. I've never commented on it publicly…"

"And that's good policy," said Peter. "All our support is coming from the left because Herod is pulling from the right. There are enough people in the middle who support gay rights that if you alienate them, you lose the election."

"But Peter, I have to be true to myself."

"Are you gay?"

"No."

"Are you dating men?"

"I just said no."

"Then you're being true to yourself."

Jesus sighed and looked over John's carefully worded statement a second time. "So, we lie by omission?"

"We're not lying," Peter said, handing his boss a pen. "You're not gay. You're just not condemning those who are. That's the political climate we're in. Let Herod condemn gay marriage because anyone who supports it will vote for you."

"I don't like it," said Jesus, wagging the pen between his index and middle finger.

"Politics is about compromise," said Peter. "This one is yours. Sometimes you have to do what you don't like to get what you want. This keeps your constituents happy."

"Right. A constituentocracy," said Jesus, signing his name on the bottom line so they could release it.

"Exactly," said Peter, taking the paper back. "There will be questions, but we'll dodge them for as long as we can. We'll promise an answer but never give one. We'll say 'we,' so that you're not implicated in any denial. You'll have no opinion on record. We'll just stay quiet on the whole gay rights thing."

Jesus accepted the compromise as much as it galled him. He had long defended the rights of the oppressed by shouting from mountaintops. This time, he would do it by staying silent.

The late-night hosts, of course, could not stay silent and were willing to keep the sex story in the headlines longer than the normal news cycle. They had a field day with jokes about Herod, which gave them reason to put the pictures, particularly the one with the redhead's posterior, in their monologues and pre-recorded bits. Baptiste was the worst, though. His show, always on the verge of insane performance art, was now five minutes of stand-up barbs.

"Herod? He should be called HeRode—as in he rode every woman he's ever met."

"Boy, is American politics divided. Our choices for Senate are Virgin Guy and Slut Guy."

"Know why Herod married Herodias? He wanted to yell out his own name in bed."

Herod fumed, but nothing like Salome. She told Herod there would be no more sex until he did something about Baptiste. He had paid lip service to her requests before, but now he was under the worst sort of pressure an adulterer can be—no love from his mistress. Herod had to set about destroying a man because a woman he had casual sex with wanted him to.

God, he loved power.

YOU SHALL HEAR OF WARS

The dirty tricks had little effect on each candidate's camp, but there was movement in the middle. For the first time since Jesus entered the race, he was in a dead heat with Herod, and his name recognition rose above eighty percent. The Happy Hippy rose to ninety percent, but Peter and Tad considered that a positive once the ten-percent difference realized they were the same person.

Herod's minions accused Christ's team of leaking the lewd photos, but they denied any connection, claiming it was just good reporting. What they couldn't deny was the impact the pictures had. They were spread across the media, particularly social media, and led to a new commercial released by an outside PAC. It showed Herod with a variety of women, each a despondent woman saying "Me, too." It quickly became known as the Horny Herod ad. The Antipas campaign struggled to fight against it, falling back on the oxymoronic, "It's old news," which made no sense because, by definition, news is new. Phobos News, which had ignored the story except to also say "old news" while unable to explain why they were discussing it now, finally found a solution. Their female reporters, each in a shorter skirt as the day progressed, accused the PAC and the networks that ran the spot of abusing the social shift created by the #metoo movement. Yes, Phobos News now wholeheartedly supported the movement they frequently attacked. And although the voices in the commercial were clearly listed as actresses and not the women in the photos, enough stations took the hint and pulled the ad, particularly if it aired on programs that

185

featured promiscuity, assault, and the degradation of women. This pulled it from more than half their line-ups.

The ad's biggest impact occurred inside the Herod campaign. Herod repeatedly claimed he was willing to debate Jesus, although his campaign made no provisions to set it up. They were following another basic political strategy: never debate your opponent when you're up big in the polls. Only debate when you have nothing to lose. After all, the last thing you wanted was to stumble in the debate with some cringe-worthy comment and drop ten points. Next thing you knew, your opponent was back in the race, equipped with a new sound bite to make you look foolish. With that in mind, his team made outlandish demands before agreeing to a debate.

1. Moderators cannot ask follow-up questions.
2. Candidates get no rebuttal and have only one minute to answer each question.
3. Candidates who take longer than one minute to answer have to skip the next question, even though his opponent may answer it.
4. The debate can only be broadcast on TV or radio and not streamed.
5. There will be six three-minute commercial breaks during the hour.
6. The podiums must be five feet high and three feet wide.

The Christ camp naturally rejected these and other demands, but now Herod's advisers pulled the most egregious ones. The media took to speculating, then actually reporting, that "according to sources familiar with the possible event" a debate appeared imminent. It was possible the two sides might even work something out before the election.

By making it look like they demanded a debate they had been dodging, the Herod camp felt confident it had regained control of the media narrative. They felt even more confident after Jesus pushed a different story in the news. One that was a waste of his time but personally important.

Jesus picked up his phone that Wednesday afternoon hoping for good news beyond the polls. He was disappointed.

"Hey, cousin."

Peter repeatedly said being on Baptiste's show was like taking the polar bear plunge—once was enough. But Jesus couldn't help himself. This was family. And though he had denied his mother, he had not denied all his relations. He asked if his cousin needed him back on-air.

"Yeah, but it…it's going to be different."

Jesus wasn't sure where Baptiste was taking this, but he knew something had happened.

"I've been suspended. The video channel says they received thousands of complaints that I engaged in personal attacks. Politics of hate. You name it."

"Herod's a public figure. The rules are different."

"Apparently not as different as we think. Their email said… where is it? Here…'You have engaged in conduct beyond unsubstantiated speculation that simulates accusations of infidelity against an individual for whom this allegation could prove substantially and materially detrimental. Your account is herewith suspended pending further investigation or evidence provided by you or an engaged third party that this accusation is factually sound or damages caused are immaterial to the accused party.' I spent ten minutes deciphering that. They've got a team of lawyers and I can't afford an ambulance chaser. All my videos have been removed. They've completely cut off my income."

"What about switching to a different video service?"

"They're the only service that offers real money. They're just another monopoly. It's like one company running all the newspapers or TV stations, only this time it's online videos. I'm going to set up a podcast and hope my followers find me. I may need to sell my own ad time or find a sponsor."

Jesus knew where this was going. His team had legal experts, too, even if little used.

"Alright, I'll talk to Peter. Maybe we can place an audio version of the Happy Hippy on your show."

"That would be terrific. I gotta get rolling on this. I can't wait. I'll be starving in a day or two without that money. I just...I'm going to need help."

Jesus had never seen his cousin so desperate. Such was the impact of tussling with Herod. It explained Lazarus' own collapse into near obscurity. A footnote in Pennsylvania politics. Jesus also realized that he now had to believe in his cousin the way Baptiste believed in him.

Jesus stood before the podium in the very room where he launched his campaign. Peter warned him not to do this press conference. He argued that he should not defend an individual member of the press under attack since the press polled so poorly—almost as poorly as Congress. A Senate candidate defending the media looked like the set-up to a joke. It also looked like pandering for a good story. Still, Jesus felt compelled after promising his cousin he would take up his cause.

He faced a smaller cadre of reporters than he had that first day, which was only natural. This story concerned a friend, so Jesus invited friendly press. A few uninvited reporters showed up because they heard about it from colleagues, although Phobos News, which had heard about it, deliberately chose not to send a correspondent so they could claim they didn't attend because they weren't invited. A half-truth on that network had just enough grains to make it a full-truth.

"Thank you all for coming on such short notice," Jesus began. "As many of you know, I recently made an appearance on *The Political Messenger*. The host of that program, Jean Baptiste, was suspended yesterday for claims that he personally attacked Herod and his mistress—a mistress Herod says does not exist. Jean Baptiste has been suspended for attacking a made-up person, or so we hear. He is a member of the press, and I believe the people in this room should be deeply offended. If it can happen to one of you, why not all of you? Why not suspend reporters across the media spectrum?"

The reporters were skeptical of this claim, as they were of all claims. They weren't on the fringes of the media landscape but working for legitimate outlets with long histories of fact-checking and fairness. Semi-fairness, anyway. Well, fair news, but slightly biased editorials. Well-meaning, well-researched editorials that constructed a logical argument that offered a pre-conceived perspective, but generally fair. Except for a whole bunch of recent outlets who showed tremendous bias. And no one in this room would write a skewed hack piece like Baptiste— unless it sold a ton of papers or got great ratings or won a Pulitzer. Then all bets were off. Still, after all that, they were not worried about being banned the way Baptiste was because none of them offered wild speculation without a solid source or photographic evidence. Or at least believable evidence from a well-placed, anonymous source who refused to go on the record.

"I firmly believe that Jean Baptiste's firing is a free speech issue. It is yet another attack on the First Amendment by Herod Antipas in an attempt to quiet the media's right to criticize, condemn, and question. Baptiste uttered no threats. He told no lies. In the end, he was utterly blameless, but that did not stop this channel, this near-monopoly of the video world, from banning him for life and robbing him of his livelihood."

The press wondered if it were true that Baptiste told no lies. He accused a man of having a mistress without offering proof. Oh, sure, they'd heard rumors he had a current mistress somewhere, but weren't accusations without proof a form of a lie?

"If any of you have proof that could clear Jean Baptiste, I implore you to offer it. Clear his good name. At the very least take up his cause and demand he be reinstated. Make his case to the public because he has been silenced before them. A wise tongue makes knowledge acceptable, and Jean Baptiste has done that. The mouth of fools spouts folly, and Herod has done that. He has been linked to many lies, and I am sure his denial here is another lie. Don't fall prey to this folly. Baptiste did not, and if you are wise, neither will you."

Peter got tense in the back of the room. Jesus walked a delicate line. It was easy to prove Herod was a liar. *The Inquisition* kept an updated list of thousands of his lies. It was also easy to prove he was a fool. Video proved that. But Jesus was crossing a line he could not step back over. The gloves were coming off.

"Isn't Baptiste your cousin?" shouted one of the reporters.

"Yes, but that is not why I support him. I support him because his loyalty to the truth knows no bounds. You see, I have a new vision of family. The world is my family. Those who seek righteousness are my family. So, this story is not about nepotism. It's about justice."

That's what you think, thought the reporter. *The public won't think that even if I quote you. They'll just think your relationship to the truth becomes a lie when it comes to family—and with your family, that's easy.*

"Do you believe Herod got Baptiste banned?"

"I do. Baptiste received thousands of complaints about his comments. That seems excessive for a channel with a few hundred subscribers. This has all the earmarks of vengeance. Don't forget that Herod threatened to sue Jean Baptiste for millions of dollars for slander. Yes, the same man who favors a cap on malpractice lawsuits—even in cases where people die—thinks that if you say something bad about him, it should cost you everything. Well, Baptiste has lost everything."

"Do you really think Baptiste counts as the media?"

"Yes. He may offer opinion-journalism, but the airwaves are filled with such tripe. You call them pundits, but the good ones are prophets. Baptiste is a prophet. He knows where our politics is headed."

The reporters scribbled away. That ridiculous quote made good copy. Whether you thought it true or untrue, sane or irrational, it would get people talking.

Jesus returned to speaking in a way sure to grab the reporters' support. "The media cannot be shut down. You know that. You've based your lives on that. A free and open press is key to American democracy."

Jesus had Peter's attention now. He knew him to be a compassionate man, one willing to fight for the insolvent and impecunious, but he never knew him to be any sort of political philosopher. Perhaps he had progressed to Political Science 102. "We love our wars. The War on Poverty. The War on Drugs. The War on Women. Well, today, there is a War on the Media, and the prize is the soul of our country. You are foot soldiers for democracy. You must protect it. Defend it. Never be afraid or discouraged. Let your voices be heard!"

A few reporters were ready to run from the room and write-up this inspiration word for word, but in every room of cynics, there is always one who must be the most cynical. Someone who doesn't just report your stumbles but pulls the rug out from under you and then laughs at your fall. The gotcha question that wasn't always designed to get you unless you didn't see it coming.

A reporter in the front row scratched his head for a second until he had his question.

"Are you saying the press is more important than the army?"

"Yes," said Jesus. "Soldiers are too often sent into battle on the rumors of wars. The press must reveal the truth behind those rumors."

Now that's a stumbling block, thought the reporter constructing tomorrow's headline. All that blather about defending democracy and Baptiste's dismissal would be in there, but his story was clear—*Christ Says Reporters Outrank Soldiers.*

Peter rushed toward the stage, thanking everyone for coming and reminding them to save Baptiste or their own skins could be next. But with a bombshell of a story to write, they were guaranteed jobs for a little while longer. Baptiste was on his own.

I AM LEGION

Herod attacked Jesus' stance on the military before the first print story hit the wires. There were so many calls for comment that Herod put two advisers on the phone to handle the overflow. He said he was proud of "our military" and had voted for every single defense-spending increase for better weapons, better training, more pay, and more soldiers. He just couldn't understand how anyone could run for the Senate and not support the troops.

While he spoke, Salome kissed the back of his neck, still pleased by what happened to Baptiste and hoping to spur him to further action. She wasn't done with either of them. Herod, for his part, would address his opponent's accusation regarding the firing of that nuisance reporter after he finished getting headlines from this story. None of that meant he wouldn't take his reward now. Salome unzipped his pants while he munched on a slice of pizza, working the phones and encouraging his fellow senators to gang up on Jesus for attacking the military. Through it all, he never lost his concentration, working in buzzwords every chance he got. He answered reporters' questions, keeping up the attack while Salome kept up hers, without so much as a moan. No one was the wiser because he kept his focus on what was important, and that certainly wasn't his mistress of the moment.

"Christ is an isolationist, which goes against the last seventy years of American foreign policy. It's the wrong approach unless we have to go it alone, and I can't support him putting down our soldiers and allies who back us when it's convenient for them or we put pressure on them to do so. Christ's whole approach is anti-military, which you'd expect from a long-hair like him. He's a happy hippie because he never had to serve, and he should get down on his knees and thank the brave Americans that make it possible for him to have such un-American beliefs."

Herod never mentioned that he also never served, having gotten out of the draft through repeated college deferments and a mysterious case of knock-knees, followed by their unexpected disappearance several years later when the war was over. The one clue that Salome was keeping him happy was the rambling claptrap that was his official statement. But it was so close to his usual claptrap it was hard to tell.

The Christ campaign scrambled to put out its own response, which they naturally called a "clarification." This was different than a retraction since the candidate was taking nothing back but merely claiming there was a possible misstatement from having misspoken, and that things might have to be cleaned up or clarified.

"Jesus Christ loves our soldiers," the statement began. "He loves them so much that he doesn't want them put in harm's way for the wrong reason. He doesn't want people listening to the rumors of wars, not because he doesn't support our soldiers, which he most certainly does, but because those rumors can last for months or years as our government threatens other nations or they threaten us, and said wars or attacks may never come. Therefore, it is wise that people not listen to these rumors since they are just that and do not represent truth. And the fact is, people rarely believe these rumors despite constant hyping by politicians like Herod Antipas or certain unnamed media outlets. This is evidenced by the fact that people hear these rumors but rarely enlist. So, to sum up, Jesus loves our soldiers."

Clarifications are always less clear than the original statement.

The Herod camp certainly thought so, arguing that the second statement contained more doublespeak than the first, and they had a point. The clarification was never meant to be clear. Or to resemble human speech. The political attack was.

"These rumors Christ speaks of are part of a well-crafted foreign policy. They are necessary to scare our enemies and keep them off-guard. If our enemies weren't a threat, we wouldn't threaten them. His little hippie world of peace and love is not reality, and our brave soldiers understand that. As do my legion of supporters. My opponent ought to back off his attacks on our soldiers before he finds out just how strong our legions are."

Herod then put out photos of him hugging soldiers from two decades ago, videos of campaign volunteers sending soldiers care packages, and various articles about him approving billions of dollars for Mars Defense Contractors. They even included a photo of him touring an overseas base wearing a flak jacket over his suitcoat. Although the smirk on a nearby officer's face indicated he thought the senator was an imbecile, Herod's team said it proved he had put himself in harm's way. That led to an additional story of the time Herod visited soldiers overseas amid sniper fire even though the soldiers on the ground contradicted him. If only those soldiers had their own channel like Phobos News, it might have gotten more attention.

By the time the Christ camp got out its reply, the media had lost interest. The story was in its second day, and no one had the attention for that. Not if they wanted to keep ratings up. Still, a few outlets ran Jesus' rebuttal. Fewer still editorialized the story in Jesus' favor. They pointed out that Herod's argument contained nothing about saving lives or constructing a meaningful military strategy. Herod's approach was pure bluster and machismo and you never looked tough quoting data and death tolls unless they were about how many your side killed.

Just as this story was about to die, it gained new life, and not from the actions of either candidate. Only a guffaw-producing gaffe gave this gasping news story oxygen.

The next day, Jesus visited a working-class neighborhood in Philadelphia. To prepare for the event, police closed off several streets so the candidate could address a crowd of nearly one thousand. Hundreds of protesters arrived to heckle Jesus and his supporters. The police feared a riot as the protesters and supporters moved closer, the thin blue line compressed and made thinner. Jesus arrived just as the combatants' temperature peaked. He raced forward as the sides exchanged blows, the police pushing them back, shields up and batons out, driving them apart. Jesus headed into the melee hoping to play peacemaker even as Peter grabbed him by an elbow to pull him away.

Jesus' presence did not have the desired effect. The protesters surged forward, pressing in again, chanting their Herod-inspired slogan, "We are legion! We are legion! We are legion!"

A single protester muscled his burly way past an officer and knocked a screaming woman to the ground. With a powerful hand on Jesus' shoulder, he spun him around to face a small army of Herod loyalists. He roared and beat his chest for a moment, like a gorilla prepping for a fight. In his manic confusion, he bared his teeth and shouted, "I am legion, for we are many!"

He then threw his hands in the air, encouraging his allies to cheer his antics, and they took up his call literally, repeating his nonsense, "I am legion! I am legion! I am legion!"

But Jesus would not let them bully him or his followers. If peace failed, anger prevailed. He stood toe to toe with the angry man, every inch the muscle-bound carpenter he once had been. Jesus was not merely the shepherd protecting his flock, he was the mad sheepdog. "You are deplorable! You are swine! Swine!"

Jesus' followers appeared to double as they encroached upon Herod's legion. The outnumbered protesters, facing a mob and its enraged and unshakable mentor, retreated, racing down crowded streets and sidewalks, cutting between cars and buses, ignoring every rule of the road. Although several parked cars were damaged as side mirrors snapped, the event ended without bloodshed. The police resumed their position in case the protesters returned, and Jesus gave a strong, powerful speech about loving thy neighbor.

But as Peter knew, this day did not occur in isolation. The cameras caught everything.

By six o'clock, and far sooner on the cable channels, footage of the near-brawl emerged. The audio was enhanced to isolate Jesus shouting "Swine!", and although the man in the baseball cap had instigated the attack, he wasn't running for office. He didn't have to know better.

Herod condemned the attack on "these fine, faithful, hardworking Americans," as he called them. He also attacked the very concept that any of his supporters were swine.

"Attack me," Herod said bumping his chest with a fist. "I can take it." Even though he couldn't and often threatened anyone who insulted him with a civil suit. "But voters are off-limits. If my opponent says this about everyday people, you know he thinks everyone out there is swine, too."

Jesus' supporters claimed that not all of Herod's backers were swine, just those at the event, and they said the video showed just how brave Jesus was. He was willing to face down a legion of angry men and women ready to rip him to shreds. They argued that Herod, whom they called Cadet Knock-Knees, would have never displayed such courage without a tank behind him.

But the damage had been done. Jesus again dropped in the polls. That sort of behavior was reserved for cable news pundits, not would-be senators. At least until they became pundits.

Peter argued that the polls were fluid and could be altered. What he feared could not be changed was its effect on Herod's true believers. They had become a movement. Thousands of them took to wearing "I am Legion!" ballcaps, the unmistakable red fabric identifiable from a thousand feet away. They walked everywhere with them, even handing them out for free, but their favorite place to appear was in the background of every TV field report in the state. They routinely stood in the background or walked through shots, often pointing at the hat. Others wore "I am Legion!" T-shirts and marched as the Anti-Foreign Legion and the Anti-Christs. The dumbest among them even claimed they had contracted Legionnaire's disease.

All of that was a mild maelstrom compared to the death threats that poured in, including several calling for people to "lynch his skinny ass," which seemed like the worst way to lynch someone. The threats were turned over to the police, who only confirmed that most were not serious and no one was arrested. Jesus gained some sympathy but little support, the poll pendulum swinging wildly depending upon who conducted it.

The next week was a rough one for the Christ campaign. Every day this Herodian movement grew, marching across small towns and medium cities throughout the commonwealth. Amateur photographers sent hours of cell-phone video to Phobos News, which aired it all in looped segments like weather or traffic reports. Even the gang at *Punch/Counterpunch* got in on the action, re-enacting the street fight as an obvious joke. Righty threw a right cross and Lefty threw a left, yelling out "Legion!" and "Swine!" before going to commercial.

All of it kept Peter and Tad brooding night after night looking for a way to attract any semblance of Herod's horde. Or at least not lose any more people in the middle. They touted Jesus' moral side whenever they were asked for comment. Jesus did the same thing, though he never apologized for his words. He couldn't. He believed them. Those men were deplorable. Oh, he shouldn't have resorted to name-calling. That was poor form. But any apology would be insincere, and he had not yet reached the low point of a campaign where a candidate is compelled to offer an insincere apology.

John wrote up dozens of Jesus' good deeds and placed them in *The Good News*, the campaign's website, and their social media pages, while Judas dug up dozens of Herod's misdeeds. Peter then placed their lists side by side and created the hashtag #belikejesus. And the response was overwhelming. From twits everywhere came countless replies:

Start a fight today. #belikejesus.
Yell at your neighbor. #belikejesus.
Shout "Swine!" at your opponents. #belikejesus.

Peter needed a new strategy. He still wanted people to be like Jesus, finally suggesting that supporters ask themselves one question before acting: What Would Jesus Do?

Within a day, Tarsus asked his listeners to send him their best answers. He could have read them for an entire three-hour program for the next two weeks straight. Instead, he picked the best ones and never chose the same answer twice.

What would Jesus do? Raise my taxes.

What would Jesus do? Become a commie and take my stuff.

What would Jesus do? Allow his father to @*#! my teenage daughter.

It was clear Peter had made the biggest marketing blunder possible. He let the public craft the message. It was back to the drawing board. He had to find a way to highlight Jesus' morality and compassion without having others question it. He could never put the accursed genie back in the bottle. Those Anti-Christ messages had taken on a bestial life of their own and would run for years. He just needed a way to blunt their impact.

SUFFER UNTO ME THE LITTLE CHILDREN

In the midst of the military bludgeoning from Herod, Jesus got good news: an email from Dr. Luke. Thanks to the doctors at Lebanon Medical, Little Mark was expected to make a full recovery. New treatments meant he could be home in weeks. He expressed his gratitude to the Christ campaign for intervening, even if the parents were reluctant. It was the right thing for the patient, and to show his gratitude, the good doctor made a sizable contribution to the campaign's coffers.

Jesus knew he couldn't make this information public. He had promised not to make Mark a prop and was bound to make sure no one else did either. Still, he planned to send the family a small bouquet of flowers and a toy for Mark. He was sure Mary at the front desk would know just the thing to get.

After telling her what he needed, he pictured the boy's smiling face. His parents, doctors, nurses, family, friends—everyone would be relieved that Mark would survive. No, they'd be ecstatic. Everyone loves good news about children. Yes, everyone.

Jesus jumped out of his chair to tell Peter his new plan for turning things around.

"Children don't vote," said Peter, not looking up from his laptop.

"Yeah, but everybody loves them," said Jesus, taking a seat across from his campaign manager.

"You're serious, aren't you?"

"Absolutely. Herod is killing us on this military story, right?"

"Yeah," said Peter, giving his boss his full attention. This felt like a worthwhile diversion from answering another voter's email about Jesus' long hair.

"Then we need to go in another direction. Warm and fuzzy. Something with children. Cute, adorable children who can shift the argument one-hundred-and-eighty degrees."

Peter twisted his lips, adopting a thoughtful pose. It was mostly for show. He'd been looking for a way out of this campaign quagmire that threatened to go on indefinitely. Desperation makes men believers in bad ideas.

"It could work," Peter said with a slow drawl. "But we need to adhere to certain rules."

"Such as?"

"Like babies and elementary-school kids are good, teens and preschoolers are bad."

Jesus mulled this over. He had hoped to see children of various ages but would listen to Peter's logic.

"Babies are cute. Everybody loves babies. If a baby smiles at you, people laugh. If a baby cries when you pick it up, people laugh. They've been there. Elementary-school kids play along. They have fun when you're there. High-school kids are a wild card. Sometimes they're great, sometimes they're not, and there's almost always one kid who yells out, 'You suck!' while the cameras are rolling. Or tells a TV crew that it was boring, and his parents aren't voting for you."

"And preschoolers?"

"Too honest. If they don't like you, they tell you. Or they're so darn cute they hog all the camera time. They suck up all the love in the room."

Jesus was surprised by how much Peter knew about children despite having none of his own. Must have come from being a big brother. It was certainly said with the jealousy of someone who had the spotlight taken from him a few too many times. As a younger brother himself, Jesus knew he often received all the attention. It was a trick he carried into adulthood, even now able to command a room through sheer charm. He remained confident he could handle this roomful of children. Except teenagers. Peter was right about that one.

"Well, I say suffer unto me the little children. Get me a preschool as soon as possible."

Peter shook his head. He could attack anyone who insulted Jesus with the ferocity of a lion, but if preschoolers ganged up on him, he would surrender immediately. You can't beat cute with political spin, even when it's being obnoxious.

To Jesus' surprise, Peter got him a visit to Pancras Preschool the very next day. It seemed many of the teachers would welcome anyone running against Herod, who had, year after year, voted to cut funding for busing, free lunches, and classroom materials from books to desks, pencils to safety scissors. He had voted for charter schools, private schools, and religious schools, and against public schools, public students, and anything involving public funding—unless it went to private schools. So, yes, although they understood this was not a stump speech, they welcomed anyone standing up to Herod.

Jesus arrived at the square brick schoolhouse thirty minutes after class began. The children had finished their breakfast and were well-fed, full of energy, and raring for fun.

"Children, *today* we have a *special* guest. His name is *Jesus Christ*, and he's running for the *U.S.* Senate, and he's going to tell us *all* about it. Can you say, 'Hi, Jesus'?"

"Hi, Jesus!" came a chorus of sweet voices outdone only by the voice of the teacher herself, whose tone was so saccharine that Jesus felt compelled to live up to her expectations. It was like listening to a motivational speaker who spoke in permanent nursery rhymes, punctuating her words like a sing-song preacher for four-year-olds.

"Hi, everyone. My name *is* Jesus Christ, and this is my brother, *James*." He couldn't believe he found himself copying her, but in this room of wide-eyed innocents, it dripped from his lips like warm honey. "Can you say, 'Hi, James'?"

"Hi, James!"

James said "Hi!" back and handed the students stickers that said *Vote for Jesus*, his brother's smiling face in the middle. The teacher objected because school, particularly a preschool, was no place for political propaganda, but it didn't matter since none of the stickers made it home. They were stuck on chairs, books, clothes, faces, and in one case, a toilet seat. James handed out a new set of stickers to the teacher. These just said *Vote*, and he encouraged her to place them in the kids' backpacks so that they might make it home in one piece. He considered fifty percent an acceptable attrition rate.

Jesus smiled. He brought James along to make this a family affair, and he had in his own awkward way. Jesus proceeded to ask the children about their brothers and sisters, wondering how many were older and how many were younger, like him. It all seemed rather easy, and he enjoyed not pounding the pulpit with an ulterior motive. He didn't have to convince them that the world was going to hell. He kept his message simple—almost as simple as Peter wanted for grown-ups.

After asking if they knew what a senator did and receiving no answers, Jesus explained, "I want to make your lives, and your parents' lives, better."

"How?"

Out of the mouths of babes.

"By helping your parents get more money and better medicine."

"How?" Several students asked that question now.

Jesus had no idea how to turn complex ideas into preschool speak. For that, he would have to be a professional politician.

"By making sure things don't cost too much."

"How?" Half the class joined this discussion. They even abandoned the pretext of raising their hands.

"By making rich people pay more, so poor people get help."

"How?"

The whole class joined in now, their curiosity a game more than an academic exercise.

Peter forgot to mention that preschoolers were pack animals, moving in for the kill without ever sniffing blood. Jesus realized he didn't like "How?" as much as "Why?" He was the master of why. Because he cared. Because he wanted people to be happy and thrive against the exigencies of the outside world. Because he loved them. But how? How, indeed. How should not be mystical. How should be obvious and plain for all to see. But how was the important question. How could he construct a plan when half the people rejected it without reading it? How could he make their lives better when half the world wanted to crush the other half and one percent had the power to do it? How could he do it when half the world preferred lies to truth, even when telling their children not to lie? When half the world shared rumors without research and didn't recognize the way and the truth and the life when it stared them in the face?

He gave the teacher a look that begged her for help.

"Okay, students, that's enough questions. Why don't we show Jesus what we do?"

Like automated ants, the children got up and went to square tables, each with four seats, never bumping into each other. It resembled a choreographed dance, children sliding through like a line of ice dancers. They'd done this before. The order was essential to get anything done but as mindless as mice in a maze.

The teacher led the class of sixteen through their letters, numbers up to twenty, colors, and shapes, and then asked Jesus if he'd like to read a book to the children. Although he was tempted to say it was time to go, it wasn't, for he had no place else to go. Faced with the truth, he took a seat in the teacher's special "reading chair," opening the book she handed him. The children surrounded him, sitting in a tight semi-circle, the smallest one sitting on his lap. Jesus adjusted himself and held the book out front so he could see the words while turning the pages.

James snapped several photos, knowing a charming moment when he saw one. Jesus, without knowing it, was glowing like he did in his official portrait without the aid of camera tricks and studio lights.

The story was an adorable tale about a lemming who wouldn't jump off cliffs with his friends. It stressed thinking for yourself, an important message, he thought, given how everything here was done in follow-the-leader fashion with the teacher a stand-in for authoritarian government. And she achieved her results the same way: by combining flattery, kindness, and the strong-arm tactics of reward and punishment.

After thanking Jesus for reading to them—a story Jesus had to admit was far less convoluted than his own parables—the students got up and wandered aimlessly about the room before settling into a few activities, the entire procession juxtaposed against the early morning's clockwork precision.

"This is unstructured time for the students to do what they want. It can last for hours."

"What do they do?" asked Jesus.

"Whatever they like. Some play on the computer, some watch TV, some talk with their friends. That boy over there is building a wall with blocks. We call it Executive Time because the children get to make their own decisions."

Jesus wasn't quite sure he understood its purpose because the students appeared to be accomplishing nothing. Corporations would call this "downtime," and his own father would have called it "goofing off." Still, Jesus decided not to make a stir and let the children enjoy their playful Executive Time.

He thanked the teacher and said a hasty good-bye to the students, none of whom noticed as they were engrossed in their various mind-numbing activities. Jesus realized that if the legislature or White House ever discovered Executive Time, they would implement it, if only because it sounded official.

Once outside, Jesus hopped in the passenger's seat so James could drive them back to the office. It had been a productive morning, and to keep it going, he called Peter to tell him his ideas for an education policy.

THOU SHALL NOT BEAR
FALSE WITNESS

The photo of Jesus reading a picture book went viral as soon as it was released. Supporters championed the claim that children are excellent judges of character and since they liked Jesus, you should, too. The airwaves became filled with anchors saying "Awww," and "How cute!" Even *Faust & Friends* had to admit the picture was cute, although Doozy joked that, "Christ is so young, it looks like one of the students got left behind in there."

The blonde added, "He could always get a job as a teacher's aide if that carpentry thing doesn't work out. He could show the kids how to build with blocks."

"Yeah, because politics isn't in his future," Doozy replied, which garnered big smiles around the couch.

The harshest rhetoric was saved for Tarsus who, like *Faust & Friends*, found a way to make his comments caustic yet comedic.

"Yeah, the photo is cute, but only because of the kids. What's that old showbiz saying? Never follow animals or children? This photo includes both. Of course, the dog in the middle is Jesus as the Shaggy D.A.. But correct me if I'm wrong—and I'm not, so you can't correct me—but isn't a grown man touching schoolchildren wrong? I'm not saying he's a child molester, but his family has history. Hell, I bet he pulled up to that school in a white van with no windows. Not saying that's the case, I'm just saying you hear rumors in this business. Anyway, the picture is cute, but what's his policy? I mean it. Where's his education policy? I—well, me and my staffers," which always meant his staff, "went to his website and couldn't find it. Not one word. So, I ask you, where's his policy?!!"

Tarsus then threw to a commercial for Venus Delicates, Body by Jove, a private school that promised it had armed teachers to protect the children, and an Italian restaurant that promised you could "taste the love in the sauce."

But within hours, Saul's insinuation became an actuality on a NeverReadIt fringe feed that claimed Jesus' hippie look was an elaborate disguise to hide him from the police because he wasn't allowed within one-hundred yards of a school. Dozens of posts later came charges that Jesus ran a child-porn ring out of a pizza shop. That one caught fire in all the wrong circles, dispersed like pepper spray at a riot in the conservative War on Christ.

Jesus knew Tarsus was right. He had no policy on improving the state's school system. He had given no speeches on it, or even put out a press release. Now, to be fair, Herod had nothing on his website about education either, but that was what made him great. As a new politician, Jesus needed to have a detailed plan about how to fix a problem he wasn't involved in creating to prove he deserved the job, or else his competitor could accuse him of not having the experience for the job, which he didn't. Herod, as a veteran politician, could offer vague policy proposals or none at all, then claim this showed his experience because he was keeping his options open to work with the other side. Having next to nothing while claiming the problem wasn't his fault because he wasn't on that committee showed that he was the best person for the job because he knew how to strike a deal even though his own side would never let him strike said deal.

Either way, by eleven o'clock, as Tarsus' rant made the rounds in conservative hubs, Peter scrambled to get Jesus' educational plan up and out to the press, following reviews from Tad, James, and Bart, who had been added because he was in charge of saying controversial things. Underutilized in this clean-cut campaign, he was now tasked with calling out anything remotely questionable.

He did, and it slowed everything down.

The plan started out well enough:

Every child deserves an education. (Only controversial to a small number of people.)

Schools should be better funded. (A standard line, and only controversial to a few more people.)

Teachers should be better paid. (A standard line, and only controversial to slightly more people.)

Teaching should be unionized. (Controversial, but sure to win points with the union.)

Greater emphasis on the three Rs. (Sure to make almost anyone over forty happy, though it might offend young voters and reformers pushing modern curricula.)

Greater emphasis on knowledge, not rote memorization. (So carefully worded it could offend almost no one.)

Bart nodded his head, bored by how bland this all was. Someone always objected to something, but those offended here could be pushed aside or won over by the next point.

Allow prayer in school. Uh-oh.

Religious studies should be an elective class in public schools. No, no, no…

The Ten Commandments should be hung in a public place. What?!

Bart was out of his chair and down the hall before anyone could skim the Ten Commandments let alone post them. To his disappointment, Jesus wasn't in Peter's office. He asked—no, demanded—to see him because men willing to take the heat for saying dumb things they didn't believe in weren't known for their patience. They had thick skins and often thicker skulls. "You can't be serious about putting up the Ten Commandments?"

"Why not?" said Jesus. "I'm not saying it should be mandatory, only that schools have the option as a form of moral guidance."

"Moral guidance?" Bart said. "That's a great argument if half the voters weren't against it. And that half is your voters. If Herod puts this up, the conservatives will applaud, but you're chasing the liberal crowd. Some of them will turn on this issue alone, and you can't afford to lose anybody right now. You're behind."

"I don't see how anyone can find the Ten Commandments controversial."

"Look, it's a great moral code," said Bart, "but atheists back you because you're a lefty..."

"I'm not a lefty," said Jesus.

"Well, they think you are, so you play to them," Peter said, figuring he better inject himself into a conversation on campaign strategy since that was his job. "And you're further to the left than Herod will ever be."

"And since atheists don't want those tablets up and are voting for you, you don't support this."

"Worse yet," Peter added, "tons of well-funded groups throwing money at us are against them."

"Why?" said Jesus, still working out the atheist issue when this conundrum struck.

"Simple. 'Thou shalt have no other gods before me'? You can't tell people that. That's bullying. Same with 'Thou shalt not make any graven images.' Opposed by groups that say their god isn't graven. 'Thou shalt not take the Lord's name in vain.' Which lord? Well, how are football coaches supposed to motivate their players if they can't say God damn it? 'Remember the Sabbath.' Which one? Should schools close on every other Sabbath, too? Schools would lose a fortune if they had to cancel games that fall on the Sabbath. And 'Honor thy mother and father?' We've been hearing about that one from anti-abuse groups for years because let's face it—some mothers and fathers shouldn't be honored. You simply can't support it. I'm telling you the Ten Commandments is about the most controversial thing you can put up. It will cost you votes and won't cost Herod anything."

"What about my other ideas?" asked Jesus.

"The religious ones?" Peter said. "Kill them, too."

Jesus paced the room. Twice he went to speak but then thought better of it. They made strong arguments about the political lunacy of using these ideas unless he was on the right side of the political spectrum. That all made sense. But was it who he was? Politics was the art of the deal, if you actually knew how to make one. It wasn't just the art of the possible—it was the art of making the impossible believable. That's why politicians lied so much about what they could do.

"But I truly believe in those ideas."

"Then let me say them," said Bart. "Take them off the platform and let me float them to a few people who can float them to a few people. Let Simon run some polling data. If it does well, we adopt it and see if anyone notices."

Peter liked that idea. Anything to duckwalk this process so they didn't get ahead of their supporters. If they said nothing now and it came up for a vote in the Senate, Jesus could always vote in favor and claim he had no prior position. That was another thing politics was: the art of making a 180-degree turn so that you could do a full 360 and agree with your original position.

"Okay," said Jesus, acknowledging Peter's grave nod. "But we need to add something. It feels incomplete." Jesus paced the room one more time, then snapped his fingers. "Got it. The whole point of this is to get well-behaved students. Well-behaved comes from well-fed. Add that I support funding school lunches and breakfasts for every student. They can't learn on an empty stomach. We'll make kids as wise as Solomon."

Peter liked that idea, too, and instructed John to add it to the official policy. Bart liked that he got to say something controversial and left the room with his fist over his heart like a gladiator about to die.

DO UNTO OTHERS

The release of Jesus' education platform met the usual partisan bickering from the right and the left, but it picked up support from the teachers union, which was its secondary purpose. It was never designed to gain the widespread support of voters with kids in school, or even voters who paid school taxes. It was meant to shore up support with the working-class part of his bloc. While it achieved its primary purpose—putting out something to silence those who said he had nothing—it never fully silenced them since now they had something to pick over, which meant they couldn't be quiet for more than two seconds of airtime.

As expected, the fiercest critic was Saul Tarsus, who said he hated everything about the plan but never got past the headline. "As wise as Solomon? Not only is Jesus a possible child molester, now he wants to cut babies in half!"

Other than the initial snide bursts of derision, the proposal got little attention. One day after its release, Bart arranged an interview with a small paper in the conservative heartland. *The Ephrata Eagle* announced that Jesus Christ backed putting the Ten Commandments in school, school prayer, and elective religious classes. The backlash was swift.

From all sides.

The right accused the campaign of pandering to traditional-values voters without any intention of delivering on this promise. The left flat-out rejected it, striking back with all the subtlety of a poke in the eye. Peter jumped into the fray, saying none of this had come from the candidate. It had been mentioned in a meeting, but the candidate did not fully support it. Bartholomew—and here Peter repeatedly used Bartholomew and not Bart because you always use the full name when chastising someone—had simply gotten his wires crossed.

As expected, Bartholomew had been thrown under the proverbial school bus.

The strategy of leading with a fake story that could be a real story if the public approved worked. Peter's explanation mollified the left and inflamed the right with I-told-you-so editorials. It had a strange effect on the middle, however. They shifted toward Jesus. Moderates leaning right felt the middle had shifted toward them, and so without shifting their beliefs, they came closer to Jesus. Aggregate polling by SixSixSix put Jesus and Herod in a statistical dead heat. That put Herod in a realistic cold sweat.

His stance, like the proverbial fever, broke.

Herod would debate Jesus in two weeks, with an agreed-upon moderator, in the state capital. They even offered concessions on streaming the debate and the size of the podiums.

Christ's supporters cheered the news. They had brought Herod to his knees, which wasn't true at all. They had brought him to the stage, where he could be formidable. Herod's supporters also cheered because Herod said they should. And the ultraright said, "Who cares?" as they accused Jesus of praising the Ten Commandments to provide cover for his pizza-shop pedophilia, which forty-six percent of Herod supporters now believed.

The media picked up the story in their usual way. The team at *Faust & Friends* said Herod would attack Jesus like a rabid dog. The pundits at *Punch/Counterpunch* showed video clips of how they predicted their respective candidate would do. Righty showed tape of a rabid dog, and Lefty showed seven men forming a circular firing squad. When asked how they thought the other candidate would do, Lefty showed the same clip of a rabid dog, and Righty showed a loop of a wet noodle whipping concrete. Saul Tarsus picked up this theme and displayed "Herod's debate style" with a five-minute clip of that same rabid dog. The only good news for Jesus in this pre-debate circus was that ten percent of Saul's listeners thought it was actually audio of Saul giving his opinion on universal healthcare.

No one—even those on the left—thought Jesus could win. Herod was too experienced a debater, and Jesus, though good with a sound bite, was too quick to confuse his audience with a meandering parable of dubious political philosophy.

Perhaps *The Morning Star* headline said it best: *Herod to Sacrifice Virgin at Debate.*

Jesus undertook debate prep within hours of Herod agreeing to it. Peter focused on the message. John wrote snappy lines. Tad picked out clothes since debate strategy was less about message and more about posh. John repeated that line, which Tad said proved his point. He thought of the line five seconds ago, and they'd already memorized it. Jesus could cast off lines you could put in a fortune cookie, but all the slick slogans in the world wouldn't help if you had to read them a second time.

Judas and Bart added their own unique skills to the mix, instructing Jesus to go negative.

They met the expected resistance.

"No," said Jesus. "The whole theme behind my campaign is do unto others as you would have them do unto you. It's why we feed the homeless, preach free healthcare, and seek better wages. We must lift people up, not tear them down. Turn the other cheek is my mantra, not a concession."

Peter leaned over to John. "Do unto others…get that in a speech. And on bumper stickers. But lose that 'turn the other cheek' bit. That'll get us killed."

Judas, however, continued to urge his boss to fight dirty. "Going negative is the positive way to win."

"We need to inspire people, Judas. Win them over. Inspired people act."

Judas all but spit out his eighth cup of coffee for the day, and it wasn't even noon.

"Inspiration? If you inspire people, you get a few extra checks in the ol' cash box. Know what gets them to vote? Vitriolic hatred. Knee-jerk reactions. Intense loathing. It's what turns mid-terms into routes—voters hate the guy in office so much they vote against him. That's been the key to conservative victories for decades. Conservatives hear a word they don't like and have spasmodic reactions that cause them to spit fire and throw up in their mouths. Liberals hear a word they don't like and spend five weeks debating whether it's the right word. If you want to beat him, get people to hate Herod!"

Lazarus had called Judas a zealot, and there was no mistaking it now. He was red in the face, his finger wagging with every word. Jesus couldn't believe his debate prep hadn't even begun and he was already involved in the most strenuous clash since he sat in Lucifer's office—and Lucifer was in the midst of getting liquored up like a barstool drunk. Judas had no such excuse. There was simply no spinning him off his position. "I am incapable of creating that kind of hatred. All I can do is inspire people to despise evil…"

"Then make Herod that evil! Link him to every despicable thing in the world. You're dead even with Herod because your core voters haven't abandoned you. Turn up the pressure on him and you'll surge ahead!"

Judas stormed out of the room. For him, Jesus had answered an age-old paradox. Jesus, the unmovable object, had derailed him, the unstoppable force, and not by physics but by psyche. He could keep going, but to what avail? If you argue politics with someone who will not change his position no matter what, you stop arguing with him. He'd seen this a hundred times with Herod's helots. He'd destroy them in an argument, and they'd blindly stare at him while repeating Herod's position. Judas called it zombie zealotry. They just kept plodding forward, grunting nonsense, looking for a brain.

And that's when Judas realized anger—not inspiration or facts—motivated voters. Anger that somebody might get something you didn't—even if you got something else they didn't—kept them in line. The line that led to the voting booth. You couldn't negotiate with blind adherents. You could argue with them until you were blue in the face, but if you held your breath until their position changed, you'd pass out. Jesus was becoming one of them on the opposite side of the aisle. At least you could negotiate with Herod if you offered him the right motivation.

Jesus spent the rest of that day wondering if Judas had a point. Not about being vicious. That wasn't his nature. But he had to get back to being the man he was at that first press conference, the man who inspired and attacked simultaneously. The man whose positions hadn't been twisted by a team of handlers. Yes, he decided, it was time to be the man he was on day one and not day one hundred. The speeches and interviews were a perfect chance to test that, but the debate would be the big stage to bring it all together.

THE UNJUST JUDGE

Peter stood in as Jesus' debate proxy for three days before the team concluded it wasn't going well. Jesus hit his marks and rebutted Peter's arguments effectively, but that was the problem. They were Peter's arguments, not Herod's. Peter insisted on playing fair, and Herod would never do that.

On the fourth day, in walked Lazarus. He was here to take command. He handed Jesus three sheets of paper: one sheet of facts he would need and two sheets of emotional talking points and insults he had to get to.

"This isn't a high-school debate. You don't get points for logic. There's no clear-cut winner based on some objective scoring system. Pundits will say their candidate won according to their political ideology, and the voters will say who won based on who moved them the most. You've said politics is emotional. Say that to yourself every second you're on stage. Just don't get emotional yourself—that's how you lose."

Lazarus spent the next two days attacking Jesus the way Herod attacked him in the debate six years ago. Like Jesus, he had been running neck and neck with Herod until that night when the tide turned and he drowned.

He couldn't let that happen to Jesus.

"You're ready to face Herod on that stage," Lazarus said, "but the debate isn't just the sixty minutes you're in the spotlight. You need to establish a strong position before you get out there. The pundits don't care much about what you say, but if you have momentum going in, they give you extra points coming out."

"I thought you said there were no points," said Jesus holding back a smirk.

Lazarus burst into a solo round of applause. "Good! Use that sense of humor. Keep it throughout the debate. You made me look foolish by using my words against me like a comedian taking down a heckler. Because that's who the real judges are—the comedians. They'll run tape of whoever looks like an idiot, and that's what sticks. They shape your image more than any campaign manager. The comedians take your complex idea, shorten it up, make it pithy, and make it funny. If it sounds convoluted, they'll cut out the b.s.—and that hurts you. That vice president never said he invented the Internet, but when the comedians used that line, that's what stuck. And that governor never said she could see Russia from her house, but when the comedians used that line, that's what stuck. Keep it short, keep it funny, get a laugh at Herod's expense, and you win the debate, issues be damned."

Jesus wasn't sure he could swing a deliberate comeback like that, a cutting line that doubled as punchline and headline. It needed to be spontaneous. Herod needed to give him that opportunity. He wouldn't bet on it, but he could be ready.

"The debate is a week away, and a week in politics is a year in human terms. Hit the stage and practice playing on people's emotions. See what they react to, then use that in the debate. Herod will know some of what you're up to, but not all of it. If you release your facts now, he'll develop alternative facts. You know—lies. Use the truth to throw him off-balance."

Per Lazarus' advice, John set up an interview with a friendly outlet: *The Bethlehem Star*. It wouldn't allow him to read an audience's emotions, but he could practice connecting with an audience through a third-party medium. Reading emotions should come naturally, at least if you're human, but doing it through a lens or microphone or ground-up wood pulp was like asking someone to marry you by carrier pigeon. You'd get a response, but it wasn't immediate. You had to trust your instincts to know if you were connecting.

"You've spent a lot of time talking about the poor. Your opponent accuses you of…" Nicole Demus pulled out a piece of paper. "…of, and I quote, 'eating with sinners.' End quote. What do you say to that?"

"I assume Herod's never been to one of his country clubs. Otherwise, he'd be eating with sinners, too." Jesus paused, surprised at how easily that insult came. It certainly made the reporter smile. Jesus then realized he had paused for a few seconds, and although not as deadly as a pause on camera, he had to treat this like he was sweating under the stage lights. He couldn't stop, he couldn't stumble, he couldn't become distracted.

"I visit the poor because if I can lift up the downtrodden, I can lift up anyone. And so I treat the poor the same way I treat the rich. I dine with them and break bread with them because that is the American way."

Great, I've got patriotic jingoism down. Now, be emotional. No, don't be emotional. Make them emotional. Got it.

If he kept talking to himself like that, he might become president after all. He sounded like a schizophresident. God forbid Lucifer was right.

"When you see their dirty, yearning faces—when you see how hungry they are—you know people aren't meant to live like this. You see people crying for their children. Crying, hungry children, and you just have to help. At least I do, and so I open my hand to the poor and the needy. Everyone should."

Better, thought Jesus, *but is it enough? It needs to be personalized. It can't be about the generally distraught and downtrodden.*

He cut off the reporter before she could ask a follow-up, or worse, go in an entirely new direction.

"You asked why I eat with 'sinners.' It's because they're not sinners. They're people. Amazing people who have fallen on hard times. Let me tell you a story. A shepherd had one hundred sheep, and one of them, a little lamb, wandered off. The shepherd left his ninety-nine sheep behind to find that one. When he did, he carried it home and called everyone he knew to celebrate with him. They thought he was nuts. 'Why do you celebrate one lost sheep when you risked your entire flock?' And the shepherd said businesses often do that. They lay off ninety-nine employees to save one CEO. We must do the same but in reverse. We must save the one who is lost and let the ninety-nine who are safe survive and thrive."

The young reporter shortened the story but got the gist of it across to her readers. The paper added a sidebar to prove Jesus' point, listing local layoffs from various multinational corporations based in the area, starting with Hades Steel. Comments and letters poured in overwhelmingly supporting Jesus' position. If only this had been televised more people would have seen it.

Jesus returned to his old stomping grounds to speak to the ironworkers union in Bethlehem. It was a rousing speech as he called upon shareholders to share their riches. He decried CEOs making hundreds, if not thousands times more than the lowest-paid employees. He urged his union brothers to level the playing field between them and their would-be overlords.

And then came his mistake.

In the midst of calling upon them to welcome new employees into their ranks and not begrudge them their wages, he told them a parable.

"A winemaker hired laborers to work in his field for a fixed wage. No matter how many grapes they picked, they received a day's pay. As the day wore on, the winemaker brought in more laborers to finish the job and clear the vines. At the end of the day, the winemaker paid everyone the same amount. Those who started in the morning complained, saying they should have been paid more. The winemaker said they had agreed to those wages and he had not shorted them. So, I say to you, do not begrudge new employees their wages, but add them to your fight to improve all your wages!"

What Jesus thought would be an applause line was met with silence. Then murmuring. Then outright, out-loud complaining. The union members took this as an attack on seniority and a call to accept poor wages and benefits until a contract was up. They saw no reason long-term members should not get more.

Jesus meant none of that, but parables were always dicey. This time, he rolled snake eyes. And all of it was captured on video by a local news station and a dozen or more cell phones scattered across the room.

The next day, Peter and John had some explaining to do. They said the candidate only meant new workers should get living wages, too, but all the parable did was fill up online threads with people wondering how a virgin could screw so many people. Of course, at least eighty percent of those comments were written by Herod staffers and their allies. For all his good intentions, Jesus found out what politicians always find out: The explanation is never remembered as clearly as the original mistake. Union leaders accepted the official response as genuine and encouraged their supporters to stay on Christ's team knowing that Herod, as a member of the overlord class, would never side with them. He had kept his chain of Herod's Hotels, resorts, restaurants, and other service industries from unionizing for years, and they were sure he would do so for years to come. They didn't have years to wait. Dwindling membership and diminished power meant they needed Jesus now. They just weren't sure if their arguments, like the candidate's, fell on deaf ears. They'd find out in a few weeks. But until election day, they were rolling craps, hoping for a seven while believing they'd been handed loaded dice.

Following the union debacle, Peter and Lazarus pushed Jesus to get out there and make another speech. Jesus, eager to atone for his sin, accepted the challenge, promising to reach this audience as intended.

Two days later, in an effort to turn the news cycle his way, he found himself in the rich farmlands of South Central PA outside Ephrata. Here, Jesus spoke of the farmer's hardscrabble life, battling weather and pests and crop yields, as well as the fickle demands of pricing, industrial needs, and corporate farming. Mostly corporate farming, always creeping closer, stripping away land and livelihood, leaving family farms to hold on against massive debts, international pressures, and poorly conceived trade wars.

And that was what Jesus encouraged them to do. To embrace their famed patience and faith and hold on till a brighter day came, not just in the weather but in the political climate. Until a man like him could take up their fight and support their cause against megafarmers backed by a certain sitting senator.

"In a town not far from here was a judge who did not care for justice. He always sided with corporate interests and wealthy landlords because they poured money into his re-election campaigns." Jesus struck a sour face, his taut cheeks barely containing his displeasure that judges were routinely elected based on political affiliation and not merit. He felt that the greatest miscarriage of justice occurred when a nation that boasted about being a meritocracy awarded the most solemn jobs to those with the right connections. It was no wonder the system sat loaded with the incompetent and the uncaring. Toadies advanced only so far in the business world, but they could run Congress, and with any luck and a little persistence, someday address a joint session of it.

Which brought Jesus back to his main point: persistence.

"Now, in this town was a poor widow whose husband died deep in debt. He worked his fingers to the bone, day after day, dawn till dusk, just to stay ahead of creditors and corporate farmers." Jesus felt no shame in embellishing the tale a little bit. In his original version, the man was not a farmer, but as Peter suggested, 'know your audience.'

"Every day, this widow went to the judge and begged for relief against the bankers. And every day the judge dismissed her, but she did not give up. She harangued and harassed him until he gave her what she wanted. He dismissed the liens against her property until the harvest came and she saved her farm."

The audience of farmers sat there without saying a word. A few wept in solidarity with the woman's struggles. There was no purpose to their fight but to save your hide for another day's fight. Broken equipment led to broken spirits, and they needed a man like Jesus on their side. A man who looked as comfortable in flannel as he did in a polyester suit. He may have dressed like them today, but it was not for show. He was one of them.

And as Jesus sought to console them while letting them weep, he realized he had done it. He had reached them the way Lazarus wanted. The way he promised Peter in the beginning. Today, politics was local, and that made it emotional.

He was ready for the debate.

IT IS YOU WHO SAYS SO

On the morning of the debate, four Sundays before the election, Jesus entered a menswear shop where he had a fitting a few days before. Mary Larnaca and Peter went along to help him pick out a suit. Peter, because his suits were always as sharp as a serpent's tongue, and Mary because Peter liked how she dressed her brother for his debate. Jesus was happy to stick with his professorial attire, even if he appeared to be more of a grad assistant at a poor, unaccredited college. Peter, Mary, and Tad convinced him otherwise, saying this was a statewide event and he would be judged by his clothes. They enlisted the help of Mary Magdalene, who further pressed him to get a well-pressed, well-tailored suit. In fact, she recommended this shop, saying she'd known the owner for years. Jesus at last accepted their recommendation but only because he had won the battle over keeping his beard and shoulder-length locks.

Jesus found the suit to be a perfect fit, the cuffs ending in line with his wrists and the shoulders square with his frame. It was snug without being constricting, and the whole ensemble struck Jesus as if he'd grown a second skin—an irritating second skin that needed to be shed to keep him from becoming a snake. He'd have to spend the rest of the afternoon wearing it around the office to adjust to the silky, too-rich feel of the synthetic fibers.

What made him more uncomfortable was when the tailor told him he didn't have to pay.

"No, no, I couldn't do that," said Jesus. "You're a working man who needs to make a living. Take the money."

"I'm afraid I cannot, sir. I listened to you the whole time I measured you. The whole time. And I was impressed. I can't stand Herod. He's no friend of small business. He'd just as soon see some chain store open up down the street until I'm out of business, all while he says how much he supports the little guy. No, sir, not this little guy. This is my gift to you."

"That's very nice of you," said Jesus, slipping on his usual corduroy jacket while the tailor wrote paid across his invoice, "but I don't think we're allowed to accept gifts."

The man smiled. He'd been told to expect this. "Then it's a political donation. People are allowed to give usable gifts as long as they are reported. Report this and consider it my donation to your campaign. Good luck against Herod. You'll be the best-dressed man on that stage, I guarantee it."

Jesus thanked the tailor and said tonight he'd be thinking about him and the thousands of small shop owners like him across the state. He launched this campaign for them and planned to finish it the same way. Jesus left the store knowing he had this man's vote.

What he didn't know was that Mary Magdalene paid for this suit in cash and instructed the tailor to donate it to Jesus. It was just one more way around the legal limit.

Jesus, Peter, and Andrew climbed out of Jesus' jalopy outside a thousand-seat theater in the heart of Philadelphia. A man called the office that afternoon offering to drive them in his sleek luxury car—another unknown gift from Mary Magdalene, who thought it was embarrassing for a Senate candidate to show up in a beater. Her only requirement was that it be American-made because she could hear Herod's team ripping a foreign vehicle and the unions falling in line behind him. Magdalene understood the pretensions of politics. Image mattered.

Unfortunately for her, Jesus understood that, too. Peter jumped at the opportunity, particularly when the man said it was his political contribution, but Jesus, when he learned of it two minutes later, said no. He ordered Peter to call him back and respectfully decline. He was going in the car with rust around the edges and the squealing fan belt because that was his image. He would not ride a stallion when a donkey would do.

An usher escorted Jesus up a back stairwell to a dressing room larger than either man's living room. Four mirrors surrounded by more than a dozen bright white bulbs, a private bath complete with shower, a fold-out couch, and a table for four set with twenty-four bottles of water and four baskets of fresh fruit. Jesus wasn't sure if he was debating Herod or restocking his campaign headquarters.

Not three minutes after Peter and Andrew left Jesus alone to rehearse his talking points under the guise of "We're going to see if the rest of the team is here," there came a loud knock on the door. A forceful knock. A knock that said, "If you don't open this door, I'm coming in anyway."

Jesus chose to control the situation by opening the door.

On the other side stood Governor Pontius Pilate. The governor, halfway through his second term despite consistently polling somewhere between the press and chickenpox, was the pictorial definition of constituentocracy. Despite the fact that no one Jesus knew liked him, and no one they knew liked him, he had beaten two better-qualified opponents. Rampant Beltway gossip even claimed he might get promoted to Cabinet secretary or agency head since he remained a "close personal friend" of President Tiberius, which he announced every time he got the chance.

Jesus invited him in. Whether because it was his nature to be kind or the nature of politics to be diplomatic didn't matter much at the moment. Jesus offered him something from the table, as well as a seat on the comfortable, overstuffed couch.

"No thank you," said Pilate, "I'm just wishing each candidate good luck tonight."

Jesus knew Pilate was being polite through duplicity. He wanted Herod to win. They'd been connected for decades, having come up through the same political party with many of the same political mentors.

"Thank you," said Jesus. "I'm looking forward to working with you after I win."

Pilate's blue eyes lit up. The hubris! No, the confidence. Then, he had a more disturbing thought. Did Jesus truly believe he was going to win or was he getting inside the governor's head? Mess with him before he faced the cameras later tonight. Maybe earn the rare cross-party endorsement. Pilate now believed he was right to visit Jesus first—he could warn Herod about the clever tactics Jesus would use in the debate.

He had to get to know this enigma from Nazareth.

"So, you're a man of the people?"

"It is you who says so."

"Yes...it is," said Pilate, a tad confused, failing to recognize that Jesus had never said that himself. He must have heard it somewhere. Probably one of those "people are saying" things without them actually saying it, or maybe one person saying it to a lot of the right people. He wasn't sure, and he didn't need to know. That was how they tricked you, stuffing your head with so much information that you couldn't do the job properly. Who needed facts when rumors got the best response? In fact, he doubted Jesus was a man of the people, being all tricky like this. No, he was too clever for his own good, but he wouldn't trick Pilate. No way, no how.

"So, I hear you're the savior of our political system. Maybe president someday."

That'll get him, thought Pilate.

"Again, it is you who says so. Me, I'm focused on the people of this state. I have no plans for higher office."

Oh, he's good! That rolled off his tongue like he meant it. Which made Pilate feel better. It meant Jesus wasn't gunning for his office either. Or was he? Maybe this was also a trick. Jesus was just trying to convince him he wasn't seeking higher office so he could blindside him down the road. *Oh, I have got to warn Herod about his guy.*

"Well, it was nice meeting you, Mr. Christ. I…"

Jesus interrupted him. "I understand you have two men scheduled for execution next week. I'd like you to pardon them."

"Why would I do that?" Pilate replied with indignity. Pardons weren't meant for hardened criminals who might benefit from mercy. Or who might commit another crime. He figured he wasn't about to flip a coin with that lot and give them a second chance, not if it came up heads one hundred times in a row.

"We need to show mercy over those we rule," said Jesus. "Judge not lest you be judged."

But Pilate was judging. Constantly. He was judging those men after they'd been judged by actual judges. He was judging Jesus. He was judging the voters. The polls. Political issues. Possible legislation. His job description may have been chief executive, but he acted like a judge. And in turn, he was being judged. No, he shook his head, he would not give up judging them.

"Then, I'm pleading with you to show mercy," Jesus replied. "The death penalty is immoral, racist, and unfairly applied. Pardon them, and I promise my followers will support you."

"Hmmm, I don't think so," said Pilate, shaking his head, stopping, then shaking it again as if confirming his doubts. "Can't lose my base. Still, if it makes you feel better, there is one criminal I'm thinking of pardoning."

Jesus scanned the carpet, wondering who. That's when he realized that the rug, which stretched wall-to-wall, was little more than fluffy cardboard. Who spends all this money making an elaborate dressing room, then skimps on the carpet? Jesus figured that people, taken in by the opulence, ignored the details of poverty that surrounded them. This room was America in microcosm, pulled in by the glitz while walking on the poor.

"Don't you want to know who?" said Pilate, smiling as if saying 'I know something you don't know.' Which was appropriate. He did. It was his pardon.

"Yes, of course. Who?"

"Barabbas."

"The terrorist?" Jesus could not hold his surprise in check.

"Eco-terrorist, actually," said Pilate.

Jesus couldn't believe it. Why would Pilate, a firm climate-change denier and anti-environmentalist, free an eco-terrorist? An archenemy, if one thought of politics in cartoon terms, which Pilate didn't, or he would have become a pundit. Then it hit Jesus. Environmentalists were up in arms over Pilate's push to roll back certain environmental regulations. Pilate was buying their silence by releasing one of their own. Even if it didn't work, he faced little pushback. He'd pardon him on the same day as the attention-grabbing executions. After all, he was killing two men convicted of killing two men while releasing someone who did property damage. A fair trade as far as Pilate could tell, since the environmentalists would celebrate and almost no one else would know. He kept his base happy on the right while mollifying, at least temporarily, those on the left.

"Well, I have to be going," said Pilate, reaching out to shake Jesus' hand before leaving. Jesus didn't offer it in return, sickened by Pilate's blatant political maneuvering. Perhaps he wasn't as stupid as he seemed, but he sure was good at faking it. Pilate, hoping not to appear put off, grabbed Jesus' hand and shook it as an aide stepped up and took a photo. Jesus looked like hell in the shot, eyes as terse as his mood, but Pilate was all smiles because he could now say he reached out to the other side and the other side stayed divisive. You could see it all over his face.

Pilate stepped to the sink in the corner, washed his hands with a splash of liquid soap and a dash of water, dried them on a towel hanging to the right, and disappeared through the door to warn Herod that Jesus wasn't the debating fool you might expect.

Jesus picked up his notes from the dressing-room table, counting down to showtime. Just ten minutes until he took the stage on the biggest night of his young political career.

THE PLANK IN YOUR EYE

Jesus and Herod walked on stage from opposite wings, meeting in the middle to shake hands. They were pinched between two podiums before a giant American flag, which Herod's camp insisted be there. They smiled and posed for the cameras, Jesus in his sharp blue-gray suit and Herod in a rich, Italian design that contained a subtle purple sheen. The photographers satisfied and the applause dwindling, the two men took their places behind their respective lecterns, Jesus to the viewers' left and Herod to their right. Jesus tried to control his squinting in the spotlight's glare. He stood immobile, holding the paneled podium to keep himself steady, save for a slight shaking in one leg. A twitch. He chalked it up to nervous energy. Despite loving a live crowd, even one buried deep behind stage lights and a press pool, he felt uneasy. He had to conclude it was the TV cameras, as if he wanted nothing he said to be recorded for posterity. Strange for a man who lived for a better future.

The moderator, a forty-five-year-old African-American woman, sat downstage facing them. She had been a compromise candidate. Early on, Herod's team pushed for a Phobos pundit, then a Phobos anchor, then a Phobos contributor, but Tad pushed back, looking for someone a little more to the left. Someone who could be fair to Jesus. And so, this woman was chosen because she shared almost nothing in common with these candidates, and that indicated she might not be biased against either of them, or perhaps both of them, but that sounded fair enough. She did not share their gender, race, political affiliation, profession, or background. Her age was almost dead center between them, as was her income. Herod never liked her professionally but found her personally acceptable and a capable journalist, which meant she gave him one good article to every four negative. That didn't make her his first choice, but she was on the list, and being that she aired the same ratio of favorable to unfavorable for Jesus, she was acceptable. Herod had been getting pressure in the media, and more importantly from Lucifer, to make this debate happen, so he conceded many of his preferences. Of course, he justified it to his supporters by saying he was so eager to "mop the floor" with his opponent that he "took the mess that came with it."

The moderator, knowing none of this but assuming all of it, opened the debate with a big smile for the cameras and a gentle reminder of the agreed-upon rules.

"Good evening, gentlemen, and good evening to our audience around the state. Our rules tonight are simple. Each candidate will have three minutes to answer my question, followed by a one-minute rebuttal. Herod Antipas will answer each question first, followed by a response from Jesus Christ. Gentlemen, are you ready?"

Herod said, "Yes," and Jesus nodded before realizing he should be heard as well as seen and said, "Yes" a second after his opponent.

"Good. A few weeks ago, the two of you had a row over our armed forces. Please clarify your position on the military."

Herod tried to hold back a smile at this softball question. He'd been talking about his love of the military since he first took office two wars and thirty armed conflicts ago. He gripped the sides of the two-foot-wide podium, a foot less than the one he requested and the actual size he wanted since it still hid his girth and made stick-figure Jesus look like a man-child with a beard, and spoke into the microphone with the familiarity of a frequent and formidable debater.

"We must be ready for any attack. Liberals complain we have the largest, most expensive military in the world, but I brag about it. We spend more than the next several nations combined because it's not enough to be number one. We must be dominant. Our military is the BMW of the world, and you don't buy a Beemer to keep it in the garage. You take it out for a spin to show it off to the neighbors. Well, invading other countries is just taking the military out for a spin so the neighbors know we have a better car. After all, it's the primary responsibility of the government to secure our borders here and abroad, and I'll see that they do."

Jesus wondered how you could secure our borders abroad, but he wasn't about to interrupt. His time was coming.

"We are safer when we have a massive military," Herod went on, "and so is the world. Guns and bombs secure our leadership. Now, everyone knows I'm a religious man, so let me leave you with this: The Lord is a man of war. Who are we not to follow Him if we are made in His image?"

Herod smiled. That last bit was a bit hyperbolic, but great red meat for his religious followers who liked war.

"Mr. Christ, your turn," said the moderator.

Jesus took a deep breath and launched into Peter and Tad's talking points embellished by his own rhetorical flourish.

"War must be just. There is a time for war and a time for peace, and a wise man knows which is which. If he rushes headlong into battle, his head will not be long for his body. We must put our sword in its scabbard lest we perish on another's blade. Why fight a guns-and-butter war when we can enjoy a bread-and-butter peace? Thou shall not kill is not just for people but nations, too. And while my opponent says the Lord is a man of war, I say He is a man of peace, and we should follow His example."

"He's a pacifist!" said Herod, as if that were a bad word like liberal. "My opponent's the type who says give peace a chance when peace isn't working. Do we really want someone who'll surrender before the first shot is fired? Someone who thinks the answer is blowin' in the wind? My opponent won't defend America—he'll offend Americans!"

Jesus remembered a piece of advice from Lazarus: When you can't defend your argument, attack the other guy. Or when he attacks you. Either Herod read Lazarus' playbook, or Lazarus studied under a master at his last debate. Regardless, Jesus was steeled for any assault Herod might send.

"I bring not peace but a sword—a sword against those who oppose justice, and for that, I don't need an army behind me." Jesus smirked and jerked his head toward Herod, hitting him with the grown-up equivalent of the schoolboy taunt, 'You and what army?' "My opponent forgets that while he calls me a pacifist, I stand here arguing with him. And I will not back down in any just fight. I will stand up to America's enemies while my opponent is still getting out of his chair."

Herod leaned into the microphone, but his guttural burst was silenced when the producer cut off his mic. He'd done a few of these debates and was determined to get one done on time. Just one. That's all he wanted. Just to prove he could. Unfortunately, for Herod, the producer picked tonight to make it happen.

The moderator jumped into the next question to fill the obvious silence.

"Please explain your position on women's reproductive rights, particularly the controversial issue of abortion."

Herod thought he was being thrown another softball, but the last question proved you could lob a grenade the same way. He needed to be more careful in getting his point across to his fervent base.

"I am, and always have been, pro-life. Firmly. In all cases, save maybe—maybe—the life of the mother, though the doctor will have a high bar to prove that the mother's life is, indeed, in danger. I cannot make it any more clear that I am pro-life."

"Mr. Christ?"

Jesus wondered if he were being set up, but he couldn't lie and say what his side wanted to hear. Not on an issue for which he held such deep beliefs. The only choice he had was to pull back the curtain and shed light on what separated his positions from his opponent's.

"Like my opponent, I am pro-life. Thou shall not kill also applies to the unborn. But women, before, during, and after pregnancy, must have the best healthcare available. They should not be treated the way my mother was, and children should not be treated the way I was. If we tell women that they must have those children, then we must give those children the best opportunities to live a good life. Free healthcare for children and mothers. Financial assistance, food, utilities—whatever it takes to protect children. If the state demands women bring these children into the world on the basis of morality, then we have a moral obligation to help raise them. Our responsibility for life doesn't end at birth."

Herod blubbered his lines over the smattering of applause that broke out in the theater.

"That's…that's socialism!" Herod treated that as a word worse than pacifist. "If there's one thing we conservatives support, it's keeping the government out of people's lives. We believe in personal responsibility. We never told those women to get pregnant. No government interference, unless, of course, it means stopping those women from having a choice."

Jesus didn't wait for the moderator to greenlight his response.

"It's funny that my opponent is against government overreach but believes the government should step in as quickly as possible to take away your children."

"That's not what I said!" Herod was firm, his voice the audible mimicking of flexing a bicep before a fight.

"That's the greatest overreach of all," Jesus said, ignoring the fact that Herod was right. He hadn't said that, but it immediately shifted the focus of this argument. "Mr. Antipas has always been spare the rod and spoil the child while my campaign is dedicated to helping you care for your children."

Jesus drew a breath. The moderator, thinking he was done, spoke, but Jesus interrupted her with a decision he knew he'd regret. He had to win this debate. That's the one thing about debates among alpha males: You try to win a pissing contest even when pissing into the wind.

"Early in my campaign, I reached out to help a very sick boy. Mark. And I'm happy to say Little Mark is doing exceptionally well and is expected to make a full recovery. That's the sort of help I will bring to families and children whenever I can."

The smattering of applause grew to half the house, although it was not for Jesus, and he knew that. It was for Little Mark. Jesus merely provided a happy ending. Lazarus was right—personalize the story.

"Very good, gentlemen," said the moderator, "but I ask the audience to please keep your applause to a minimum so that we stay on schedule. Now, gentlemen, question three. Please explain your position on the death penalty."

Herod launched into this question without hesitating. He had convinced himself after the last question that the surest way to make a misstep in a minefield was to worry about where you were stepping.

"The death penalty is underused. While some criminals can be rehabilitated, those on death row are beyond hope. Kill them, don't cure them. Death is the permanent cure."

Fifty or so people, the equivalent of the first row, erupted into applause, even as the moderator called on them to quiet down. Jesus, aware that Herod had barely used any of his three minutes, waited for the applause to stop so that it didn't step on his lines.

"Earlier, I said I am pro-life. Well, I am pro-life in everything, despite the fact that in today's world, that is a political oxymoron."

"Well, it's moronic anyway," said Herod, taking a cheap shot.

Jesus struck back as Lazarus instructed—not below the belt but with a knock-out punch.

"You want moronic? My opponent has voted to expand the death penalty to include minors. He says he's pro-life but supports killing children. That's moronic!" Herod tried to jump in, but Jesus kept his words tight, knowing he was on the clock. "Compassion brings out the best in us. It inspires us. Just backstage tonight…"

Jesus caught something out of the corner of his eye. Herod had wandered away from his podium, aimlessly crossing the stage in front of one of the cameras. Jesus checked the monitor, and sure enough, Herod was behind him, in the shot, half a head taller than his opponent. It looked like he was trying to intimidate Christ, a man not given to fear. Not after growing up an outcast. He tossed his head toward Herod and said, "He looks lost back there. Somebody get him a map." A small chuckle followed, but Herod stayed put, wandering another half-step toward Jesus. "It's a good thing he wasn't in the desert with Moses. They'd still be out there."

That line got a big laugh, and Herod, realizing the audience was laughing at him and his unusual tactic—if it could be called that—retreated to his lectern and pretended to read his notes before raising his head as if to say, "What? I've been here the whole time."

Jesus returned to his point, annoyed that Herod had broken his rhythm. Shifted the power of his argument. But maybe that was the point.

"Anyway, backstage tonight, I asked Governor Pilate to spare the lives of two men scheduled to die next week."

Herod chuckled just loud enough for the TV audience to hear it. "Give me the rope and I'll do it myself. An eye for an eye!"

The producer chose to let this violation go. They were a few minutes ahead of schedule, and a good back-and-forth might be good TV. Jesus was glad he did.

"You hypocrite! Remove the plank from your own eye so that you can see to remove the speck in your brother's. You want to grab the rope? You want to stone someone to death? Well, I say let he who is without sin cast the first stone. Given all your sins, you better get in the back of the line and hope there are a few rocks left!"

Even a few conservatives in the audience laughed at Herod now. They knew a good insult when they heard one. They'd certainly heard enough of Herod's over the years. The only people who didn't laugh were the religious conservatives who had to ignore Herod's many sins so they could vote for him, though the more honest ones who could not overlook his offenses simply told themselves he was the sort of sinner they felt good about forgiving. Often.

"What would you do if that had been your wife who had been raped and killed?" Herod snapped. "Or your mother? Your daughter? Would you be so cavalier then?"

It was a fair question, but if its goal had been to show Jesus as a hypocrite, Herod needed another plan.

"I'm not saying it would be easy," Jesus said, looking directly into the camera before turning to his opponent, "but I would turn the other cheek."

In the back of the auditorium, Peter hung his head. *Stick to the bumper stickers...stick to the bumper stickers...*

"What does that mean?" Herod said in a snippet of anger.

"It means I would forgive the attackers. I am a man of principle, and I can't violate that because something terrible happened to my family. Terrible things happen every day. The strong find it in their hearts to forgive. To lift up. To heal themselves and their loved ones, the wronged and the wrongdoers. I will not ask others to do what I cannot."

"That's a coward talking," snapped Herod, playing to the everyman's need for revenge brought on by bravado.

"No," said Jesus. "It takes courage to go against an easy opinion. Cowards change their position on a whim, flipping like paper in the wind. That's not me. I am a man of high morals that I must follow. Enforcing the laws must not make justice blind. We must rehabilitate, not recriminate."

"You see?" said Herod, once again addressing the audience, still unsure whose rambling answer was scoring points. "Soft on crime. He wants inmates to run the prison. We must show criminals that we are stronger than them!"

Jesus let Herod dangle in the wind for a second like a stuffed piñata that didn't know it was about to be split open. But he should have known what was coming when Jesus changed his tone, ever so simple, ever so Socratic.

"Do you believe you're a powerful man, Senator?"

"Of course."

"And naturally those who oppose you are weak."

235

"As weak as you are."

Both men smiled but for different reasons. Herod for thinking he had scored a point his followers would long remember and Jesus for knowing his enemy's pride preceded his fall.

"And yet you don't know that that which gives us strength gives us love and self-control. Being strong doesn't mean crushing your opponent, it means forgiving them or ignoring them because you're so powerful that they're no threat. But you react like a school bully precisely because you're scared that you're not strong. If you're strong, you can forgive, but your very actions prove you're not strong!"

"That's psychobabble!"

"Appropriate for a man who babbles."

The piñata had split open, but the candy that spilled out was tart. Bitter. Herod's eyes glowered with a fury that would never forgive Jesus. His opponent must now taste the venomous sting of defeat.

"Gentlemen!" bellowed the host, reminding the combatants she was still there. "Please remain civil. Remember the dignity of the office you seek."

The producer remembered to whisper in her earpiece, "Dignity doesn't bump ratings."

She fought the urge to throw down her notes and go home. This wasn't what she signed up for. If the producer wanted an onscreen rumble, he should have grabbed a daytime talk-show host or primetime prima donna. Still, she could forbear a little conflict if it got people talking about the debate—naturally using her name—come tomorrow.

"Our fourth question, gentlemen, concerns immigration. How would you reform the system?"

Again, Herod went first, a format he accepted so he could strike first blood, never expecting a counterattack. Now, he had a choice: choose his words carefully or fire up his base. Unlike most politicians who sought some middle ground because higher ground was too hard to maintain, Herod chose low, flooded, swampy ground which was hard to attack. A few bombastic militants were better than a million sappy dabblers any day. But that required a vociferous rant and a shift in tone. It was time to pull out his bumpkin act and go schizophresident.

"I oppose all forms of illegal immigration and most forms of legal immigration. I'll tell ya why. This country is bursting at the seams. Maybe we could let in people from more of the white countries, where they share our language and values. I've supported the wall to keep Samaritans out, but we can use all sorts of things that are like a wall—restricted work visas, no foreigners in colleges, stuff like that, to throttle immigration. You like that word, throttle? It's a good word. The best word."

Jesus caught the underlying violence in the word throttle and had no doubt Herod would go full-throttle to secure his Senate seat. He wondered if his opponent had crafted this response himself, relied on a speechwriter, or pulled it from some xenophobic website where they used small, powerful words to convey their arguments because the only big words they knew were invented to prove their racism to believers and hide their racism from the uninitiated.

"But we have to stop the Samaritans from coming in," Herod went on. "They're clogging up our jails. They're killers and rapists. I mean, I ask myself, who's doing the raping? Who's doing the raping? You gotta ask yourself that, and when you do, you say it's the Samaritans. And that's why we have to keep them out."

"Mr. Christ?"

The fingers of Jesus' left hand tapped the podium. He didn't have a schizophresident character to draw upon or a base to feed raw meat. Maybe one day he would, but for the moment, he had to hope they came to him as he spoke the truth.

"Our government is a government of the people—and all people once they enter this country. They must live by our laws, but our culture is broad enough to include every last immigrant. We cannot eliminate whole groups while slandering them with made-up crimes."

"They're not made-up." Herod lowered his voice to make that line more powerful. He hoped to throw Jesus off his game, but his opponent just kept swinging for the fences.

"Alright, let's say they're not made up. If that's the case, I beg people not to stay at Herod's Hotels. He hires hundreds of Samaritans a year, and if they are the murderers and rapists he says they are, they will rape and kill you in your sleep. Please, for your own safety, don't stay at Herod's Hotels. Now, are they still as bad you as you claim?"

"I only hire the good ones." Same tone, same tactic. Say the line so fast the moderator couldn't stop him.

"Let me tell you a story," Jesus said.

Peter unofficially pulled out a clump of hair. Not another damned story. He was sure to be bald before this was over.

"An American was beaten and robbed and left for dead on the side of the road. A priest found him, but it was his holy day and he was in a hurry. He walked to the other side of the street and didn't help the man. Then, a politician found him, but he was an important man and had to get to a meeting. So, he crossed to the other side of the street. Then, a Samaritan—an illegal Samaritan—found the man. He bandaged his wounds, gave him some medicine, and took him to the hospital. Which of these men was the better man?"

The audience sat in uncomfortable silence amid the occasional rustling of a squeaky seat or crumpled program. It felt inappropriate to answer a rhetorical question aimed at hundreds.

"Mr. Her—" the moderator began.

Herod spoke over her. He was going into blitzkrieg mode—strike with lightning speed to get thunderous results.

Whatever. Let him talk, she thought.

"That's a lovely story. You should publish your fantasies. But this is reality, and we don't need to embrace other cultures. Whatever cultures shaped this country are already here. It's what makes us the strongest country in the world. We don't need foreigners. This is America, so speak English. I mean, people speak it everywhere. They certainly do on TV. Even in outer space. It's the most popular language in the universe. English is the language of America, and it should stay that way!"

Herod's backers offered up wild applause, but Jesus was prepared despite their broad enthusiasm for narrow minds.

"We are the strongest country in the world because we incorporate the world. We take the best of what other cultures have to offer. Music, clothing, food, you name it, we take it."

Herod jumped in again as the moderator attempted to move to the next question.

"I'm not eating foreign food, I'll tell you that. I'm sticking with American staples like hamburgers, hot dogs, french fries, pizza, spaghetti, taco bowls, bagels…you know, the classics."

Jesus sighed, resisting the temptation to look at his watch. If anything, he'd look at a calendar to show Herod what year it was.

"Mr. Christ, you're allowed a response in the overtime."

Jesus looked directly into the camera. "My opponent is free to eat whatever he likes. It's not what goes into a man's mouth that makes him evil, it's what comes out of it."

An audible gasp arose from the audience. Jesus had just called his opponent evil in the way politicians are supposed to— without actually saying it. But there was no doubt he'd hit Herod hard enough to make his knees wobble. The only question was whether the champ had enough in the tank to go the distance.

"Gentlemen, our time limits us to one final question. My apologies to those who wanted to hear about topics we didn't get to, but I'm sure you can find the candidates' positions on their websites."

This made Jesus wonder why they were doing this at all. The best he could guess was to let the public see how fast they were on their feet, or how well they handled pressure because honestly, there was no other reason to be here.

"Our final topic tonight is welfare. What steps would you take to reform…"

"I believe in limited welfare," Herod began without apologizing for yet another interruption. He saw no reason to wait when he knew where the question was going. Had she been with Phobos News he might have let her finish, but a middle-of-the-road traditionalist who didn't like him? Not a chance. "Call it restricted welfare with strict work requirements in order to get checks, food stamps, and medical benefits. My own companies, especially my hotels and restaurants, would happily train them for new and rewarding careers."

"Of course they would," said Jesus. "You get free workers while the government picks up the tab."

"I have held these beliefs for years," said Herod, turning away from the cameras to face Jesus.

"You've owned your hotels for years."

"Gentlemen, please stick to your times."

Both men ignored her, though it was Herod who pressed his case before his young opponent could get in another rejoinder.

"I favored workfare long before this whelp ever got into politics. And the voters back my position because they know it's the right position. They know that too many people abuse the system, stay home, watch TV, and don't work. They take far more than their fair share."

"Right," said Jesus, "and you think that's the right of the rich."

Jesus knew Lazarus was smiling somewhere in the back of the room.

"The rich earn their money. If you knew any of them, you'd know that."

"If you knew any poor people, you'd know they're struggling to get off welfare."

"Gentlemen, stick to the format..."

"Americans aspire to be rich, which is why they frown on welfare," Herod went on.

"Americans do aspire to be rich, which is why they look for ways out of poverty."

"Need I remind you that your beloved poor, young man, vastly outnumber the rich. They are the ninety-nine percent. If the poor want to change the welfare system, they can do it. They can overturn the system legally and ethically." Herod caught his breath, afraid he just started a revolution. "But they don't. The poor don't vote."

"If they did," said Jesus, "we'd get better politicians." Herod glared at his opponent but before he could come up with his own comeback, Jesus continued. "They don't vote because we restrict them. You want limited welfare? Change the voting rights. Let freed criminals vote. Find daycare so the working poor can go to the polls. Let everyone vote. That is the definition of democracy. Make Election Day a national holiday!"

"That's just a power grab," said Herod.

"And how!" said Jesus. "A power grab for the majority. A power grab for the eighty percent who own twenty percent of the wealth. A power grab for the people!"

The back row burst into a chorus of *Power to the People*. The TV director switched off the audience mic's to keep from paying royalties. The producer yelled at the anchor to keep them on topic and on time.

"The topic is welfare!" shouted the moderator before he could finish.

But who could hear her over that singing?

"Then you admit it!"

"I admit that it's a way to end welfare! Give the people a voice in policy. If you want to help the poor, talk to the poor. Give them a say in how they can get out of the system and into the workforce. You say Americans aspire to be rich. Well, they also aspire to stay rich. That's why the rich rig the system by backing politicians who pass laws to benefit them. Let the poor do that, and they will find a way to lift themselves up. What you want is taxation without representation, but if you give the poor a chance to vote on policies that benefit them, we all benefit. They will lift themselves out of poverty."

Herod scoffed. "Commie!"

"Fascist!"

The men bristled, their chests puffed up like roosters before a cockfight. The audience grew tense, eyeing their neighbors to see who would throw a punch. They were ready to reduce this historic theater to rubble as the ushers raced toward the heavy double doors in back, ready to run rather than stop a riot. Minimum-wage security did not get you crowd control. Their vests were made of polyester, not Kevlar, and they'd be gone before the first punch landed.

The theater director, pulling at her collar, told the stage manager to flip on the sprinklers if things got any more heated. It might not be legal to yell fire in a crowded theater, but that didn't mean you couldn't have an unplanned fire drill.

The moderator had the same idea.

She threw her clip mic on the table in front of her and walked off stage right, shaking her head, sad she did this and thrilled for the ratings. Still, she'd keep this off her resumé while knowing it would be in her obituary.

The two candidates mingled for a minute with their teams and spoke affably with those who dipped into the orchestra pit before walking to center stage, shaking hands, and saying goodnight. And why shouldn't they be friendly? If politics makes for strange bedfellows, this moment was their make-up sex. Rough-and-tumble, ready-to-keep-the-fight-going-just-to-do-it-again-tomorrow make-up sex.

FIG LEAVES

Ten minutes after the debate ended and the tech crews were breaking down equipment to reset the stage for tomorrow night's hip-hop romp of *Oedipus Rex*, Jesus led his team upstairs to a room meant for cast meetings and wrap parties. It had a functioning Pullman kitchen, some tables, chairs, and two couches, enough to hold the twenty people attending Jesus' post-debate soirée. Herod and his team ducked out a side door and climbed into the limos waiting to whisk them away to what he called "the most splendid, swankiest hotel in Philadelphia" because, after all, he owned it, even though travel guides ranked it sixth due to its faux marble, gold-plating, average customer service, and high prices. For him, such surroundings made good news better and bad news palatable. He wasn't sure which he was getting, although he was sure the sycophants surrounding his campaign would tell him he was fantastic. They were the equivalent of putting salve on a third-degree burn: they meant well, but it only helped a little. An unnoticed little.

Jesus, however, had no such worries. He had no sycophants in his camp—just a few doubters, and once they expressed that doubt they were free to tell the truth. And every single person in the room from paid staffer to paying donor shook his hand, patted him on the shoulder, hugged him, and told him how good he looked tonight. Facing Herod put him in his element, like Daniel in the lion's den, unafraid of the beast in front of him.

At the end of the line stood Mary Magdalene, bedecked in jewels so opulent she could easily be mistaken for a Herod supporter. She gave Jesus a quick embrace and a showbiz kiss followed by a smile big enough to hide the creases in the corners of her mouth.

"You did it. You scared Herod."

"He made it easy by playing the fool." Jesus' modesty was not for show. He was unsure what to think until tomorrow when his mind—and the public's response—would be clear.

"You look good in your new suit," Magdalene said, tugging at the lapels.

"Thank you, though it feels more like a costume. Perfect for the theater, I guess. I had to play the part, but the message would have been the same had I been out there in a fig leaf."

"I'd like to see that!"

There was that winning smile again.

Jesus couldn't determine whether she was joking—there was certainly a small titter afterward—or hitting on him.

"I'm afraid it's better to cover our nakedness with fine linen."

She smiled, blushed a light crimson, and gave him a curious eye with a twinkle inside. He couldn't believe it. His attempted retreat had become innocent flirtation. Linen suits apparently made her think of linen sheets.

Mary covered her embarrassment by asking him if he wanted a drink, and he covered his unease by accepting. They each got a glass of red wine, spending the next thirty minutes discussing what steps the campaign needed to take now. Before long, they found themselves on the couch, though Jesus kept a throw pillow between them under the pretense that he needed an armrest. At this distance, she smelled like lilies in the early summer, and Jesus knew her perfume would remain on his suit for the rest of the night. He started to slip off his jacket but couldn't decide whether that was to preserve the scent or escape it. He stopped when Mary reached out to help him, flipping it back up with a thrust of his shoulders, believing that removing it was too suggestive. It served better as a suit of armor, the pillow his shield. Her only way through his defenses was poignant conversation and the occasional touching of his hand.

The discussion turned to their upbringing. Neither came from money, though Mary's father made it soon enough. Both had declined marriage, instead devoting themselves to work and charitable causes. And each thought Herod to be among the most vile and vicious senators in the chamber.

A few stragglers—Judas, Thomas, and Barney—lingered in the room when Peter came over and said he'd see Jesus at the office first thing in the morning. His wife had already texted him a dozen times, upset that he was out later than he said he'd be. Two hours later.

Jesus took this as a hint that he, too, should be leaving. He said goodnight to everyone, which told the remaining three that they had better head on home. Jesus walked Mary to her car, where her chauffeur waited without a word or look of disapproval. He opened the door for Mary and stood by like an armed sentry. Jesus said, "Goodnight," and while prepared for an embrace, he got more. A first kiss more. It was as soft and gentle as the tips of angel wings and briefly brushed away the pressures of the campaign. Mary's "Goodnight" escaped as a soft sigh seconds before she disappeared into the night with her driver at the helm.

Jesus reached his car and told himself to be at the office early tomorrow so he could focus on work because tonight that would be impossible.

Mary Larnaca was already collating news stories about the debate when Peter arrived at the office a few minutes before 7:00. She also sent the top advisers links to Herod's answers to reporters' questions. Yes, he'd held a press conference at the hotel while Jesus partied. That was never a good sign in a candidate. The job had to come first. Still, he looked happy talking with Mary Magdalene. Maybe he needed a little of that, too.

The bags under Peter's eyes looked as dark as the ink on the pages Mary handed him, but at least he was here. He understood the job.

Peter ducked into his office, impressed by how much Mary had already gathered. Best damned assistant he could ask for. She may have benefited from her time in her brother's campaign, but he had more than a sneaking suspicion she'd always been this good. If Jesus won, they would have no choice but to bring her on board. They might even have to pay her. No one could run the office better.

An hour later, Jesus arrived to find a screenful of emails and more than a dozen voicemails, all from reporters with questions about the debate. Of course, the screen would only have been half full and his voicemail almost empty had the reporters showed any patience and not called and emailed three times each.

Before Jesus answered any of them, he had to get an update from Peter. After his compliments last night, which Peter called the best debate performance he'd ever seen, Jesus wouldn't have been surprised to see an open bottle of champagne on his desk, but Peter was up to his eyes in paperwork and studies.

"This is fantastic!" said Peter, jumping up from his desk and handing Jesus several sheets of paper. "You're up in the polls. For the first time, you're up in the polls! *The Inquisition* has you up fifty-three percent to forty-seven. SixSixSix has you up fifty-two/forty-eight. Even Phobos has you even money, and they always have you down. Everything is within the margin of error, but you're up! No money, a skeleton staff, little media coverage, and you're up, baby, you're up!"

Jesus accepted being called "baby" as a sign of Peter's investment in winning.

"Of course, it would be a lot bigger if you hadn't pulled that abortion stunt, but right now, I can't be mad at you."

"It's my position."

"I know. Mine, too, in as much as a campaign manager can have a position, but our constituents are mostly pro-choice. We can remain pro-life but say we back people's personal choice by keeping the government out of the bedroom."

"I can't do that, Peter. I have to be true to myself—without compromise."

"Boy, are you in the wrong line of work."

"There are times I think so, too." Peter's face soured at his candidate's admission, but then he had long believed more than a few more politicians should reconsider their careers. "So, how did the public view the debate?"

"A split decision. The majority of radio listeners thought you won. A small majority of TV viewers thought Herod won. And those who watched online thought the moderator was hot."

"What?" said Mary from Peter's doorway, walking in with a cup of coffee for Jesus.

"That's the results of an actual poll," Peter said, shaking his head and clinking Jesus' coffee mug with his own. "Same poll said your suit was better than Herod's. He looked like purple mountains majesty in that thing. Anyway, the good news is that online viewers thought you won, too. Split decision in your favor, baby!"

Again with the baby. Jesus was sure it was a natural thing to say in Peter's world of campaign manager cum talent agent, but he really wanted it to stop.

"Of course, he did," Mary said. "Most of the people watching on the web are under forty. They like what a young candidate has to say. They see themselves in him." She turned to Jesus and said, "Well done."

Her tone was soft yet confident. Jesus liked how easily she got her message across, without any of Peter's histrionics or hyperbole. She never called him "baby."

"He's young, alright. A young candidate on the rise. I see a great future for you, Mr. Christ!"

From baby to Mr. Christ. Jesus knew he must be doing well to get a promotion like that.

"I've got you booked on Baptiste's show this afternoon. You'll pre-record a podcast for tomorrow. In the meantime, let's go over these questions. Anything sounds better than 'No comment,' or 'The campaign did not respond by our deadline.'"

Peter took to email and Jesus returned phone calls, occasionally checking with each other to make sure they weren't duplicating their efforts, though a few reporters thanked them for providing two responses. Although it made the campaign look disorganized, it always made for a better piece when two people gave two opinions no matter how similar they were. It gave readers a change of pace and made it so much easier to hit the word count.

Half the questions focused on whether Jesus truly thought Herod was a fascist. Herod had doubled down on his claim that Jesus was indeed a communist and that people should expect another Commie Christ ad in the coming days. Jesus kept his response simpler, saying Herod's history spoke for itself. When asked what that meant, he told reporters to investigate Herod's record of backing far-right groups, voting for corporate takeovers of government functions, and hugging the flag so much he thought they should marry in a public ceremony.

Another common question concerned his views on immigration. Jesus defended immigrants by pointing out they had a lower crime rate than American-born citizens. He also pointed out the obvious: thousands of Samaritans worked legally and illegally throughout the state, adding that if they weren't good employees, "Apollo-Mart wouldn't have locked them in the stockroom to keep them there."

Peter and Jesus got back to every reporter on the list to answer every question—except those concerning abortion. Jesus had gone against his base, and Peter worried that repeating his opposition would make it a live grenade glued to his cheek. There was no way to keep it from blowing up in his face. Jesus worried it was a ticking time bomb, getting ever closer to the hour when it would finally explode.

Only one of them could be right.

For now, Jesus had an interview to do. He realized too late he should have gotten more sleep because he needed all his energy to keep up with his mad cousin.

Baptiste gave Jesus a bear hug before his cousin could get out of the hallway, but as excited as he was to see him, he was even more excited to get him on the air. He was, after all, Jesus' most devout supporter. He'd been preaching about his coming before the public knew his name. But there was a practical side to this. Since being banned from the world's preeminent video channel, his viewership had fallen from thousands to hundreds to dozens. Viewers couldn't find him, or weren't interested in a ranting Baptiste they couldn't see. Even he had to admit he was an on-air spectacle, a wild man suited to an era of visual stimulation. With so few listeners, his advertising revenue plummeted. He hoped Jesus could boost listenership enough to gain him a few dollars. Enough to eat for the first time in two days.

Jesus took care of that problem in the short-term by handing him a bag of food containing every one of Herod's "American staples," from hamburgers to hot dogs, tacos to bagels. He hoped it would last his cousin until at least one payment came in.

Baptiste began the show with a lengthy introduction of the day's topic. It was too long for a podcast, the host unable to hold people's attention without his antics. Jesus tried to step in several times to get the interview going, but a hungry Baptiste rambled at a fanatical pitch, attacking Herod, the system, capitalism, and anyone opposed to Jesus, who could not stop his cousin's raging. Baptiste did not put on the brakes for a full ten minutes before he turned to the man sitting next to him. He embraced Jesus again, a terrible gesture on radio but a sign of a man desperate to hang on.

"This man here," said Baptiste, dabbing his eyes on the frayed cuff of a burlap bag he was forced to don as a shirt, "has been subjected to relentless attacks, and yesterday's debate was just one long ad for Herod to attack the greatest candidate the world has ever known." Baptiste paused, but this was not the deliberate, drawn-out silences of the more seasoned Tarsus. This was an honest inability to go on, the tear trickling down his cheek brought on by exhaustion, failure, and empathy for his besieged cousin. "Oh, we hear your attacks, Herod. You call Christ a commie, but I say he is the common man! And I say you are a fascist because you are facile! Yes, Herod, I attack you because Jesus will not. He is not tempted by your childish arguments because he is above you!"

Jesus at last found a moment to address the listeners before this interview became a monologue. "I agree that we must not be led into temptation, although it's all too easy to tempt people. Apollo-Mart, Uranus, and Vulcan Investors have built empires on that premise."

"Oh, yes, Herod," Baptiste said, blasting the airways again with his own incomparable vitriol. "He attacks the companies that back you. Jesus will not discuss your theoretical politics in the theoretical. No, he will come like a thief in the night when you least expect it and set the world aright. And there is nothing you and your fascist supporters can do about it!"

"I would not be so harsh," said Jesus, liking the analogy but knowing it would be used against him, "for I am no thief. I face Herod in the bright light of day and do not bow before his criticisms. And I'm no communist, though I believe in giving everyone a helping hand. And Herod should know that because he claims to be an expert on foreign affairs."

"The only affairs Herod knows about are those in his bedroom!"

"I don't know anything about his private life," said Jesus, his voice so quiet it got lost in Baptiste's boom.

"Well, I do!" said his host, carrying on more resolutely than ever. His idol inspired a return to his old form, aware that listeners would line up to see him tear into Herod. "His affairs are legendary, his love life a feast of tabloid fodder were the tabloids not in his pocket. And I don't mean in his pocket the way his mistress is in his pocket, if you know what I mean."

"I think they do," said Jesus.

"Of course they do. My listeners are smart!"

Jesus thought they didn't have to be smart to get an obvious innuendo that was about to become a full-blown charge if Jesus failed to stop it. "I'm not interested in Herod's private life..."

"His private life is the only thing interesting about the man," Baptiste went on. "His policies are a boring trope of conservative politics. A regurgitation of the party line. No, what is interesting about Herod is what he keeps secret. And I have a secret for my listeners. I know something they don't. Something Herod doesn't want you to know. He has a mistress." Baptiste gave his first Tarsus-style pause. "No, not Herodias. No, this mistress is a pretty young thing, a devotee of the despicable Herod." Another long pause. "I should share her name with you."

"I don't think that's…"

Baptiste silenced his cousin's mic. "I know she's listening. I'm sure of it. Those with secrets always listen to the truth-tellers. So, here is the truth. Herod's new mistress is…" The pause was so long Baptiste could have made himself a burger from his new stash of food. "…Salome."

Baptiste was right about one thing. Jesus increased listenership, but nothing like the bombshell he dropped about Herod. Ten times as many people downloaded the broadcast as ever watched his vlog. Reporters called in wanting to know his source. They weren't the only ones.

"How did you hear that?" Jesus asked after the program ended. "Did it come from my team? Did it come from Judas?"

"Iscariot gives me nothing. Worst dirty trickster I've ever seen. No, I got this on my own. I heard two of Herod's lawyers discussing it. Probably thought I was homeless. The homeless are invisible. People say anything around them. But if his people know, the press will know, so I beat them to it. I got the scoop that will bring down Herod Antipas!"

Jesus kept his eyes downcast, overcome by sadness. His cousin was delusional if he thought this would ruin Herod. It was an act of revenge and nothing more. His cousin had given in to an eye for an eye, the very act he had condemned in the debate. Herod had survived his last sex scandal, an escapade that involved an adulterous affair with his sister-in-law. Sleeping with an intern wouldn't even scratch his reputation. Being a known philanderer made him immune from future philandering scandals, unless, in someone else's wise words, it involved "a dead girl or a live boy." And this one involved neither.

TV crews scrambled to prove this by getting on-the-spot reactions from voters everywhere. At best, people feigned shock and went about their day. At worst, they said "We're not shocked" and went about their day. Herod supporters still planned to vote for him, opponents said they could never vote for such a man—even though many had voted for such a man when he was in their party—and the Internet filled up with comments rating Salome anywhere from a two to a ten depending on personal tastes . Many joked that she was an obvious improvement since Herod had moved from family member to employee while skipping the logical step of family employee. This surprised many of them, who thought he would naturally date his daughter since she fit both bills. To no one's surprise, however, the scandal did not shift the polls in any meaningful way.

The only person to come out of this damaged was Jean Baptiste because he was right about one other thing.

Salome was listening.

DEN OF THIEVES

Fifteen minutes after leaving Baptiste's apartment, Jesus reached the outskirts of town where he crossed paths with an old foe. Not the physical sort that challenges you to "step outside and settle this" but rather a site that is always outside, taunting you with its mere presence, symbolizing everything you oppose.

Jesus pulled his car into the jammed parking lot, finding an open spot near the back. His car fit in with the row upon row of jalopies sequestered hundreds of feet from the building. As he got closer, the cars got nicer. The front row, just twenty feet from the door, featured the finest American sports cars and European luxury models, their bright coats dazzling in the midday sun.

This injustice brought up the bile in the back of Jesus' throat. Inspired by his poll numbers and believing voters wanted to see the real him, Jesus stepped inside the one place he always avoided: The Reverend Deacon Dollar's Megachurch for Enriching Poor Souls.

The golden doors, surrounded by a beveled glass frame, opened into a world of unabashed hucksters pitching wares as if they were bull-rally brokers in the exchange pit. Vendors from dozens of tables yelled out prices and the benefits of buying. They had golden idols, prayer books, apples and other foodstuffs, memorial plates, holy grails, coats of many colors, gold-trimmed clothing, foreign currency, tax-prep help, and much more, the line so long the signs diminished in size and importance.

253

"Did you get your gun blessed?" a woman asked, tearing Jesus from this reverie for money.

"I'm sorry, what?"

"Did you get your gun blessed? It's Bless Your Gun Day."

"Why would I get my gun blessed?" asked Jesus.

"To be ready for the Apocalypse! It could come any day now. If you get your gun blessed, it will shoot straighter, fire faster, and never miss its mark. It's the best way to have the grace of God with you during the dark times."

"If the Apocalypse comes, I'd rather have a prayer shawl than a shotgun," said Jesus.

"We have those, too," said the woman. "Table Seven. Just fifty bucks. A great bargain!"

Jesus pulled away without another word, his anger growing. He thought people hit bottom when they blessed their pets, but at least those were living creatures capable of loving you back. But a gun? A means for killing someone? What cult had he fallen into that thought God would save them through violence? At least their violence, not His.

Jesus pushed deeper into this well of despair selling hope as a commodity. He did not see the deacon but figured he was somewhere close selling his soul to the highest bidder.

Jesus reached the entrance to the church beyond this lobby-turned-rummage-sale, its hundreds of red-cushioned pews leading upward like a tiered Mayan pyramid to the summit, the deacon's pulpit where he pounded out profit as the surest sign of God's undying love.

"Ten dollars, sir," said the woman behind the table, one hand reaching out to take his money, the other firm upon the till.

"For what?" Jesus asked.

"For admittance to the sermon. It's a wonderful bargain. Your ten-dollar donation goes right back to you."

"You give me my money back?" said a confused Jesus.

"No, the Lord will. For every dollar you give us, you receive one hundred back. The Reverend blesses your money, and then that money is returned to you a hundred times over. Maybe you'll find money on the sidewalk. Get a raise at work. Win the lottery. Start a great GoPayMe campaign. God works in mysterious ways. Your good deed will ensure God's providence. And for just ten dollars!"

"I'm not paying to attend a sermon," Jesus said with a tone so terse his jaw hurt. He turned to walk away, but the woman was not done.

"Give what you can! Ten dollars, twenty, thirty, fifty, a hundred!" She swooned in ecstasy. "Ten dollars gets you a thousand. Ten thousand gets you a million!"

She couldn't go on and collapsed in her seat, her hand never leaving the cashbox. Five seconds later, when Jesus was gone, she was back at work. "Ten dollars, please."

Jesus stood at the midpoint between the woman seeking buyers for gun blessings and the woman seeking donors for a once-free sermon. The masses pushed around him, crowding him, shuffling like sheep through ornate barn doors to seek their fortunes. It was the same scene as the homeless shelter, but with more despair. Hunched old ladies crept forward like the Sphinx's three-legged man. Couples dragged children in ragged clothes. Old men wheeled their oxygen tanks before them. It was the definition of decrepit and derelict, plodding one miserable step in front of the other, purchasing magical talismans and amulets, each as worthless as a tin trinket passed off as gold.

And then Jesus realized something else. For every one hundred poor people, a well-heeled couple passed, flashing furs and jewels and dressed more for the opera than a sweaty revival. As they reached the doors, not a single penny left their pockets. They bragged about how much they'd made by giving, giving until it hurt, to the Reverend. "And look at us now!"

If it worked, they'd give again. They'd gain more riches to prove that the rich got richer. But they kept it all for themselves.

They were plants.

Jesus could no longer contain his rage. He flipped over the first table he came to, its "magic money candles" flying end over end, "pet prosperity rocks" sailing like missiles through the air. A second table and a third followed until he grabbed the nearest parishioner by the shirt collar and yelled in his face.

"Have you given before?"

"Y-yes..." the man stammered.

"Are you still poor?" The man nodded as Jesus touched a woman tethered to an oxygen mask. "Still sick?" As each person around him nodded, Jesus yelled, "Do not give to the rich when you can give to the needy. He has no more connection to God than the beggar in the street! I promise that God will sooner reward you for giving to the man in the gutter than he will this lecher! Love your neighbor! Give to..."

Before he could finish, armed security guards, who likely had their guns blessed, surrounded Jesus and ordered him out of the church, seizing his elbows and dragging him away. But even that could not silence him.

"You have made this house of prayer a den of thieves!"

The heavy front doors flung open and Jesus sailed through the air, landing on the concrete walk as the new dead with their zombie debts took no notice and shuffled by.

DOUBTING THOMAS

Throughout the night, Jesus found himself the number one trending topic. When churches have security cameras and banks have security cameras, a church acting as a bank was sure to have them. The cameras captured Jesus from the moment he flipped the first table until security escorted him from the building in a none-too-ceremonious way. Phobos News ran the clip in a variety of ways, from uncut to chopped up, creating comedic effects by splicing together violent movie scenes, or running clown music underneath it, or speeding it up to create a slapstick silent film complete with tramp-like ending as Jesus bounced along on his backside. Tarsus returned to the air for a special one-hour, online-only commentary dedicated to his "most devoted followers." But the coup de gras came from the Herod camp.

Having yet to catch Jesus in a lie, they released his press conference tape as proof that he was a crazy man, or as they delicately put it in their press release, "a mentally deficient candidate." They amped up the audio on his "I am the way and the truth and the life" statement, sending it off to Phobos, *The Morning Star,* and select outlets.

Every station and paper—particularly those inclined to endorse Jesus— covered other stories, but they couldn't ignore a story this big for long. Or several stories this big. There was the accusation that Herod was dating an intern (a new twist on an old story), and the firing of Jean Baptiste for reporting it. With his proof little more than hearsay, he was out. The public, more than willing to accept scurrilous accusations from sources they trusted, demanded photographic evidence, if not pornographic evidence, from the fringe media. Several columnists took up Baptiste's firing as a First Amendment issue, but that proved as popular as a foreign film battling a superhero franchise. The mistress angle was a tired romance, the Baptiste firing a political opine, and the Megachurch Madman, as Phobos called it, an action film complete with video footage of a lunatic attacking a church.

It was clear who the winner was going to be from the first minute.

Missing from it all was Jesus' denial that he was a communist. Once upon a time, it would have appeared on page twelve of the daily paper, but papers now ended at page eight, so there wasn't room for it. Without it appearing in print, cable news had no way of knowing it existed and so couldn't air it. This meant that Herod was free to run another Commie Christ ad, which featured Herod calling Jesus a "Commie!" at the debate, followed by a bunch of people saying, "I hear he's a commie," "I heard on TV he's a commie," and "I have it on good authority he's a commie," which covered all the basic demographics of the simple, the intelligent, and the gullible who believe whatever they hear on TV.

It was enough for Peter to finally lose his cool, knowing Jesus had just blown all his hard work trying to clear things up. The commie label went from sticking with cheap tape to Super Glue.

"What were you thinking?" he bellowed, his voice filling his office and the other ones, too.

"I wasn't thinking," Jesus said, turning away from the television. "My zeal overcame me."

Peter paced the room, his half-clenched fist vibrating, frustration looking for a way out. "Alright, alright, that's how we're going to play this. Just like that. You went in on a religious excursion, and you saw a con man ripping off the poor. Simple as that. You lost your head because you're sick of seniors getting scammed. You had to draw attention to it, and you did. And that is how strongly you will fight for the working class in the Senate."

Peter picked up the phone and laid out his pitch to John, James the Great, and Thomas in rapid-fire succession. He told them to scramble the boys, particularly Tad, and get a few of them on the air to present the campaign's side of the story. Mary had gathered a list of reporters calling in, at least as fast as she could take them, which gave Peter a good place to start.

"I can do it, too," said Jesus, equally ashamed and proud of his outburst. It was out of character, but it was done out of necessity.

"No, you're off the air tonight. We can't risk you losing your temper if someone gets in your face. You start interviews with a clear head tomorrow."

Apparently Peter just couldn't reconcile countering the charge that his candidate was a madman by putting him on the air when he was mad.

Today's papers were filled with yesterday's bad news. They ran stills of Jesus rampaging through the temple. Editorials condemned him, as did TV commentators and radio callers, but the worst cut was yet to come. Within a day, Herod's team had an ad up featuring the security camera footage of Jesus flipping over tables, blown-up frames capturing the crazed look in his eyes. The narrator's commanding voice spoke over the action. "This man hates God. A man who does not fear God does not fear you. Vote for a man who respects you and loves God. Vote Herod." Immediately thereafter, Herod's staff and his media allies flooded the airwaves with their opinions.

Among these allies was Dr. Monet Goode, Herod's personal spiritual adviser, host of the evangelical program God Is Goode, and pastor of the Goode Fortune Church for Prayer & Prosperity. Her doctorate was real, having been granted to her by Goode University, a theological school she established twenty years ago in her honor. She claimed that, "As a humble woman of God, I know that Jesus is an atheist whose life is entirely antithetical to God's plan of making believers rich. God is anti-tax," she went on, "which we can prove by the fact that houses of worship don't pay taxes!" When it was pointed out to her that that was the Constitution and not from a religious text, she responded with "Then why does God print our money with In God We Trust? When Jesus attacks a temple, he attacks God and can't be trusted. So trust God, elect Herod, and get rich by sending me money!"

As further proof to prove a negative, other commentators said there was no footage of Jesus singing *God Bless America*, putting his hand over his heart during the national anthem, or going to a temple except to destroy it. When video appeared of Herod not putting his hand over his heart during *The Star-Spangled Banner*, his supporters said, "Yes, but his head was bowed because he was praying," though none of them could explain why he was praying during "bombs bursting in air."

Only *The Inquisition* ran a new story. Of course, their top story remained the rampage which, online, included the Atheist Christ ad since algorithms had determined those readers wanted to see it. But in the lower right corner of the print edition was a smaller story that one writer argued was more important: *No Women Among Christ's Top Advisers*. The story listed all twelve of Jesus' senior advisers, pointing out the obvious—they were all men. The only woman in the office, the article went on to say, was Mary Larnaca, an unpaid volunteer despite the fact that she had extensive political experience.

The paper had only one quote from the Christ campaign.

Ms. Larnaca said she had no knowledge of any payment arrangements within the campaign. She added, "I am happy to volunteer my time and service so that Mr. Christ can defeat Senator Antipas."

When Peter arrived that morning, he wanted to rip into her for not alerting the campaign to *The Inquisition* call, but they were smart. They reached her at midnight, too late to put a plan in place, with the side note that if she didn't pick up, they would use the standard, 'The campaign did not respond in time...'"

Damn that saying!

And her response was perfect. She had said Jesus was such a tremendous candidate that she'd work for nothing—and to prove it, she was. That wrong would be righted immediately, even if he had to take it out of Levi's hide.

Now, a few trolls said Mary sounded like a woman scorned, out for revenge against Herod at any cost, including fair wages and self-respect. The right echoed these sentiments, saying the Christ campaign was filled with former Larnaca staffers and volunteers, including Peter Cephas, Judas Iscariot, and a few others. They claimed Christ's election bid was driven by petty revenge and not any real opposition to Herod's policies—policies, they argued, that helped the state tremendously.

By the time Peter called an emergency staff meeting at noon, more than a dozen women were outside the office picketing with signs that read *Fair Wages for Women, No Women No Votes,* and *Christ Chreeps Women Out.* Several organizations filed paperwork to oppose Jesus, choosing names like Christ Against Women (CAW), Women Against Christ (the WACs), and WATCH (Women Against the Christian Hierarchy, which was led by a man).

What had been a blazing fire last night was a three-alarm inferno by the afternoon. Simon Z summed it up best. "We've dropped ten points since yesterday."

"In one night?" said Tad, who'd never seen a drio that fast. Not among supporters.

"SixSixSix has us down twelve."

"And that's all coming from women?" said Tad, shaking his head in astonishment.

"Not all women," replied Simon. "We're up slightly among older white women." Tad raised an eyebrow, which brought a shrug from their analytics guy. "They seem to like the abuse."

A standing Peter punched the table with a downward stroke. "That story is everywhere. Alright, we need a strategy to hold on to our supporters. Any…"

Before he could finish, Mary stuck her head in the door at the opposite end of the conference room, which kept everyone quiet. Some felt guilty about getting paid while she slaved away, while others knew she never interrupted unless there was big news.

"Tarsus says he has new information about us."

Yep, worth every penny they hadn't paid her.

Before Mary could close the door, Simon Z was already on his laptop loading the online broadcast. Ten seconds later, Saul's bombastic voice filled the conference room.

"Folks, I have been promising you this all morning and now is the time to deliver."

And it was true. Tarsus couldn't have addressed it in his first two hours because that would have driven down his ratings in the third hour. So, he spent the early part of his program firing up his religious base by describing the church film in lurid detail. This chewed up a great deal of airtime, particularly when he had to examine it from different angles. He concluded, only half-jokingly, that there was so much damage on this film that there might have been a second ranter. He encouraged the cops to look at the footage for themselves and investigate the campaign in case someone else was there. It was all suspicious and conspiratorial—and it made for damned good radio. Now it was time to deliver the closing bit.

"First, you need to know that I received this news—this monumental piece of information the likes of which you can't begin to imagine—from a highly trusted source who got it from inside Christ campaign headquarters itself. That's right, Christ campaign headquarters! Right from the top! Or maybe the bottom. Right out of Christ's a—" His airhorn cut him off, lest the FCC levy a fine against this wholesome family show.

"Now, you may have heard this morning," Tarsus pushed a button which unleashed trumpets announcing a royal decree, "or maybe even read yourself…" He pushed another button and a crinkling, then snapping, newspaper crossed the airwaves, "that the Christ campaign does not have a single woman—not one!—among their senior advisers. That's right, that liberal hippie doesn't have one woman on his staff. Now, I'm nothing if not fair. This story was broken by that liberal rag *The Philadelphia Inquisition,* but as you might expect, they didn't get the whole story. They left out significant details like they always do. But I got 'em. It turns out that that one woman on his staff... oh, are you ready for this? That one woman—yes, you may have heard it's Mary Larnaca, younger sister of Loser Lyin' Lazarus, but that's not important. That doesn't matter. It turns out Miss Larnaca, the one woman they found to work on their campaign, was a prostitute."

Dead air. Dead silence. Dramatic effect.

But at the front desk of campaign headquarters, a single tear rolled down Mary's cheek. The first of many because not all tears should be fought back.

"Yes, Virgin Guy may not be such a virgin after all. He likes whores! Sorry, political commandants, sex workers. Is that the right term? Sex workers? Prostitutes, ladies of the evening, call them what you will, but how does he know her? Was it through Lazarus or some tawdry affair? We'll never know because you always pay cash!"

The entire Christ campaign sat crestfallen, silenced by Saul's charges. After Simon closed the webpage, the only sound for the next twenty seconds was Mary trying to hide her weeping. At last Thomas found the courage to speak up, even if his courage was brought on by despair.

"We can't win." Everyone except Judas stared at him. He kept his eyes on the table, his voice low. "Herod has us on the defensive. We're reacting to everything his team says."

"How did Tarsus get this information?" Jesus said, pointing his question to Judas.

"Who knows?" said Judas, wrapping a hand around his coffee mug. "All it takes is one person. A client, a bellhop, a guest with a good memory. How the hell do I know? The point is, they found out, and if we deny it, we look guilty."

"How can denying it make us look guilty? That's the whole point of denying it."

"In a court of law, yes. This is the court of public opinion. Only the guilty deny their guilt, which keeps it in the news for an extra week or so, giving the press time to investigate. They may already have a corroborating witness, photos, receipts, I don't know. What I do know is that lying about it makes us look worse than denying it. It's like tacking ten years onto a life sentence."

Jesus rolled a pencil back and forth on the table. Good news never appeared when you wanted it, except in John's newsletter, and that news was not good enough to bury this.

"We can't give up," said Peter. "Not at this late date. We can still get out of this."

"You always say that," said Judas, his voice a subdued growl.

"That's because I believe it. And I believe it because I believe in this man." He pointed at Jesus with a firm finger, one that challenged anyone to contradict him. "Anyone who doesn't believe in this man should get out now because it's going to get rough from here on out."

All eyes turned first to Thomas, then Judas. Neither moved.

"Alright then, we're in business," said Peter, his exuberance over a good fight hard to conceal. He'd be damned if he was losing to Herod again.

Jesus turned to Levi with a question presented as a command. "I thought I told you to see that Mary gets paid."

"With what money?" replied Levi. "The campaign is barely solvent. That's the problem when you ask for five- and ten-dollar donations and court the poor. It's like cutting taxes while saying you won't cut entitlements. Eventually you run out of money."

"Do we have enough to pay Mary now?" Peter said.

"Maybe. We'll be cutting it close."

"We'll have to run a fire sale," Tad said.

"I don't care how we do it. I want a check drawn up, no matter what, with back pay, so that we can show the press we always intended to pay Mary for her work. Now, is there anyone else here who hasn't been paid?"

Not one hand went up.

"Anyone who hasn't been paid everything they're owed?"

Every hand went up.

"Alright, John, draft a press release saying that Mary is not the only one who hasn't been paid, but our staff so deeply believes in this campaign that they've stayed on to help."

"That will never work," said Judas. "You'll just look poor, and people hate the poor. That's why they vote for the rich."

"Do you have a better idea?" said Peter.

Judas thought it over for a second. Not that he was trying to craft an idea. He had that before he spoke up. He just wondered if they'd let him get away with slipping something negative into the release.

"Yeah. Say that every one of us has given up our wages in solidarity with the contractors Herod has screwed over at his hotels and restaurants. Turn us into martyrs, not victims."

Peter looked at Jesus, who raised an eyebrow before giving in. It was the campaign's fault, but Mary had stayed on, as had all the others.

"Alright, John, you heard the man. Maybe this will even help us turn around that prostitute story they're running." As John got up to work on the campaign's counterargument, Peter added, "But don't put that in your press release!"

After the meeting broke, the campaign's website ran deep discounts on its merchandise—from What Would Jesus Do bumper stickers to Do Unto Others T-shirts and I Come to Serve aprons. The Christ team also set up one last fundraising dinner with Jesus talking to his union brothers again, raising the suggested donation price from ten bucks to fifty, though saying any amount would do. With business out of the way, Jesus walked into the lobby to console Mary.

"How are you doing?" he said, handing her a tissue from a box on her desk.

She took it but didn't use it right away, patting her eyes with the one in her hand. "Just peachy, can't you tell?"

Jesus said nothing. He simply sat on the corner of her desk, waiting for her to talk. His father often told him that the best way to show a woman you cared was to let her open up. They'd accuse you of not caring because you didn't push harder, but they would eventually tell you what was on their mind.

"My brother is going to kill me. I always told him I was going to work, but I changed clothes in the car, or in a rest area, or someplace far away. Always far away, so I didn't have to be reminded of home." She dabbed her eyes with the tissue Jesus gave her, picturing her family's once lovely home now tarnished as a house of ill repute.

"Lazarus is a man of the world. He'll see beyond this. He knows the things Herod can reduce people to."

"Herod? Herod? Herod had nothing to do with this. This was my decision. My...sin..." The tears came harder now, though Jesus admired this sign of character. If she wasn't wholesome, she wouldn't care. Mary's tears brought back memories of his own mother crying when the neighbors leveled accusations at her. He sometimes thought the tears would never stop.

"You took care of your family."

"No, no, I didn't." Mary let out a huff that became a laugh as she sniffled back a tear. "Oh, I tried, but I couldn't. I never actually...I couldn't. And now the world will believe something I never did."

"Then Judas was wrong. We have to deny it."

Mary put a hand over Jesus' to thank him. She couldn't believe he would risk everything to put forth the truth. But a lie could cost you everything, too. Within hours, hundreds of posts appeared from men claiming to have paid Mary for her company. Most came from foreign addresses and were quickly disproven, but the few with ties to Bethlehem gave the story credence and convinced those with deep religious convictions that Jesus was an atheist. Only a sinner would consort with prostitutes and tax collectors, and he was busy doing both.

To win now, Jesus needed to pull in votes from every one of his most ardent supporters—if he could overcome his own brewing sex scandal.

HIS HEART IS STEADFAST

The moment Jesus sat down at his desk the next day his phone rang. It was rare that he ever got a call at 7:10 in the morning, and although he had a sneaking suspicion it was a reporter asking for comment on the Larnaca story, he picked up anyway.

He was half right. It was someone calling for comment on a story, but it was no reporter.

"Have you seen the front page of *The Inquisition*?" said Mary Magdalene, anxiety masking an underlying anger.

"No," Jesus said, jumping to their website. If a picture is worth a thousand words, the rest of the front page could have been blank. The color photo said it all.

It was Mary kissing Jesus after the debate.

Video would have shown it to be a quick peck, a friendly goodnight kiss. The still image made it look smoldering and passionate. It was a kiss frozen in time—a never-ending caress between two people deeply in love.

"How did they get that?" said Jesus, shocked by the image. A man who had devoutly avoided the distractions relationships bring found himself ensnared in a sex scandal that wasn't a scandal. Or had sex in it. In fact, it was less of a scandal than what Mary Larnaca was going through. At least she tried. This was a goodnight kiss between two single people in their thirties. But reporters and political opponents can find the seamy underbelly to any beast, and this one was a hydra, creating two questions for every one answer.

"I don't know," Mary said. "Maybe a reporter stayed behind to catch you leaving."

Jesus skimmed the article. The details were light. Only that Magdalene served as an early supporter and primary donor to the campaign. She and the candidate had been seen speaking at the party, though one eyewitness referred to it as "shameless flirting." They were among the last people to leave the after-debate party when this photo was captured by someone passing the back of the theater.

"They left open the idea that we might have left together," said Mary.

"But they weren't specific," said Jesus, hoping to salvage some of her reputation. "It simply says the photographer didn't know what happened next because he left the scene."

"The 'anonymous photographer.' Did you notice that?"

"Yes," said Jesus, knowing this source didn't have to worry about being perceived as fake or imaginary. He or she provided solid, verifiable, and very real, photographic evidence.

Jesus wondered if these witnesses were all the same person, even though the article indicated they were different people. A lot of chance had come into play to land this story. If fortune favored the bold, it blessed Herod because he was downright brazen. But there was something else that favored Herod because they were as brazen as him: trolls.

The Inquisition played the story straight without exaggeration or implication. Those willing to comment on the story felt no such compunction. They implied Jesus slept with her so she'd finance his campaign. They stated without reservation that Mary slept with him to increase her power. They spoke of unverified corruption, tax dodges, and money laundering, and wondered if anyone had nude pictures of Mary. It started ugly and got uglier, without any hint a swan would emerge. One didn't. Trolls roll in the mud; swans do not.

Jesus promised Mary he would do his best to debunk it. To explain it for what it was, even if he wasn't sure what it was. A smooch between friends? The culmination of hidden feelings? He only knew one truth: *Faust & Friends* was already covering the story, and Tarsus would jump on it later today. Even less-biased sources ran with it because they trusted *The Inquisition's* journalistic judgment. And there was no denying the evidence. Like the news running with the video of him in the megachurch, this one had "film at eleven" written all over it. They finally had their romance film to match their action flick.

What Jesus didn't realize was that this story was the best news he'd get today.

At 10:00 a.m., an hour after Doozy said goodbye and Tarsus took to both boasting and bemoaning into a microphone, coordinated social media posts rocked the Christ campaign. It had technically started days ago but was timed for this morning to maximize impact days before the election. The campaign had guessed wrong, and its opponents didn't want to give them a chance to respond.

Peter had misplayed the abortion question.

One-issue voters never forget the one issue they care about.

It started in small fashion. A few dozen complaints about Jesus' pro-life position being unacceptable exploded into thousands of posts, memes, emails, phone calls, twits and retwits. It would have included calls into liberal radio shows if one could be found. This flood of complaints, which overwhelmed Mary Larnaca and James the Great, grew worse outside their office windows. Twenty women marching to protest the campaign's dearth of women became two hundred to protest his pro-life stance. Their quick gathering caught the Christ camp off-guard and prevented them from contacting counter-protesters. Jesus hoped this would keep the cameras away. Conflict is the key to a good story, but other than their anger at him, there was little to draw their fury.

Unfortunately, no opposition had the opposite effect. More protesters came because no one yelled at them or got in their faces. Demonstrators called friends and fellow activists, cajoling them into getting down there without delay. Within the hour, those two-hundred protesters doubled. This created a sea of handheld signs telling the candidate *My Body My Choice* and *Anti-Choice Means Anti-Christ.* The clustered signs made a great photo, and the local press made sure to capture them. Marchers chanted while speakers climbed a makeshift soapbox. Without a microphone, their voices all but fell silent until someone delivered a bullhorn that allowed the speakers' voices to carry far and wide and sound a whole lot angrier. The cheap bullhorn didn't allow for nuance since subtlety was not necessary for crowd control.

The police, who didn't care that this was a peaceful protest, set up sawhorses and barricades to corral the crowd. A few diehards donned riot gear and used bullhorns of their own to drive people back, creating a crossfire of angry voices. It made great, stirring video as the police braced themselves while the protesters marched, and absolutely nothing happened. It made a less-than-explosive ending, but as a ten-second clip on the evening news, it made a terrific backdrop.

The protesters led the news that night, two stories ahead of the Mary Magdalene photo, with the same soundbite running everywhere. "An office with no women can't tell us what to do with our bodies!"

Nowhere in the evening news, and only in a few newspapers and websites, did it mention that Jesus went out to talk with the protesters while his staff offered them snacks, water, and coffee. Jesus wanted to take center stage and speak through the bullhorn, but the organizers were not giving up their power. Unable to make his way through the throng, Jesus resorted to speaking with scores of individual protesters along the barricades despite police opposition, delivering his defense with all the vehemence of a lawyer looking to win his first case—against a stacked jury.

"I support all life. I want to end abortion, assisted suicide, the death penalty, war...We must care for our brothers and sisters from cradle to grave, before they arrive and after they're gone. Understand my love for humanity. I'm on your side. Please understand I'm on your side."

But Jesus got another important lesson in politics that day.

Religious people can hate you but will vote for you if you support their issues.

Rich people can hate you but will vote for you if you support their issues.

Poor people can hate you but will vote for you if you support their issues.

Single-issue voters can love you, but if you don't support their one issue, they won't vote for you.

Jesus felt these voters slipping through his fingers because neither he nor they could bend. Yes, politics made for strange bedfellows alright, but at some point you realize you still have to wake up next to that person. This time, both sides wanted to wake up with their self-respect. Their love affair was over.

NO ONE WAS GREATER

The biggest story the next day was not about the campaign. Not directly anyway. It seemed murder could push it to the margins for a few hours.

The doctor at the city morgue pulled open the bottom drawer in a row of cadavers encased in stainless steel. The chill that surrounded the body gave death an icier hand than expected.

"Is this your cousin?"

Jesus stared at the gaping wound marring a large part of Jean Baptiste's skull, the fiery eyes that could light the sky forever doused. His perennially dark skin was drained of color, but his bearded jaw, still set as if ready for another blow, remained unmistakably firm.

Jesus nodded, unable to take his eyes off his cousin until the drawer slid closed, not to be opened again until it was time to prepare him for his final, permanent silence. Jesus touched the drawer and spoke as though his cousin could still hear him. At least Jesus hoped he could. "Goodbye, Jean. There was no one greater than you."

The morgue couldn't release any of Baptiste's personal effects, which amounted to thirty-four cents, a blanket, and a Styrofoam cup, since the cops were keeping them while investigating the murder. Those personal items were all they had because they sure didn't have a lead. Nothing. And they weren't sure they'd ever get one.

Baptiste lost everything after being fired from his podcast. His landlord evicted him yesterday for being three months behind in the rent. Baptiste went to the park to preach to anyone who passed about Christ's vision for America's future, or the "coming miracle" as he called it. People thought he was a madman, but a few kindhearted souls threw him a couple bucks. It was enough to get him a disgusting last meal of day-old hotdogs on stale buns from a nearby gas station. At some point, Baptiste curled up on the bench to sleep. Shortly after three in the morning, someone shot him in the head. There were no witnesses or security footage.

"Did he have any enemies?" the cop asked.

"Thousands," said Jesus. "Anyone in an 'I Am Legion' hat."

That seemed a bit broad for the officer, who knew he'd never get a warrant based on the flimsy evidence of a flimsy hat.

"Anyone close to him?"

"Anyone who fears my coming," said Jesus.

"Right," said the officer, finding it hard to believe that anyone feared this scrawny, if intense, Senate candidate. "We'll start with the landlord and anybody who posted threats. That kind of thing."

"Don't forget the Herod campaign."

"Right," said the officer again, simply placating a grieving relative. There was no way he was going near the Herod campaign without evidence, a warrant, and a good pension plan. That was career suicide, and at thirty, he wasn't ready for that. Let a cop close to retirement handle it. Someone who could ask the right questions that didn't get any answers so that he wouldn't upset the senator. Someone who could pull off saying, "I'm just doing my job" because after three decades on the force he couldn't do much else.

As Jesus left the station, the young officer gave him one last bit of discouragement. "We'll do our best, but don't expect much. A lot of homeless are murdered by random strangers."

Jesus left the station fighting to keep his head up. There was a campaign to wage. Only now, he was doing it in memory of his cousin. The man who convinced him to start this journey would be there in spirit when it ended.

The press dutifully reported Baptiste's death with a few front-page pieces and several glowing obituaries about a man they had paid little attention to. The columnists, however, sang his praises. They railed in support of a journalist twice fired for criticizing a candidate a thousand times, whether commenting on published articles or unproven rumors. They claimed it was his First Amendment right to say foolish things for profit. Politicians had been doing it for centuries, and it was now a cottage industry online. They pointed out that scores of anti-Christ websites existed, from Twit pages to NeverReadIt chat rooms, thriving on the margins and the repetition of lies so egregious and so vile they had to be true. They pointed out that Jesus had been accused of stealing money meant for disaster relief, frequenting gay sex clubs, and murdering a friend to cover up financial crimes. Defending Jesus against these charges in online threads had become full-time jobs for Andrew and James the Great, who were called cuckolds, cucksters, cucksuckers, cucklickers, cucklikers, and commie cucksters by the trolls they encountered. The press contended that Baptiste was only being punished because he had the courage to include his name. Anonymity, it seemed, was the key to free speech. It was the only way you could say exactly what you wanted without repercussions. Not that the reporters had a problem with repercussions. Hate mail meant readers, which could get you a raise. The more controversial the column, the more you stood to make. In fact, building a sufficient hate base was a key to journalistic prosperity. No, it was the anonymity part that bothered them. People who said the most outrageous things should face the greatest consequences.

The one punishment the reporters couldn't abide was getting fired for your opinion when you were a columnist or pundit, or in Baptiste's case, a fringe journalist with a semi-popular and hard-to-find vlog. They argued if you could fire him, nothing would stop media executives—an ever-shrinking number of people and corporations—from moving up the food chain and firing them. If they didn't speak out against this firing, they feared no one would defend them when their turn came.

Herod, professional that he was, got ahead of this story the moment it broke. He put out a statement before Jesus could because his opponent was tied up with next-of-kin duties, which meant Herod squeezed out an additional press release discussing his enemy's death before Baptiste's family could. Herod's statement came in the two words that best described his personality: blunt and provocative.

"I am sorry to hear about the death of Jean Baptiste. We had our differences, but I always defended his right to speak to the death. Unfortunately, his death came prematurely. There has been wild speculation on the lunatic left that my campaign was involved in his terrible murder. Anyone who knows me knows that I am a great defender of law and order and would never, nor would anyone I know, stoop to such action. Mr. Baptiste had a loud voice, one that was often unfairly critical of me, my policies, my staff, and my family, but his voice will be missed by the few people who actually listened to him. I never met or interacted with Mr. Baptiste because I only surround myself with winners. It's what winners do, and as anyone can tell you, and as the voters of this great state know, I am a winner. Jean Baptiste was a loser, and his life reflected that. While I didn't wish him dead, I can't say I'm not happy he's no longer on the air. He harassed me for too long and muddied the waters of an otherwise great campaign."

After issuing his statement, Herod did what so many other rich and powerful "winners" did. He spent a few hours with his mistress, who was even less sorry to see Baptiste dead.

Herod couldn't hold back his smile.

Salome got what she wanted, one way or another. She wanted Baptiste's head on a platter, and whether by hook or by crook, serendipity or scythe, she got it, and with no splatter on him. No political splatter anyway. He didn't know if she did it. He didn't know if she called someone to do it. For all he knew, it could have been some other offended target of Baptiste's rage, a supporter in a red hat, or a stranger in the park. All he knew, despite aspersions, was that he did not do it. He may have once boasted he could shoot someone on Broad Street and not lose a single vote, but the truth was he didn't have the balls or the bullets to do it. The investigation would never tie things to him even if his inner circle fell like dominoes. Let them take Salome. It would be the most unique way yet to break up with someone.

Much of the news condemned Herod's statement as insensitive and self-serving on the basis that he had spoken ill of the dead, though Tarsus and others on the right said this showed Herod's tough side. He was no wilting wallflower who took half a day off because some cousin died. They claimed this showed that Herod had the iron will the people needed. It's why he won time and again. People like winners.

That was a hard point for the press to counter, in as much as Herod often won. Meanwhile, the press liked losers, endorsing their fair share of insufferable candidates simply because they had a penchant for honest and fair-minded politicians—and those people almost never won.

Still, it was those very attributes Jesus hoped would let him prove Herod a loser once and for all.

THE WEDDING FEAST

The Friday before Election Day, Jesus returned to familiar ground, making one last pitch to his union brothers and working-class buddies. He used Jean Baptiste's murder to galvanize them.

"Herod has inherited his wealth and power. He has been granted such things as should not be his, or taken them from their rightful owners. Fame, property, women…the list is as long as my beard. The one Herod is not man enough to grow."

Bitterness over Baptiste's death crept into his speech, but this audience laughed along, caustic jokes their favorite genre. Peter, however, cursed Jesus for not using that line sooner. If only they had emasculated Herod from the start. No Virgin Guy. No homophobia. Just a tough candidate doing unto another before they did unto him.

"We spend years learning our craft until we master it. We train our apprentices to be like us so that someday, when the time comes, they can replace us. Well, the time has come to replace Herod because if we do not, he will train his apprentice to be like him, and the corruption that mars his reign will continue for generations. Replace him with an honest craftsman and return integrity to government!"

The gathered artisans appreciated him including their livelihoods in his speech, but his analogy didn't receive the same enthusiastic applause it would have months ago. Most had already made up their minds, and when Jesus told them "to vote for your own interests because this will let you shape the interests of your progeny," more than half had already concluded that voting for Herod was in their best interest. Jesus may have been one of them once upon a time, and at times still spoke like them, but few of them believed any politician could change their economic lot. Work, get paid, and do it again, and so they voted for candidates based on social issues, and that led them to Herod. He might not know a ball-peen hammer from a ballpoint pen, but he lined up with them where it counted. He hated foreigners and loved the flag. He supported tariffs, hated free trade, and supported "Made in America," even if his own line of ballcaps, ties, suitcoats, shoes, and wallets were made overseas. And sure, he voted several times to make outsourcing easier, but at least he verbally encouraged domestic production. Maybe somebody would listen. Or actually make something in America. It was okay to vote against your economic interests as long as you did so with a clean conscience.

Jesus, unaware of this shifting dynamic, stayed late to thank them for coming, although he left without enjoying the feast they put out afterward. He told them he had a big day tomorrow. With every hand shaken, Jesus and Peter left for the brown bomber of a car parked on the street.

As Jesus bent to duck into the car, he stumbled, lurching forward against the open door. Peter's arm shot out and caught him, his candidate twisting like a spineless child, his jacket and shirt rising up mid-torso until Peter caught him in the armpits. He held Jesus for a moment, asking him if he was alright.

Jesus nodded and said, "I guess I tripped on the sidewalk. I'm fine."

Peter said, "Okay," but guided him into the backseat of the car anyway. He then got behind the wheel, having given Andrew the night off to fight Internet trolls with any gruff tone he liked. The campaign, in its final days, was hitting back as hard as it could.

A reporter covering Jesus' speech caught his stumble on the sidewalk and almost immediately posted it on the station's website and social media outlets, where it went viral in under a minute. This was bad for Jesus but good for the station, which knew clickbait when they had it. The tape had no real news value, but at pay-per-click rates on several platforms, it could cover the cost of the reporter's trip that day.

The late-night comedians were the first to jump on it, the worst of them rolling it into a full and recurring bit that ran throughout the program. It featured an actor dressed as Jesus tripping while getting into a car, then a different car, then on a bike, then falling on roller skates, falling off a Segway, falling down stairs, catching a ball with his face, and hitting his thumb with a hammer, alluding to his days as a carpenter. The program ended with a bit of visual trickery that showed Jesus walking off a cliff that turned out to be, as the camera pulled back, a chart representing his falling poll numbers.

Peter, Tad, and the team were on it the moment the video went up, explaining that Jesus had not eaten that day after learning of his cousin's death. It finally caught up with him late that afternoon, and he tripped. It was nothing to be concerned about. The Herod camp, though, said that Jesus appeared sick. They claimed getting into a car was too strenuous for him and that this was more than just "a few hours" without eating. Network pundits soon followed, asking what was wrong with Jesus. The most gentle of them said he might have a cold, maybe a fever, while the worst said he had cancer, dysentery, dropsy, leprosy, and worms. A few claimed he had multiple conditions and could be dead by next Tuesday. Doctors were brought in to offer their expert opinions without ever examining him, which they were always quick to point out seconds before they gave a diagnosis of "something serious, perhaps [insert disease here]."

Jesus' detractors showed side-by-side pictures over a six-month period to prove he had shed excessive weight. Peter, though he wanted to, couldn't deny that Jesus looked gaunt. But not being able to deny something didn't mean a good campaign manager couldn't find an alternate explanation.

"This shows just how hard Mr. Christ has been working for the people of this state. He gives everything he has morning, noon, and night for the voters. While his opponent has gotten larger, Mr. Christ has sacrificed his health to carry out his message. And when he's elected, you can expect more of the same."

To which one comedian joked, "You mean more falling down?"

That became the next day's meme—a screencap of Jesus falling with Peter's text above it: "Expect more of the same."

Faust & Friends commented on the story often, returning to it after every half-hour newsbreak. Their conclusion was that Jesus' stumble was a metaphor for his stumbles along the campaign trail. And by the end of their program, they had a big announcement—a new campaign ad from Herod Antipas.

"It's brand new," said Doozy. "Just put together last night by Herod and his team, and boy, do they work fast."

"They do," said the blonde. "So fast."

"Which is why he gets more done for the people of this state than anyone," said dark-haired guy.

"Of course, we shouldn't endorse people on a news program," a line that made his co-hosts and at least two people off-camera laugh, "but this ad is amazing."

It opened with Jesus stumbling, followed by various video rolls of Herod chopping wood, riding a bike, riding a horse, off-roading, and lifting weights, most of them clearly done in a studio and a few of them taken at least two decades ago given the clothing, slimmer waistline, and lack of gray hair. The ad concluded with several women ogling Herod, enamored with the man for no other reason than they were paid to. Although the women were in a studio and not at a campaign event, it conveyed the image Herod wanted, and to make sure they saw it, the announcer's voice said over their gawking, "Vote stamina. Vote Herod."

When the screen brought up the hosts of *Faust & Friends*, they looked like giddy teens fawning over a top-of-the-charts pop star. A reasonable viewer could assume they were in love. An honest viewer would call it lust.

The ad quickly joined the Phobos rotation but landed on other stations and websites, too, a Herod ad running somewhere in the state every minute of the day. They ran in a cycle—Hot Herod popping up between Commie Christ, Commie Christ II, the Happy Hippy, and Atheist Christ. Despite being preposterous, it was effective. But the worst ad was yet to come.

Peter had promised Jesus a big day on Saturday, and it was finally here. Mid-morning, minutes before 9:00 a.m., Jesus arrived at campaign headquarters in his best suit, but the spectacular change in wardrobe wasn't what Peter noticed first. In fact, Peter couldn't have been more shocked if Jesus had shown up naked, and it was a valid comparison because he almost had.

Jesus had cut his hair and shaved off his beard.

"Well, that's a new look for you," said Peter, who couldn't stop staring at his candidate's shorn face. "So...uh, what prompted you to do that?"

"You asked me to."

"No, seriously." That may have been the sternest tone Peter had used in this campaign.

Jesus drew in his breath before answering. A long breath, as if contemplating the best answer he could give. For him, that always meant the truth.

"I did a lot of soul-searching last night about how badly I want to win this. I don't need to win for me—I need to stop Herod for the people he's hurting. And I am willing to do whatever it takes. Jean's outcast Bohemian look got him nothing but contempt. TV pundits say the same things but get respect because they look like *Bible* salesmen. Then, they attack me for looking unhealthy or dirty, as if I were a caveman covered in lice. Well, they can't say that now. It's time to look the part. It's time to look senatorial."

Unfortunately, from Peter's perspective, and he was sure for the public at large, that no longer looked true. Jesus didn't look like a senator at all. The beard had aged him. Made him looked wizened and experienced. Now, he looked like a freshman congressman in need of legislative seasoning. And as for healthy, his cheeks appeared sunken and hollow, the beard having filled out his face. His bony demeanor was all the more apparent now. Jesus had gone from rugged outdoorsman to ninety-eight-pound weakling overnight.

Peter hung his head. He had been wrong. The candidate was right to trust his instincts. He knew who he was. Some men just look better with a beard.

There was nothing he could do about that now.

He, Andrew, Jesus, and John piled into the campaign's best car—John's—because he was the last to hold a steady job. The compact car was a tight fit, but it was the best he could afford on a reporter's salary in a mid-size market. Still, it reinforced Jesus' image for this big event. He had been invited to a wedding in the town where he'd already had one big event, Canaan, and Peter was damned certain they were going, even if his boss objected.

"Peter, the optics on this are bad. I'm here to help the hungry, not enjoy a feast."

"First of all, it's not a feast," said Peter sitting beside him so he could cut off any protests. "It's a banquet. And second of all, poor people get married, too. I'm told this is a tiny affair, which means the optics are great."

Jesus' face told Peter he had yet to overcome his skepticism.

"Alright, look, Simon says your image is growing in a reverse positive cycle." Hearing that in his head, Peter understood his candidate's skepticism a little better, but that's how campaign managers talk when they don't want to give bad news. "You're dour and serious. We need to show people the real you. Funny Jesus. Man of the people. This is a chance to show you having a good time…"

"I'm all for having a good time," Jesus said, "but everything has its place. To everything there is a season, and this is not that season."

"It's always wedding season!" Peter said with a laugh, looking out the window at the orange, red, and yellow leaves clinging to the trees. "Okay, so it's not June, but it will be a lovely fall wedding in the mountains."

Jesus stared out the opposite window. He had to admit he loved the splendor of the mountains. Their majesty and solitude. He'd live there if he could, away from the big-city hustle of hustlers like Herod. If only the people didn't need him. If only he wasn't consigned to cure their suffering. Perhaps after a long career as the people's servant, he could settle here amid the peace that escaped him now. The struggle that followed him as much as he followed it.

"Canaan, huh?"

"Yeah," said Peter with a reassuring smile, knowing he was winning over Jesus. "The site of your greatest speech. Your... your Sermon on the Mount. Hey, John, write that down. We should call it that later today. Every good speech should have a name. The Gettysburg Address. The Cross of Gold. Thousand Points of Light. Make sure we tag that one." As John nodded his head, redrafting the latest draft of today's umpteenth social media post, Peter continued. "That fits in with what we've already released. How cool is it that you've been invited to a supporter's wedding? This couple loves you almost as much as they love each other..."

Jesus raised an eyebrow. "Really?"

"Okay, so that's the angle we're playing, but the couple agreed to it. These supporters love you, so they've invited you to their special day. They want you to be part of their lives."

At last Jesus smiled. He liked the idea that he was so beloved he could impact them even at a distance. It was every politician's dream. Jesus leaned his head back against the seat, figuring he'd better compose a toast to the young bride and groom.

The four men climbed out of John's car after a little more than a ninety-minute drive. They arrived early, but like most of what Peter did, that was by design, too.

He had a surprise.

Ten minutes later, another car pulled into the parking lot. One that did not belong any more than John's among these luxurious automobiles. The person inside, however, was worth the world to him.

Outstepped Mary.

Not Magdalene.

Not Larnaca.

THE Mary.

His beloved, sainted mother.

Jesus stood there, unable to move, the shock setting in. Or maybe the embarrassment. This was the woman he denied in public for a three-decades-old scandal.

He ran across seven car lengths to hug her. To embrace her more fully than he had his calling or career. They held on for five seconds, ten seconds, the time passing without either saying a word. The charade for the campaign's benefit was over.

And Peter made sure the cameras caught it all, Andrew on video and John clicking away like the paparazzi at a premiere. Peter had arranged for this to happen early, away from the press. If it went wrong, no one would know, but if it went as he hoped, the campaign would have a story to tell. The public loved to see a man knocked down, groveling for their acceptance, abandoning everything to win their approval before basking in his happy ending. This story gave them that, and he was going to sell it to every buyer who came along. He insisted John capture mother and son praying together during the ceremony and sitting together at the reception. Most important, he had Andrew capture them dancing across the floor. He couldn't ask for a better way to show a happy and healthy Jesus than having him grooving at a joyous occasion like this. Jesus hadn't had this gleam in his eyes since that first press conference.

As Jesus returned from the bar, wine glass in hand, the head table called upon him to make a toast to the loving couple. Knowing he would have few chances to speak publicly before Election Day, he placed his mother's wine glass in front of her, her sparkling eyes showing how proud she was of her son.

"I want to thank you for inviting me to this tremendous celebration. I was invited here by people who don't know me but who want to honor my message of doing unto others. And so, I am reminded of a different wedding."

Jesus paused, expecting Peter to rush the dais and stop him before he launched into another parable. Perhaps the wine had overtaken Peter's good senses because he let his candidate go on uninterrupted.

"A king invited the richest people in town to his son's wedding. No one came. Disappointed, he invited businessmen and merchants, but none of them came either. Disappointment turned to rage and the king razed the shops and homes of everyone who rejected him."

Jesus smiled and raised his glass, not to toast the confused couple but to salute someone who wasn't here. "He was a petty tyrant, like some of the senators we have now."

A general chuckle spread across the room, deepening as it went, his reference to Herod unmistakable.

"Finally, the king invited the poor—the sick, the impoverished, the undocumented. Every one of them came, but one man did not dress for this feast and the king had him bound and gagged and tossed outside."

The confused couple, and anyone with even the mildest curiosity, wondered where this was going. They were torn between waiting, gasping, or having this lunatic escorted from the premises.

"What I mean is—many are called, but few are chosen."

The happy couple applauded, joined by a blotted Peter, but the rest of the room sat in stone-cold silence like the early press corps. He had to put this in contemporary terms because many will hear, but few will understand.

"You have all been called to share your wealth and resources with others. If you want to be chosen—truly chosen for greatness—you must help the poor and the indigent. I once said, in this very town, that the rich are accursed, but today I offer you an addendum. The rich are blessed if they thirst for justice. Use your resources to bless others. Our happy couple understands that, and for that reason, they are blessed. They are chosen!"

Jesus raised his glass to the happy couple, followed by cheers of "To the bride and groom!"

After they kissed, the newlyweds thanked Jesus for coming and said they considered him family, promising to do as he asked, today and always. They went out on the street and invited anyone who passed to partake in their feast, although no one took them up on it because it felt weird crashing a stranger's wedding. They did, however, wish the couple luck, the same couple who, come Monday, donated their riches to the poor. It was the best vote Jesus could ask for.

But the real vote—the one that counted—was just three days away.

THE FOUR HORSEMEN

John and Andrew posted the images of Jesus at the wedding before the wedding was over, which meant the trolls came out before the honeymoon began. The first thing they attacked was also the easiest: Jesus' clean-shaven face. They pointed out how ghastly his face looked. The Herod camp said this was a clear case of Jesus pandering for votes because his hippie look hadn't worked, but they otherwise ignored it. This left the issue wide open for social media, where the most circulated meme was a parody of a missing-child milk-carton poster featuring Jesus' former look. It said, "Have you seen this candidate? If so, please call 1-NO VOTE 4 HIM." It quickly earned one thousand Likes and two thousand laughing emojis.

Others focused on the various wedding videos. Most found Jesus hugging his mother adorable and were happy to see them reunited, although critics called it saccharine and cloying and hypocritical. He only condemned her four months ago. When Jesus' supporters pointed out that, at fourteen, Mary was the victim and should never have been condemned in the first place, the trolls quickly disappeared. You never win a battle defending a child molester. It just didn't look good, even if you acted anonymously. With this skirmish sinking into Waterloo, the trolls took on a new front, one fraught with far less danger but much more foolishness.

The dance video.

#danceshame became the raging hashtag, attached to almost every comment on the subject.

That's not dancing. That's drunken stumbling. #danceshame

It's like watching my dad dance—without the good moves. #danceshame

Anybody got video of the people he hurt? #danceshame

I've seen drunks with more rhythm. Was it a frat party or a wedding? #danceshame

Did he try to sleep with his mother, too? That family is effed up. #danceshame

A thousand of those comments in an hour got the dialog flowing, with Jesus' dwindling followers defending it as a candidate letting loose and being human. The majority found it humiliating and shameful that any serious Senate candidate would act that way. They wouldn't abandon that argument even after someone posted video of Herod dancing—well, bouncing entirely out of step—with a West African dance company. They said Herod was working on improving international relations, the true job of a ranking member of the Senate Foreign Relations Committee. Even embarrassing footage of Herod line dancing at a nephew's wedding couldn't deter them, nor could tape of him dancing like a spasmodic robot while groping a young woman. Nothing stopped Herod's supporters from attacking Jesus' missteps, claiming they had video of him break dancing, moshing, dubstepping, and spinning like a drug-induced hippie. No such videos ever surfaced, but people kept saying they "serve as proof Jesus is an alcoholic junkie who should never be senator. #voteherod #danceshame."

All of this entertained Herod's team, but it hardly solved their problem. Legitimate news sources wouldn't condemn it the way loyalists and amateur comics did. They showed it as a fun piece before moving on to the big story—Jesus reuniting with his mother. He could see saps across the state sucking that one up. Almost everyone loves their mother. Even Herod loved his mother, and she was downright demanding, telling him he'd never be as good as his father. Herod couldn't let last-minute good news, complete with video, tighten the polls. He needed to change the conversation, and there was only one way to do that.

"Release it."

"Sir?" said his young aide.

"The ad. Release it."

"But, sir, that's set to go Monday."

"Did I stutter? Release it. Now!"

The aide picked up a phone to dial out. Herod shook his head and yanked the phone from the kid's hand. If he wasn't a sycophant, he'd be stupid. At least he had enough brains to suck up.

"From a burner phone. I don't want this traced back to us."

The aide stepped into the hall and headed for the exit. He wouldn't be anywhere near here when he placed the call, just the way Herod wanted it. The one-minute spot would be released through a super PAC. Technically, Herod wasn't even supposed to know it existed, let alone having seen it three or four times. There was supposed to be no coordination between the campaign and outside groups, and so there wasn't. Herod made all his recommendations through an intermediary or two, then let the group make their own decisions, which meant implementing exactly what Herod wanted under the guise of them having been that sneaky on their own. All in all, it offered him one of the biggest advantages of modern politics: believable deniability, which was much stronger than the old system's plausible deniability. Back then, everything went through the campaign, so the candidate should have known about it. Now, the Internet and federal law created a new Wild West in which he was a sheriff working with a posse of rogue gunslingers. *Try that in your average democracy,* he thought with a chuckle.

Within an hour, People for the Ethical Treatment of Antipas had the ad on their website, Twit account, NeverReadIt, and a host of other outlets where their followers were bound to see it. There was no time to get it on TV before tomorrow morning— even Phobos had their spots booked unless Lucifer himself called in—but there were plenty of ways to reach the masses. By midnight, the ad spread, forcing a few newspapers to post commentary about it. The media was sucked in again.

A camera opened on a young girl holding a daisy. She plucked off the petals, counting up in the convoluted way four-year-olds do before a siren split the air and a mechanical voice counted down. Four Horsemen swooped across the screen, nuclear missiles trailing them. Cities burst into flame and bodies vaporized on the spot. Looters gunned down innocent families while Death, on his white horse, galloped closer, breaking from the pack, until his skeletal face materialized over the young girl's. Throughout the video, a stern voice warned: "These are the stakes. To make a world in which all of God's children can live, or to go into the dark. We must either love each other, or we must die. Don't vote for an atheist. Vote Herod. You can't sit this one out."

That ad terrified some people, but Herod slept like a baby. It had the desired effect. The press wasn't talking about Mary.

The Sunday morning shows, and Phobos News all day, focused on the Apocalypse Ad as it became known, though a few trolls tried to stick it with the #deathchrist tag despite his antiwar views. If the ability to function while holding two opposing ideas in your head was a sign of intelligence, these people were geniuses because they simultaneously believed two opposing ideas: Jesus was a pacifist and a hawk. Anti-military and pro-war. They said it was part of his master plan to destroy the country by getting us into a war after weakening our forces.

Reporters questioned if the ad was ethical, saying people couldn't truly believe Christ supported nuclear annihilation. The talent at *Punch/Counterpunch* went back and forth as if it were an actual war. The only point either side conceded was that it had put Jesus on the defensive. Lefty said it "turned Christ into the little girl under attack," which made Righty laugh. "Couldn't have said it better myself. Jesus is a weak little girl."

Herod moved to condemn the ad before lunch, calling it "over-the-top" and "entirely unnecessary since it's obvious my opponent is weak on defense." He called for the ad to be taken down, which the super PAC did, knowing the ad could never be taken down. It spread across the Internet, propped up by the Anti-Foreign Legion and the Anti-Christ Alliance and watched by people on both sides curious to find out what the hubbub was all about. The ad generated so many clicks it produced enough revenue to pay for itself. Of course, it helped that the little girl worked for scale with no royalties. The PAC even fired the "beast" who created it, Nero Germanicus, who landed a job at a Madison Avenue firm within twenty-four hours. Controversial meant ingenious, which meant selling another million pairs of jeans, cars, and booze to people who didn't need them.

By Monday morning, Simon Z gave the team the new poll results from SixSixSix. Jesus was even further down. They had one day to turn things around. Now was the time for a miracle.

THE LAST SUPPER

Jesus woke up Monday morning for what was to be the busiest day in the campaign. Peter had a strategy that required a lot of travel and a lot speaking, but unable to make inroads in advertising, they had to use the old-fashioned approach. Meet the voters. Get local press. Glad-hand and press the flesh. The one thing he told Jesus not to do was "kiss any babies. That will remind people of those stupid sex-ring allegations."

Peter laid out a map showing where Jesus was polling well. His plan was to go into those areas and galvanize the vote. It was a get-out-the-vote campaign like no other. Barney would reach out to rural voters, and James the Less would work the phones to pump up the union vote, while the online team pushed out email and social media reminders. But the crux of this plan was Jesus' ability to drive the voters like sheep to their polling places. He would rely on in-person persuasion to ensure his voters came out in force on Tuesday. Done in enough towns enough times, picking up one or two percent everywhere they went, convinced Peter they could win this thing.

And so, Jesus made his first speech at seven in the morning at a prayer breakfast in Nazareth, followed by stops at a donut shop and a coffee shop on the way out of town, where he shook hands, spoke to customers, and encouraged the cashiers to get out and vote. Not yet being full but sure it was coming, Jesus spoke at a late breakfast in Bethlehem, where he was unable to finish his eggs and hash browns and couldn't take any more coffee. Later that morning in Emmaus, he again filled up on coffee because his hosts insisted. He nibbled on some coffee cakes but had to save room for his lunchtime speech in Zionsville.

By this time, the food, drink, and speeches were running together as Jesus ran through a medley of his greatest hits, reminding audience after audience, voter after voter, to do unto others. Live by the sword and die by the sword. He is who first shall be last. I come to serve and not be served. Each crowd remained fired up as Jesus drew on his draining reserves. Peter plied him with a cup of coffee or two before every speech and reiterated his notes so that Jesus hit the highlights. Like a trained seal he always delivered, becoming as inspired as his audiences, adrenaline driving him to his big finish.

"Blessed are the meek, for you will be strong! Blessed are the poor, for you will be rich! Blessed are the peacemakers, for you will survive! My opponent will bludgeon you with his rhetoric, but you must resist. When he says, 'Vote Herod,' I say vote him out of office!" Jesus paused for the applause which varied in length from room to room but was always there. It gave him a moment to admire how John had punched up his lines to make them bumper-sticker perfect. "I say vote for Jesus and send a just man to work for you! Thank you, and God bless!"

He would leave on that applause line, shaking hands as he exited the stage, audiences chanting his name. Jesus and Peter were sure they would come out to vote tomorrow.

After Zionsville, the team headed into Lebanon to speak in a library conference room where, out of habit, Jesus kept a low tone so as not to disturb anyone enjoying a good book. Peter instructed him to speak louder and draw them in, but his soft tone had the same effect as the audience leaned in to catch every word. The worst part of this speech was that the group that sponsored his library visit put out more cake, obligating Jesus to stuff himself once more. His bloated stomach could barely handle another bite. For a man who spoke against gluttony, he was certainly doing his part to partake in it.

Waddling out of the library, Jesus and Peter made a quick stop at the Lebanon Medical Center to visit sick patients. At least that was Jesus' intention, but Peter knew these people, many of them terminal, would not be voting. Any vote they cast had already been done by absentee ballot, and so he kept finding ways to delay Jesus, dawdling at the nurses stations to discuss universal healthcare and other concerns. The nurses, of course, were far too busy to talk, making this strategy an immense failure. Except at one station. The one Jesus dreaded.

Peter urged Jesus to see Little Mark, but Jesus refused. He had given his word to leave the boy alone. The angels were smiling upon him, however, because after a few minutes kibitzing with the oncology staff, a loud voice called out behind them.

"Jesus Christ!"

Jesus turned, expecting to see Mark's angry father racing toward him, fists up, wondering why this ambitious carpenter couldn't leave his son alone. But it wasn't his father. It was a young doctor in a lab coat pushing a laptop on a cart.

"I'm Dr. Luke," the young man said, extending his hand.

"It's good to meet you in person. We…" Jesus said, gesturing with his thumb toward Peter "…were just going."

"I understand. The election's tomorrow. But wait a second."

Dr. Luke dashed behind the nurses station and rumbled through a drawer to their left. While Jesus thought a hospital drawer would be more organized, it apparently resembled a kitchen junk drawer because it took more than half a minute for the doctor to find what he wanted. At last the doctor pulled out a small white envelope and handed it to Jesus. He lifted the flap of the unsealed envelope to find a small square card with flowers on the front.

Thank you for everything you did for our son. Your help will never be forgotten.

Although clearly in a woman's handwriting and containing a heart after "forgotten," both of Mark's parents signed it. The biggest surprise came when Jesus flipped the card over. On the back, in a man's thick scrawl, was another message.

I tried to go on Phobos to tell them what you did for Mark but they wouldn't put me on anymore because I wanted to say good things about you. Jesus' broad smile spread across his face when he read the next line: *You got my vote!*

Dr. Luke patted Jesus on the shoulder. "Yes, Mark will live. Good work."

That news fired up Jesus, who vowed to deliver his remaining speeches without pause or nourishment. He had to win this for children like Mark who would not survive under Herod's drastic healthcare proposals.

Jesus spoke with energetic fury in Bethesda, Shiloh, and Bethel before heading home to Nazareth. He regained his appetite, feeling strong enough to eat like one hundred men. Which was good, because that night he planned a very special supper with his innermost staff.

Jesus took his seat in the middle of a long table. Although he thought it was an odd arrangement that made conversation difficult, particularly if he wanted to speak to anyone on the ends, the man of the house said this would keep his wife and daughter from interrupting their conversations with annoying questions about water, wine, and dessert, or having to slip in to clear away the dishes. Jesus dropped any further debate, hoping to keep the family's vote tomorrow by not being demanding tonight.

The advisers filed in, taking their seats in a first-come, first-gets-to-sit-next-to-Jesus manner. There was no rhyme or reason to it—no place cards or seating arrangements. That violated Jesus' sense of equality. He wasn't even sure he should be in the center seat, but since he would be doing most of the speaking, it made the most sense. John and James the Great won the seating lottery, finding themselves to Jesus' immediate right and left respectively.

Jesus let the group engage in small talk for a few minutes before his speech. Peter and Andrew, halfway down the table to his right, discussed Herod's last-minute approach, equally similar and disparate to their own. He had gone into several Philadelphia neighborhoods where he was polling poorly to convince these unlikely voters to switch their vote to him. Peter thought the whole idea was a ridiculous gamble, calling it a major mistake on Herod's part. Herod needed to gather his supporters and tighten his grip on the election, not court people who would never vote for him.

At the other end of the table, nearest the door where they came in, Simon and Tad dissected that morning's polls, the last they'd see before the official polls opened tomorrow at 7:00 a.m. Before that conversation grew too bitter, Jesus tapped his wine glass with his fork. He didn't want them discussing bad news tonight. He knew what the polls said, and it didn't look good. Tomorrow's news, good or bad, would arrive unchanged by what they said tonight. Let them rejoice, for the hours of their hard work were at hand.

"Gentlemen," he said, rising to his feet, "thank you for standing by me during our many trials. I could not ask for more loyal friends."

"Hear, hear," they mumbled like a restrained committee of British parliamentarians.

"This part of our journey will soon be over. Someone is going to our nation's capital as a senator for the first time or the last time. Let's hope it's the former. But win or lose, we are in a fight for this nation's future. It is not enough to convince thousands of our righteousness when millions are waiting to rise up!"

His advisers cheered and banged on the table, and Jesus realized he should probably reel this in a bit. This was a large upstairs room in an otherwise modest house, not a campaign rally thrown by raucous supporters.

Jesus picked up a bottle of wine, open but unpoured, that he specifically asked be placed in front of him. He slipped by those to his right until he reached Bart on the very end, filling each man's wine glass as he moved up the line. Peter objected, saying they should pour for him, but Jesus reminded him of his core purpose. "How soon you forget that I come to serve. Follow my example. Continue to serve no matter where you are."

Having finished pouring the wine, Jesus broke bread for all of them, placed it on two plates, and passed it down each side of the table. The symbolic act done, Jesus told them to enjoy their meal as the family brought in plate after plate of roasted potatoes, roasted chicken, beef brisket, and glazed carrots. Jesus, like his team, dug in. If things didn't go well tomorrow, it might be a while before they had a good meal again.

Toward the end of the dinner, Judas, who had been drinking since noon but still managed to finish half a bottle of wine at dinner, rose from his seat next to John.

"The people hate Herod," he said in alcohol-infused tones, putting his hand on the back of Jesus' chair and leaning forward so that his boss got a full whiff of his wine-soaked breath.

"Yes, they do," replied Jesus, pulling back a bit and trying not to make it obvious he was wrinkling his nose. "That's been our greatest advantage."

"Our wasted advantage," said Judas with a dismissive wave stylishly demonstrating his drunkenness. "Like my skills. Wasted!"

Jesus handed Judas the last chunk of bread in an effort to soak up some of the wine—and some of that anger.

"I had all these ideas for attacking Herod, but nooooo, you had to stay above the fray. You don't do that when they hate the other guy! Attack! Attack! Attack!"

Judas' outburst silenced the table from one corner to the next, and downstairs, a plate shattered against the floor, dropped by someone spooked by all the yelling upstairs.

"Also, when they like the other guy. Attack! Attack! Attack!"

"Judas, this isn't the time to talk politics. It's..."

"It's always time to talk politics! Don't you get it? Thanksgiving is ruined because everyone's talking politics. 'Don't invite Uncle

297

Joe and Aunt Mable, or Starchild and that boyfriend of hers. They're crazy!' We're all crazy! And we're all crazy because we're always talking politics!"

Judas staggered to his left, steadying himself with one fist on the table. It looked like he would vomit any minute, and so John leaned away, as close to Peter as possible, giving Judas all the swagger room he needed. Somehow, Judas kept his dinner down, but his face remained flush, his eyes swimming about his head in a dead man's float.

"Come on, let's get you some air," said Jesus, putting a steady hand on Judas' shoulder and leading him toward the exit. The chairs between the table and the wall created an obstacle course for the drunken trickster, but his guide stayed patient, letting him untangle his feet from two chair legs and a long tablecloth that threatened to trip him up as he rounded the corner near Tad. Jesus figured it was best if his inebriated companion berated him outside, away from the staffers. The campaign ended tomorrow. He saw no point in picking a fight on the final day.

As they descended the stairs, Jesus supporting Judas on one side, the railing on the other, Judas invented a sing-song chant that was part opera, part child's rhyme, and less serious than either. "Down, down, down! We're going down! Down like the polls. Like the voter rolls. Down, down, down. Downnnnnnnnn!" He gave the last word the deepest bass he could, but it didn't reverberate the way it should. It only filled the air with alcohol, the stairwell resembling a rotting vineyard. Jesus now longed for the open air and took his first deep breath the moment they passed through the door. Judas kept singing, though whether this was a new song or a second verse, Jesus couldn't tell.

"We're sinking, we're sinking like Babylon, like a ship at sea. Like...like Jonah in the belly of a whaaaaaaaaale."

Jesus wrenched his hands free, letting Judas stand, or rather teeter, on his own. "What did you say?"

"We're sinking...like a...we're sinking."

"No, about Jonah."

298

"We're sinking…like Jonah in the belly of a whaaaaaaaale."

Jesus' stomach unexpectedly twisted in knots. He hadn't expected to see those words again. He dismissed them at the time, but now he understood.

"You betrayed me."

"You're crazy. Just like the rest of them." Judas pushed off toward the sidewalk, but Jesus stepped in front of him.

"No. Two weeks ago, a reporter from *The Inquisition* sent me an article about someone leaking campaign strategies to Herod. It had copy from all these emails. I denied it, but the strategy was ours alright. I simply refused to believe it came from inside the campaign."

"So, what's that gotta do with me?" Judas said. "Good ol' Tad's your strategy guy. Coulda been me, but I wasn't good enough."

"There was a line in the article quoting one of the emails. It said this info would sink me like Jonah in the belly of a whale. That was you. You sent those emails from an outside account."

"No way!" said Judas, lurching forward to push his way past his boss. But Jesus was a muscled carpenter, even if out of shape, and easily held Judas back, keeping him on the walkway in front of the house, trapped near the wilting mums in the front garden.

"Why? Why did you do it?"

"Leave me alone!" Judas struggled to push his way through but couldn't overpower Jesus. His boss had the strength of an army driven by anger, disgust, and disappointment. The coward in Judas did not have the strength of a feigning possum.

Jesus wrestled him backward, the drunkard's arms flailing to stop him.

"Why? Why?"

"Because you're a fraud!" said Judas. "A downright fraud! A false messiah! You can't beat Herod because you won't fight him. All your pretty talk about peace and love and caring for the poor and bringing us a new world, but you can't make it happen."

"But Herod will never make it happen!" Jesus was confused. He saw no logic in Judas' position. Lazarus said the man was a zealot, but Jesus could not identify his cause.

"I know. In six years, I'll be fighting him again, working for a candidate who can beat him. Better the devil you know. Better a false messiah who knows he's a false messiah than one who believes the lie." Judas at last pushed past Jesus, mumbling as he reached the sidewalk. "Fight him again in six years with a real candidate, not some loser. I can't support you…"

Jesus talked to Judas' back, unwilling to stab it like he'd been stabbed but willing to hit this traitor with a meaningful, even painful question.

"How much did Herod pay you?"

Judas stiffened his back before turning to face Jesus at a crawl, his movement so slow it guaranteed he wouldn't fall.

"You're a loser!"

"Mm-hmm," said Jesus, not buying this lie. Not from a traitor pushing to make this his fault. "How much?"

The moon shone across Judas' face, enhancing his sneer.

"Thirty thousand dollars. Four times what you paid me for six months of work. So I gave him everything. Every plan, every speech, everything. I even gave him the photo of you and Magdalene, so take that." Judas swept his arm wide as he shuffled off, his way of telling Jesus to go to hell as he disappeared down the sidewalk. "Loser."

"That's it," Jesus said, "go, and go quickly. Do what you must do. Herod and Caiaphas and Lucifer and the whole crew are waiting for you. They don't share your beliefs, but that's okay because neither do you."

Jesus went into his last supper with his staff and told them Judas would not be returning, though he did not say why. They'd learn the truth soon enough. As the evening wound down, Jesus went for a walk in a nearby park. Peter and Andrew, with him since the beginning, insisted on accompanying him. Neither thought he should be alone at a trying time like this. As they meandered between trees, encountering voters here and there who wished him well or asked how he thought he'd do, he replied, "Thank you," or "That's up to you," but he was otherwise silent.

Despite his comrades beside him, he was utterly alone because it was his name on the ballot. For all the love he received during this campaign, he could only share so much with others. The weight of the vote was on him.

And tomorrow he would find out whether that weight would be lifted by joy or depressed by sorrow. That was the one thing he wished Lazarus had taught him: the solitude of the final moment, win or lose. It was all his. And like every other politician, he would accept the blame or spread the credit, and the only ones who would understand were those who ran before.

Yes, Jesus was utterly alone, and tomorrow's results couldn't change that.

...SHALL BE LAST

Jesus met Peter at campaign headquarters a little before the polls opened. Coffee in hand, the two of them strolled to their local polling place just as the protesters arrived to remind people not to vote for Nazareth's favorite son. Jesus waved to them as he and his campaign manager departed. After voting, Jesus encountered Nicole Demus, as well as a TV camera crew, both of whom wanted to know how he thought the day would go. He gave the same reply as last night, adding only that he had "faith in the voters to do the right thing."

Peter and Jesus, joined by Andrew, made a few additional stops that day, including greeting employees as they came in and out of Hades Steel. Lucifer watched Christ's last-ditch efforts with a blend of anger and sadness at what could have been. But when a candidate would not carpe diem, it's se la vie, or some other trite saying. What wasn't trite was what he would do next. Jesus, his one-time favorite, gave up a chance for greatness, which meant Lucifer would seek to destroy him and everything he stood for. It was not enough to consign him to the dust bin of history. Lucifer would work day and night to turn him into a mere speck in that rubble heap.

Jesus and the team, minus the conspicuous absence of Judas, spent the rest of the day calling supporters, urging them to vote. A little after dusk they were joined by Mary and Lazarus Larnaca and a handful of local well-wishers. There would be no fancy hotel or giant spreads. It wasn't in the budget, and it wasn't his style. Mary Magdalene, who arrived ten minutes before the polls closed, offered to fund a ballroom in the grandest hotel in Bethlehem through an Election Party Fund, but Jesus refused, wanting to stay low-key and close to home.

Herod, of course, retreated to his Philadelphia hotel, where he, or rather his donors, paid for a large buffet, band, dance music, mirror balls, and hundreds of red, white, and blue balloons. It was every ten-year-old's idea of a grown-up nightclub.

At five minutes to eight, Peter turned on the headquarters' only television, a beat-up set they picked up at a thrift store a few months back. Herod had a giant, drop-down screen that ran the news throughout the party, even though the news was barred by law from giving results prior to the polls closing. He was trying to create an exciting atmosphere, one that made everyone eager for the results.

The Christ headquarters had atmosphere, too. An atmosphere called apprehension. Most of the people were too stressed to eat or drink anything, and Simon Z kept running to the bathroom every ten minutes, though he swore it wasn't to throw up from nerves, no matter what sounds they heard coming through the plywood door.

At 7:59, the anchor who handled the debate appeared on-air—not to give the results but to tell everyone that she would give the results in one minute. Stand by, enjoy the commercials, and they'd be right back. As if torturing Jesus, the first ad was from Hades Steel bragging about what they had done for this community. The second spot was for Uranus Furniture, reminding everyone that these elections results would be "more comfortable on Uranus."

True to her word, the anchor reappeared promptly at eight. Jesus' eyes narrowed, as did Peter's, each wanting to be the first to see the results and steeling their emotions either way.

"In today's biggest race," the anchor began, "early numbers, with more than fifty percent of precincts reporting, the race between Herod Antipas and Jesus Christ goes to..."

A split second before she spoke, the numbers flashed on-screen.

92%-8%.

"...Herod Antipas. We are calling this election for Senator Herod Antipas."

The room fell silent. All they could do was stare at those numbers. This wasn't a loss—it was a grotesque beating four times as bad as Lazarus' loss six years ago. It was the worst defeat in U.S. Senate history that didn't involve a dead candidate or a live criminal.

Mary Magdalene put a hand on Jesus' shoulder to comfort him, but he didn't need it. He knew this was coming. He knew the odds were stacked against him in a way they almost always are against a candidate who isn't close to the middle of the electorate but in the middle.

Jesus picked up the phone to call Herod and concede the race.

Herod could barely hear his opponent over the cheering, chanting, and impromptu conga line in the background. Despite all the obsequious clamoring, Herod remained humble and gracious on the phone, accepting the conciliation with unusual grace. That didn't mean he wasn't gloating in his head. He was telling himself he was the greatest campaigner ever—if he forgot the two times he never escaped the primaries in his presidential bids.

The Christ campaign was a more somber affair, a funeral amid bright colors and appetizers.

"As you heard, I've just conceded the race to Herod Antipas." There were a few groans and almost inaudible no's, but sadness made the rest too numb to respond. "I don't know why the voters have forsaken me, but we must forgive them for they know not what they do. They voted against their own self-interest to reward an oligarch, one who will be blind to their needs. But they have spoken, and we must respect that. A house divided against itself cannot stand. Anyone who is angry with a brother or sister will be judged. Do not be what you hate. And so, I leave you with these words—though the voters have forsaken me, they have not forsaken our ideals. I will live to fight again, and the next time will be different."

Jesus hugged his advisers and friends and then exited through the front door. The protesters were gone, except for a few who stayed to jeer at him as he passed. Both Magdalene and Peter wanted to offer any small solace they could, but sometimes people need to be alone in their misery. Each thought Jesus would resurrect his spirit and return tomorrow. They could rejoice and lament equally then.

Peter stayed behind, the last to leave. He could not take his eyes off the screen, listening to the analysts for hours on end. Phobos News turned itself into an entertainment channel that was nominally news, with partying in the background and primetime heads calling Jesus a political hack and Herod a political genius without ever admitting it didn't take a genius to beat a hack. They might as well have said Herod was powerful because he defeated the powerless. Tarsus offered a one-hour online special that he didn't previously announce so he could cancel it without anyone knowing should Herod lose. But he, too, mocked Jesus' campaign skills while lauding Herod's ability to connect with the common man. The sharpest analysis came from the team at *Punch/Counterpunch,* which should have been renamed *Punch & Punch Some More.*

Righty jumped in first, accusing Christ of having no message or theme. "Was it do unto others? I'm here to serve? He who is first? What would Jesus do? They were just throwing things out there hoping something would stick. All wonderful phrases, but either too long or too confusing. Which was a big part of his problem. He spoke in those rambling, confusing stories..."

"Parables. He called them parables."

"Call them whatever you want, but when people mocked that first one, he should have dropped all the rest. Keep it simple stupid! Otherwise, people will think you're stupid, and they won't vote for you. Unless you're truly stupid. Then people will vote for you because they can't believe you're really that stupid."

"That's a good point," Lefty said, continuing their lovefest. "People hate a smart guy pretending to be stupid to get votes, and they hate a stupid guy pretending to be smart to get votes. Be yourself. Unless you're really good at being stupid, it won't work for you."

"Speaking of stupid, some of those scandals…"

"Plenty of politicians have survived campaign scandals far worse than this, from extramarital affairs to taking bribes, working with foreign governments, breaking into your opponent's office—hell, Tiberias bragged about sexual assault and still won the election."

"Yeah, but Christ had stupid scandals," Righty said. "The campaign finance thing at the diner? Stupid. Not hiring one woman for his staff? Stupid. Not paying the only woman in the office? Stupid. And that kiss with Magdalene? Stupid! I mean, they did it on a public street, and he wasn't even getting any. Stupid!"

"Entirely stupid," said Lefty, caving in so often viewers thought it was on the teleprompter.

"And what was his central issue? Help the poor? Attack the rich? Healthcare? Welfare? Jobs? Buy American? Open borders? I never knew where the guy was headed. He had no big issue. Pick one and hammer it home."

"Hammer it home," said Lefty, taking up the role of talking dummy in this debate.

"Herod did, that's for sure," said Righty. "And it was a classic. Taxes, taxes, taxes. Cut the people's taxes."

"Even though there aren't many left to cut," said Lefty, interrupting with a perfectly logical point that had to be overlooked during Righty's rant.

"And the people ate it up. At every speech—I will cut your taxes! And keep the immigrants out, but that was Herod's B-side. His big hit was cut rich people's taxes. That's smart."

"It's dumb policy, but smart politics."

"No, it's smart campaigning," said Righty, warming up under the heat of the TV lights. "And that's what this was about. Herod worked his base. Jesus worked the middle."

"You can't work the middle," said Lefty, shaking his head, not because he agreed with that but because it wasn't what he wanted to say. What he wanted to say was that you could indeed work the middle. What you couldn't do was work for the votes of those who had their votes suppressed: minorities, ex-cons, the poor. You can't win appealing to those most unappealing to the powerful. But Lefty never got his argument right. It's tough to make a good point when your job is getting pointed at.

"You throw the other side one or two issues so you can pull in the moderates while the rest is strictly party line so people know they can vote for you. Don't deviate from the left or the right. Don't be both pro-life and pro-pardon. Be consistent. That's all we're saying."

"That's all we're saying," said Lefty, who spoke while Righty took a sip of water. The people at home thought it was a tremendous trick.

"Look," said Righty, pushing Lefty aside and pulling a ventriloquist's dummy from under his chair, bringing not only their segment to a close, but their charade. "Jesus alienated the left and right by attacking both, and you just can't do that. This guy formed a circular firing squad all by himself. The public couldn't trust him. The voters showed him no loyalty because he had no loyalty to their ideals."

"No loyalty!" squeaked the dummy. "Now…what's an ideal?"

Peter donned his heavy coat as the laugh track kicked in. He had told Jesus much of what they said. Don't speak in parables. Have a slogan. Don't disagree with your base. And for God's sake and your own, fight back. If only his candidate had listened they might have stood a fighting chance. Jesus gave them the moral high ground, but with no message and no money, he couldn't win over an amoral mass looking to be entertained by a master of misdirection. For generations, politicians believed politics was show business, and now the masses did, too.

There just weren't enough believers to cast a vote for Jesus.

Peter couldn't get over that tally: 92-8.

No one would ever forget that.

Peter put on his hat as the station rebroadcast Herod's victory speech. It was a stunning example of modern political oratory.

"I am the chosen one! Chosen to lead this state! Chosen to right the economy! Chosen to defeat all-comers! Chosen to save your souls!" His supporters raucously applauded every word. After all, he must be the chosen one. He arrived with trumpets blaring the way the chosen one would. "I refudiate anyone who says otherwise. I won't tolerite it. They thought Jesus was going to win, but he got schlonged!" The crowd laughed, which hid any shame they should have experienced. From there, Herod was free to go full schizophrenic as the shackles fell away. He lied with every line, which drove the crowd into a frenzy. "Tax cuts pay for themselves! Deficits don't matter! Guns don't kill people! Samaritans love me! Windmills cause cancer! Cold weather means no global warming! Slogans save lives! Ich bin ein jellyroll! Erg ack blagger! Republic dog vote! Fibbertigack and trumperdoozle! U.S.A! U.S.A!"

Peter switched off the TV. He couldn't take any more nonsense. The voters had rejected an honest, humble man for one who never made a brag he couldn't make bigger. The man he shaped to be an American populist—with the added benefit of bringing integrity and purity to the political landscape until that failed—lost in a landslide. And there was no reason to think it wouldn't happen again.

Peter turned out the lights and shut the door behind him with the thought that Jesus Christ, savior of American politics, had been crucified.

REVELATIONS

Although our story could end there, as Jesus acknowledged, the fight went on. People's lives continued. Here's what happened to our most important people.

Saul Tarsus: A burst of bright light struck Saul while driving to a political rally in Damascus, PA. He claimed Jesus emerged from the light and asked why Saul persecuted him. Wracked by guilt and realizing he had backed the wrong man, Saul quit his radio program, changed his name to Paul, and launched a highly entertaining podcast promoting denture cream, ED meds, and the policies of his one-time nemesis.

Peter Cephas: Peter denied he was Christ's campaign manager in his next three interviews, unwilling to take responsibility for such a debacle. Finally, unable to deny it, he embraced his position, began a large foundation to espouse Christ's ideas, and financed it with vast real estate holdings and a massive media empire. Women continued to play secondary roles.

John Patmos: John put his tremendous writing skills into creating some of the most original, provocative books about Jesus. He became a highly respected author, even though other staffers refused to back many of his inside stories.

Mary Magdalene: Magdalene contributed large sums of money to various charities and did all she could to convert women to the ideas Jesus espoused. Various hate groups linked her to prostitution without providing evidence.

Lazarus Larnaca: Lazarus resurrected his career in politics by bragging that he coached Jesus for that impressive debate performance. He rose through the ranks to become a highly sought-after political consultant and lobbyist. He hired his sister because he knew a good thing when he had it.

Mary Larnaca: Went to work for her brother, rose to the pinnacle of his organization, and commanded a hefty, upper six-figure salary because she knew she was worth every penny.

Herod Antipas: Herod finished his term but was soundly defeated in the next election by a distant cousin who showed him no mercy. That cousin was so corrupt, he went to prison before finishing his term. Herod Antipas was forever stuck with the nickname Herod the Lesser because he never matched his father's accomplishments.

Pontius Pilate: Pilate finished his term as governor with the lowest approval rating in modern history and retired to the southern part of the state, abandoning his presidential ambitions.

Dr. Luke: Dr. Luke continued to treat patients, wrote prodigiously to spread Jesus' message, and fought hard for universal healthcare.

Little Mark: Never forgetting that Jesus saved his life, he grew up to become an author and scholar on Christianity, as it became known. His work was boring compared to John's.

Lucifer: He got richer. That's what people like him do.

Judas Iscariot: Judas could not land another position in politics because no one trusted him. Word spread about his betrayal, and when his $30,000 ran out, he hung himself in his apartment.

Jesus Christ: Jesus disappeared after the election. Word spread that he went to the Promised Land, as in Promised Land, Pennsylvania. He lived in a small cabin in the woods and worked as a carpenter. Rumors abounded that there would be a second coming, but he never ran again. He figured the world wasn't ready for him, but if it ever was—if it ever truly wanted to embrace his ideas of peace and love—he'd come back. But until then, as he told his neighbor, "You guys can work it out."

ABOUT THE AUTHOR

John Briggs is a former stand-up comic and nationally syndicated reporter. Although he has written topical jokes for TV, radio, and the Internet, he is best known for creating the stage show *Left-Wing Laughs* and its signature bits *Yeehaa or Jihad* and *Showdown: Apocalypse*. After earning a bachelor's degree in Political Science from Temple University, John briefly did lobbying work before turning to journalism. He has worked a variety of beats, from hard news to sports, entertainment, and features and counts among his proudest moments attending the White House Correspondents Dinner. He later studied Creative Writing at New York University. A native of Philadelphia, John was raised in the Pocono Mountains and currently resides in New York's Capital District.

Printed in Great Britain
by Amazon

31217317R00178